Green
with
Envy

Richard G. Brooke

<u>Acknowledgement</u>

The author gratefully acknowledges his debt to the work of
Ayn Rand, a novelist-philosopher of genius.

To Alexandra.

PART ONE: GUILTY

1

Blake Hardwicke screwed up his eyes as the sun hit them through a gap in the curtains. He smiled. It wasn't a bad way to wake up, even after only an hour's rest.

He turned to look at his wife Marisa, sleeping peacefully on the pillow beside him, her long, blond hair spread out across it. They had been too busy making love to sleep. It had been amazing and long, long overdue. He grinned until his lips cracked. And then he felt a lump in his throat which he had to swallow back. She was going away again this morning.

~

In the room next door, their son James was also woken by the February sunlight. But instead of rolling over and burying his face in his pillow, as most teenagers would, he lay looking out of the window with a big smile. Today the car was being delivered.

He'd slaved away at his maths, physics and chemistry A-levels for two years, well more than two years, what with tutoring and retakes, and now he would have his reward. Of course, he knew he would now get into Cambridge, like his father, and that he'd achieved an important step on the road of his career, but what he really wanted was something tangible, right now. Something to justify all the nights he had stayed in studying, instead of playing rugby at the club or spending time with Emma.

Emma. His smile broadened. He couldn't wait to take her out in it. Perhaps he could get away with a quick visit to her place this afternoon. Then a short drive together. His father wanted to be the first passenger. James was going to drive him to a special meeting that evening, and his father had been true to his word in buying him the car in return for good exam results, so he should really give him the first ride. But he could picture himself at the wheel with Emma smiling and excited by his side. It was too good to wait for.

Emma. She wasn't a stupid greenie like his sister and a lot of his peers. For God's sake, it was electric! Emma liked cars. She wanted the freedom to drive where she wanted, when she wanted, and, like him, she looked forward to the privacy. Her parents insisted she save up her wages from her weekend job at the supermarket, and then they would help her buy one. In the meantime, she would enjoy riding in his car. He just had to figure out how to get away with it. Maybe he could convince his mum somehow. Then he remembered somewhat guiltily: she was going back to prison again today. So actually, it would be easy.

He got up and opened the curtains. It was starting to cloud over, but that couldn't dampen his enthusiasm.

~

Blake watched the smile on his son's face broaden

into euphoria as they all witnessed the shiny blue car being driven up to the house, and the garage salesman handing James the key.

"Thanks Dad," James said, as he looked directly into Blake's eyes.

"You've earned it," Blake said, and he put a hand on his son's shoulder to feel the boy who had, somehow, grown into a man so quickly. He sighed. Time passed so rapidly sometimes. And sometimes, like today, when he had an all-day meeting with the government electricity quota officials, it would drag like a horse-drawn plough in wet clay soil.

When the salesman had gone, Candice turned to James. "You know your new car is still guzzling fossil fuels somewhere, even if it *is* electric?" She threw this at him, almost spitting, while staring at him from under her blond fringe.

James grinned at her. "Well, it's got to move somehow, hasn't it?"

"And you know how many resources have gone into making it? How much energy and raw materials that could have been used for more deserving projects than your personal pleasure trips?"

"Well, you clearly do."

"And you don't care?"

"Not really."

"How can you be so selfish?"

"How can you be so annoying?" James raised his voice and stared at her.

But before either parent could intervene, Candice said, "Urgh! I hate you. I'm going to my meeting now, where we discuss people like you. "

She turned and hugged her mother, but when they

separated she couldn't look at her.

"Have fun," said Marisa, with a half-hearted smile. She wanted her daughter to have friends and interests, but she wished she'd chosen differently.

As they watched her stride away down the drive, her head down, a dark blue car passed her travelling at a slow but determined pace, heading towards them.

"Already," sighed Marisa, as she submitted to Blake's bearhug.

Two men in dark uniforms got out. Blake clutched his wife tighter. Then he kissed her lips until she pulled away, needing to breathe. The men stepped forward, one reaching for a pair of dark steel cuffs.

"Take care, Mum," James said through an angry sob. "Now I've got a car, I can visit you more often."

She smiled back, then hugged him.

Putting on a bright face, she said, "Now, you be sure to get your father to his meeting on time tonight. You know how important it is."

James nodded and stared at her, his face distorted, as she released him from their hug and the man stepped forward to put the cuffs on her wrists.

As she stood there, her hands bound but her head high, Blake rushed forward and embraced her again. She could only rest her head against his and then kiss him.

One of the men coughed. Blake and Marisa reluctantly separated and she was helped into the back of the car.

As it travelled slowly and silently back up the drive on its electric motors, Marisa turned awkwardly in her seat and stared out of the rear window. Blake blew her a lingering kiss and waved, holding back the urge to scream with frustration. Not only was she leaving them and returning to Ironview Prison, but she would be spending most of her days sorting rubbish for recycling, when she used to be a city executive.

He watched the car turn the corner then channelled his feelings towards what he could do.

"James, make sure the car is fully charged and you're ready to take us into town at six. Don't take it anywhere before then. I want to be with you on your first journey."

"Yes Dad," James said brightly.

"The BCF is—" Blake paused, "—the *only* hope we have for saving the country, and ultimately helping your mother."

"I know. I'll be ready."

"Good. I'll see you later then." He gripped his son's arm and turned to get into his own car, an ageing Bentley.

He hadn't exaggerated, he was sure of it. The Business Carbon Forum was a sorely needed organisation if industrial civilisation in Britain was to survive. It really was as bad as that. Its charter was to independently research the science of global warming, what CO_2 actually did, to get a true, non-alarmist picture of the risks they all faced, and to develop alternatives to fossil fuels, particular nuclear.

The governments of Britain had long since abandoned research, funding or objectivity in such matters. All they did was channel money into 'green' pressure groups, including his own brother's Ecoist Party, and complain about big business. Blake and those he had persuaded to join the BCF knew that without a viable energy policy, businesses would collapse, and with them, the country. The launch event tonight had to succeed, regardless of the death threats. He was used to those. His Internet server company, Caelum, had constant pickets outside it, complaining about wasted energy and carbon emissions, and wishing him dead. He had to fight back against the lunacy and find a way forward.

He sped on, but groaned as he remembered who he would be spending most of the day with.

#

By the time she reached the end of the drive, the venom against her brother had somewhat worn off, and Candice waited a few yards along the road.

As her mother was driven passed, her face looking drained through the back window, Candice waved and saw her mother's surprise and joy.

She loved her mother. A surge of warmth and an irrepressible smile confirmed it. But she also hated her. Hated her for being in prison rather than at home where she could talk to her, woman to woman. Hated her for getting herself locked up by retaliating when 'eco-warriors' started smashing up the building she worked in – unfortunately one of them fell down an escalator and suffered permanent brain damage. And hated her for the out-of-date and wrong-headed ideas she held about the climate. Everyone knew there was a planet-wide emergency that needed urgent action if disaster was to be avoided. But her mother had continued to work as an oil and gas trader in the City, insisting that fossil fuels were a boon to the world's prosperity instead of a threat. How could she be so obtuse?

It hadn't helped Candice's social standing at school,

but joining the 'Green Shoots' had shown that she had different ideas from her mother. That she cared about the planet. She was going to learn about the climate emergency, then explain to her mother where she'd gone wrong.

Her friend Lucinda was in a similar boat. Her father was a merchant banker – a group that were largely to blame for the current economic crisis. Hopefully, they'd have time to console each other at today's meeting. She'd been walking in that direction since her mother had disappeared from view but the sky was growing ominously darker.

She swore as the heavens finally opened and she forced herself to run the last half mile to the Green Shoots meeting hall. The weather app on her phone was often wrong. It hadn't said anything about rain yesterday. In fact, it had been wrong a lot this whole summer. They were supposed to have had boiling-hot drought conditions, but actually it had been largely cloudy with regular showers. There was no other app to try instead, since the government had banned all but the Great British Media Company's on the grounds of 'fake news'. Why couldn't they get it right? It was James's fault. Him and his stupid car. If he hadn't made her so angry, she wouldn't have left in such a hurry, and she might have looked at the sky and taken a brolly.

Panting for breath she reached the hall and, finding it unlocked despite her early arrival, she went in. Had she always been so tired after running? She didn't think so. She knew she should do more exercise like her father, and admittedly her brother, but none of her friends did more than they had to in games lessons. It wasn't cool to waste energy – especially on trivial things like sports.

She pulled her phone out and checked the weather app: 'Rain expected 2 p.m.' Pathetic. It was raining now. She could see it with her own eyes. One day she would write computer programs that got it right.

She checked her wet hair in a mirror app and was glad she'd stuck to her short style. Then she went into the main hall.

Mrs Oakley, the Green Shoots leader, was preparing the flag for their usual opening ceremony. It was the same image as that used by the Ecoist Party: a large green tree on a solid red map of the UK. Candice sometimes thought the tree looked more like a mushroom, but she didn't tell anybody. Mrs Oakley was folding the flag reverently and tying it ready for unfurling.

"Hello," Candice announced.

"Ah, Candice," Mrs Oakley said, turning her bird-like eyes and thin figure towards her.

"Sorry I'm so early, Mrs Oakley. I had to get away from my stupid brother and his new car, and then I had to run to get out of the rain."

"The weather is so chaotic these days. But we all know the reason for that, don't we!"

"Yes, Mrs Oakley." Everyone from her school, to the news, the documentaries, and of course Green Shoots, said it was man-made climate change. Even her father seemed to agree with most scientists despite trying to fight the latest legislation to reduce carbon.

As if reading her mind, Mrs Oakley asked, "And is your brother still driving your father to his ridiculous pro-carbon launch party this evening?"

"Yes, I'm afraid so."

Mrs Oakley tutted and sighed, and gave her a sympathetic look. "We can't choose our families, dear."

Seeing Candice brooding, Mrs Oakley said, "Well, as you're here, why don't you help me set the chairs out? We've got a very interesting talk later about the effect of climate change on poor countries."

"Okay," Candice said brightly.

She began moving the chairs in stacks using a trolley, and lifting them off one by one. It was tedious work but it felt good to be useful.

She'd just finished a row beside the sign on the wall that read *"Who's more important – the planet or the people?"* when Lucinda arrived, also rather damp. Candice knew her father didn't agree with Green Shoots and wouldn't drive her.

Mrs Oakley greeted her and Lucinda smiled back, but Candice could tell that Mrs Oakley didn't like her. She wondered if it was because Lucinda lived in a very large house, while it was known Mrs Oakley had a small flat in a social housing scheme. Her dad said it was envy. But that didn't make sense. How could people want Lucinda's wealth when they despised her having it? Did they want to be shunned and spat at themselves? Another mystery to try to understand. She smiled and went over to her friend. They laughed at how bedraggled they both looked.

#

Blake slumped in his office chair and stared out of the window, thinking about Marisa. It could be nine more years before her sentence for GBH was over. One day out of every six months was better than nothing, but... He stopped himself thinking about it. He knew he couldn't think rationally when he was this tired.

All day 'negotiating' with the government inspector to extend his partial exemption from energy quotas had left him exhausted. He realised there was a shortage of electricity but how could he, or anyone, run a business when they had to justify every kilowatt hour they used?

Congo had refused on principle. Congo UK no longer existed. But Blake's Internet server company, Caelum, was not Congo – it only had the UK – so he'd had no choice. He had planned to expand into South America after Brexit, but the imposition of electricity rationing by the British government and the ensuing blackouts had taken away his energy, his customers, his revenue and his time.

He looked outside at the weather rather than reaching for his smartphone as many people did. It had rained earlier but it was now a clear, windless, winter afternoon – not good for turbines, but perfect for running – so he left his office early and drove towards the hills. It would take his mind off things. There was plenty of time before his big speech tonight.

He parked in a suburban street on the edge of town. Tightening his laces, he looked up at the dusky sky and smiled. It would be deserted but still light enough up on the heath. He rarely got out these days, what with all his business problems, so he'd make the most of it.

He stood up and started running gently to warm his muscles. As he passed a couple of teenagers sitting on the back of a bench vaping, they shouted abuse at him: "Oi, mate! Where's your number plate?" Absorbed in the pleasure of moving his body through the air, it took him a moment to decipher the taunt. It was about the latest Ecoist Party proposal that those exercising in public should obtain a government permit. The idea was to reduce CO_2 emissions and wasted energy. Sports teams could apply for a year-long permit covering all members at a discount. Blake thought it was ridiculous, and ignored it as yet another pointless, environmentalist gimmick.

Sensing easy prey and with no one else around, the two teenagers started running after him. Blake heard them coming and moved into a sprint, grinning. It had been ages since he'd raced. After ten seconds they gave up, panting, bent over double. Were they just unfit or was the trend for veganism taking its toll? He didn't care to think about them any more, but as he settled into a normal pace and his mind relaxed, his mind turned to his children.

Candice's veganism worried him. Was she doing herself any harm by having too little iron in her diet while she was still growing? He had tried to persuade her it was risking her health but that had just riled her, so he'd backed off. He didn't want to push her any further into the arms of the green movement. He sympathised with their aims – yes, pollution was an issue; yes, the climate was uncertain (possibly due to carbon dioxide) – but disagreed with their methods. Banning things, fining people and regulating them to kingdom come didn't work. They just got everyone bogged down in politics and legal action. Instead, they should be allowing businesses to develop new technology – like nuclear power – to solve these problems. That's what companies were ultimately for, he reasoned. Stupidly, the government had reduced the amount of science teaching in schools – they said it would only lead to more ways for mankind to exploit the Earth – and he'd had to give James remedial maths and physics lessons. These had paid off handsomely though and James was set for a great career. Hence the car. Candice, on the other hand, he struggled to help. He was pleased and relieved when she'd taken one science subject – computers – and she'd occasionally asked him questions. Mostly she liked to work things out herself, which he admired. On the other hand, what was she going to do with her computer knowledge when her other subjects were environmental studies (not a true science in his book) and history? He knew his own position caused her distress, but he couldn't make himself believe something he didn't. He could only try to explain.

The incident with the vaping teenagers made him think of all the other green 'attacks' on him over the years. The media enjoyed picking on any businessman whom they thought wasn't 'doing their bit' against climate change. Blake was a favourite target since he spoke out against the energy regulations and instead emphasised the importance of expanding the economy through more computers and better internet access. 'How could anyone break such a social taboo?' asked the media. Only by being purely 'selfish' they explained. So Blake was not welcome at many social functions. Only those where businessmen wrung their hands in vain as they discussed how to keep their firms afloat with the electricity supply becoming more and more unreliable.

Now that the light was fading, from high up on the heath Blake could see a patchwork of blackness in the town below: probably areas switched off by central control for rationing. The government issued a timetable of when each blackout was to happen, but of course, it didn't always work out like that. Blake wondered how people coped with such uncertainty. His business relied on electricity to power its servers, so he had several backup generators, including a small one at home. But it wasn't enough to charge a car. He hoped James had already done it.

He stumbled slightly on a rock he hadn't seen. Last time that had happened he'd damaged a bone in his foot which still creaked. It was only late February, he reminded himself, and darkness still came fairly early. He moved to the centre of the path, where there would hopefully be fewer stones, and carried on enjoying his run.

After a mile he reached the far end of the park, where there was an exit, a bench and a bin. As he turned around to retrace his steps he noticed an old, discarded copy of the *National Voice* newspaper lying on the bench. The headline read: *"Carbon Crime Crusade Reaches Commons"*. Blake knew the issue well. It referred to a parliamentary bill, not an actual, bloody crusade, though its consequences would also be gruesome. The bill planned to imprison those business executives who failed to accurately record every emission of carbon they incurred, or who exceeded their carbon quotas as laid down by an army of bureaucrats. This would be much worse than the electricity quotas. Tens of thousands of businesses would close rather than take on the extra burden of regulation and the risk of prison. It would cost hundreds of thousands, if not millions, of jobs. How could politicians be so short-sighted?

He recalled the paper's owner and editor Manny Schweizer. Thanks to him, the paper now had no serious competition in the physical newspaper industry. Ignoring the niche *Financial Times*, there was only the *National Voice* and the *Green Times* – a pure propaganda rag.

A year ago, Schweizer had taken the owner of the other major titles to court over an article he claimed breached the Climate Change Denial law. He had mounted a private prosecution and staked his paper's reputation, as well as his fortune – and had won, bankrupting the other side. Some said he had bribed the jury, but there was no proof. What was certain was that Schweizer had pushed hard for the CCD law to be created in the first place, having been a fervent ecoist for years.

And now there was the Carbon Crime Bill. It would ruin Blake's business, which provided cloud servers, mainly to industry. If he couldn't add and remove servers to meet customer demand without asking the permission of a bureaucrat, Caelum would grind to a halt. The great irony was that his business, when used to host online newspapers, consumed far fewer resources and 'emitted' far less CO_2 than the printing and distribution required for physical media. Yet the *National Voice* had shut down its Internet site in a blaze of self-righteous glory six months ago, citing the evils of Internet consumerism. Schweizer would be delighted if the Carbon Crime Bill passed. At least Dalton's upcoming debate with him at Oxford might bring him down a peg or two.

Blake's brother Fabian would not be so easy to challenge. He had led the increasingly influential Ecoist

Party for several years now and had been given a seat in the Lords by a Tory government keen to placate green interests. Blake had given up debating with him. Fabian just danced around the contradictions Blake raised, as if logic and reason were only applicable some of the time.

He could feel his blood pressure rising, even above the level caused by his run. He took some deeper, steadying breaths and reminded himself it was only a bill, it could still be stopped, and the BCF would try to do just that. He was excited about the inaugural meeting tonight. Despite the threat of protests, he hoped a sizeable number of business leaders would attend, along with at least a few scientists – if they dared to flout public opinion. He was particularly looking forward to hearing Dalton's speech.

Dalton MacDermot was a philosophy professor at Oxford, and since they'd been corresponding regularly about the BCF, Blake had begun to think of him as a friend. Dalton's approach to thinking was a revelation to him. One exchange had been particularly fascinating, yet also distressing. Blake had asked, "Why does ecoism have so many followers when it's clearly destroying their lives?" Dalton had replied, "Why do you assume they want to live?" which Blake had dismissed as unthinkable. But then Dalton had added, "Isn't man evil?"

The title of Dalton's speech tonight was: 'The logical errors in climate change reasoning.' He just hoped Dalton would be careful – if what he said was construed a certain way, thanks to the CCD law, he could end up in prison.

All the members of the BCF knew they were taking a

risk, which was why the membership list had been kept secret up to now. At this first public meeting the plan was to reveal themselves as a united front and thus appear, and feel, less vulnerable. Clive Donaldson of English Telecom, Sam Tillman of Tillman Foods, Paul Williams of Western Energy, Liz Blackwood of Blackwood's Bank and Gobind Grewal of Serpent Pharmaceuticals were all scheduled to appear. He hoped they would stick to their guns.

Relaxing his face, he smiled at the half-set sun. Tomorrow was another day – there was still hope.

Suddenly his phone buzzed ferociously in its armband. It was a text dated an hour ago – probably delayed by the blackout. Texts were allowed by government regulations since they were deemed most eco-friendly. And there were three missed calls, all from Candice. The text read, *Come to hospital now*. He tried calling her but it just kept ringing. He couldn't call his wife since she wasn't allowed a phone. Still clutching the phone in his hand, he sprinted back to his car. He thought his legs would have rejected his demand for speed, but they didn't. As he ran for the car, he gave silent thanks to the phone makers who carried on despite constant attacks for using rare earth metals.

When he reached it he saw '*Selfish Carbon Criminal*' had been sprayed in green paint down one side, along with a cartoon tree. On the corner of the street fifty metres away, he recognised the two teenagers from before. There was no time to pursue them now. Instead, he yanked open the car door and drove off, shutting it as he went.

#

Blake drove the Bentley as fast as he could across town towards the hospital. Smiling bitterly, he revelled in the lack of traffic – few people could afford the tax on fuel or the electricity to charge a car – but cursed the potholes, horses, bicycles and pedestrians who wandered all over the streets, there being no need any more for maintenance, traffic lights or lanes.

Averaging 20mph, he felt frustrated by his powerful car being reduced to the pace of a bicycle. Still, if business kept declining he wouldn't be able to afford the car anyway, and that would solve the problem. Right now he had to find out what Candice's message had meant. Was it about her? Maybe not, if she had sent it. Then who? His heart rose into his throat as he tried to focus on the road in the fading light.

After nearly twenty minutes, he arrived at the hospital. It was pitch dark. Surely hospitals were exempt from rolling blackouts? But on such windless days it was not uncommon for whole cities to get blacked out. Focusing on driving, he hadn't noticed, but now he realised there had been no lights on in any of the houses he'd passed. They had just been dark lumps against the twilit sky.

He leapt out of the car but then couldn't see the entrance. Suddenly, out of the shadows, a torch emerged bouncing towards him.

"Dad?" It was Candice.

"What's happened?"

"Quickly, this way. James is in the operating theatre. His head got injured when he crashed his car!"

Blake flushed cold. Head injuries were dangerous. Difficult to fix. The best surgeons, like a lot of the best entrepreneurs, had left the country.

"I texted Emma. She's already here."

"I see," was all Blake could say.

They stumbled past groaning shadows on trolleys, bumping into one or two and apologising.

"Why the hell isn't their generator working?" Blake cursed, to no one in particular.

After a couple of wrong turns and backtracks, they arrived in a booth outside the theatre and found Emma staring through a window looking stricken. Blake smiled at her then followed her gaze. The inside of the theatre which should have been bright as a sunlit sky was dim like a savage's cave. He could just make out a surgeon hunched over James, who was unconscious on the table. Two nurses illuminated the scene with dynamo torches, occasionally squeezing them frantically to charge them up. Batteries had been banned within the NHS for not being environmentally friendly.

"Can we go in?" Candice asked.

"I don't think so," Blake said. "There's a risk of infection."

Where they stood was some kind of observation room, perhaps for training doctors. Blake could hear heaving breathing which wasn't coming from Candice or Emma.

"Keep that bloody light still," cried a voice. It was the surgeon shouting at the nurses. The theatre must be wired for sound. Blake noticed the surgeon's scalpel hand was shaking slightly.

"Sorry, Doctor," mumbled the nurses and they tried to alternate squeezing their torches.

Blake could just see his son's damaged skull. Its right side was concave. He felt a shot of adrenaline in his throat as his mind caught up with his vision. James was seriously injured. He might have severe brain damage. He might not... He wanted to ask for professional advice, but he daren't interrupt the surgeon, or the nurses. He noticed the anaesthetist for the first time. He was holding a cloth mask over James's face and taking his pulse manually – his usual equipment stood idle, dead without power. Blake held his breath.

The surgeon continued gingerly removing pieces of bone from James's wound with surgical tweezers. Blake realised how much he depended on this team of medical experts. He'd never been a fan of the NHS, but he gave silent thanks that these people had dedicated themselves to saving lives, despite the constant, overbearing interference from the government.

"Suction," the surgeon said curtly. There was no machine, so one of the nurses put down her torch while she used a large syringe to clean the wound of fluid.

The other nurse wiped her sweating brow with her spare arm. She realised she needed to relieve her aching left hand and swapped the torch to her right.

It never got there. Unused to the muscular effort, her left hand lost its grip as she tried to pass the torch and it clattered to the floor, making a brittle shattering sound.

Blake looked desperately round for a spare.

The surgeon suddenly swore. "I can't see," he shouted. The first nurse grabbed her torch, and shone it on James's head.

Blake gasped. Clear fluid and blood were now flowing out of his son's brain and onto the surgical sheets.

The surgeon turned to stare at them through the window. "I couldn't see," he wailed, and Blake realised what had happened. His hand had slipped in the dark and cut into James's brain, making the injury worse.

The surgeon was shaking even more now. The team were all looking at one another, helplessly.

James's body convulsed.

Emma groaned.

"I'm going to bring him round," the anaesthetist said. He took off the chloroform mask and reached for a syringe, then plunged it into James's arm. James jerked slightly, struggling against the impossible situation, fighting to escape his trapped, enforced sleep, and rekindle his dying brain. But he could not. His loved ones looked on helplessly.

Eventually the anaesthetist let go of his hand and looked up at the surgeon. "He's gone."

The nurses bowed their heads.

The surgeon ripped off his gloves and mask, mumbled, "Sorry," into the mic, then ran from the room.

Emma pressed her hands and tear-stained face against the window. Candice looked with fury at her father.

"It's your fault, you know."

Blake was gobsmacked.

"No, it's mine," whimpered Emma.

#

Lee Procter closed the door to his dingy flat and lowered his hoodie. The owner of the Internet cafe had stared at him on the way out, but he couldn't have seen the birthmark that well.

He wiped his sweaty hands on his jeans and sat on the lumpy sofa. It would be okay. The car must have dropped a good hundred metres. That should have been enough. He'd had to improvise. Why had they gone that way to the meeting? And why leave so early? It didn't matter. He was pretty sure he'd done the job.

He was proud of his disguise as a government safety inspector, which had enabled him to change the car's remote control software while it was still in the garage. It was lucky the blackout hadn't happened until after the crash. That would have bollocksed things up. Now it was all right, and he could look forward to his reward. He sat back and turned on the TV.

2

The small but noisy crowd of protestors in the street outside made it difficult for Dalton MacDermot to reach the Oxford Union's debating chamber, but not impossible. There were placards saying, *MacDermot Must Go* and *We're Marching for Life*. He supposed the latter was a reference to his recent book, *Marching to Death*. In it he'd argued that ecoism was against free speech and respect for person and property. Were they against those things or merely questioning his reasoning? Without a discussion he couldn't tell. That was the problem with slogans.

Once through the crowd he exhaled deeply, then smiled. He was looking forward to demolishing Manny Schweizer's arguments. As a professor of philosophy, he knew he shouldn't allow disagreements to get personal, but Schweizer was partly responsible for his wife Grace being in a full-time nursing home.

Ten years ago she had contracted cerebral malaria on a trip to Cameroon to see her parents. Schweizer and his newspaper had been vociferous in backing Fabian Hardwicke's plan to ban all pesticides worldwide. This had been achieved in Cameroon after Britain threatened to withdraw its foreign aid, but at the price of a massive increase in the mosquito population. Grace had been bitten by one. Unfortunately, she had also been pregnant with their child. Their future son had been lost, and she had been hospitalised ever since.

Dalton visited her almost every day. She was well enough to talk a lot of the time and he was still in love with her. Yesterday the BCF launch meeting had been cancelled due to a tragic accident, so he'd changed plans and gone to see her. They had been talking and smiling for an hour when there was a blackout, and the emergency lighting had not come on. Given their mental state, some of the patients had panicked and injured themselves, including one who fell down some stairs, luckily only breaking his leg. Dalton had stayed with Grace for two hours until the lights came back on. Afterwards, he'd asked the staff about the lack of backup lighting – they had simply blamed a lack of NHS funds.

Today he would have some slight revenge, exposing the non-sequiturs, fallacies and wickedness that lay behind Schweizer's latest campaign supporting the Internet Regulation Bill, legislation that would massively diminish the right to free speech. The audience would be mostly young students, with a sizeable peppering of visitors and dignitaries. But these were impressionable students who usually went on to hold government offices.

Dalton was trying to change the future, but for that he needed free speech in the present. The culmination of his life's work was going to be presented in his forthcoming book, *The Proper Purpose of Government*, if he could find time to finish it, and only if it was allowed to be published. The law against Carbon Crime Denial meant he had to tread carefully, but if Internet Regulation happened, if the government could decide which websites were allowed on grounds of carbon usage and which weren't, he would have huge difficulty in reaching his target audience. Bookshops still existed in some towns, but the carbon tax on fuel and paper production made books relatively expensive. As for broadcasting, the so-called Great British Media Company had been biased for so long and had such a monopoly on the airwaves that his book would not even be mentioned. Then there was also the fact that in his book he argued for it to be disbanded and privatised.

Smiling to himself he caught sight of his ex-pupil and now high-flying barrister Roger Newton, who was standing in the entrance to the Union and smiling back. Roger was to be his seconder in the debate. Dalton was looking forward to this. He walked up to him and shook hands.

"Roger! How are you? Did you need your chain mail on the way in?"

"Oh, you mean the protestors? No, I just smiled and nodded at them, which seemed to disarm them. Of course, being black they couldn't conceive of me being on the 'bad' side."

Dalton laughed and they went in.

The debating chamber was set up much like the House of Commons, which was its model. Dalton had always admired the reverence that was given in Britain to settling disputes by words rather than by weapons.

Did they realise how much in jeopardy this practice was? He looked around and realised the entire room was lit by candles. Scores of them. Were they magic candles that somehow didn't emit CO_2 and soot? He glanced at the high ceiling. It would be a tricky, wasteful job for someone to clean.

He took his place with Roger on the opposers' side of the room and looked about him. The large hall was packed with students wearing all manner of clothes to keep warm on this chilly March evening. He knew they had voted in a previous debate not to heat the room. That was consistent at least, he thought, as was the increase in wan rather than ruddy faces due to veganism. He wondered how long it could last, this trend towards self-abasement, but he knew it was no mere fad, and that the debate tonight was not just a training opportunity for future Parliamentarians, but a battle in the long, protracted war against reason. He surveyed his opponents.

Manny Schweizer – short, pudgy and balding in his early fifties – looked like a disgruntled older version of Tweedledum but without the shorts. Yet thanks to his newspaper, he was probably the most powerful man in the room, and would be more so if the Internet Regulation Bill was passed. Next to him was the seconder, a rat-faced man whom Dalton didn't recognise.

There was a loud shout of "order, order" and the student chairing the Union made some announcements and introduced the speakers, before introducing the debate.

"This House would regulate the Internet to save the planet. The floor is yours, Mr Schweizer."

Schweizer stood to loud applause, and after acknowledging the cheers, began to speak. Perhaps the protestors were somehow listening, thought Dalton, as the background noise of their chants suddenly diminished.

"Ladies and gentlemen of the Union, and honoured guests, it gives me great pleasure, as I'm sure it gives little pleasure to the opposition—" he grinned malignly at Dalton, "—to make the case for this vital step in our mission to save our beautiful planet from greedy human exploitation." Again he looked at Dalton, who merely raised his eyebrows.

"The Internet has been a great invention and a powerful tool for mankind. It has enabled the spread of information around the planet more quickly than ever before. It has permitted contact between families and businesses, continents apart. And it has allowed news of events in war zones and troubled regions to come to the attention of the rest of the world. But it has come at a terrible price.

"The cost has been to our planet, due to the increase in economic activity it has fostered, and to our national cohesion due to the prevalence in its pages of fake news."

Dalton rolled his eyes. Many of the students "hear, heared". The room was warming up now from their breath. Dalton could see condensation running down the windows, and wondered if the Union had elected a 'mould officer'.

Schweizer gripped the sides of the lectern, his eyes darting around the room. "Our planet, Mother Earth, who has nurtured us from the cradle of humankind, has had enough of our arrogance. Of our refusal to obey her laws and listen to her warnings. We have all heard about the ozone crisis, the biodiversity crisis, and the global warming crisis. But still we continue pumping out carbon and behaving as if life was one long freshers' party."

The crowd murmured. Dalton wondered if Schweizer hadn't alienated his audience.

The editor wiped his hands on his trousers and waited for the noise to subside. "I was a fresher once myself, at a college of this great university. And I know the importance of having fun before a difficult task, of building friendships, of camaraderie, of celebrating our achievements. But with the climate crisis upon us, we must redirect our energies towards saving the planet. Otherwise we will have nowhere to celebrate. The Internet Regulation Bill proposes to sober us up, and focus us together on what must be done.

"It will have a dramatic effect, both on our civilisation and our planet. But that is what we need. Some cry 'censorship', but that is scaremongering. The bill will create an independent body for deciding which websites will be allowed. The criteria will include the amount of CTS – Carbon Tonnes Saved – that using the web brings compared with other means. For large organisations, such as the government, the likelihood is their CTS will justify the carbon and energy use of the servers their websites require. But to stop businesses joining together and pooling their CTS, the bill specifies another criteria – downstream emissions.

"These are emissions of CO_2 caused by the actions of other parties as a result of using a website. If these, when added up, exceed their CTS threshold, then the originating website will be shut down. For those that do not comply, the bill recommends fines and disablement by the security services.

"These measure seem strict, even severe, but they will be applied fairly and they are necessary, if we are to save the planet. And don't forget, not long ago we all managed quite well without the Internet. Businesses will continue. People will always be allowed to communicate by traditional means. There is no intention here of preventing free speech. Laws already exist to protect us from those who advocate crimes against humanity." Here he looked pointedly at Dalton.

"As I come to the end of my opening remarks, and leave the floor free for the next speaker, let me say this. Mankind has made great strides in conquering nature. But now he has gone too far and nature is taking her revenge. Now is the time to recognise our mistakes and our limitations and sacrifice our modern, Western conveniences for the sake of our future on this Earth. I propose that 'The Internet must be regulated'."

There was thunderous applause, cries of "hear, hear," and some stamping of feet, as Schweizer wiped his hands and walked quickly back to his seat.

When it had subsided, the chairman indicated to Dalton, who unfolded his tall frame and stood staring at the audience with his piercing blue eyes framed by his head of wavy, grey hair. Then, rather than heading for the lectern, he began pacing up and down the length of the floor. As he stopped to speak, silence fell.

"A wise person once said, 'don't pause to examine a folly, but consider its effects.' Regulating the Internet would be an act of extreme folly, and we will not examine here the truth of the claims that seem to justify it, particularly that humans are destroying the Earth. To do so would be an act of folly itself, and as my opposite number has kindly reminded me, there are laws already in place regarding 'that which must not be said'."

Schweizer was poised with pencil and notebook as if hoping Dalton would commit CCD there and then.

"Instead, we will examine the actual, unmentioned consequences of passing this bill into law."

Dalton resumed pacing the room.

"Firstly, the degree of power that would then rest in the hands of an unaccountable few, such as my opponent opposite. With dissenting voices on the Internet silenced, he and the few like him would hold a monopoly on the publication of news."

Schweizer glared back as Dalton paused and looked at him. The noise of chanting from outside rose slightly, but it did not deter Dalton.

"As a publisher of physical newspapers, when websites are shut down and apps stop working, his views will come to dominate cultural debate. Is that something a debating society should welcome?"

He looked pointedly at the society's chairman, then continued pacing.

"Furthermore, it will stifle actual thought. Imagine you have an idea for a new medicine. You develop samples and you want to try them out. How will you find volunteers and how will you assemble a team to conduct a trial? You could apply to a well-known journal, but there is now a backlog of two years' worth of articles to be published. Yours will be at the end of that queue, and by then you will have left the university. You wake up the next day feeling disheartened but you go and discuss the situation with your peers. After a week of physically going round and talking to them, because your messaging application has failed the CTS test, and the company running your email has become involved in a legal tangle regarding the consequences of downstream emissions, you learn that they would like to help, but can't, because without the Internet, their own research and studies are taking much, much longer. You feel more disheartened. The following day you wake up and decide to do something else, giving up on your idea because you can't see it ever being made in practice.

"That is the worst consequence of the suppression of publication. The death of new ideas. If you want to see the consequences of a society with a low transmission and acceptance of ideas, read up on the Middle Ages.

"You might argue that there is always the printing press, but paper-making is an energy intensive process, which usually involves emitting CO_2. Assuming, as is likely, that the Carbon Crime Bill becomes law, do you think a paper-making company will be allowed a decent quota? Perhaps it will depending on the political views of the company's owners and its customers."

Schweizer was fidgeting on his ancient wooden bench. Dalton continued.

"Which brings me to the issue of bias. When the so-called 'independent panel' decides which website to allow, will it be—"

There was an almighty crash of breaking glass. Dalton whirled to face the sound. Cries of pain came from students sitting under a massive stained-glass window. There was a dull thud at his feet. Looking down in the candlelit gloom, he saw shards of coloured glass from the shattered images of saints and benefactors – and a brick.

He picked it up and strode from the room, his don's robes flowing behind him.

#

Dalton arrived at the door of the Chancellor's office only fifty yards away and barged it open. The stooped, aged Chancellor, who had been gazing out of his study window, turned to look at him.

"Ah, MacDermot, I was expecting you to show up."

Dalton dropped the brick on the floor with a thud. "You saw what happened? Have you called the police? An ambulance?"

"No," said the Chancellor, slowly.

"What about the mob outside? It must have come from them. Have you called security?"

"Again, no."

"Why the hell not?"

The Chancellor took a tired breath and said, "What do you expect, given your recent publication?"

"My book is the cause of criminal damage and actual bodily harm?"

The Chancellor said nothing.

"Have you even read it?"

Again the Chancellor was silent.

"Yet it was thanks to yous –", he realised that his emotion was exposing his Northern Irish origins, but he didn't care, "– that I had to self-publish, because you told the OUP not to touch it. Your predecessor had no problem with my books."

Keeping his gaze safely averted from Dalton's, the Chancellor looked wistfully out of the window. "Times

33

have changed, Professor MacDermot."

Fuming, Dalton went on. "You had no trouble publishing Professor Unwin's recent book, *The Wages of Sin*, which, if I recall correctly, advocates suicide pacts as a way to save the planet. Surely that is far more inflammatory than my work?"

"You forget, perhaps, that Oxford was originally a Christian institution. Self-sacrifice is a virtue."

Hardly believing his ears, Dalton remembered the Chancellor had been Head of Mediaeval Theology before accepting his current exalted position. Still, he battled on, through the wall of non-integration that was the Chancellor's method of thinking.

"But it's sheer vandalism," he said, hoping this appeal to the fabric of ancient Oxford might reach him.

"Some might call it that," mused the Chancellor. "But they do have a right to protest."

As Dalton stood speechless with indignation, the Chancellor took his opportunity.

"Professor MacDermot, these are not the first protests against your work. A number of students have come forward expressing their fear at being intimidated on the way to your lectures.

"By protestors that you refuse to confront.

"And some are considering withdrawing from your course."

"Despite the fact that I have the highest pass rate for philosophy in the university?"

"With fewer students willing to take your courses, it will become very difficult to justify your position here."

"You mean you want to sack me?"

"These are difficult times – financially as well as

politically – for the university."

"But I need to finish my latest book. It's the culmination of my career. I need the Bodleian and I need my colleagues' input. And I need the income."

"I'm sure you can manage at some other, less prestigious institution."

"But I'm settled here. My wife is in a good care home here. Moving would not be good for her."

The Chancellor smiled weakly. "That's as may be, but you're putting me in a very difficult position."

Dalton couldn't absorb what was being said to him. As he stood staring at the floor, the Chancellor continued.

"A few years ago I helped start the 'no-platforming' movement. As you know, it was, and still is highly successful at rooting out unsavoury people and opinions from university life. The Chancellor at the time was very grateful for my reducing the level of confrontation among the students. What we want is peace and stability, so people can continue their studies. That is all."

Dalton looked up. He could feel his hands sweating and his heart racing. He would have liked to punch the Chancellor for his cowardice and his betrayal, but with a deep breath he said, "So you're not reporting this incident?" and pointed to the Union.

"No."

"But you are aiding and abetting thuggery. If you won't go to the police, I will." Professor MacDermot stormed out.

As the main door slammed shut, the Chancellor noticed his side door creak open and the wasted, greying figure of Lord Fabian Hardwicke emerge.

The Chancellor wiped his hands on his robes and asked, "Did you hear all that?"

"It would have been hard not to," intoned the leader of the Ecoist Party.

"I've never known anyone more arrogant in my life. To say he has a 'closed mind' is rather an understatement."

"Yes, Manny was trying to open it a little this evening."

"Manny?" asked the Chancellor, curiously.

"Ah, Emmanuel Schweizer. At the Union."

"Yes of course," said the Chancellor, who then remembered his own chief concern. "This business with the brick through the window. It would be so much better if the press didn't make a fuss, don't you think?"

Fabian fixed him with his worried yet wild-looking eyes, then said, "Naturally. I'll see what I can do. I take it you will continue to allow the protests, then?"

"Yes indeed. Young people must be able to air their views. And I'm sure you'll agree that Oxford is one of the best places there is to encourage young people to understand the world properly. It would be such a shame, if the cost of repairing this ancient institution meant that future generations were denied the same opportunity."

Fabian took the hint. "Rest assured, Chancellor. When our party comes to real political power, Oxford will be high on our list of those in need of subsidies."

"Thank you, thank you," said the Chancellor. Then he remembered the risk to another source of income. "Er, there is also the sensitive matter of the ethical lending laws."

"What about them? They are part of a sensible, responsible strategy for ensuring money flows to sustainable organisations that don't harm the planet. You're not objecting to that, are you?"

"No, no, I wouldn't dream of it. But in the course of our wide-ranging research here, Oxford has to have many partners in industry, and, well, we wouldn't want any question mark over their green credentials to affect us."

Fabian simply stared at him.

The Chancellor clasped his hands and clarified. "We couldn't afford to be taken off the approved list." He waited and could almost see Fabian silently calculating behind his eyes. Finally, his visitor spoke.

"I, of course, have no direct influence over such matters. An independent body decides such things. However, given your accommodation of green principles and support of many ecoist intellectuals, I don't think you have anything to worry about."

"That is most reassuring, thank you," gushed the Chancellor.

Fabian smiled. "Of course, I do share your concern about the safety of the students and staff. Perhaps I could go down and talk to the protestors, if you think it would help? Make sure they behave responsibly?"

"That would be very much appreciated."

He shook the Chancellor's moist hand and left.

#

Fabian permitted himself a smile as he descended the creaking staircase. The Chancellor had been most amenable. It felt good, it felt powerful. Certainly compared to his student days in Oxford. Back then he had not been as successful as his friend Manny. He could admit that now. He had been a bit lost. Especially when the Berlin Wall came down. He had jumped off that bridge. If it hadn't been for Manny … And then Ursula, his only ever girlfriend, had left him and…

As his feet touched the stone floor at the bottom of the staircase, he was reminded of the solidity of the earth. He stopped and played with his cracked wooden ring. He'd have to replace it again soon. It was in 1989, at his lowest point, that he had discovered the green movement and bought his first wooden ring to remind himself of his 'marriage' to the Earth. "To love and cherish it over and above myself." Those were the words he had recited at the time, and they formed a sacred vow that he had kept. Never allowing himself to be deviated from his cause. Never allowing himself the indulgence of another intimate relationship. Sacrifices had to be made. There were too many people anyway. He took a deep breath and stepped outside.

The night air was chilly. Particularly so since his suit jacket had still not quite dried from that rain shower earlier. The government weather app had been wrong again. Yet more evidence of climate chaos, he reasoned. And he focused again on why he was there. Another unpredicted event had happened, and he had to rectify the situation.

Marching across the wet grass to the noisy group of ten protestors, he noticed, with satisfaction, that many of them wore the Ecoist Party badge. Apparently some people thought it looked like a mushroom cloud. He didn't mind that – it scared people, and they needed scaring to take action.

As he neared them, one of them recognised him and

pointed him out to the others, who stopped chanting and began cheering. Fabian smiled as he stepped into their midst and was surrounded by them. He shook the hands of a few he'd seen at party meetings and greeted some others, before gesturing for them to quieten down and listen.

"I salute you all, and thank you on behalf of the party, and all those who care about the planet, for confronting one of the worst enemies of ecoism – Dalton MacDermot."

They made angry noises.

"Your protests are particularly important at the moment, as we garner support for the Carbon Crime Bill. It will make all businesses account for every speck of carbon they produce, every bit of damage they do to the environment, and make them afraid to fart without government permission."

The small crowd emitted guffaws.

Fabian continued. "This is not just metered use, but a detailed account of cars parked, cars driven, the reason for each journey and a calculation of the carbon used. And it will apply to all energy they use, from the canteens they eat in, and the sources of their food, to the pens and paper they write with. And each year, the government's Carbon Audit Committee will determine if their carbon use was justified, and if it will be permitted to continue the following year. Make no mistake. This bill, and your efforts to support it, will change the world for generations to come."

He signalled he'd stopped speaking, and was greeted with enraptured applause. The audience slapped him on the back and shook his hand, but as they started chanting again, Fabian managed to manoeuvre a protestor with a large purple birthmark on his face away to one side.

The short, wiry man looked up at him with a worried face.

"Well done with the brick, Lee," Fabian said.

"It was a pleasure," Lee grinned, relaxing.

"But you failed regarding my brother."

"Yes, I know," Lee said, looking down at his dirty trainers. "It was all going so well, the device in the car, the Internet cafe…"

"But he wasn't in the car."

"I couldn't have known that. I did exactly what you said."

Fabian stared at Lee while he considered this. Yes, loyalty and obedience were highly valuable.

"You did your best. You risked your freedom for the cause. And for that, you should be praised."

Lee beamed.

"Now you must follow through. He still thinks it was an accident. Send him a threatening note that says, 'Candice is next.' You know how. I know him. He won't carry on with the BCF if he thinks his other child might die."

Lee nodded and grinned.

Fabian reached into his suit pocket and surreptitiously handed over an envelope of notes.

"For the cause."

"For the cause," repeated his acolyte, grinning wider as Fabian slipped back into the crowd. Addressing the nearest beaming face, Fabian asked it, "Do you know about the long-running protest at the Tilcot power plant?"

"Of course," said the pale face belonging to a

dreadlocked boy. "Do they need us there?"

"I'm sure they'd welcome anyone who hates carbon. I'm off there later tomorrow, as it happens. Would you like a lift?"

Speechless, the boy nodded.

After several more minutes of general encouragement, they left together.

#

Behind him, the main gate to Tilcot Power Station opened. Brigadier Timothy Campbell – the Brig – put down his binoculars from scanning the crowd of protestors and turned to look.

A shortish man with a closely cropped beard and a solemn face was walking towards him.

"Brigadier, I must try to talk to them again."

"Mr Williams…"

"Paul, please."

"Paul. I admire you trying to make them see reason, but I think it's gone beyond that now. It's too dangerous."

He gestured to the large, chanting crowd and their array of banners: '*Electricity is Evil*', '*Fossil Fuels are Murder*', '*We're Carbon Free, Are You?*' There were also several Ecoist Party tree banners on show.

"But they have to understand. We supply ten per cent of the country's electricity here. If they turn back the coal lorries, or break in again and try to destroy the equipment, they will bring misery to a very large number of people, including countless pensioners."

"That won't happen. Not while we're allowed to do our job." They had been ordered there a week ago at the behest of the President. He nodded towards the couple of hundred armed soldiers guarding the perimeter.

"I don't want this to turn nasty. Troops and civilians are a bad combination."

"So are pensioners and cold weather."

Paul smiled weakly.

The Brig didn't want an escalation either, but he had his job to do. "Look, you can try talking to them again, but we'll accompany you."

"And your guns?"

"We'll leave some of them behind."

"All right."

"Peters?"

A lieutenant colonel stepped forward.

"Yes, Brig."

"You're to accompany Mr Williams and me to a talk with the 'enemy'." He used this term lightly, but he knew his troops were there because of the violence that had been meted out to the police previously. "Leave your weapon, but have a platoon follow us. And ask Major Windsor to join us if he'd be so kind."

Peters gave the orders and they advanced towards the crowd.

"Where do they all come from?" asked Paul.

"All over," said Peters. "They're very organised, rotating people in and out of the camp every two weeks, but there's a core who've sat it out all winter."

"Burning fossil fuels or wood to stay warm, no doubt," Paul sighed. "Where do they get their supplies?"

"There's a regular delivery by truck every day. It's a diesel," the Brig said.

All three of them smiled sardonically.

"I was hoping the BCF would expose this kind of

hypocrisy and start to turn the tide of public opinion."

"The BCF?" Peters asked.

"Business Carbon Forum. I'm a founding member. But the whole thing's been suspended since Blake Hardwicke lost his son."

"Aye, of course," commented the Brig, who'd read about it in an intelligence report. "He's a brave man, going against public opinion like that."

"Or what appears to be public opinion," Peters said, pointing towards a camera crew. "The GBMC have been here for months, egging them on."

They all stopped and looked. There was a man in a bright blue puffer jacket with a camera on his shoulder, panning across the crowd. Behind him was a mobile broadcasting van. They saw the exhaust from its generators.

As they paused, a tall, lean soldier in battle fatigues marched up to them. He had a slight limp.

"You wanted to see me, Brig?"

"Ah yes. Paul, may I introduce our own secret media weapon, Major Arthur Windsor."

"How do you do," said the man, scowling at the Brig as he shook Paul's hand.

Paul was taken aback, then he bowed slightly. "Your Royal Highness, I didn't know you were defending us."

"Please, just Arthur."

"We still call him the Prince," the Brig said.

The Prince grimaced. "I really don't have a title any more, as you well know," he said as he addressed the Brig.

The Brig smiled. He enjoyed winding Arthur up. He had no children himself, and he was proud to have an

43

ex-royal under his command. The only member of the Royal Family to stay after their ignominious departure. The only one with his country truly at heart. He also knew Arthur would always indulge him. The Brig had saved his life in the Middle East by opening fire against orders and evacuating him swiftly. Since then, the Prince had never complained, though he had gone on a bomb disposal course. Along with serving in the RAF too, Arthur had become quite a man.

The Brig signalled the platoon behind and they moved off again towards the protestors. As they got closer he could see them handing round steaming mugs to each other. Before he could suggest otherwise, Paul had stepped forward to address them.

"That soup," he said, pointing to a cracked, wooden mug leaking into the mittened gloves of a wild-eyed woman, "that you heated up on a fire, you must have wasted seventy per cent of the energy literally going up in smoke. If you really want to preserve resources and avoid pollution, why do you do it?"

"Look, mate," said a tall, grizzled man of about forty. "What we're doing here is going to bring you and all your carbon-loving friends down, eventually. If we have to make sacrifices along the way, so be it."

Paul studied the man's pinched and frowning face, and noticed a Bluetooth earpiece hidden under his knitted hat. Another concession to technology for the sake of the revolution, he presumed.

Paul tried again, hoping that at least some of the others would listen and try to process what he was saying, but as he was recognised they moved to surround him, and he had to explain over their shouting.

"Do you realise how much worse your lives will be if we go on denying ourselves cheap, reliable electricity? Every business, every job, every home relies in some way on energy. Wind power can't provide that. What happens on days like this, when there's hardly a breeze?"

"We've got solar," someone piped up from the crowd.

"You have now. But you see those clouds?" He pointed to the horizon. "In half an hour they'll be here, you'll be cold, and solar will generate almost nothing."

"Fossil fuels are murder," said the pinch-faced man.

"A lot more people will die without cheap and reliable energy," Paul retorted. "Look at last winter's figures on deaths among the elderly. Twenty per cent up compared with five years ago."

Some of the protestors mumbled.

"Lies," the man said. "Put about by industries like yours so you can carry on polluting the world and lining your own pockets."

The crowd hollered in agreement.

"But don't you see it makes sense?" Paul tried. "You know there are more blackouts now than five years ago. You know we've got an ageing population. You know it was a cold winter last year. There's only one possible outcome."

"Don't try your capitalist logic on me," croaked a pungent, wiry-haired woman nearby. "You're just telling us what you want us to hear. What about all the things you're not saying? All the things that are hidden?"

"Such as what?" Paul asked, genuinely bewildered.

"For those that understand, no explanation is

necessary. For those that don't, none is possible," she intoned, raising her voice. "We just know that carbon is wrong, unnatural, and has to be stopped, for the sake of the world, and for all future generations. We are the pioneers of a new, forward-thinking, progressive mankind. One that loves and cherishes the Earth. You exploiters have had your chance. Your time is over, your damage is done. We are the future now. We are leading the way to being carbon-free!"

The crowd erupted into rapturous chanting, whistling and cheers.

Paul could see the slogans were having their effect. He turned to look for help but the Brig, Peters and the Prince were already pushing through the crowd to extract him.

"It's Prince Arthur," someone said, and the protestors stopped harassing Paul to get a better look.

They were silent as the Prince's party met up with Paul and together they made their way slowly back towards the power station. Then someone in the crowd shouted, "Carbon traitor," and a gob of spit landed on the Prince's cheek.

As he stopped, wiped it off and turned, the Brig and Peters braced themselves and the crowd went quiet, withdrawing slightly.

"I'm only doing my job, " said the Prince into the crowd. "Why can't you act like civilised people?"

Then he moved off with the others and the crowed stopped following them.

As they rejoined the platoon and headed back to the perimeter fence, Peters spoke up. He was fuming.

"I accept that the environment is important. We all live in it, for Christ's sake. But how did 'saving the planet' become spitting on people, attacking power stations and causing people to suffer?"

"They think the planet is more important?" the Prince suggested.

"But the planet isn't alive, not like people."

Paul chimed in, "They think it's necessary now to preserve the world for future generations."

"But what kind of life are these future generations going to enjoy if they're legally banned from lighting a barbecue? And if all the world's resources are basically off-limits? How are they going to live?"

"So full of questions, grasshopper," the Brig chided.

"You may laugh," said Peters, "but remember Sun Tzu. 'Military leaders must struggle to understand the unfathomable plans of their opponents.'"

"Indeed," smiled the Brig.

With the platoon around them, it wasn't until they reached the main gate that they could see a large black car pulled up beside it. Standing next to it was the figure of Fabian, Lord Hardwicke. He was holding binoculars.

Paul went over to meet him.

"Lord Hardwicke," he said, not shaking hands. "To what do we owe the pleasure?"

Fabian paused, taking the measure of them. He raised his eyebrows when he recognised the Prince, but otherwise ignored him. Then he spoke. "I see it's getting quite dangerous here."

"Well, it felt a bit uncomfortable just now," Paul admitted, "but I was in safe hands." He smiled his thanks at the soldiers.

"I didn't mean for you," Fabian said. "For the protestors."

The Brig coughed.

"You see," Fabian continued, "it's not a sustainable situation. A large, democratic crowd exercising their legal right to protest, and a mob of armed troops. These things have a tendency to escalate and we wouldn't want that, would we, Brigadier?"

The Brig bristled. "You know we're only here to protect the power station."

"But in doing so you're attacking the future of everyone in this country, everyone in the world. Climate change is a real threat to people. You've got to expect them to get angry."

"We have democratic means in this country of dealing with situations like that."

"We do. But sometimes they are not enough. Sometimes those with more knowledge and with the best interests of the world at heart need to take direct action."

The Brig and the others glowered at him.

"However," Fabian continued, "you have just given me a good idea." He retrieved a mobile phone from his pocket and stood staring at them as he waited for a number to connect.

"Put me through to the President, would you? This is Lord Hardwicke."

It was less than a minute before he got a response.

"Yes, it's me... It's about the Tilcot protests... I'm up here now, and it's looking like the situation is getting out of control. Things could easily escalate here... There have been confrontations between the army and the peaceful protestors. Paul Williams has become personally involved, as has the ex-Prince Arthur... Yes, I believe it is getting quite dangerous... The GBMC are here, you could ask them. By the way, how is the coalition holding up…? Indeed? …Thank you. I'll see you in Cabinet later… I'll pass you over." Fabian handed his phone to the Brig.

"Brigadier Campbell speaking," he said, frowning. "No sir, it's not like that… We did take some men over to them, yes… No, we did not… How do I know how they feel…? It's a matter of doing our job and protecting the power station and those working there… No sir, I can't recommend doing that… I'm afraid, sir, I would need that order from my chain of command… I see." He thumbed the phone angrily and tossed it back to Fabian, who fumbled but caught it, then walked away to make another call.

"Well? What was that about?" Peters asked.

"He thinks we should leave."

"What? Abandon the power station?"

The Brig nodded.

"But that's crazy. It'll be chaos. The staff here won't be safe. The protestors might cause real damage."

"I know."

"It wouldn't look good for the army," the Prince joined in.

The Brig gritted his teeth as he and the others looked at Fabian, who seemed to be giving instructions. After another minute or so, something buzzed in the Brig's breast pocket and he pulled out his own phone.

"Yes sir." He looked worriedly at Peters. "We can't do that… I'm here on the ground and it's not the right course of action… I know there's a lot at stake… my point is… I'm afraid I can't do that, sir."

He held the phone to his ear for a full minute. Then he let his arm drop to his side as he directed his gaze at the protestors, at the power station, and finally at his men, before raising his arm and continuing the call.

"That is my final answer… Yes sir." He handed the phone to Peters, who took it with a look of shock.

"Lieutenant Colonel Peters here… Yes sir… Can you repeat that, sir… I see." He looked aghast at the Brig, who nodded slowly at him. "Yes sir. I'll make those arrangements right away… Yes sir, I will." He gave the phone back to the Brig. Then he looked at his boots and swallowed hard.

"Brigadier Timothy Campbell, I am placing your under arrest on a charge of disobeying orders, until you can be court-martialled." To the Prince he said, "That was General Kettle. He's put me in charge. We've got to move out by tomorrow."

~

The Brig looked out of the staff car window as they joined the column of army vehicles driving away from the power station. Also in the car were the Prince and Paul Williams, both looking shell-shocked. Behind them was a hastily requisitioned coach full of Tilcot's staff.

As they drove away, they looked out of the rear window. From the woods where the protestors had been camping came a swarm of dark-coloured figures. They reached the unguarded but locked main gate, but some must have had bolt cutters as it was soon wide open and the hordes surged inside.

"At least we had time to close it down safely," Paul said, looking at the smokeless chimneys.

"Can it be started up again?" the Prince asked.

"Only if they don't do too much damage."

"I fear the damage has already been done," the Brig

said. He was thinking of what had made the President capitulate so quickly, and of how he could ever serve his country again.

#

Fabian relaxed on the back seat of his government car as he was driven back to London for the Cabinet meeting. Things had gone well at Tilcot. Better than he'd expected. Now he would have to explain it to the Cabinet and ensure it stayed shut down. Given his recent record of success, he felt confident about it. After all, it was he who had been instrumental in having Parliament closed on both Wednesdays and Fridays to save CO_2. No more time wasted at Prime Minister's Questions. More time to persuade people in Cabinet to get things done. The climate wouldn't wait. In fact, today's meeting would be a good opportunity to make his latest demand, now his power was becoming obvious.

Just as he relaxed and thought of this, there was a screech of tyres, the car lurched, and Fabian was thrown out of his seat.

"Sorry, sir," the driver said. "Horse and cyclist."

Fabian lowered his electric window and wanted to shout abuse at them as he went past. Couldn't they see the flags on the bonnet? But instead he forced a smile. They were being better ecoists in this case.

He dusted himself down and tried to enjoy the rest of the long journey back to the capital. The roads were much emptier thanks to the carbon tax on fuel, but there was now a distinct lack of discipline. At least the motorway part of the journey should be easier, non-motorised vehicles still being banned from them.

Several hours and traffic mishaps later, he

recognised the hotels of Park Lane, and they were soon driving along Constitution Hill. Fabian smiled as he recalled the night the Royal Family went into exile. Their lavish lifestyle had been criticised for decades, although a few apologists claimed it was simply part of their tireless service to the nation, but what eventually made them leave, except for Prince Arthur, was their objection to the regulation and taxation of charities. Fabian had campaigned tirelessly and as a result the government had insisted that no organisation should be exempt since they all, especially large charities, emitted tonnes of carbon, which had to be monitored and paid for. When the royals all objected, a lot of people accused them of being political, and when there was only a paltry crowd for the birth of the latest royal baby, they had decided to go and live in Canada.

It had been a left-wing dream for over a century. Fabian smiled as he thought of how he'd helped bring it about. Britain now had a President, who combined the roles of Prime Minister and Head of State, and who occupied a modest number of rooms at the Palace as well as Number 10. Fabian didn't think much of him, as he was a Tory, but he accepted the necessity of having someone good at compromising to hold the Tory, Labour and Ecoist coalition together.

He girded his loins as he stepped from the car into Downing Street. These meetings were never easy, especially when dealing with his non-Ecoist colleagues, but it was all temporary, he told himself, until the next election.

The President shook his hand as they walked into the meeting room together. Once they were all settled, he asked him what he had to report.

"Thanks to the prompt action of the President," he smiled at him, "two disasters have been averted. Firstly, the deaths of any protestors at the hands of the headstrong army, along with the civil unrest that would doubtless have followed."

The others "hear-heared".

"Secondly, the last and largest of the CO_2-polluting power stations has ceased belching its poison into the skies."

Again they expressed their approval.

Then the Minister for Energy and Environment, a thin-faced man with glasses, raised his voice. "Unfortunately, while obviously done with the best of intentions, the sudden and unexpected loss of Tilcot to the grid has led to unplanned power outages across the country."

"Has anyone complained?" asked the President nervously.

"The banks have been on the phone explaining that they only have diesel backup for three days. Many of them are accelerating their plans to relocate to America."

"Good riddance," said the Minister for Justice.

The rest banged the table in approval. The President fidgeted in his seat.

"There's also the likely effect on patients," said the Minister for Health. "As you know from my report, accidents are increasing while quality of care is falling."

"Yes, that's an unfortunate consequence," said the President, "but you must realise this war against carbon is a war. There will be casualties." He looked sternly at the Minister for Health.

She feared for her job and said, "Yes, Mr. President, naturally."

"Are there any more concerns regarding Tilcot?" the President asked.

The Minister for Industry studied his lap as if he was trying to escape observation by not making eye contact. The Chancellor of Exchequer was staring fixedly out of the window.

"Good. Tilcot will remain closed. Organise a press release, will you," he addressed the Cabinet Secretary, "highlighting the victory over selfish capitalist industries and our determination to save the planet."

"Did Paul Williams raise the issue of compensation?" the Chancellor piped up.

"No," the President said, glancing at Fabian, "but I'm glad you mentioned him, as this brings us to our next agenda point: making the sentence for Climate Change Denial custodial, rather than merely a fine."

Fabian smiled as the President turned to him again. "Do you have anything to say, Lord Hardwicke?"

Fabian still enjoyed hearing his full title. He had been given it for 'services to the environment' two years earlier. It vindicated his existence and his direction in life, as did his presence in the Cabinet. As the leader of a major party in the coalition, a seat was always available for him. He was also a key advisor to the Ministry of Health on veganism – a post which had proved extremely useful.

"Only to reiterate what I think you all know," Fabian said. "That the climate is still in chaos. Scientists now think it might never be stable again, due to the damage industrialisation has done."

The Cabinet shook their heads sadly.

"But we must try not to make it worse. People must be made to take the issue seriously, and not just pay lip service and a fine as if it were as trivial as a parking ticket."

He was starting to raise his voice now as it followed his blood pressure, but he knew this was not the time – the conference in April would be better – so he took a breath before continuing. "Therefore, I fully support the plan to lock up climate change deniers. It is the only safe place for them."

The Cabinet enjoyed a good speech that made them feel part of a group doing something important. They banged the table in approval.

"Right, that settles it – unless there are any objections?"

The Chancellor and the Minister for Justice both shook their head.

"Good. Can you announce it in the press release as well?"

"Yes, Mr. President," the Cabinet Secretary said.

Suddenly, just as the President was looking at the next agenda item, the lights went out.

Without hesitation, they all reached into their pockets or handbags and brought out their hand-charged torches.

"Shall we continue?" the President asked.

3

The April sun was shining, the birds were singing, the cherry trees were blossoming, but Blake's heart felt like a heavy, dead lump as he sat next to Marisa in an open-top carriage being driven towards the crematorium behind a horse-drawn hearse. Candice sat opposite, looking tearfully but resolutely away from him. Marisa was pressed up next to him, within his arm's embrace, clutching his other hand and staring at the floor from under her black veiled hat. The prison had let her out for one day's compassionate 'leave', but he could feel the electronic ankle bracelet against his leg.

They had created James together, they had raised him, shared it all, from birth, through illness, parties, holidays, schools, but not this – Blake alone was to blame for his death.

The note, made up of letters cut out of newspapers, had been pushed through the door two days after the crash. It read:

STOP THE BCF FOR GOOD OR CANDICE IS NEXT. YOU DESTROY THE PLANET, WE DESTROY YOUR

FAMILY.

He had taken the note to Inspector Smith at the police station but so far he'd had no ideas, except to say it was probably just some opportunist trying to scare him out of his views. The investigation into the car crash had revealed nothing untoward. The police were treating it as an accident. Yet Blake had been to the steep drop where James's car had swerved off the road and he could see no reason for it. The car was new, the model had no history of accidents, James was a spirited driver, but not reckless. Besides, these modern electric cars were nothing like the powerful, rear-wheel-drive vehicles of old. They had all sorts of safety devices and warning signals. No, he had to take the note seriously. And he had to take some, if not all, of the blame.

He couldn't tell Candice. She would be scared to death. She would demand he give up his leadership of the BCF and keep quiet about his views on ecoism in general. All while they were trying to rebuild a family life now down to two. She would have a point, but he couldn't change his views, they were part of who he was. And if he said nothing about them again in public, all his friends and colleagues would want to know why, and the ecoist propaganda machine would continue, relentlessly mowing down his and his country's freedom.

And he couldn't tell Marisa. Not when she would be suffering alone in prison, grieving for James with no one to comfort her. She shared his views on ecoism, but having already lost one child, she too might insist they all kept their views private. But what was the point of having ideas in your mind if you couldn't express them or act on them in the world? It would crush his ability to think. It risked tearing their marriage apart. It was hard enough already, with Marisa in prison.

He sat listening to the slow clop of the horses' hooves, the birds in the trees and Marisa's shuddering breaths, feeling as if his will to move would never be effective again.

As they turned in to the crematorium and rode slowly up the curving drive towards the entrance, Blake saw someone who was possibly feeling as guilty as him. Emma, James's girlfriend whom he had been driving to see, was standing alone in a long black dress, her chin on her chest, sobbing and unable to look at the hearse.

Thankfully, as soon as they stopped, Candice got out and went over to comfort her and, Blake surmised, herself.

He helped Marisa out of the carriage and into the small, secular entrance hall, where mourners waited whispering on agnostic benches.

He saw his brother Fabian, thin and grey in a black suit, reminding him of their mother, except for the permanent worried look and – today in particular – his constantly shifting eyes. Fabian would not meet his gaze, though he did manage an exchange of weak smiles with Candice.

Moving slowly, as if in a muffled dream, he and Marisa felt the hands and sounds of sympathy as they processed slowly into the chapel.

As they sat on the front row of hard, pine pews and held onto the white service sheets like polystyrene swimming floats, Blake finally allowed himself to think about his son.

James would no longer run with him, through the mud and the leg-scratching fields, up the slopes and onto the sunlit hilltops. He would no longer turn his smiling, sweaty face towards him and jibe Blake as he arrived second. They would no longer share their thoughts about the state of the world or their own future plans. Blake would no longer help him with his science homework. And James would no longer give Blake that reflection of himself in earlier days that lifted his spirits and made his heart sing.

No. Now all that life, all that love and all that promise, was suffocated in a box. He felt a large tear roll down his cheek and left it there.

Escaping the pain of the personal for a moment, he recalled the national debate over cremation versus burial, and which was more eco-friendly. Cremation had won, because despite the carbon pollution from burning a body, it left less of a human mark on the Earth in total. He wished James had lived long enough to leave a decent sized mark.

At last the service began and they all stood to sing, not a hymn, but a favourite pop song of James's: 'Sunrise over Salford'. Blake smiled between the tears that tried to wash away his grief and his guilt. He remembered James blasting out that song at the top of his voice in his room, while Blake had tried to work in the office downstairs. He'd never had the heart to ask him to stop or turn it down. The song was about feeling uninhibited joy and confidence that would last forever. He knew the lyrics by heart, having heard them so often, and he croaked them out now as best he could , in salute to James's spirit.

The service continued with a mixture of songs, some

readings by a humanist priest and a eulogy by Blake.

He'd written down what he wanted to say, so with some pauses to clear his throat, he managed to get it out. It seemed so inadequate to describe what a person meant to you in a few sentences. But as he looked out at the tear-streaked faces he realised everyone accepted the convention of a limited public acknowledgement of the unlimited private volumes within.

Then came more music, and finally the curtains. He'd had his arm around Marisa throughout as she sobbed quietly, and now, having endured the worst of silent pauses, knowing the crematorium was impatient to stick to their schedule, but also knowing that getting up was a sign of acceptance, he took a deep breath and guided her up and out into the harsh sunlight.

They listened to more sympathy and appreciated the displays of flowers until the carriage drew up and they proceeded solemnly back to their house for the wake.

As they came to a halt outside the front door and got out, one of the horses pulling their carriage left an enormous, steaming mess on the drive. Fabian, who had been following in the carriage behind, came over.

"Never mind. I'm sure it'll be good for the roses."

Blake exploded. "Why don't you come round and dig it in for me, then? It's your fault—" he nearly said 'some ecoist nutter killed him', but couldn't, not now, "—we have to use horses these days anyway."

"And it's your fault James is dead, as you bought him that ridiculous car."

Everyone froze as they witnessed the escalating verbal fight between the two brothers.

Blake looked at Marisa, and realising this wasn't helping the situation, became reconciled to leaving it there. Then Candice spoke up.

"I agree with Uncle Fabian."

#

"So she's living with you now, is she?" Manny Schweizer asked Fabian. They were sitting in Manny's office on Fleet Street.

"Yes." It had been a surprise to Fabian that Candice had vehemently wanted to move in with him. But it was logical. She was a member of the Green Shoots and her father was, at least in principle, its sworn enemy. Nevertheless, he'd had to weigh the pros and cons before agreeing to it. Blake couldn't have told her about the note, or perhaps he had. Either way, Fabian couldn't admit to knowing about it. On the other hand, it would definitely be one more victory against his brother and further diminish his credibility. So he'd agreed. He'd had to clear the spare room for Candice but it hadn't taken long. In fact, he was almost enjoying getting to know her as they chatted about her new school – where he was soon to give a speech – and her new friends at the local Green Shoots meetings. What she could tell him about Blake was most interesting. Most helpful.

His mind went back to Manny, to whom he said, "She's a remarkable young woman, who's come on a remarkable journey."

"Not just literally, I presume?" Everyone acknowledged travel was far more of a challenge than it used to be.

"No. Blake is one of the most selfish capitalists that exists, but she's somehow managed to extricate herself from his mindset, mostly."

"Only mostly?"

"She still considers it possible that she might become a software engineer."

Manny groaned. They both hated the Internet.

"Yes, I know. But she's young. She can learn. I'm going to invite her to the party conference at the end of the month. Put her on the platform."

Manny murmured appreciatively. Fabian thought he even detected some jealousy.

"Did the police find out any more about how her brother died?"

Fabian flinched but he didn't think it showed. Manny was a journalist, after all.

"No. It seems James just lost control. Most unfortunate."

"It was convenient though, wasn't it. I mean, I'm not saying it was a good thing he died, but it did stop the BCF in its tracks."

Manny did like to ferret away, ruminated Fabian, but then he had saved his life all those years ago. "It seems to have, for now. But there's always the possibility that Blake will get it going again. Candice has mentioned that he has a long list of members and donors. People who haven't come into the open yet."

"I'm not surprised," Manny said, "especially now Carbon Crime Denial is custodial. But we know Dalton MacDermot is a member. He's not shy about it."

"No. You'd think that brick through the window would have put him off, wouldn't you, but I hear he's pressing on with his latest book."

"God, I'm glad I knew it was coming – the brick, I mean. It was pretty dramatic. Glass everywhere. That Lee has a strong arm."

"Thanks for putting me onto him. He'll make a good

party member, I'm sure of it."

"But what are we going to do about MacDermot? His book will doubtless be filled with libels against ecoism. The trouble is, his writing does have a habit of reaching into public consciousness, despite being full of nonsense."

Fabian enjoyed seeing his old friend riled. Manny's own attempt at book publishing had not been so successful. But he was starting to have an idea. "What was that top fifty book he wrote a few years ago?" Fabian asked, goading Manny slightly.

"*Capitalism versus Ecoism.*" Manny almost spat the words out.

Fabian smiled to himself. "Yes, that one. Well, didn't it contain a lot of criticism of climate change? Didn't it question the science and the politics?"

"It claimed to. It was just a lot of reactionary rubbish."

"Would any of it be considered today as Carbon Crime Denial?"

Manny paused. "Probably. You did help draft it to be as wide-ranging as possible."

"One of my better efforts, I think. Look, I'm not being obtuse, I'm just wondering if you'll see it the same way I do. The book may have been published years ago, before the Denial law, but it's still being printed and sold today, after the law."

Manny sat up.

"You see where I'm going with this? Technically, he's breaking the law. The only way round it would be to withdraw the book and pay an enormous fine."

"He won't do that," Manny said gleefully.

"I think you're right. Definitely grounds for arrest.

I'll get onto my party members in the police."

"And while they're humiliating him in his house, they could seize any computers or manuscripts he's got. We don't want any more of his ideas endangering the public."

"Good idea," Fabian said. "You know, you'd be a great asset to the party if you joined."

"That's very kind," Manny said, "but I do need to appear impartial, for my readers' sake."

"Of course. But you'd be able to inform them so much better from the inside."

"I do have staff, you know."

"Well, I was just thinking, in recognition of all you and your paper have done for ecoism over the years, we could honour you somehow at the party conference."

Manny leant back in his chair. "That would be... acceptable, I'm sure. Only nutcases are against the environment. What did you have in mind?"

"How about a special seat on the main platform? You can make a speech if you like. Preferably in favour of the Carbon Crime Bill."

Manny's face widened. "I'd be delighted."

#

Blake sat in his office at Caelum with his head in his hands, feeling drained. It had been a month since James's funeral, Candice moving out and Marisa going back to prison. A long, painful month: seeing the sun outside and planning a run, then realising James wouldn't be coming with him; hearing a noise upstairs that turned out to be a bird hitting the window; straining to hear James's singing and getting only silence in return.

He had tried repeatedly to make up with Candice over the phone, but she still blamed him for buying the car and causing James's death. There was no getting through to her at this stage, he knew, so he had returned to work, to get away from the large, silent house and to try to take his mind off his family. He smiled wryly as he realised how that had panned out. It was no use resisting his mind's attempts to reconcile itself to his strange new childless world, so instead he let it wander, and the image of Fabian consoling Candice as he led her away came to his consciousness.

It made him think about how they'd grown up together, how their family had functioned. His mother Evelyn had been an actress, then after bringing up him and Fabian, a charity fundraiser. She had always doted on Fabian much more than on him. His father, Lorenzo, a test pilot and the owner of an aero-engine company, had always had more time for Blake.

He recalled how Fabian had always acted the victim in their childhood. If he'd been hurt while playing a game, like hide and seek, he was always quick to run and complain to their mother that it was Blake's fault, even though Fabian had just tripped while running. When Blake was summoned before his parents to explain himself he had protested his innocence, but it had been simply his word against Fabian's. If his mother was there alone, Blake was usually punished. If both his parent were, then not.

Whilst this practice annoyed Blake intensely, he never really disliked his younger brother. Of course he'd enjoyed playing the odd trick on him, as older brothers do, such as hiding his toys or putting spiders down his shirt, but Blake saw that as training, simply toughening him up. He'd never done anything to really hurt Fabian. And yet his brother had always complained to their mother that Blake hated him and was continually inventing slights to prove it.

The time Blake came closest to hitting his brother out of anger was when Fabian had burned Blake's toy cars by putting them in the garden incinerator, saying, "Cars are bad!" Instead of turning on him, Blake had doused the fire with water until the cars were cool enough to touch, then carried them as evidence to his parents, expecting them to exact a far greater punishment than he could inflict. Unfortunately, his father had been away on business at the time, so Fabian got away with confinement to his room for a day. When Blake's father returned, he made Fabian pay for new cars with his pocket money over the next six months. This had been no major hardship for Fabian, as he preferred receiving presents and sweets through begging for them, rather than spending his own money.

When he and his brother were in their early twenties, both their parents had died in a plane crash during a test flight, so they had never known their grandchildren and Blake was unable to turn to them for consolation.

His office held no signs of life, just the bank of monitors opposite his desk showing the volumes of data flowing through his company's servers and the health status of the various machines and services involved. Blake stared at them with more detachment than usual. Like a dying patient, they showed a steady decline as businesses closed down or moved abroad, and as more people in general cancelled their broadband subscription. But there were still hundreds of thousands of people relying on him and his servers to work. If the generators ever failed during a blackout, he thought, his company would be out of business in no time. Why on earth would a hospital let that happen to them, he wondered, when their work literally involved life and death? He was eager to do something for his son, so he decided he would go to the hospital and find out.

#

Candice felt so excited and proud, she gripped the sides of her chair and beamed constantly as faces in the audience kept turning round to look at her with admiration. She was loving her new school. A clean break from all that family history. There was the excitement and hustle and bustle of living in London, and now she had provided the school with a speaker who was one of the most important people in the country.

When he'd found out Fabian was going to address the school on climate change, her father had offered to speak himself. But the school had refused. Good. She did miss her father, sometimes, but she felt a greater empathy talking to Uncle Fabian. He was genuinely interested in her views rather than dismissive of them.

She missed her old friends more. It had been a sudden break, but now she lived in London, she was making plans for them to visit her and explore the city together.

She missed James. It was hard to admit because they had argued so much. But it had shocked her deeply, seeing him die at the hospital, and she had forgotten her recent hatred of him, remembering instead the games they had played together, the times he had helped her with her maths homework and the songs they had sung together. It had galvanised her into action. She had to make the most of her life, and if she could help save the human race from self-destruction, that was a good start.

The whole school was now in the assembly hall and most of them clapped enthusiastically as her uncle emerged from the back of the stage, was introduced, and then walked to the lectern.

"Thank you for taking time out from your regular lessons to listen to me," he began and the children fell silent. "Time is precious. Time is all we have. You are young now and see your lives stretching out infinitely before you. But I must warn you. Your time on Earth will be much shorter and more brutal than you expect, unless we address climate change today."

The room was silent.

"The older generations have exploited the Earth, used it for their own, selfish gain. Look at the result. Climate chaos, plastic-filled seas, vanishing species and dwindling resources. Such lifestyles are unsustainable and you have been disinherited."

Murmurs of discontent echoed round the room.

"But it is not too late. There is still time. If we act together, we can save ourselves and the planet.

"You all know the science from your ecology classes, but let me just remind you of the biggest threat we face: CO_2."

Her uncle pressed a handheld button and the screen on one side of the stage lit up with a jagged, but steeply climbing, graph.

"The blue line shows the level of CO_2 in the

atmosphere over time. This red line shows the average global temperature."

Candice could see the timeline ran back several thousand years. She wondered how they got the data from that long ago. She'd heard of ice cores. But there weren't any thermometers, let alone satellites. It must be tricky.

"As you can see, the two lines continue in a stable manner, until here—" He jabbed his finger at the graph. "—where there is a dramatic change upward. Now, who can tell me when this happened? Who's brave enough to raise their hand?"

A serious looking boy from the sixth form raised his.

"Well done. Yes?"

"It's the start of the Industrial Revolution around 1760."

"Very good. As you can see, CO_2 and temperature have been on an upward trend ever since."

Candice began to wonder what had happened off the far left of the graph, maybe hundreds of thousands or even millions of years ago. She knew the dinosaurs had existed then and that plants had been bigger in order to feed them. She knew from biology that plants liked CO_2, so maybe there was more of it back then. But if so, where did it come from? Humans weren't around.

"And that is the battle we have been fighting, and are now starting to win. To reverse this trend by achieving zero carbon."

A girl with plaits just in front of Candice put her hand up.

Fabian was about to continue when he noticed her.

"I see a hand. Yes, do you have a question?"

The girl cleared her throat and stammered, "Is it because we all breathe?"

Fabian slanted his head to one side. "I'm sorry. How do you mean?"

The girl knew everyone was looking at her but she spoke again with sincere concern. "We learned in biology last term that human beings exhale much more CO_2 than they inhale. Is our breathing causing CO_2 to rise like that?"

Fabian paused briefly. "In a word, yes."

Candice could hear the girl and hundreds of her schoolmates take in a collective breath and try to hold it.

"What you've learned is true. And the more people there are on this planet, the worse the problem becomes. But it is the lifestyle, the energy consumption, the fossil fuel burning that has the biggest effect, not our breathing."

Candice knew this already from her Green Shoots meetings and she began to feel the nervous urge to ask her own question about the dinosaurs.

She remembered a time when she was twelve and had been asked a maths question in front of the whole class and her father, who had been visiting as a governor. She had got it wrong. She knew the mathematical rule but had misapplied it in her head. Despite the shame, she tried to redeem herself in the next lesson by asking a question herself. She'd asked the teacher why the rule was true. He had just replied brusquely, saying that it was beyond her understanding and to trust the experts. "Just learn it for the exam. It doesn't matter why it's true." She had felt like she'd been 'shut down'. But he wasn't the only teacher like that – seemingly full of knowledge and what the examiners were looking for, but unwilling or perhaps unable to teach it, to really explain it. The urgency to raise her hand abated. It needed a longer discussion than would be appropriate in an assembly. She'd ask her uncle later. He was still talking.

"For the last two hundred and fifty years, society has all been about 'we versus me', with the emphasis being on the 'me'. To tackle climate change effectively, the emphasis must change. Acting together as one, as 'we', pooling our efforts, sharing our money and our property, so that everyone can enjoy a decent basic standard of living. Stopping the endless scramble for resources to be richer and better than our neighbour, and securing a sustainable future for the human race. That is my mission. I hope it will also become yours. Thank you."

The children burst into wild applause. Most of the teachers were clapping too. Fabian descended from the stage and moved down the centre of the hall, shaking hands and receiving touches from those who could reach. That was a bit sad, Candice thought. He wasn't Jesus.

Eventually he reached the back of the hall, where there was a table already laid out with Ecoist Party pamphlets, which he distributed while chatting to the children.

Candice had seen most of them before. But some were in a different, unfamiliar style. She picked one up and looked at the date. It was over thirty years ago. She flicked through it. There were the usual claims, and also some she hadn't heard of, like the Himalayas melting. As far as she knew, that hadn't happened.

How had the human race survived if it had been destroying the planet for so long? It got her thinking.

#

Driving across town in the daylight, it was easier for Blake to see the potholes, horses and the number of people loitering about, not working. He focused on these things rather than the memory of the last time he'd driven to the hospital.

When he arrived, instead of parking in the front, he decided to try to see the generators for himself and drove around the back. He passed a number of 'Authorised Access Only' signs but their loud red letters lacked conviction when no one tried to stop him.

He saw some likely-looking sooty funnels over the top of a low roof, and drove towards them. As he stepped out of the car he noticed that the generators and their fuel tanks were inside a wire cage, probably for safety and theft reasons. However, the door to the cage was wide open, with no guard in sight. That couldn't be right. Blake looked around a few corners until he found someone – a man in a dirty green jumpsuit putting bags labelled 'medical waste' into a truck. Assuming the role of a manager, Blake walked up to him briskly and asked what he knew about the generators being unlocked.

The man in the jumpsuit looked for a while at Blake, trying to assess his importance. But then he thought, it doesn't matter who he is, the facts were the same for everybody.

"The tanks have been dry for several weeks now, since before the last big power cut in February. So you see, there's not a lot of point in locking or guarding them, is there?"

"Quite," Blake said through gritted teeth. He thanked the man and marched off to find the hospital administrator. After various attempts by members of staff to put him off, he discovered the name and location he needed.

When Blake stormed into his plush office unannounced, Mr Goadby was sitting at his desk reading a nature magazine. Blake noticed his tree-like silver badge, then began his excoriation.

"How can you possibly let the generators run dry when there are lives at stake?"

Somewhat surprised by the interruption, but confident in the security of his position that a friend in the party had arranged for him, he spread his arms in a manner of helplessness and explained, "The thing is, Mr…"

"Hardwicke."

For a moment, Goadby was shocked. Could this chap be related to the Ecoist Party President? Quickly he calculated that, if he was, then it would be fine, they'd be on the same wavelength. If he wasn't, well, something close to the truth couldn't hurt. After all, being green was what everyone wanted.

"The thing is, Mr Hardwicke, it's the company that supplies us with diesel. It's had glitches with its distribution system."

"Well, why haven't you tried some other companies?"

"If only it were so easy, Mr Hardwicke. As you probably know, the number of companies licensed to perform such carbon-rich services is very small. And there's a very close check on who they supply. The amount of paperwork we would have to fill in to get permission to change supplier is gargantuan. But I'm sure you'll agree that's a good thing. We can't have carbon being used left, right and centre without careful monitoring, can we?"

"My son has just died on one of your operating tables during a blackout, so no, I don't agree."

Slightly caught out, Mr Goadby looked down at his desk.

"I'm very sorry to hear that, Mr Hardwicke, but you can see what a difficult position I'm in."

Blake turned and walked out in disgust. As he drove back to his office, his hands shook with rage on the wheel.

Once at his desk, he phoned the fuel company and asked what was wrong with their distribution system. They denied all knowledge of a problem until he mentioned the hospital. It then emerged that there was a computer glitch with that particular customer. He asked the woman on the phone if she supplied any other hospitals, to which she snappily replied, "No."

Blake didn't believe her, especially given how difficult it was to obtain a carbon licence. There wouldn't be that many of them.

He rang the next nearest hospital, which was about twenty miles away.

"Is that accounts payable?"

"Yes."

"This is Sunshine Fuels. I've got a query I wonder if you can help me with. We've checked our records and it seems odd, but you haven't paid our last bill. Could you have a look for me please?"

There was a minute's silence. Eventually the clerk

came back on the line.

"You're right. But it's because we haven't had a delivery for weeks. According to our records we don't owe you anything. What invoice number are you referring to?"

"I see, I'm so sorry. Could you put me through to the hospital administrator? I'd like to apologise directly to them."

Surprised but gratified by such responsible behaviour, the accounts clerk put him through.

Seeing an internal number, the administrator answered the call, unprepared.

Blake switched to his own persona and took charge. "I'm ringing on behalf of the patients in your hospital. I've just discovered your backup generator tanks are completely dry and you haven't had a delivery of fuel for weeks. What happens if there's a blackout during night-time surgery? How are the doctors supposed to cope?"

"What business is it of yours?"

"My son died in on an operating table due to the lack of light."

"It's not my fault. The supply company said they had a problem with their distribution system."

"Couldn't you have found another supplier?"

"We tried that, but when we applied for permission to the Department of Health, we got a call back telling us to wait, as this was being dealt with centrally."

"While you're waiting, more people might die."

"But you can't expect me to fight the government."

"What about your patients? Don't you think they've got a right to a decent service? After all, they're paying for it through their taxes."

There was a pause.

"Well it's not very green, is it, diesel generators pumping dirty great clouds of carbon into the air."

Blake hung up in disgust, but with a sense of unease. That was two hospitals. What if there were more? It was clear James had died unnecessarily. What if he was not alone? He had to find out.

He locked his office door from the inside and logged on to one of the maintenance consoles that had access to all of Caelum's computer systems, including the ones they were obliged to keep by the government for storing copies of all the emails, website visits and texts that had passed through their network over the previous six months.

He thought of the irony of using the government mandated copies to check up on the government. He didn't think that what he was doing was illegal. If he found something, he'd be helping the police. If not, it didn't cause any harm.

He started by searching for emails to or from the fuel company. Luckily, it turned out that they did use his network. There were thousands of emails stretching back over the last year. He didn't know the name of the woman he'd spoken to there, so instead he searched for any emails between the fuel company and '.gov.uk'. Unsurprisingly, there were dozens. He started reading them. Some were to do with tax payments. He eliminated the government address they'd been sent to. Some were about permits and reporting the quantities of fuel purchased, stored, and sold on. This was all part of the tight regulations surrounding anything carbon-related. They all seemed to be from one place: the Department of Carbon, Energy and

Environment. He eliminated those too. He was left with about sixty emails to a set of almost random addresses within the government. He studied them for a while and one stood out, simply from its brevity. It read, "*Please proceed (or not) as discussed.*"

That was odd and strangely informal, coming from the government. Was it an in-joke? He searched and found others to the same address: sam.hult97@doh.gov.uk. There were about half a dozen. All similarly cryptic. All referring to discussions.

He wondered what else he could find out about that email address. Poking about on government websites, he couldn't link it with anyone in particular. Just the Department of Health. An anonymous, innocent bureaucrat? Or something else? It certainly wasn't an example of 'Open Government'.

He tried searching all the emails through his system that were exchanged between that address and anyone else.

It wasn't long before he recognised one of the recipients: mgoadby@nhs.gov.uk. Again, the message was brief: "*Remember the plan. We'll fix the numbers.*" Definitely the same individual. But what was he or she planning?

He kept looking and turned up half a dozen more cryptic emails from 'sam.hult97'. One was to the second hospital he had quizzed. He looked up the name of the administrator: Wendy Carson. It matched the email recipient. There was a pattern emerging here.

Blake looked up the other recipients' addresses. They were all care homes in the local area.

He phoned the first one, again pretending to be from

Sunshine Fuel's accounts department. Again, the care home hadn't had a delivery for months.

He phoned the second one. There was no reply. He checked the number online, and came across a news story: "*20 Die in Care Home Fire.*" He read the article. The fire seemed to have been caused by candles being used during a blackout. A chill went down Blake's spine. Was there a plot here to deliberately starve the most vulnerable in society of fuel?

He remembered that Dalton MacDermot's wife was in a care home. Dalton had left him several messages since the crash, but Blake hadn't had the courage to call him, fearing he would break down. Now his anger overcame his fear. He phoned his friend.

"Dalton?"

"Blake! Is that you? How are you? How are Marisa and Candice?"

"I'm…" he sought for the words, "…still reeling from the shock, to be honest. But I'm back at work, trying to distract myself. Marisa is heartbroken, but I've been visiting her regularly in prison. Candice has moved in with Fabian."

"You're kidding?"

"Yes, I know. It's a long story. I'll tell you when we next meet up."

"Any news on the BCF?"

"I'm going to restart it. Another launch event. Can you send me the latest draft of your book? I want to plan some talks and press releases around its ideas."

"Of course. I could do with an editor I can trust. You know it's not finished?"

"Yes, but you've got, what, two to three months left of work to do on it?"

"About that."

"Fine. I'll run my plans by you first, just to make sure I haven't got the wrong end of the stick."

"Okay."

"And there's something else you can help me with, perhaps. It concerns Grace."

"Go on."

"I know this is an odd question, but have there been any accidents related to power cuts at her care home that you know of?"

"Actually yes. I was there during one of the blackouts. They had no emergency lighting and no backup power. It was very scary for the residents. I stayed with Grace, but one of the others fell and broke her hip. She died not longer after from complications."

Blake let out an expletive.

"I think it's being done deliberately."

"What?"

"By someone in the Department of Health."

"Why?"

"I don't know, but I'm going to blow it wide open if I can prove it. Whoever's behind it may also be responsible for James's death."

"Oh, my God," Dalton said slowly.

They talked a little longer about the incident at the Oxford Union and the threat to free speech of the CCD law becoming custodial, but Blake was keen to get back on the trail of sam.hult97.

He had to find out what these emails had been referring to. He had to listen to their discussions. But how? His company dealt with email, websites and text messages in transit, but not telephone services. There was a way to find out, but there was a risk. What he was thinking of doing could land him, and others, in prison. Candice already had one parent behind bars. He knew he was being impetuous but he did it anyway. He had to know.

He phoned Clive Donaldson, CEO of English Telecom. Although they were rivals, they had recently agreed to collaborate on a larger cause.

"Clive?"

"Blake! May I just say how deeply, deeply sorry I was to hear about James."

"Thank you."

"If there's anything I can do for you, or your family…" Clive was thinking of his wife Fiona and his son Keith. If anything happened to them, he would – well, what would he do?

"That's very kind, Clive."

"Or if you'd like me to take over organising the BCF until you're ready?"

"Thank you. I might take you up on that. I do want to reschedule the launch as soon as possible. But right now, I need your help with another matter. I concerns James."

"Of course."

"Are you alone?"

"Yes. I was just reading."

"Clive, we've got to know each other quite well recently, I think."

"I'd say so."

"And I think we agree that we've got to fight the Carbon Crime Bill together, or the economy will collapse."

"I'm afraid so."

"And I know what your feelings are about

government regulation."

"I'll admit I've made a lot of ill-judged concessions in that area. Some things I wish I'd never agreed to." He could feel the twinge of his stomach ulcers and reached for some medicine.

"Well, how would you like to fight back, to redeem yourself? What would you say if I asked you to break the law for the sake of uncovering a conspiracy within the government? One that makes the expenses scandal look like children spending their bus money on sweets?"

Clive felt his stomach twinge again. He'd had a very mixed relationship with various governments over the years. Some he had done favours for, some he had accepted favours from. He knew it was dangerous to cross them. After Brexit, the EU's anti-competition law had ceased to apply and left-wing elements in the government had seen an opportunity: face a breakup, renationalisation or heavier regulation. He'd reluctantly taken the last option. But it had never sat comfortably with him. "Tell me more."

Blake told him about the generators, the hospitals, the emails and all the evidence he'd uncovered so far.

Clive was gobsmacked. "Why don't you go to the police?"

"Because I've already committed enough crimes to be put away for twenty years, and I'm not sure I'd get off those lightly even if I proved the whole case."

"Neither am I," Clive said ruefully. He was currently in the spotlight, accused of price-fixing. "So what do you want me to do?"

"Retrieve the phone calls made between sam.hult97 and these other people. It would mean some digging around to try to correlate the emails with phone calls. And, of course, it would also put you straight in prison if you were caught."

Clive thought about his family. He couldn't stand to be away from them for long. They were the antidote to all the turmoil of the last few years. On the other hand, if Blake was right, this wasn't the kind of world he could have his son grow up in. He was in a position where he could help uncover one of the worst atrocities Britain had ever seen. Probably a unique position. If he didn't act, no one else would, and evil would go unpunished. His sense of righteousness would not allow that to happen.

"I'll do it."

Blake heaved a sigh of relief. "Thank you so much, Clive. I know we're often fighting against each other for business, but in this case, I think we're fighting alongside each other, for a decent world."

Clive smiled at the moral certainty of Blake's words. There was a reason he was chairman of the BCF. "Send me the details you've got – you'd better encrypt them – and I'll start on it right away."

Blake spent a restless night going over what he'd found out in his mind. Who could be behind such a thing? What was their sick motive? How on earth would someone like that get into government? Governments had been rocked by all sorts of scandals in the past. But they'd always had some kind of sordid, personal motive, whereas this... He eventually drifted off.

~

Despite his lack of sleep, he was at work early the next morning waiting to hear from Clive. All day, when he should have been focusing on meetings, he kept checking his phone. Eventually, when everybody else had gone home for the day, it rang.

"Clive?"

"Yes. You're not going to believe this."

Blake took a breath and braced himself.

"Go ahead."

"It's your brother, Fabian."

#

Blake had been apoplectic when Clive told him. He'd wanted to go and confront his brother there and then. Clive had to point out that the last day of the Ecoist Party Conference was probably not the best time. Now they were off the phone, Clive ran his hand through his thinning red hair and sat back stunned. Not only had he worked in concert with an arch rival, not only had he broken the law by snooping on his own customers – something he'd sworn never to do – but he'd discovered that the leader of a major political party was actively starving hospitals and care homes of fuel. Why?

As he repeated this slowly to himself, the answer became scarily obvious. He turned to the Consultation Paper on Internet Regulation he'd been reading when Blake had called. He turned to the front to remind himself who'd written and published it. He'd only just finished reading the list of names when suddenly the lights went out. He automatically reached for his solar-charged light, and then stopped. He checked his luminous watch. It had just gone 8 p.m. Offices weren't allowed power after that time. He chuckled bitterly as he realised how quickly he'd adapted to 'intelligent supply'. He sat back in his chair in the dark. He didn't need light to think.

The paper had been championed by the Ecoist Party, but put forward by all parties in the coalition to placate the Ecoists' followers, and no doubt try to win some over for themselves. It called for the ceasing of all Internet traffic, apart from that deemed essential by the government, which of course included its own.

Its rationale was that the Internet, and all the devices attached to it, used up enormous amounts of electricity on essentially trivial activities. Even worse, it enabled trade and production on a global scale, increasing pollution and wasting precious resources. After all, we managed perfectly well without it for centuries. In addition, the paper pointed out, the Internet was divisive – the poor and the old were effectively excluded by the price and complexity of modern electronics. Finally, the paper said it would reduce porn and terrorism.

As usual, there was a clever, divisive enforcement mechanism. While putting up a website would be technically illegal without government approval, the carrier of the traffic to the website, e.g. Blake or Clive, would be the one who was fined. That way the government had a small number of targets compared with prosecuting every individual website owner. It was always easy to punish 'big business' as opposed to small individuals.

Clive realised how trapped he was and smiled grimly at the logic of it all. If he refused to support Internet Regulation, which would clearly decimate his business, he'd be accused of hypocrisy. That mud would stick, since five years before he'd happily supported the introduction of low price controls to wipe out his smaller rivals, which he'd then bought at a cheap price and made millions from.

On the other hand, if he did support regulation, he'd be called a mere puppet of the state and lose the admiration of his wife and the support of his colleagues, not to mention his own pride.

Now he had a third alternative – expose the ecoist plot. This would distract everyone from the Internet Regulation issue and make him a hero. His pulse quickened at the idea. Then he reconsidered the jury's probable verdict. Wasn't it more likely they wouldn't believe him? After all, the government was always trying to help people and he was just a greedy businessman. Wasn't it more likely that he would be ridiculed for trying to cover up his own problems with such a preposterous idea?

He felt a weight on his stomach and sat back in the dark. He couldn't cry 'freedom' any more. He'd sacrificed it long ago. His son, Keith, had spotted his compromises over the years. He feared it was partly what had led him to become a rabid ecoist. He'd thought his father had more integrity. Clive cringed inside.

Perhaps freedom was also a value that had ceased trading long ago. When the freedom to smoke was taken away with such little complaint, even in private clubs. When all businesses were so regulated as to be largely under public control, what did people really care about using the Internet, which had been around for far shorter a time?

He knew he was in a hole, but didn't know how to dig himself out of it. Who could he turn to in confidence? The BCF? He was a founding member and major sponsor, but without Blake, it was currently stalled. His mind felt paralysed. Looking around his office for a way out, his eyes lighted on the shadow of a book that had sat on the corner of his desk, waiting to be read since Blake had given it to him. Its title was *Capitalism versus Ecoism*, and its author was Dalton MacDermot. Clive switched on his emergency light and began to read.

#

As their limousine was driven past the public entrance to the arena, Candice looked out and saw dozens of ticket touts flogging access to the last day of the Ecoist Party Conference. Scores of green supporters were milling about, some trying to buy them. It had been a highly publicised and well-reported event, and only party members had been guaranteed a place. But Candice, as Fabian's niece, had special privileges. He was treating her seriously, unlike her father, reserving her a place on the platform. She was somewhat daunted but she wanted to please her uncle, who had kindly let her live with him. She was also somewhat excited.

At the VIP entrance round the back they stepped out into the chilly April air, but were quickly ushered to the warm, ugly, but functional backstage 'green room'.

Here Uncle Fabian introduced her to various important-sounding people who apparently ran the party or contributed to it in some way. The only one she remembered, because her father often spat out his name, was Manny Schweizer, the newspaper owner. Other than that she saw no one she recognised apart from Mrs Oakley, who gave her an unusually friendly smile. What was a youth group leader doing back here?

Suddenly Candice heard, or rather felt, a huge, resonant rumble, followed by some booming music.

"To the stage now please, ladies and gentleman," said an usher and they processed out of the fluorescent-lit room along dim corridors, the sound getting louder.

At the back of the stage they paused and Candice could just see the top level of the audience at the rear, waving banners such as '*Save the Earth*' and '*Pastures before people*', and swaying their arms.

Then they were shown up the steps and onto the stage. The sound of thirty thousand people bellowing about England's 'green and pleasant land' was deafening. Candice wanted to put her fingers in her ears but thought it might look bad, so instead kept her hands in her pockets as she was shown to her seat, unexpectedly on the front row.

On recognising her uncle, the volume rose even more. He began vigourously shaking hands with the other people on the stage, even though he had only just been talking to them behind the scenes.

His last and longest greeting was reserved for Manny Schweizer, who sat fidgeting in the front row, centre stage. As Fabian left him to begin his speech, Manny looked pleased but slightly uncomfortable as he wiped his balding forehead with his handkerchief and added to the applause.

After much acknowledgement of the crowd through open arms, and his own applause, the music came to an end and Fabian signalled for them to quieten down.

As he took a deep breath, readying himself to speak, Candice held her breath. Was this man really her uncle?

"Thank you, thank you all so very much for coming, and for your committed support over many, many years." He paused for the cheers to subside.

"Nature dictates," he intoned.

"We obey!" came the refrain from the euphoric, steamed-up crowd. Candice's father had once told her it was a cruel adaptation of Francis Bacon.

She could see Fabian's face on a screen pointing up at him. He smiled beneficently. "In return for your magnificent support, I pledge to go on fighting for the values you hold dear: low carbon (*cheers*), Earth-Peace (*cheers*), and sustainability (*loudest cheers*).

"But you must be ready. For I have it on good authority that the rumours you've heard are true. There will soon be a snap general election."

The crowd roared and stamped their feet. It was a frightening sound. Fabian continued.

"We already have a quarter of the seats in the House of Commons, and we often hold the balance of power. But this election will be a big opportunity to blow away the coalition with its murky deals and shallow compromises. This is our chance to lead Britain back to her natural state. To the time before greedy capitalists raped our countryside, and greedy businessmen made us all wage slaves. To a greener, fairer Greater Britain."

The crowd roared again. Fabian was basking in the warmth of their adulation. Candice could see masses of red and green Ecoist Party flags flapping and swaying with the crowd.

"As you embark on this mission of gathering support for our victory, do not forget to attack our enemies. It is vital that we protect Britain's environment by keeping out foreign businesses and foreign workers. They are exploiters, polluters – out to destroy our green and pleasant land."

This passage drew particular approval from one section of the crowd. Candice thought it came from an area dense with St George's flags.

Her uncle continued. "And there are enemies at home we must tackle. Loathsome anti-green figures with a message of pure hatred. People such as Dalton MacDermot." The audience booed in unison. "Fortunately, he is being spontaneously opposed by protests whenever he appears among the true British people. They recognise his evil. Britons want to be green!"

The banners and flags waved frantically, the massive concrete shed vibrated again to the cheers and stamping of the crowd, and the odour and humidity emanating from them almost made Candice gag.

Eventually, Fabian carried on. "To this end, we have pushed forward the Carbon Crime Bill. With enough support from the press and the public, this will become law, and those who bleed this country dry – the truly evil egoists, who stop at nothing to make a profit – will be faced with jail if they continue their immoral ways."

Applause rained down on Fabian and he couldn't help taking a small bow. Candice could see his autocue was stationary and that his next words were not on it.

"If I had my way, Climate Change Denial and Carbon Crime would not just mean jail time. They would be capital offences." The crowd emitted a guttural roar and Candice felt the bile rise towards her throat. Nor were his next lines part of the script, or she would at least have had a warning.

"And to show you that we can win, that we can convince people to join our cause, even from the most unlikely of places, I present to you my niece, Candice Hardwicke."

He turned and pointed her out then started clapping.

Candice didn't know what to do. She was honoured, but she knew she hadn't done anything to deserve this. What was her uncle embarrassing her like this for?

She smiled and nodded but clutched the edge of her seat, willing the attention to pass away. Soon it did, and Fabian continued his speech and Candice was able to relax sightly.

As she drifted out of focus, recognising the slogans and ideas she'd heard a million times before, she looked at the powerful lights, the booming sound system and the massive TV screens, and wondered if they could all be powered by solar or wind energy. Would rallies such as this be possible in the planned, ecoist future?

4

Blake ran down the stairs, partly to warm himself up. The cold shower had been necessary due to a power cut, but it had also helped. He'd hardly slept for thinking about what he would do to Fabian.

He quickly made a cheese sandwich he could eat in the car, then started to phone Marisa. But before the other end rang, he hung up. There were only certain times she was allowed to access a phone and this wasn't one of them.

He phoned Dalton instead and got a network voicemail service. He left a message explaining Fabian's guilt, saying he was going to confront him and requesting that he take over the BCF if anything should happen to him. He didn't know what he might do when he came face to face with his brother.

Just before he put away his phone, he noticed that Dalton had sent him his manuscript. That was something he could look forward to.

He grabbed his jacket and ran out of the room.

As he drove towards the motorway, he knew Fabian might be anywhere in the country now the conference was over, but the radio had mentioned a celebration at the party headquarters in London – so that's where he pointed the car.

In the old days, he would never have considered driving and would have taken the train instead. But now there were so few cars and lorries due to the carbon tax, he took the M4. It was a bitter benefit, he thought. On the one hand, he could now get to the capital much quicker. On the other, it meant people and goods took much longer to get where they were wanted, and hence everything was slowing down. This was exactly what the ecoists wanted. But it played havoc with businesses. Caelum was still waiting for the replacement hard drives they'd ordered three months ago. As a consequence, two major customers had been unable to run their payroll. They were now ex-customers, looking for someone else to manage their data and simultaneously dealing with a very angry workforce.

He parked easily in Pimlico at a meter that was no longer checked and walked a short distance to the Ecoist Party headquarters.

The receptionist was hidden behind a crowd of activists and reporters, presumably trying to get into the event. When the security guard was looking the other way, Blake slipped past him and up the stairs. He wanted to catch his brother unawares. He also wanted to burn off some of his adrenaline with the exercise.

Several floors later, Blake was about to open his brother's office door when he heard some kind of singing from behind it. He recognised Fabian's voice but not the tune. Good, thought Blake, I'll catch him off-guard.

He threw open the door.

Fabian was alone, and was indeed singing from a manuscript. He stopped abruptly and looked at him with narrowed eyes.

"Blake. You're lucky. You've just caught me between meetings. Did you come to congratulate me on my party's surging popularity? Candice enjoyed the conference last night."

Blake's arms and fists tensed. "I know you killed James."

"Me?" Fabian dropped his manuscript.

"You're sam.hult97."

"Oh." Fabian seemed to relax. Didn't he care? Blake struggled to keep his voice calm.

"I've uncovered what you've been doing with the diesel supplies to hospitals and care homes. You're starving them of fuel. You're freezing people to death in the winter, then when blackouts occur, and the lights go out and critical machines stop working and surgeons can't see, people have accidents. Mistakes are made. People die."

"What's the source of your evidence? You don't know anyone in a care home."

"But I know someone who does – Dalton MacDermot." He wished he'd kept his mouth shut but he couldn't help himself.

"Ah yes," said Fabian.

"And the Internet."

Fabian looked surprised. "You must have hacked into your own systems. You must have violated countless privacy laws. Are you sure all this sleuthing won't backfire?"

Blake ignored the attempt at diversion. "Why? Why

are you doing this? What on earth justifies the deliberate killing of people like this, on a countrywide scale?"

"You've seen the result of the economic crisis. Rationing of electricity. Empty shelves in supermarkets. Queues for basic necessities. We've been saying for a long time now, there are too many people for the planet to support. Those in hospitals and in care homes have already been naturally selected. I, and a small number of my closest party colleagues, are simply hastening a normal process. We're helping the rest of the population and the planet."

Fabian had uttered his justification with a straight face, but Blake was gobsmacked. "You feel no qualms about killing your own nephew?"

"Ties of blood are not as important as our shared responsibility for the planet."

Blake suddenly felt cold. "You're mad. This is insane. Do you know what you're saying?"

"Only the same thing that's been said for years. We're just acting on it rather than talking."

"But if you're found out, the public will crucify you. They're not all paid-up ecoists."

"But they won't find out. Will they?"

"I can't keep this to myself. In fact, I've already had help uncovering your tracks."

Fabian kept his expression calm while his eyes darted about, then he said, "Well, you and your helpers must have broken several laws in the process. That could be very awkward to explain in court."

"You think it will matter when I expose what you've done?"

Fabian's face was immobile. "We shall see." Then he

turned his attention back to his lyric sheet.

Blake shouted, "You bastard," and ran at his brother, shoving him onto his desk.

Fabian spat in Blake's face and managed to roll out from beneath Blake's torso. Scrambling to his feet, he ran to the wall and hit an alarm switch.

Blake didn't care now. He grabbed Fabian by the lapels and forced him to the windows overlooking London. They were old-style, not hermetically sealed. He slid one open with one hand while gripping Fabian by the throat. Then Fabian kneed him in the groin.

Crumpling slightly, but still hanging on to Fabian's jacket, Blake stopped him escaping, but in moments the security guards had arrived and it was too late.

The two large, meaty men were carrying batons and wearing Ecoist Party badges. They grabbed Blake's arms.

"Take him outside," Fabian gasped, nursing his throat.

"Nothing else, sir?" the taller guard asked.

"No," Fabian said, staring at his brother. "It's just a family quarrel."

They manhandled Blake down the stairs and shoved him out of a basement exit. Blake saw a nearby bench and struggled over to it. He needed to recover and to think.

~

Fabian's smile dropped as soon as his brother left the office. He paced up and down beside the windows that looked out over London, feeling his neck and toying with his wooden ring. After a few minutes his smile returned, revealing the irregular, yellow teeth that his inverse vanity had been too proud to fix.

He used his mobile phone. "Smith? …Are you alone? …How would you like to prove your loyalty to the party once more and perhaps earn a promotion? … I've compiled a case against Professor Dalton MacDermot. …Yes, him. It proves that he is currently breaking the Climate Change Denial laws. All it needs is some physical evidence. I need you to go to his house and arrest him, then take away any laptops, computers, tablets, phones or manuscripts that might show he is committing CCD. …I'm certain it will stick. The CPS will have no problem with it. They're headed by a party member. …Tomorrow will be fine. Now, I have another opportunity for you. I've had a tipoff that somebody at Caelum has been hacking into government emails to try to disrupt the electoral process. …Yes. The same company my brother runs. … It *is* a big firm with thousands of computers, but you know how they say corruption begins at the top. I think you should start by checking my brother's office then his house. Tonight. …You might well need to arrest him, yes. But democracy comes first, I'm sure you agree. …Yes, I will be in a powerful position if we win. …Thank you. I know I can count on you. Goodbye."

Fabian wiped his sweaty palms with a freshly eco-washed handkerchief. It smelt mouldy but that didn't bother him. He replaced it and took out his phone again. Of course, he was leaving a trail with his calls. He shrugged. It didn't matter now. Blake wouldn't get the evidence he'd need in court. He'd see to that. But it was important that Blake's 'research' didn't spread. He called another number.

"Manny? Is this a good time? …Listen, I have a

couple of scoops for you…"

~

Manny put his phone away and frowned. MacDermot he was looking forward to, but what was going on with Fabian's brother? Surely Blake wasn't that stupid? He felt a twinge of conscience urging him to investigate – not just witness – the arrest, but he swiftly pushed that aside. It would be a great story. His readers loved to find out the faults of the rich and famous, and undermining democracy was a major no-no. Everyone agreed with that. If the basis of the story was true, the details could wait until later. They could come out in court. It wasn't his job to censor the information given to the public. He phoned his political sub-editor.

~

Besides his rupture, Blake knew he was shaking too much to drive. After a few minutes, he hobbled over to a bench on the Embankment and sat looking at the Thames, but thinking about his brother.

He would have killed him, he realised, if he hadn't been stopped. The adrenaline coursed through him again as he remembered having his hands around Fabian's neck. But what good would that really have done? Millions of people would still believe in the Carbon Crime Bill and all the other economic-suicide ideas of the ecoists. Fabian was just the current figurehead.

His blood pressure lowered as he started to think of a rational plan.

He did need to stop Fabian starving the vulnerable of fuel. That had to be made public. If he didn't kill him, he had to expose him. Perhaps it would undermine people's belief that ecoists were always acting for the best interests of society. To make it stick and be widely publicised, without the possibility of a cover-up, he'd have to take Fabian through the courts. But what if Fabian got there first? He couldn't run a prosecution if he himself was incarcerated for eavesdropping.

Who could he turn to? The BCF? But it wasn't fully launched yet. Dalton and Clive knew. Would they be able to fight the case if he couldn't? If not, who would protect the vulnerable?

Candice!

His face reddened as he realised how long it had taken him to think of her. He rang her number but had to leave a voice message: "Don't trust your uncle. Pack your things. I'll pick you up in the morning and explain." He couldn't go there now. He had to go home first. He'd been so angry with Fabian he'd forgotten to bring his laptop, and it was the only source of evidence.

Blake lifted himself off the dolphin-embellished bench and staggered towards his car.

Blake drove as fast as he could but he was hampered by the horses, pedestrians and cyclists wandering the streets and ignoring the road signs.

Despite the May midday sun shining into his car, he shivered as he thought of his brother. Fabian had always been political. His support for communism in his teens, his speeches at the Oxford Union, his visceral hatred of Margaret Thatcher and his switch to environmentalist activism. He was fifty-two now – two years younger than Blake – and had spent his entire life organising rallies, trespassing at power stations and giving rabble-rousing speeches. Once, when interviewed, he'd explained that he had no children because it would increase man's impact on the environment. Blake had never met a girlfriend or boyfriend of Fabian's. Had he become so psychotic from a lack of love? Blake didn't think it was that simple. But understanding his brother was not the issue at hand. Stopping him was.

He sped up the drive to his house, expecting it to be empty, and came to a gravel-showering halt. Two police cars were stationed by his open front door. A tall, thin bobby was looking in his direction and speaking into his radio. It was too late to turn back now. The truth will out, Blake thought, and he stepped calmly out of his car.

The bobby approached him.

"Are you Blake Hardwicke?"

"Yes," Blake said with pride. Ultimately, he had done nothing wrong.

"Come with me, sir."

Blake was led through his own front door and into his kitchen.

"This is Mr Hardwicke, sir," the policeman said to a tallish, bearded, overweight man in his forties.

"I'm Inspector Smith," the man said as he continued chewing a sandwich. He put the remainder of it down on a rectangular object covered in plastic bubble-wrap. The state always allowed itself exceptions, Blake thought. He peered at it and recognised a laptop inside.

"Is this yours, Mr Hardwicke?" Smith asked, unwrapping it for him to see.

"Yes," he said indignantly.

Smith made a note in his book and told the sergeant to take it away.

Turning to the open-mouthed Blake, he said, "I'm arresting you on charges of political espionage."

"What?"

"This morning we received a tipoff that you were using your privileged position in the telecoms industry to spy on political opponents in an attempt to destabilise the election. We obtained a search warrant and we found these in your office."

He pointed to a sheaf of papers in another plastic bag. Blake took them out and glanced through them. Some were indeed printouts of the email and phone call trail he had been following to Fabian. But others he didn't recognise. One was headed '*SECRET*' and seemed to be from the Department of Climate Change. It must have been planted.

Blake looked up at the bearded, crumb-strewn Smith and noticed his silver oak tree badge. Smith was a proud member of the Ecoist Party. No doubt Fabian had used him to arrange this charade. The evidence was partly false, but true enough to stick. After all, he had broken the law. Would a jury see it like that? Surely once they knew the full story they would. Then, as he watched his desktop computer and his tablet also being removed, he realised the full story might never come out. He didn't trust these police. His evidence was being taken away, to where it could be doctored to fit the charge.

"We'll need your phone, if you please," Smith said, holding out his sticky hand.

"I need to call my wife," Blake said angrily.

"Just the one call, then," Smith said.

Blake phoned the prison. Again, it was not the right time, but he was able to leave a message for her. The officer at the other end laughed when he said he'd been arrested. Blake struggled to keep his temper. He hung up and handed over his phone.

"I'll need my solicitor," he said sharply.

"All in good time, Mr Hardwicke. When we get to the station, you'll be able to call him."

Smith signalled to the sergeant, who led Blake away. As he left, Blake saw Smith pull out a mobile phone from his pocket, walk to a corner of the room, and make a call.

#

Candice yawned and lifted her head off the pillow. It ached. She'd been out partying with her new schoolmates the night before. Why couldn't alcohol just give you the pleasure without the consequences?

Her uncle didn't seem to mind her staying out late, unlike her father.

She remembered a voice message from him that she'd ignored the day before. She didn't have to speak to him now, she lived elsewhere. The separation had given her more confidence in their relationship, and so, with a feeling of nonchalance, she lay back on the pillow and phoned the voicemail service.

The message baffled her: "Don't trust your uncle... I'll pick you up in the morning." What was that supposed to mean? Would he be waiting outside any minute? It made her head hurt. She phoned him back.

"Dad?"

"This is Sergeant Ashwin speaking. Who is this?"

Candice sat bolt upright, her hangover forgotten.

"What's happened to my father?"

"Is that Candice Hardwicke, daughter of Blake Hardwicke?"

Candice felt sick.

"Yes?" she faltered.

"Your father is under arrest for political espionage. We've taken his phone while he's in custody. I'm exercising our new search powers to investigate his contacts."

"Political espionage?"

"Yes, Miss. It's the election coming up, you see. We can't be too careful."

"I see." Candice felt the wave of nausea pass, to be replaced by anger. "What on earth has he done? Can I see him?"

"You'd best talk to his solicitor, Miss. Apparently a Mr. Atkinson."

Hanging up, she tried Xavier Atkinson who's number she'd saved during her mother's trial, but all she got was his voicemail. She left a message and put some clothes on. She couldn't have both parents in prison! What the hell was happening? At least she had her uncle. But her father had said not to trust him. Then again, he would, given their different political views. Perhaps the two things were unrelated. She would try to find out.

Downstairs in the kitchen, she found her uncle smiling over the front page of the newspaper. As he saw her come in his face switched to concern.

"I've just tried ringing my father and he's been arrested for spying or something," she blurted out.

"Yes, I've just found out myself," said Fabian, and he showed her the newspaper.

There it was, in black and white and colour. A picture of her father's grim face as a policeman pushed his black head of hair into the back seat of a car.

"It doesn't give many details," Fabian said, "but I imagine it's part of his desperate attempt to stop the Carbon Crime Bill. Perhaps he's been trying to hack into the government's computers to manipulate their statistics somehow. I expect it will all come out sooner or later. He is – sorry to say this Candice, but I think it's true – deranged."

Candice was angry now with her father. What was he thinking? It made her situation even more difficult. She didn't know what to say, so she looked at her uncle helplessly. She noticed he had some red patches around his neck.

"Are you all right, Uncle?" she asked. "Your neck, it's…"

"It's just a rash I get from time to time. A sort of eczema. Nothing to worry about. Anyway, enough about me, let's talk about you. I enjoyed speaking at your school the other day. There were some very intelligent questions."

"Lots of people thanked me for organising it."

"Perhaps I can visit again. Have you thought any more about your future career? About your choice of subjects?"

Candice was temporarily thrown by the question. Her father never discussed this with her. Her uncle had actually picked an issue she needed help with.

"You know I'm taking environmental science, computers and history?"

"Yes, quite a range."

"Is there a… can computers be useful in saving the

environment?"

Fabian pondered this for a moment. "That's an interesting one. Yes, computers are helpful for quantifying the damage done by mankind to the planet. They are able to measure and graph a lot of data, showing what trouble we're in. But on the other hand, computers and the Internet have been largely responsible for the mass consumerism that is stripping the world of its resources. Indeed, there are plans under the Internet Regulation Bill to close a lot of websites down in order to reduce CO_2. Cloud computers themselves emit CO_2 as well as enabling globalisation. And you know how much CO_2 that has generated."

"Mmm. Thanks," Candice said. "I'll have to think about it some more." Her uncle nodded and went back to his paper. She knew those arguments already. But she really enjoyed programming classes. Surely laptops were okay, especially if you ran them on solar? And what about the masses of information that computers could send electronically? Surely that was better than reams of paper being delivered by carbon-emitting trucks?

Her head started hurting again, so she made herself some porridge with water. As she sat down to eat it she wondered for the umpteenth time about the effect of veganism on her health.

"Uncle Fabian?"

"Yes?"

"You've been a vegan for a long time."

"About thirty years."

"Do you get tired often? I've read about lack of iron being maybe a cause of tiredness, especially in young women."

"Well, I'm no expert, Candice, but from my own experience, yes, perhaps it's true that I do feel slightly less energetic than when I ate animal products. But you know what? Whenever I do feel bad, I remember the thousands of animals whose lives I've saved by sparing them from our speciesist, exploitative culture. That always makes me feel better."

Candice smiled back and continued with her nearly tasteless breakfast. She'd heard it all before. Right now, she could murder a bacon butty. But then it was her fault she had a hangover.

#

The dew stood on the grass in the quad as Professor Dalton MacDermot navigated round it on his way to the lecture hall. He could hear the sound of chanting from the street beyond but nothing could spoil his mood this morning. He had spent the whole previous evening at Grace's care home, dining, chatting, laughing, playing cards and watching an old film on DVD. He knew that such evenings were rare and that she would spend the next couple of days recovering, but she had been like her old self. He was sure, overall, she was getting better. Among other things, they had discussed his nearly finished magnum opus. He smiled as he remembered her insight about selfishness – "why is looking after yourself wrong?"

He loved how philosophical she could be without any effort, seeing right through to the fundamentals of a situation. Could he impart any such ability in his students today? He strode into the building, ducking his head under the ancient doorframe on the way in.

A dozen or so yawning students met his gaze as he

approached the lectern and opened his tablet computer.

"I apologise for the early hour, ladies and gentlemen," he addressed them. "And for the noise we have to contend with." The sound of a jungle beat vaguely breached the cloistered hall. "In fact, the reason we are so early is ultimately down to them. To make better use of daylight and avoid blackouts, all lectures this term have been moved forwards by two hours."

The students collectively groaned.

Raising his hand, a young man asked, "What makes them so angry, sir? The protestors, I mean?"

"I'm proud to say it's probably me, though I don't recall any recent burst of rationality that would particularly upset them. As for the final cause of their emotion, you should first clearly identify it. Are you sure it's anger?" No one answered. "What else might it be?" Again no one proffered a suggestion. He smiled to himself – they were only freshers. He continued. "Unfortunately, neither ecoism nor mysticism is this term's subject. If you can't wait for the answer, read my book, *Capitalism versus Ecoism*."

Again he smiled to himself, but more grimly. He didn't enjoy writing such negative books, but it had to be done. As he listened to the protestors and looked around the hall at its mediaeval Christian features, it occurred to him how much they too were like an ancient cult. The chanting, the self-immolation, the group mentality. Why could mankind not learn from its mistakes? This recalled him to the purpose of his lecture, and his life.

"Today, we shall continue our overview of the

branches of philosophy, with politics. This branch also answers a question applicable to men across all time – how to live together in society. Should we…" The noise of the protestors rose outside. Dalton's voice rose to match it.

"Should we, for instance, listen while others speak their minds, or drown them out with a cacophony? If there are more chanters than listeners, does applying the rule 'the greatest good for the greatest number' mean the chanters should win the day?"

As he stared at the students on their benches, hoping he'd kindled a spark in their minds, there was the sound of the hall door creaking open and a thickset man with a straggly beard entered, followed by a policeman. He noticed the first man had a shiny silver oak on his lapel.

"Professor Dalton MacDermot?" he asked.

"To what do I owe the pleasure?"

"I'm arresting you for Carbon Crime Denial. Anything you do say will be taken down and may be used against you in court."

"I trust it will," Dalton said, sighing. Having expected it for years this was rather an anti-climax. "Why did you decide to visit me today? I've been denying dangerous anthropomorphic climate change for decades."

"We have built a case against you based on your previous writings, and have reason to believe you are in the process of writing more illegal material for publication. Take his tablet, Sergeant."

The policeman snatched Dalton's computer before he could reach for it.

"I hope you realise there is still meant to be a right to

free speech in this country?" Dalton said, mildly irritated.

The bearded man scoffed. "You can tell that to the jury. Put the cuffs on, Sergeant."

"I don't think that'll be necessary," Dalton said.

"That depends what we're trying to achieve," said the bearded man, grinning, and the sergeant secured Dalton's wrists.

As they attempted to pull him towards the door, Dalton bellowed, "Wait!" The policemen stopped. "There is something I must attend to." He turned and faced the class.

"Your assignment this week is to write two cases, one for and one against utilitarianism, to be handed in on Monday. Now you may go," and he nodded to the police.

As they processed back across the quad, this time straight over the wet grass, Dalton looked up at the Chancellor's window and, seeing him, smiled and nodded.

#

It was just after the early evening rush that Sam Tillman left the checkout he was working at and began a tour of the aisles.

He liked working on the shop floor of his flagship supermarket branch. It got him out of the tedious meetings he had to have regarding the latest regulations on food 'waste', and into the real world. He knew it made a difference when he opened a checkout to reduce customers' waiting time. He also knew it made a difference – he frowned as he actually did it – when he moved products to the front of shelves where customers could actually reach them.

The lines on his mid-fifties face smoothed over as he stepped back and admired his handiwork. An old lady smiled at him as she reached with little difficulty for a tin of peaches he'd just moved forward.

After checking all the aisles, Sam finally arrived at the front of the shop, where the newspaper stand was and where an evening edition of the *National Voice* was being restocked by a member of staff called Jaromir. Sam saw how neatly he arranged the papers and praised him.

He looked at the main headline: *'Carbon Now a Crime.'*

So, the bill had passed. Sam wasn't surprised but he felt the weight of dread in his stomach. He had campaigned against it. He had joined the BCF. But he knew that the coalition members only cared about out-greening each other to garner more votes in the election next month. His stomach told him he was not looking forward to the endless lobbying that would now be required to ensure his business's carbon quota.

Turning away from thoughts about what that would do to the whole economy, he read the page two headline: *'You're Nicked Prof!'*

Under it was a picture of Dalton MacDermot in handcuffs. He felt a sting of cold sweat on his forehead and read the story.

After a few moments, he looked up to check the world was still there. The story could not be real. MacDermot had always been anti-green. Why would they arrest him now? What about the other members of the BCF ?

These days he was always on the lookout for the *National Voice*'s fake news. Once, they had mounted a campaign against big supermarkets, especially his, for not using enough local staff and instead hiring and recruiting abroad. They were clearly pandering to a surge of fear and xenophobia after the Brexit vote. Rather than admit that, they had attacked him for wasting energy and exploiting people like a trafficker. The comparison disgusted him. He gave his staff the chance of a better life which they gladly took. If the *National Voice* had bothered to interview any of them, they would have found that out. Instead, they had obtained grumbling resentment from people he'd turned down for a job because previous employers had told him they'd been dishonest. Despite the lack of facts, the campaign had built up pressure on him and other big employers. The government had threatened to force him to employ 90 per cent of his staff from within a five-mile radius of each of its stores, for the sake of localism and to cut travel emissions. That was when he and the other retailers had struck a deal he regretted – a 25 per cent extra tax on meat in return for leaving his staffing to him.

It left a nasty taste in his mouth as he recalled the incident. But what had they cooked up against MacDermot?

He re-read the newspaper article. It seemed there had been some shift in legal circles regarding retrospective law. Then he read the linked editorial. The vitriol in the writing was unmistakable. It concluded, *"an unrepentant climate change denier and full-blown egoist has had his comeuppance."*

Disgusted, Sam gathered the entire pile of *National Voice*s in his arms and marched out of the shop to the nearest large bin, and dumped them in it. He knew the board of directors would probably sack him but he didn't care. It wasn't the first time they had clashed with him over 'green' issues.

As he returned to the newspaper stand, he met Jaromir.

"I want you to spread out the other newspapers to fill this space. I'm cancelling our entire contract for the *National Voice*."

"Okay," Jaromir said, smiling. Sam wasn't surprised he didn't like the paper either – they always blamed immigrants when it was clearly not their fault. How could it be when governments since Brexit had reduced immigration to a trickle?

An elderly customer stood nearby, and poking Sam with his stick said, "You can't do that! It's my favourite paper. I've got a right to read it."

Sam turned to him and said, "You'll have to find someone else who'll grant you that. There isn't room in my world for both the *National Voice* and a hero like Dalton MacDermot."

5

Blake walked out into his garden and marvelled at how light and warm it still was despite being after 6 p.m. While his year had been completely thrown off course, the Earth and the Sun had continued their intricate but unstoppable dance, unconcerned. It almost made him smile.

God, he wanted a cigarette. But it had been twenty years since he finally quit, and he knew it was more a memory of past enjoyment now rather than an actual craving. Besides, he needed to control his high blood pressure for what was to come, not make it worse. But he did need to relax somehow. Not particularly looking forward to it, except as a distraction, he went inside to fetch the newspapers and then sunk into a garden chair to read them.

He had heard the headlines already from Xavier, his solicitor, who had brought the papers with him – Blake being under house arrest – but he needed a change from thinking about his own case. Since all his computers and smartphones had been confiscated as evidence, he had no other contact with the outside world.

He opened the *National Voice* and started reading about the details of the Carbon Crime Bill that had now been passed by Parliament. The majority had been 335 and it would come into force in two months' time. Businesses would start off with a zero carbon quota but could start applying now for permits to increase them. The fines were unlimited…

Clive! His face sprang into Blake's mind as he put the paper down. What would he do now? Would he beg for permission to continue running English Telecom, or would he quit? What should Caelum do? Blake forced himself to refocus on the paper.

There would be an independent body set up to review…

Independent? What a joke, Blake thought angrily. Just like all the other quangos. Power without responsibility or accountability and acting as a screen for government coercion.

He could feel his blood pressure rising. But it was better than the anxiety he had felt during his meeting with Xavier. He had explained the police's refusal to give Blake access to his computers until the trial. They had cited 'National Security' as their reason, but it had left Blake in a dangerous position. The entire case depended on the evidence he had gathered and stored on his laptop and company computers. What if they didn't provide them on the day? What if they were tampered with?

Then he thought again about Clive. How much danger was he in? Xavier had contacted him discreetly and so far he had not been approached by the police. Blake could use his evidence of the 'sam.hult' phone calls, but it would also implicate Clive in spying.

He sat and stared at the blue sky, thinking how inspiring it was, all that unimpeded space, but knowing he would he have to fight to be allowed to see it again, when he wanted to.

He glanced at his watch. It was another half hour before he was due to call Marisa. No doubt their conversation would be monitored. How much could he – should he – say?

"Erm, Mr Hardwicke?"

A young policeman was standing next to him, holding a tablet computer.

"The governor has said you can have this, for keeping in touch with friends. But it will block access to non-approved sites, including Caelum – sorry. It's to do with evidence." He handed it over with a sheepish smile.

"Thank you, Johnny," Blake said. "That's extremely helpful. I appreciate you asking for me."

The policeman nodded and walked back to his guard post by the house. Blake recalled him laughing with delight as he'd jumped into their pool years ago at James's tenth birthday party. He sighed. How things changed.

He switched the tablet on and tried accessing various websites. Most were blocked, but some – such as the GBMC – were not. It didn't seem a very sophisticated blocking algorithm. He tried accessing his email but it wouldn't connect.

He glanced at his watch. There was still time. He checked where Johnny was, then shut the tablet down and restarted it in diagnostic mode, giving himself 'root' permission. He spent a few minutes locating the blocking software and then the key-logger and spyware that were checking everything he did. It wasn't anything he hadn't seen before. Soon he had added a software switch disabling it for his new, hidden 'root' account. Perhaps later he might risk some kind of contact with Clive. But first he checked the online backup service for his email. He could still access it. He downloaded his recent emails and was relieved to see they included the draft of 'PPOG' from Dalton. Then he stored them in encrypted form in a hidden drive on the tablet. Checking his watch, he logged out and beckoned to Johnny for a phone so that he might call Marisa.

As it was prearranged, this time she answered.

"Hello, Blake?" He could tell from her tone she was worried.

"Hi darling, it's me."

"Thank God. Where are you?"

"I'm at home, in the garden. It's nice and sunny."

"Lucky you. I'm in a room with no windows. It smells of disinfectant."

"Could be worse. It could smell of wee."

They both laughed. It was a reference to a birthday trip of Blake's years ago, when it had rained and they'd ended up in an odorous shelter on a remote train station platform.

"Listen, how much time have you got?"

"Ten minutes," Marisa said. "Will they let you come and visit?"

"No. I'm under house arrest, but the trial is in under a month. Then I'll be free."

"If you win."

"I will. There's no real case against me. It's all

trumped-up charges because of my anti-green stance. I've seen Xavier today. We've got a very good defence. It'll be fine. I can't talk about it openly over the phone, but don't worry. It'll be all right. More to the point, as the parent actually in prison, how are you?"

"Oh, much the same. The diet's boring but at least I don't have to do any cooking. There aren't any bills to pay, which is good. And I've made a few friends among the felons. We're starting a glee club."

"A what?"

"Singing. A choir, sort of. We're working on our set list. 'Jailhouse Rock', obviously, 'Chain Gang'…"

Blake laughed.

"I think about James a lot," Marisa said, suddenly serious.

"Me too. I was remembering when he was born." There had been complications, and Marisa and James had both nearly died. "We survived that. And we'll survive this too."

"I hope so."

"When I'm acquitted I'm going to get the whole weight of the BCF behind a campaign to have you released."

There was a pause. Blake thought he could hear her snuffle. "Are you all right?" he asked.

"I'm fine. Have you… have you heard from Candice? She's been writing to me regularly. I got a letter yesterday."

"Aren't you the lucky one." He hadn't had any contact with her since leaving her the warning message about Fabian, but it sounded as if she was okay. He couldn't tell Marisa about Fabian's murderous plans. Not over the phone. Anyway, until it was all exposed at the trial, the fewer people that knew, the better. "I'm glad she's keeping in touch," he said eventually. "Have you heard about Dalton?"

"Yes. We get papers in the canteen. Surely they can't apply retrospective legislation like that?"

"You'd have thought not. Of course, I can't go to the trial, but I bet it'll be quite a show. He'll make mincemeat of them."

"He should do. What are you doing about Caelum?"

"I've taken a paid sabbatical until all this blows over. As soon as I'm back, I'm going to persuade them to launch a test case against the Carbon Crime Bill, with the help of the BCF."

"You will be busy."

"Then there's the Internet Regulation Bill, again it's the same underlying—"

"Sorry darling, they're signaling me to hang up. I've got to go. Good luck. Don't forget, I love you."

"I love you too. It won't be long. We'll be together again soon."

"I hope so. Bye darling," and the phone was disconnected.

#

Liz Blackwood's stomach rumbled. She had been at the bank since seven, as usual, and the sandwich on her desk was begging to be eaten. Crayfish and rocket with cocktail sauce. She knew how good it would taste. She'd been enjoying them for years, whenever there was a fresh delivery to her favourite sandwich shop on St Swithin's Lane. But no, she would put it off until she'd seen Fabian Hardwicke, who was late. He had invited himself over to discuss his party's finances and she couldn't afford to refuse. But Liz had arranged it for lunchtime, so as not to interrupt her other plans. She'd also arranged to meet him in her office, as she didn't want to be seen with him in public.

She tore her eyes off the paper bag containing the sandwich and went to stand by the window. She looked down at the City of London's streets and remembered fondly how much busier they had once been. There had been a brief surge in trade after Brexit when a lot of the EU regulations had been removed and international trade had become easier. But then power quotas had been levied on businesses and most banks, which used energy-hungry IT extensively, relocated around the globe.

On the side of a bus was an advert that read, "*Vote Ecoist – It's Your Future*", and the picture of a tree. As she cast her eye along and up the street she noticed the same slogan and picture in a number of windows. The City was going green, she thought. Strange for a community that prospered from industrial progress. Couldn't they see that reducing business meant less help available to the poor? Seeing the same advert on another bus, she wondered how the ecoists could afford it, especially as they eschewed riches. Then she recalled the purpose of the interview she was waiting for.

There was a knock at the door. She turned and uttered, "Come in." Her secretary showed in the President of the Ecoist Party. Liz had never seen him in the flesh and noticed that his thin frame didn't quite reach the potential his height demanded. He seemed to be smiling at her.

"Come in, Lord Hardwicke," she said, and gestured him to the seat in front of her desk while she went and sat behind it. She did not want to shake hands with him.

"Thank you for taking the time to see me," Fabian began.

She waited for him to be seated, scrutinised him for a moment, then said, "You wanted to discuss party funding."

Hardwicke looked uncomfortable and quickly broke eye contact.

"I'm sure you're well aware," he eventually began, "how unusual your bank currently is, Ms Blackwood."

"What do you mean?" she asked.

"It is one of only two private banks left in the City —"

"Which is something we are very proud of," she interrupted. "Especially considering the economic mess this country has been brought to by its politicians."

"Nevertheless," Fabian continued, "it is not a status you may continue to enjoy, especially if my party wins the election."

"How so?"

"Some people are upset that your bank appears to be breaching the eco-ethical lending laws and getting away with it."

"We've paid the necessary fines."

"Yes, but you are going against the mood of almost the entire country. That could be a very dangerous position to be in. You remember the May Day riots of the late nineties?"

"Of course. I helped clear up the mess."

"Well, that's the kind of thing that can happen when people feel they're not being listened to."

"Or when politicians refuse to protect people's property."

Fabian smiled half-heartedly. "Times have changed, Ms Blackwood. A lot more people feel like those rioters nowadays. A future government might have to nationalise your bank for your own safety."

"I see," Liz said.

"And then there's the issue of carbon quotas and, if it's passed, the Internet Regulation Bill. Both of those present you with significant problems, which I will be in a position to help you with – provided I win the election, of course."

"How on earth do you expect to do that? Most people still realise that ecoism is economic suicide. How will you convince them?"

Fabian smiled again, but this time he showed his teeth. "It pains me to have to act like this, Ms Blackwood, but it is my sworn duty to look after the planet." He took a deep breath while this time holding her gaze. "If your bank were to become a significant donor to the Ecoist Party, it might change people's minds."

Liz shot up out of her chair. "Over my dead body."

Fabian appraised her for a moment or two, then stood up himself. "I don't see why it should come to that."

"Lord Hardwicke," she replied, "we at Blackwoods believe in the market of freely made choices, not in favouritism and threats."

"But if I win anyway," Fabian said, his brow furrowing, his smile dropping, "your life will become much, much harder."

"Then I'll have to deal with it. But do tell me how

you think the country will function if you completely suffocate the banks."

Fabian rose to leave, a scowl on his face. "I suggest you check your premises," he said in a low voice, and then left the room.

Liz got up from her chair and opened a window. The sound of the City came in. What would be left of it when her daughters grew up, she wondered? Would banking exist? Would freedom?

She had joined and helped finance the BCF, but its founder was in deep trouble and opposition to ecoism had stalled. She admired Blake Hardwicke for taking such a stand, but if he went to prison, it would much harder to convince the bank's partners to continue her policy. How could his brother be so different?

#

As Dalton accompanied his ex-pupil and now legal counsel into the courtroom, he reflected that at least he hadn't been under house arrest like Blake. Dalton had lost his laptop, tablet and phone to the authorities, but he had his freedom – enough to prepare Grace for the worst.

Freedom – that was, of course, the whole issue, not whether the government's pronouncements on climate doom were true. He looked around at the packed visitors' benches and at the jury in their box. Did they care enough for their own freedom to defend his? Or were they here to see him punished for non-compliance with society's norms, whatever the personal cost? He noticed the familiar glint of silver oak trees on a number of lapels and tops. It wasn't going to be easy. Then he noticed, as the court got underway, that the judge wore one too. He also noticed

Manny Schweizer sitting with the prosecution counsel, no doubt looking forward to his demise. He would do his best to disappoint him.

The jury was sworn in, Dalton pleaded 'not guilty', and the trial of his life began.

Roger stood and said, "I call Dalton MacDermot to the stand."

Dalton strode to the dock and took the non-religious oath. He examined the jury. Most were looking away absently or staring at their shoes, as if they didn't want to be there, but one young woman was looking back at him expectantly. He knew it was people like her that he had to reach.

Roger began as they had planned. "You are accused of breaking a law which did not exist at the time you broke it. What do you think of such retrospective legislation?"

They had hoped to call on a respected professor of law rather than open Dalton up to cross-examination, but they could find no one willing to act as a defence witness.

Dalton responded, "It makes a mockery of the law and renders man's mind, by which I mean any human's mind, helpless."

"Can you explain?"

"If we are each responsible for supporting our own lives through mental and physical effort, it is bad enough that future laws can seize the *output* of that effort. But it is far worse if a law may be made tomorrow that finds us guilty of simply *making* that effort. How can anyone work, plan, or hope without fear under such a threat?"

The young woman was intensively making notes.

Dalton smiled.

Roger continued, "Moving on from the timing of your alleged offence, what can you tell us about its nature? Do you recognise the legitimacy of the Climate Change Denial law as such?"

Dalton replied firmly, "I do not."

The jury and the public collectively gasped and started talking to each other.

"Silence in court," said the judge, banging his gavel and frowning over his spectacles at Roger. "Do you intend to allow the witness to grandstand against the legal system, Mr Newton?"

"I would never be so presumptuous, My Lord. We only beg to be allowed to treat this as a test case, it being one of the first of its kind."

The judge scowled but waved at Roger to proceed.

Roger took a deep breath, drew himself up, and spoke again to his client. "What would you say is wrong about the law of Climate Change Denial?"

Dalton knew this was now no idle debate, no lecture hall of yawning students. His future and that of the entire country rested on what he said next. He felt excitement mixed with fear, but he also smiled to himself. His whole life had been preparing him for this. He knew what he had to do.

"The Climate Change Denial law is an attack on all of you." He pointed to the jury and to the public benches. "It is an attack on your very power to reason, without which you will die. And it is an attack on your ability to act, to obtain a job or funding or a platform if you do not agree with the status quo. Without such action again, you will die."

They were sitting up now, straining to hear. He

summoned all his powers to speak as clearly and comprehensively as possible.

"Let me explain. If *you* cannot talk about something for fear of arrest, in order to arrive at the truth and make decisions, *someone else* will. But who? It will not, in fact, be experts, because who is to say which of them is right? It will be bureaucrats and politicians. Because they make the law, they are the only ones allowed to debate the issue, including deciding which experts to listen to. They are allowed to think about it and express their thoughts, while you are not. And if you believe you can think without being able to express those thoughts in some form, I suggest you try it. Your thoughts will not flourish, they will disappear."

"Professor MacDermot," the judge interjected, "we are not here to listen to some theory of cognition. We are hear to listen to the facts. Would you kindly stick to those in future."

"My Lord, as I understand it, free expression is essential to establishing the facts. The jury are free to make of my speech what they will are they not?"

"That is their function, to decide who and what to believe."

"May I proceed then?"

The judge nodded reluctantly.

Dalton took a deep breath and continued. "So what is the supposed justification for nullifying your thoughts like this? Individual incompetence. Individuals, they say, are incapable of seeing things clearly, of reasoning accurately about the world, without their individual biases and experiences distorting their view. Such distortions are built into each human mind, they say, by genetics, upbringing, or even the very nature of the brain itself. Yet this leads to a fascinating irony, ladies and gentlemen. What makes politicians and bureaucrats less biased than you? And when they disagree among themselves, who will make a final decision? One person: the President. But if they too are human, how can their decision be more valid than yours? Unless they think they are a god."

The room swelled with murmurings. Questioning the President was tantamount to treason in some people's minds.

Dalton pressed on. "There is a further consequence to legally limiting debate that opposes an opinion. It weakens that opinion itself. The Climate Change Denial laws force any discussion of it underground, where it cannot be defeated by argument. As a result, its opposite, Climate Change Affirmation, loses any arguments that might have supported it. If it is illegal to argue against something you have no reason to believe it."

"Are you now defending Climate Change?" asked the judge looking perplexed.

"No my Lord. I am merely trying to enable fair debate. May I continue."

Again the judge nodded, frowning this time.

"Furthermore, without debate, the discussion around climate change will become fossilised. It is now illegal to discuss its boundaries, its duration, its history, its causes, or its effects. When you discuss climate change, which version will you refer to? The one predicting a five-degree rise, or the one predicting a one-and-a-half-degree rise? The one that predicts cooling, or the one the predicts warming? Without free debate your ideas will become frozen at one particular 'legislated' time and cannot, legally, be made more accurate or improved.

"That is what happened with the Catholic Church…"

"My Lord, do we have to listen to the Professor's views on religion? Are they really relevant?"

The judge looked quizzically at Dalton.

"I am merely making a comparison, your lordship and as I've nearly finished, I hope you will indulge me."

"For a brief time only Professor MacDermot."

"Thank you my Lord. Now, as I was saying about the church. Doctrine was fixed by the popes, then eventually, after centuries of persecuting heretics, full-blown wars broke out, all because people were denied the legal right to question an idea. 'The science is settled' may be one of the most evil things uttered by a leader in modern times. Do you want to consign free thinking to history? Do you want wars?"

There was a stunned silence in the courtroom. They had never heard such things said before.

Roger waited, then said, "No further questions," and sat down.

Dalton watched as Zac Rutter, a well-known prosecutor of businesses that broke regulations, conferred with Schweizer. Rutter seemed hesitant, but as Dalton waited, he pushed his glasses up his narrow nose and stepped towards the witness box. Dalton got the feeling he wasn't the only one on trial.

"Did you write and publish the book *Capitalism versus Ecoism*, in which you questioned the science of climate change?"

"Yes."

"Did you profit from it?"

"People paid me for my work, yes."

"Have you withdrawn that book since the introduction of the law against Climate Change Denial?"

"No."

"Why not?"

"Because it was written before that law came into force."

"That is beside the point. Every new copy produced or sold since then is a breach of the law. Would you not agree?"

"No. If that were the case, what about the second-hand market? Surely taking into account the spirit of the law, they should be banned too. In which case, in order to stop existing owners of the book from selling it, the proper course of action would be to hunt down every existing copy and burn it. I think a search by the police of everyone's house followed by a bonfire in each town of every book found would be the legally proper course of action, if your interpretation of the law is correct."

Rutter looked awkward, but then he went back to his bench to make some notes. Dalton waited. It was like arguing with a four-year-old. Eventually, Rutter began his questioning again.

"So you do not deny denying climate change?"

"I assert the right to question it."

"On what grounds?"

"On the grounds that humans must think in order to survive, not merely obey."

"And if your thinking leads you to conclude that climate change is wrong, you would deny it?"

"One must follow where the evidence leads, Mr Rutter. Isn't that the point of a court?"

"But…" Rutter spluttered. Dalton would have enjoyed it more if the outcome were not so serious.

Eventually, after refitting his glasses several times, the prosecution continued. "So would you agree that Nazis should be free to spout their bile?"

"The spouting of ideas, whether good or bad, makes no difference to me, as long as they are not acted upon. As Jefferson said of religion, 'It does me no injury for my neighbour to say there are twenty Gods or no God. It neither picks my pocket nor breaks my leg.' The alternative to free speech is controlled speech, and I have already given my rebuttal of that."

Rutter fumbled through his notes, then glanced at Schweizer, who had his bald head in his hands.

"Mr Rutter," asked the judge, "do you have any more questions?"

"No, Your Honour."

"Do you, Mr Newton?"

Roger shook his head.

"Then the witness may step down." The judge's voice held an element of disappointment, Dalton thought.

#

Dalton had not slept well. To be fair, he hadn't actually tried. He'd spent the night making plans for his probably incarcerated future, which mostly meant making plans for Grace. He did not generally expect failure and disaster in life, but as a philosopher he knew what he was up against.

Walking calmly through the courtroom and back to the dock, he noted the faces in the audience – he thought of them like that because it was a kind of show. A showdown, in fact, in an epic intellectual drama that had been playing for centuries. The faces were a mixture of tight belligerence, yearning sympathy and pretended evasion. As he reached the dock, he turned to review the jury.

The young woman was there again but in a different outfit. She smiled half-heartedly. The others still looked away. There was a slight cause for hope, then.

The judge arrived, and as they all re-seated themselves Dalton looked at Roger. His white wig contrasted strongly with his black face, Dalton noted. Roger looked as if he was struggling to contain a fierce emotion.

The judge called for order and the clerk asked the jury for their verdict.

"Not guilty," the foreman replied.

"By what margin?" the clerk asked.

"Nine guilty, three not guilty."

The young woman lifted her chin.

"I see," said the judge calmly, as if he already knew. "As you are aware, a conviction normally requires at least ten decisions of guilty. But you may not be aware that recent changes in the law have given *me* the power to vote as well. I vote guilty, making the total ten. Dalton MacDermot, you have been convicted of Climate Change Denial and I remand you in custody for sentencing at a later date."

The audience erupted. Manny Schweizer clapped excitedly then stopped himself.

"But that's outrageous," Roger shouted. "You can't just alter a verdict like that."

"I think you'll find I can," the judge said. "The

change was brought in to make sure more criminals paid the price for their crimes, and now Mr MacDermot will pay for his. Now, if you stay quiet I will overlook your outburst, Mr Newton. If not, you will be in contempt of court."

"It's a complete travesty," Roger shouted, "a farce. This isn't justice, it's vindictiveness."

"That's enough," the judge shouted, banging his gavel. "You too will spend the night in prison, Mr Newton. Take them down," he instructed the policemen.

Roger looked pleadingly at Dalton. Dalton looked at the judge. The silver tree on his lapel glinted in the strip lights.

6

The nanny stood in Green Park and watched the little girl in her charge, unable to supress a smile. Dressed in a smart, red coat that offset her curly blond hair, she looked a picture – not that the girl cared about that. The June shower had just stopped and she'd been allowed out to play for the first time in what felt like ages. So she jumped two-footed into puddles, fed the squirrels, chased after pigeons with a stick, and kicked some old leaves stuck under a bush. She was happy and blissfully ignorant of the 'Keep Off the Grass' signs.

The nanny wasn't going to stop her. She'd had enough of authority and was sure its intrusiveness would only increase with the new government. She looked wistfully through the trees to Buckingham Palace, where she'd worked happily as a chambermaid, but which she'd left when the Royal Family did. She'd thought that seeing it again would make her bitter, but her young companion made her see what really mattered in life.

~

Fabian had woken that day as a normal human being, but now, thanks to a ceremony he'd just been through at Buckingham Palace with the Archbishop of Canterbury, he was partly divine.

Only he didn't feel like a god. The gilded walls and grand paintings chided him as he stole along the corridors of the palace, away from one ceremony and towards another.

He deserved his position, he told himself. The people had voted him in. They were tired of the weakness of governments ever since the most recent economic collapse. Tired of parties constantly changing direction as they pandered for support. People wanted a decisive, moral government and it was Fabian's task to give it to them.

But he didn't feel worthy. He knew there was a risk that his surreptitious fuel-rationing scheme would be found out, or his manipulation of his opponents, including his brother. But he had all that under control. It would never come out. And anyway, people would realise he was doing such things for the good of the country, of the planet. Somehow, though, he still didn't feel reassured.

Putting these doubts to the back of his mind, he passed through the palace doors, into the June sunshine, and then straight into the shiny, black ex-royal limousine. He was glad they'd kept the flag on the front. It reinforced his authority.

As they drove up The Mall he tried a little wave as he'd seen monarchs do. Under the plane trees he saw a small girl smiling and waving back. But then the woman with her pulled her arm down and scolded her.

Fabian shrunk back into his seat as the chauffeur

drove them under Admiralty Arch and around Trafalgar Square with its series of statues looking down at him. They proceeded down Whitechapel and towards Parliament, or as it was officially known, Westminster Palace. It was indeed a huge, imposing building. Fabian wondered what its carbon footprint was and whether he could now reduce it.

Fabian disembarked, and after a few more tentative waves followed Black Rod slowly into the Lords. Looking round at all the berobed figures standing to attention, he reassured himself that the Second Chamber was just pomp. There were no hereditary peers now and all members were appointed by the President. The longer he was in power, the more irreversible his decisions would become.

When he came to the throne and sat down – crownless, however – Fabian felt a sudden shock of anxiety. He felt almost naked in his simple suit, inadequate compared with the ermine-covered peers and the grand figures from previous centuries who had watched him from their effigies as he'd ventured in. But as the ceremony unfolded and the Commons flooded in just as usual, he gained confidence, and when the time came he began his President's Speech with an almost unfaltering voice.

"My Lords and members of the House of Commons.

"My government will legislate in the long-term interests of this country. It will improve the environment for everyone, both present and future, by rewarding those who preserve the precious resources of this country, and punishing those who selfishly consume or pollute them.

"In order to enforce this approach, my government

will bring forward legislation extending the number of crimes for which capital punishment is mandatory, beginning with Climate Change Denial.

"My government will be one of order and justice. Legislation will be brought forward giving more cash back to low electricity users, higher fines to those exceeding their quotas, and more severe punishments to those who evade their smart meters.

"Measures will be introduced reducing the quotas of energy-intensive industries.

"My government will also bring forward legislation to strictly regulate the use of the Internet. The Internet has become the driver for excessive, throwaway consumption and the purveyor of dangerous ideas. As such it will be largely reserved for government use. Some businesses will be permitted to pay for exceptions.

"It will also introduce custodial sentences for those who assist others to abuse the environment, such as non-ethical money lenders.

"To further preserve our nation's resources, my government will halt immigration. It is widely acknowledged that this small island is overcrowded, and so those who would exacerbate the problem must go elsewhere.

"Other measures will be laid before you.

"I trust that the blessing of green wisdom may rest upon your counsels."

The triumphant ecoists cheered and Fabian relaxed, grinning broadly. Little did they know what else he had planned.

#

The hot June sun penetrated even the thick window of

the prison van that carried Dalton back to court for sentencing. He closed his eyes and felt the heat on his face. He had been trying to feel nothing during the last month as he'd waited for sentencing, and the solitary confinement had helped that. But the walk to the van in the warm, bright air had unavoidably made him happy. He knew that he should not get too wedded to life again, as today it might be taken away from him. But despite all his troubles, he still relished being in existence. He smiled irrepressibly at the guards in the van with him, but they only presented faces of stone. Perhaps that was how they got through their day, he mused.

As they arrived at the court, the van slowed to a crawl and Dalton felt dozens of fists banging on its metal walls.

He wondered what motivated them. Were they rabid ecoists, kicking him when he was down? Or the hired mobs used to bolster a weak case on the TV news? They were all possible in London.

After a while he heard the sound of heavy gates being closed, and then the van doors were opened. The guards gestured for him to climb out, which he did without much effort as they hadn't cuffed him. Either they thought he was no threat at sixty-six, or they sympathised with him in some way. He glanced at their inflexible faces but he couldn't tell which.

As they walked across the yard into the court building, he turned his face to the sun and breathed deeply, making the most of it.

Inside, the courtroom was packed. He'd become quite a celebrity, he thought bitterly, for reasons he had never intended. They all rose and quietened as the judge came in. He was enjoying the publicity. Dalton could tell from his new glasses and almost repressed smile.

After the court was settled, the judge began.

"You have been found guilty of Climate Change Denial by the judgement of your peers. As you may know, this has recently been made a capital offence."

The judge's smile crept out of the corners of his mouth as he leant forwards to retrieve the black cap. As he picked it up, he seemed to be relishing the power of such a simple piece of cloth in his fingers.

He was about to put it on, encouraged by the gasps he'd heard from the courtroom, when he remembered something and put it back.

"Is there anything you wish to say?"

"Yes, there is," Dalton said calmly. The judge looked nonplussed. Roger was aghast.

Continuing unhurriedly, Dalton spoke. "This trial is a travesty of justice. It relies upon several logical fallacies, but I shall describe only three.

"Firstly, a punishment cannot be justified if it was invented after the crime took place. This commits the fallacy of reversing cause and effect. This is not justice.

"Secondly, 'a million Frenchmen can be wrong'. While the jury system is a useful guard against authoritarianism, there is, in fact, no truth created by the numerical counting of beliefs. The truth is out there, for each of us to discover and identify using our own rational minds. That is why the freedom to question climate change and anything else is essential. If any juror felt safe voting for my conviction simply because the others did, he or she is committing a fallacy.

"Finally, you are all guilty of the fallacy of 'rewriting reality'. Denying climate change does not justify you treating me like a murderer. It's the other way around. You might wish it to be untrue, but it is man's interventions and actions on Earth that save lives and promote longevity. Not passively resigning ourselves like dumb animals to the effects of nature. By hindering science and industry, and letting nature 'take its course', you, are the murderers of men. Not me.

"To live in a world where my countrymen prefer cowering to courage, and envy to justice, makes death a less appalling prospect."

There was a pause.

"Have you finished?" the judge asked.

"I have, for now," Dalton replied.

The judge snorted, then with all the pomp he could still muster, reached for the black cap and placed it on his head.

"I sentence you, Dalton MacDermot, to be hanged by the neck until you are dead," the judge said, and smiled.

The court gasped, then broke into loud conversation. Zac, the prosecutor, grinned at the judge. Manny Schweizer patted him on the back. Roger bit his lip and said to his client, "We will appeal."

The hard-faced guards moved to take Dalton away.

"Wait, just a moment," Dalton said. Turning to Roger, he said, "I want you to appeal. But I also want you to go ahead with what we discussed, for Grace's sake."

"But where will you live, if you win the appeal?"

"Please, just sell it, Roger. I'll worry about that later. We must get Grace safely abroad, to her family in

Africa. That's what matters."

Roger bowed his head and Dalton was led away.

#

Manny leant back on the leather seat and breathed in the luxurious smell of polish as the official car drove him from Fleet Street to The Mall. As the owner and inheritor of the biggest newspaper in the country, he was used to luxury, but this was something else. This was class. As he relaxed into the car's plush upholstery, he enjoyed the view of London through the oversized windows, designed to afford onlookers the best view of the occupants. However, even though it was a warm June night, he didn't open them. There were some dangerous people with grudges about, and he didn't want to be mistaken for someone responsible with an official position.

As the car passed the security checks and crawled through the imposing black gates, Buckingham Palace reared up in front of him, seeming much bigger than he'd ever seen it before. The famous balcony from which the Royal Family had given their last wave before emigrating seemed much higher than on television. That departing gesture had been quite poorly attended, he remembered with some pride. Partly thanks to his paper's anti-monarchy campaign – in which the royals had been accused of being out of touch with the nation's economic ills – people had decided not to go.

The car drove into the courtyard and drew up outside the main entrance. As he waited for the driver to open his door, Manny wondered how someone as frugal and self-denying as Fabian was enjoying such a home.

A guard led Manny through the entrance hall and along a plush corridor endowed with old masters and expensive marquetry. They must have been owned by the state, he pondered, or else the royals hadn't had enough room in their plane to take them. All the better for the new, more equal nation left behind.

They approached a large door. On either side was a row of guards standing to attention, wearing the same uniform as his escort and carrying pistols at their sides. The last one in the row also carried a large, purple birthmark on his face. Stunned, Manny recognised Lee Procter – the ex-con whom he'd paid for special services to the newspaper many a time, and whom he'd recommended to Fabian. How on earth did someone like that become a national guard? Thankfully, Lee showed no sign of having recognised him.

As Manny was about to say something, the door magically opened and he was let into a bright, yellow-painted room with large glass doors and steps down to a garden. There was a large desk and again a collection of valuable paintings, but no people. Manny ventured in and was scrutinising a Constable when Fabian finally entered the room.

"Yes, it's rather good, isn't it. Being the President of Great Britain does have its perks."

"Very impressive," Manny said, indicating the room and the whole palace. "Are you settled in yet?"

Fabian grinned. "My few possessions? It didn't take long. In fact, there are plenty of spare rooms. You'd be welcome to stay whenever you like."

Manny wasn't sure whether he was joking. "That's very kind, but my wife complains she doesn't see enough of me as it is."

Fabian smiled. "Ever the loyal husband, Manny. Well, I suppose I could turn some of them into offices for the party staff. It would save a lot of transport carbon."

Manny nodded, deciding not to bring up the issue of heating such an old building in the winter, then remembered something. "Talking of staff, I noticed a smart array of guards on the way in. Are they new? I didn't recognise the uniform."

"Yes, they're part of my Inner Circle guard. Loyal believers in the cause, whom I can trust completely."

"I see," Manny said. He wondered why the normal Household Guard were not enough, but decided it might be inappropriate to ask. Instead, he said, "That reminds me, what happened to today's Cabinet meeting? They've been on Wednesdays for years, but we received no briefing."

"Yes," Fabian said, and he smiled directly at Manny. "I've decided to have fewer Cabinets from now on. It will allow me to spend more time with friends."

Fabian stepped towards the unlit fireplace and pressed a button. A moment later, a smartly dressed butler appeared carrying two glasses of champagne.

"I hope you'll join me," Fabian said as he took his own glass from the tray.

Manny took the other and the butler left. He asked, "What are we celebrating?"

Fabian reached for a folded newspaper lying unobserved on top of the mantelpiece. As Fabian opened it, Manny could see it was quite old. The headline read, '*Be Green, Be Good.*'

"One of your finest works," Fabian remarked with a

smile curling one side of his mouth.

Manny recalled the story from five years before. It was an investigative piece exposing how much more damage to the environment the rich did than the poor, through their running and support of large industries and their excessive personal levels of consumption. It focused on the richest man in Britain at that time, a property tycoon.

"Thank you," Manny acknowledged. He had overseen and edited the work himself.

"Didn't that chap with all the houses subsequently give it all to charity, and go and live in Africa?"

"Yes. Herbert Orgrave. He did. On a farm."

"It really turned the tide, that event. Soon after, we had a huge surge in membership, which has been growing ever since."

"And here you are," Manny grinned.

"It's the will of the people," Fabian said, "and I'm sure they were as pleased as me at how smoothly the Carbon Crime Bill went through Parliament. It won't be long before we start to benefit from its effects."

"Well, quite," Manny said. He began to sip his champagne, then stopped, realising there had been no toast yet. "But I presume the exceptions we discussed for essential services such as newspapers will still hold?"

"I think there's a very good chance that they will."

"That's good to hear. You know, it's remarkable what effect even the threat of legislation can have on a business. Since the rumours of the Internet Regulation Bill surfaced, people have been offering huge sums for the *National Voice*."

"But you wouldn't sell, would you?" Fabian asked

quietly.

Manny had in fact considered doing so, several times. Newspaper hours were very unsociable. He would have been able to retire and spend a decent amount of time with his wife and daughter. But he would miss the thrill of controlling which ideas the nation got into their heads along with their breakfast. And he could tell from Fabian's manner what was expected of him. He wondered what Fabian had to be nervous about, now he was on top of the world.

"No. It's never been about the money, as you know."

Fabian smiled more broadly and his shoulders relaxed. "The bill will go before Parliament shortly. I don't expect it will take long to pass."

Manny stood before his friend and began to feel awkward, holding a glass without permission to drink from it. Fabian was staring at him but saying nothing. After a long silence, Fabian made an announcement.

"I'd like to offer you the position of Director General of the GBMC. The current one has expressed his doubts about our new 'regime' rather too openly. Whereas you, Manny, I know, are completely loyal. We do go back a very long way."

Manny was speechless.

"Do you accept?" Fabian asked after a pause.

It was beyond Manny's dreams – controlling the most trusted media organisation in the world. Why was Fabian so keen to offer it to him? They were friends, but he didn't know anything about television or radio. Never mind your doubts, he told himself. This could be the chance of a lifetime. The level of control of the narrative would be extraordinary. He focused on only one snag. What if it was only temporary?

"Presumably I could still run the paper?"

"Of course. I don't see any conflict."

"Then I accept," Manny gasped and shook Fabian's hand vigorously.

"To your new post," Fabian said enthusiastically, and they drank.

After a long draught to calm his excitement, Manny said, "If the Internet Bill passes, it will put a stop to fake news and…" He was about to say 'any competition for the newspapers, television and radio,' but he managed to suppress that remark and said, "… people like your brother spying on the state."

"Yes, that will be of some benefit," Fabian remarked. "I shall just have to make the most of trying him for his current crimes. Shall we?" and he gestured towards the expansive gardens.

#

Blake felt nervous. He was riding in the back of a police car with the rear doors locked and two burly coppers up front. It was all designed to give him the appearance of being a criminal before a trial had taken place. Well, today the truth would out. Fabian would be stopped and justice would be done. As he said this to himself, he sat up straight, emboldened. But part of him felt a degree of dread. It couldn't be that simple, especially given the election result.

Rather than being tried at the Old Bailey, for some reason they had been told to attend a building on Whitehall. Blake was hoping his supporters had got the message. He was not disappointed.

As he was released from the car into the July sunshine, he could see the founding members of the

BCF in a group clapping and cheering. Clive Donaldson, Liz Blackwood, Sam Tillman, Paul Williams and Gobind Grewal were all turned to him smiling. They were outnumbered by others shouting abuse and holding placards saying 'Climate Traitor'. But there were a few independent onlookers who cheered him on. He felt emboldened again.

Then he saw Candice. She was with a couple of girls her own age whom he didn't know. Part of her new London life, he thought, and felt a stab of longing. He went to go and speak to her, but the policemen tried to usher him inside.

"Wait a minute, can't you?" he shouted.

"Sorry sir, but we have to get you inside. It's for your own good," one of the plods said.

"I think I'll be the judge of that," Blake retorted.

At that moment Xavier, his solicitor, appeared. "Excuse me officer, I think you'll allow my client the right to speak to his own daughter, unless you enjoy having disciplinary charges filed against you?"

The two policemen exchanged glances.

"That's not what we've been told, sir," one of them said. "We're not to allow any communication between the accused and anyone else."

"What about me, then? I'm his legal counsel."

"Sorry sir. The trial's to be held in private. No conversations outside and no one allowed inside."

"But that's outrageous," Xavier cried. "It goes against every legal precedent since Magna Carta."

"It's a matter of state security."

"But what about my client's rights to be properly represented?"

"I'm afraid they're being overridden in this case."

"I can't allow it," Xavier blustered.

"You won't be allowed in, sir." Turning to Blake, he said, "We will use handcuffs if necessary."

Blake shivered despite the warm morning. Something was hideously wrong. He wanted to turn and run, but he knew that wouldn't work. If he was cuffed, it would upset Candice and he would look even more guilty. Would they take the cuffs off inside? He didn't know. Then he thought of Roger Newton's contempt of court. He couldn't get Xavier into any trouble. Not only would it be poor repayment for all his work, but he would need him in person for any appeal. He had Xavier's notes in his tablet. That would have to do.

"You won't need the cuffs, officer. Xavier, could you find out what's going on here? Get the Lord Chief Justice involved if necessary. I'll be okay on my own, but I imagine I'll be needing your services later."

"Right," Xavier said, and stormed off to a quieter spot, pulling out his phone.

Blake turned and smiled at Candice. She smiled back, lifting his heart. Then he waved at the crowd, looking as confident as he could, and began walking up the steps between the two officers.

At the top, he turned back one more time to wave and saw the severe but concerned face of Liz Blackwood staring back at him. He smiled grimly and went in.

After being led through a labyrinth of corridors, he was deposited in what was presumably the courtroom. It was unusually circular in shape. Even more unusually, the ceiling was covered in large gold stars. A distant memory of schoolboy history came to his mind, but Blake could not recall the details.

There were three judges in wigs sitting at an improvised bench on a raised platform. The two nearest ones wore silver badges that glinted in the daylight streaming down from some small, high-up windows. Blake was fairly certain the badges were in the shape of trees. The one without a badge sat at the far end.

Fabian was sitting in the middle of the room, at a table piled high with documents. Very little could surprise Blake now. Men with holstered guns and wearing a strange uniform guarded the various doors.

Conspicuous by their absence was any kind of jury, or a place where they would sit.

Blake shuddered. He would be doing this quite alone. He went and sat at a bare table off to the side.

The central judge banged a gavel, and Blake thought of an auctioneer completing a transaction. Was justice being sold?

"This special court is now in session," the judge declared.

Addressing the guards, he said, "You may wait outside."

They all marched out and closed the doors.

Seizing the initiative, Blake stood up.

"Before we begin, I would like to be clear what kind of court this is. Why, for instance, is there no jury?"

The central judge replied, "This is a special court held 'in camera' to protect the interests of the state."

"What about my interests?"

"They are overruled when state secrets are involved."

"I see," Blake said, and he noticed his brother

smiling at him. He continued, "I would also like to question the presence of two members of the Ecoist Party among the judges. That's hardly fair, given the President of that party appears to be acting as prosecutor."

"It is not an offence to belong to a political party," the judge returned, "especially a major one that has just won an election."

Blake couldn't think of anything else to say. It was a sham of a court but he would play along. If he exposed Fabian as he planned to, that might make the judges think twice. He sat down.

Then Fabian quickly strode to the judges' bench and handed the central judge a sheet of paper. The judge read it, raised his eyebrows slightly at Fabian, then nodded before Fabian returned to his seat.

Then the judge said, "Will the accused please stand."

Blake knew that the formality helped legitimise the trial, but he did it anyway. He would bide his time.

"You are accused of intercepting government communications during April this year in order to discredit your political enemies and upset the election. You are also accused of committing Carbon Crime through your IT company, Caelum, thus polluting the planet, damaging the climate and stealing precious resources from present and future generations. How do you plead?"

Fabian had just made up the second charge, Blake realised with indignation. But it didn't really matter since it was easily dismissed, he thought.

"Guilty of the first charge, but with exonerating circumstances. Not guilty of the second."

The judges all conscientiously made a note, at which

point Blake realised there was no official clerk or recorder. His stomach sank.

The judge without a badge asked Blake, "What were these exonerating circumstances?"

Blake looked at his brother and wondered how he could sit there so calmly, even smiling slightly, when his vicious plot was about to be exposed.

"I was investigating how the backup power supply had failed during my son's operation at a local hospital, causing his death. I found the diesel fuel tanks had been dry for weeks, and that there was an arrangement between the hospital, the fuel company and someone at the Department of Health, to deny fuel to many hospitals and care homes. This lead me to investigate the electronic communications of the Department of Health, in an attempt to uncover who was overseeing the plan."

"Why didn't you go to the police?" asked another judge.

"I was upset by my son's death. I couldn't wait to find out the truth, and I didn't want police delays to jeopardise finding it."

"And did you find out who it was?" the badgeless judge asked, leaning on the edge of his seat.

"I did. It was him," and Blake pointed at his brother.

The judges' jaws dropped as they turned as one towards the President of Britain. Fabian sat rigidly in his chair, staring at the starry ceiling.

Recovering himself, the other badged judge asked, "Do you have any evidence to support such a serious accusation?"

"It's all on the computers in my office that the police seized. This was on the day I got back from confronting my brother in London. I presumed they would be produced as evidence for the prosecution."

"Does the prosecution have these computers?" the badgeless judge asked, happy to be following a simple procedure.

Fabian stood up quickly. "Your Honour, we have printouts here of all the relevant documents and records showing when and how the accused broke into government systems. But I can assure you, there is nothing to indicate a conspiracy. The only criminal activity they reveal is that of the accused." He brought a box of documents up to the bench.

"But what about the computers themselves?" the judge pressed, gently.

Fabian smiled in mock apology. "The police tell me they have wiped them as a matter of national security."

Blake felt a rush of adrenaline and shot up. "My Lords," he said. "Surely the prosecution can't get away with such a blatant abuse of legal procedure?"

The judges shifted uncomfortably on their chairs as they conferred. Eventually, the nearest one asked Blake, "Do you have any witnesses?"

Blake thought about calling Clive. The problem was, Clive was just as implicated as he was in the so-called 'spying'. He didn't want to get him into the same trouble. He thought of Mr Goadby and the staff at Sunshine Fuels. Maybe one of them would support him.

"Not at present. But if we suspend these proceedings for a day or two, I expect I could present some."

The judges put their heads together again. Blake looked around the room and then up at the ceiling. He tried to remember what it had been used for.

The central judge finally said, "Since you've already pleaded guilty to the first charge, the reasons why you did it are of little importance. Lord Hardwicke, please continue with the second charge."

"You can't do this," Blake shouted, his fists like lead. "There is a huge, deadly corruption at the heart of this government, which is doubtless causing more unnecessary deaths this very day. Do you want to be party to that?"

"Mr Hardwicke," the central judge intoned, "it is you, not us, who are on trial."

Blake sat down stunned. His mind reeled. Were the ecoists really so embedded in the system that the truth would never be allowed to come out? Was there any procedure for an appeal against a court like this? Was there any point? He looked at the judge at the far end, who wore no badge. But when their eyes met, the judge quickly looked away and busied himself tidying his papers. Blake felt sickened. If ever there was a role in life where evasion was a cardinal sin, surely being a judge was it.

He looked towards his brother and saw him standing with a sheaf of papers shaking slightly in his hands, facing the judges.

Fabian cleared his throat twice and began. "My Lords, I accuse this man, my brother, Blake Hardwicke, of pre-murdering future generations, by his reckless emission of carbon through his company Caelum.

"Under Section 32, paragraph 11b, of the Carbon Crime Act, it is an offence punishable by prison to 'emit excessive amounts of carbon, regardless of the absence or presence of a relevant quota'."

Blake wondered how that kind of loose language

had found its way into the law. It was a catch-all clause that could be used against anyone, arbitrarily. Wasn't Parliamentary scrutiny supposed to stop that kind of thing?

"Furthermore," Fabian continued, his face growing redder, "I accuse him of causing untold climate damage through his demand for energy to run his beloved computers, and the burning of fossil fuels that implies. A healthy climate is the birthright of every human being and he has stolen that from everyone, present and future."

The judges and Blake looked at him, waiting for a further legal offence to be named. But he just stood there, his face drawn, out of breath. Eventually, he sat down. He may not have cited a crime, but what he'd said cut to the heart of the case. The trouble was that after decades of propaganda in the media, then generations being taught environmentalism in schools, nearly everyone took green ideas for granted. Blake, however, was a scientist and an engineer, who'd made a business out of understanding cause and effect. He knew how to use logic to get to the bottom of things, and over the years, every time he'd examined the claims made by environmentalists, he'd found huge holes in their arguments and skews in their data. For some reason, though, the juggernaut had rolled on regardless, and now it passed for truth. Still, he had to try convincing the judges otherwise. What else was open to him?

He stood up. At least he still had his tablet with Dalton's manuscript on it. He was sure there were some passages in it about government interference with science that he could use. Meanwhile, he needed to play for time. "I'd like to examine the evidence purporting to show that burning hydrocarbons 'damages' the climate. I'd also like a definition of an undamaged climate, otherwise, since the Earth can't speak for itself, how will we know what I've done? Finally, if your claims are true, then everyone who ever benefitted from a fire, or a steam engine, or a car must be guilty. Shouldn't the whole of mankind be hauled before the courts?"

As Blake slowly sat back down, Fabian leapt to his feet.

"I don't believe the court should trouble itself with indulging my brother's hyperbole. Everyone knows that the climate is being damaged by man's activities. It's obvious to anyone who's had their eyes open long enough to observe the weather. And it's obvious how this has happened. Mankind is an unnatural curse upon existence. He is forever overreaching himself and changing the natural order, always growing and expanding over the Earth, eliminating other species and their habitats, in his quest for a longer, easier life. It's common sense." Fabian's eyes bulged and he had to stop to breathe again.

Blake rose, while Fabian remained standing. "It's not common sense to me," Blake said, remembering a phrase from Dalton's new book. Turning to the bench, he asked, "Might we have an adjournment so I can call a variety of scientists as witnesses who will bolster my case?"

The judges huddled together, then after a minute the central judge replied.

"As this is a special court, in camera, we cannot allow unauthorised people into it."

"But the Carbon Crime charge has nothing to do with national security," Blake pleaded.

"But it does," the judge persisted energetically. "Someone who threatens our whole country with extreme weather, global warming and costly flooding is clearly a danger to the nation's security."

"But it doesn't make sense. From the way Fabian was speaking, it's not me that should be on trial, but the whole of humanity – and not even that, but whoever, or whatever, made human beings the way we are."

The judges froze. They obviously still had some regard for logic but were unable or unwilling to act on it. They all turned towards Fabian for guidance.

"Indeed," came the President's reply. "And the atonement can start with you, my arrogant brother." Fabian wiped his hands on his trousers. "The prosecution rests, and in the absence of any further witnesses or evidence, I suggest you reach a verdict."

The judges obediently huddled together.

In a split second, Blake realised what was going on and why. He thought of something Dalton had said to him once: the science of climate change had never been the issue, mankind's moral code was, and that he, as an exemplar of selfishness, would have to be sacrificed to atone for man's sins. It was exactly what was happening now. But selfishness was wrong. It was the epitome of wrong. He couldn't untangle it. He was frozen in his chair.

He observed the judges' furtive discussion. The furthest judge – the one without a badge – was making some exasperated appeal to his colleagues. But they answered him vociferously and then all three turned to glance at Fabian, who was still standing and smiling. The badgeless judge threw his hands up in a gesture of defeat and then, after a further short conference, they resumed their positions facing forward.

The central judge spoke. "Blake Lorenzo Hardwicke, you have been found guilty on all charges, and will be remanded in custody for sentencing."

Fabian closed his lips, still smiling, and nodded to the bench in mock deference.

Blake didn't wait for them to call the guards. He sprinted across the circular room and burst through a door marked 'Fire Exit – Emergency Only'. Outside in the fresh air he saw Candice, pacing in a courtyard. He ran to her.

"It's a trap," he gasped, grabbing her shoulders.

"What is?"

"The whole thing." And then he ran, clutching his tablet under one arm as he vaulted over some railings and continued sprinting into a park, grateful he'd kept his body and mind fit. He had to get out of this world.

PART TWO: SELF-DESTRUCTION

7

Blake awoke with a start and felt a stick digging into his back. It was broad daylight. Why hadn't he woken up sooner? What had woken him up? Was there some animal nearby? He looked up and down the ditch and raised his head over the side. Nothing. He lay back and laughed to himself, grateful that Britain hadn't reintroduced wolves to the wild for the sake of 'nature', unlike France.

His deep sleep must have been the product of all that walking he did yesterday, he thought. How far was he now from London? Remembering some of the road signs he'd seen last night, he guessed it was about thirty miles. He blessed the warm July weather. No need to book into a hotel or inn where he might alert suspicion.

But his clothes would. Plenty of other people walked the roads these days, but not usually in bespoke tailored suits. He looked at his watch. It was only 6 a.m. No shops would be open. But actually, that was what he wanted. He checked the state of his tablet. It was safely untraceable in airplane mode, but it was still losing charge. He needed to do something about that. He also checked his wallet which he'd filled with cash on his way out of London. He hoped he had enough. He couldn't take any more out without revealing his position.

He set off towards a town signposted from the main road, and realised he had a raging thirst. He'd bought a bottle of water on the way out of London yesterday, but that was long since dry. Wondering how few shops he could visit, and so leave the fewest clues to his whereabouts, he suddenly spied a solution: a garden centre. They'd long since become the go-to shop for anything and everything, not just plants. It must be because they were considered 'green' and therefore attracted less regulation, he mused.

Walking round the outside of the huge shop-cum-greenhouse, he found an open window – they had to let the heat out at this time of year. But it was twenty feet up and within the sloping roof. He didn't want to break in. It might set off an alarm, and he didn't agree with destroying others' property. Anyway, he was fifty-four not a hundred and four. He could still climb.

As it was a very practical place, it didn't take him long to find a ladder. He propped it against the shop wall, climbed up, then dragged himself across the roof, towards the window. If he went in head first he'd have to turn somehow to get down safely. Instead, he slid around awkwardly on the roof until his feet were in the opening. Then, with some effort, he pushed himself backwards, up the roof, until his waist was over the window's edge. Finally, he pivoted his legs down into the space below.

There was nothing but thin carpet tile on a hard

concrete floor below, so he let his whole body down gradually before jumping. He fell the final ten feet but his legs, strong from regular running, absorbed the shock without injury.

He looked around for what he needed and soon had quite a collection: some casual outdoor clothes, walking boots, a sleeping bag, a plastic survival bag (somehow exempt from the ban), four litres of spring water (one for immediate consumption), dried food (including plenty of sweets), a packet of teabags, two nested metal pots, a wire saw, camping cutlery, a large tin mug, some matches, a knife, some fishing line, some snare wire, a wind-up lantern, a solar charger and a rucksack to carry it all in. As was common in these days of unreliable electricity, each item had a price sticker as well as a barcode on it.

He went to the unmanned tills and counted out enough cash from his wallet to cover what he owed. Blake knew most people would laugh at him – he could easily have got away without paying. But he had never felt that life was some kind of poker game, where you had to be on the lookout for cheats all the time, and where any successful cheating should be applauded. After all, if he didn't pay, who would? The workers might have it docked from their wages. Whoever did the last stock take might be sacked. Or the business might pay in lost income and increase its prices to compensate. Then every future customer would pay for his act of thievery.

He put the money in the manually operated till. As he did so, he noticed a book, surreptitiously hidden under the counter, presumably for reading during quiet moments. The cover looked familiar. It was

Capitalism versus Ecoism, by Dalton MacDermot. You could never tell people's hobbies or interests from their job, he noted. In need of some mental stimulation, he left generous compensation under the counter and took it.

His watch said 7:30. The shopworkers would be arriving soon. He hurriedly changed out of his suit and into his new purchases. Just as he was pulling on his second boot, he heard the sound of a door being opened. He tied a quick knot and searched desperately for a fire exit. He could see one about twenty yards away. He hoped it wasn't alarmed.

Keeping low, he crossed the floor. Just as he was gently opening the door, he made the mistake of looking back. His eyes met those of the woman opening up the shop. Whatever he did now, she had the ability to recognise him and he had lost the advantage of anonymity.

Not waiting for her reaction, Blake slipped through the door and ran towards the main road. When he reached it he could see a lorry trundling towards him a hundred yards away. Hoping his brand new clothes didn't give him away – he hadn't got around to removing the tags – he thumbed for a lift.

The lorry drove closer, then slowed and signalled to stop. As he drew alongside, Blake shouted through the open window, "Going north?"

A bearded face leaned out and said, "Aye." Without looking back, Blake opened the cab door and climbed in.

As Blake Hardwicke glanced out of the lorry window, the shopworker smiled and waved, then closed the fire exit and went back inside.

Had he met that woman, Blake wondered? Unlikely. But she seemed to recognise him. He wasn't famous, unless… He glanced at the driver. His eyes were on the road.

"Where you headed?" the driver asked.

Quickly, Blake calculated a plausible story. A man in his mid-fifties in new outdoor gear…

"I'm off on a walking holiday with some friends."

The man nodded.

"My car wouldn't start," Blake added, trying to fill in the gaps the man must be spotting.

"Aye, it's hard to keep them going these days, what with garages closing and the lack of spare parts, never mind the cost of fuel."

Glad to change the subject, Blake asked, "What are you carrying?"

The man looked at him quickly, in an appraising way. Blake realised that neither of them were able to trust the other. He wondered why, and he wondered what had changed in the last fifty years to make people so wary.

After a pause, the driver explained in one word.

"Coal."

"Ah," Blake said, and worked out the rest of the story in his head. Electricity was unreliable, so people needed another fuel. There was a super-tax on fossil fuels to try to prevent global warming. Like tobacco and alcohol duty in the past, this led to a thriving but dangerous smuggling business. The driver probably took him to be a shoplifter. A pair united by crime.

Blake smiled and said, "God knows we need it."

The driver smiled too.

They drove on in conspiratorial silence, Blake

slaking his thirst with the spring water. For a while he enjoyed just looking out of the window. The sunlit landscape of fields and hedges, with barely a car or person in sight, seemed to beckon adventure. James would have enjoyed it, he thought, and a painful lump swelled in his throat. Had he really grieved properly for him yet? What with tracking down the cause of James's death and then his own arrest and trial, he realised he hadn't. Well, he'd have plenty of time for that soon, now he was an outlaw, hiding from society. But where would he go? Where would he be safe?

"Can I look at your map?" he asked the driver, pointing at a road atlas.

"Go ahead, pal."

Blake found where they were by using the road signs and the index, then looked for any large areas of green nearby. He turned over a few pages heading north until he saw the words 'Sherwood Forest', and smiled at the irony of being Robin Hood while his brother was the Sheriff of Nottingham. That had to be where he went. But for good measure he continued turning the pages, as if planning to go somewhere else.

It was a weird experience, living in fear of others, worried they'd discover his secret. He'd always tried to be open with people, admitting to any mistakes he made, forgiving others in genuine error, then sharing in their successes and values. Playing games was not his style. But now, he remembered, he had to play for his very freedom.

The driver turned the radio on and they listened to the presenter's harmless banter between songs as the miles passed them by.

At nine o'clock there the usual news bulletin.

The lead story was about some executives who'd been arrested for Carbon Crime. Blake's heart jumped as he heard the names: Clive Donaldson, Liz Blackwood and Sam Tillman. Had they been picked because they'd tried to witness his trial? Had they spoken out in his defence then quickly been silenced? He suspected Fabian was behind it. It was too coincidental. He tried not to show his emotions.

The second story detailed the number of 'carbon tons saved' in Britain in the last year. The government was taking credit for the sky not falling in.

Thirdly, the newsreader announced, "…ex-CEO of Caelum, Blake Hardwicke, is still missing. Police believe he is still in the country and have issued alerts for him in all counties."

Blake had stopped breathing, he realised.

"I used to get my Internet from Caelum, back in the old days," the driver mused, still looking ahead.

"Was it any good?" Blake finally exhaled.

"Aye, but then me computer died and I couldn't afford a new one, so I left."

"Too bad," Blake said. He was about to go into how the import tariffs and carbon taxes were affecting the price of computers, when he realised he shouldn't reveal too much about himself. Again, it was an unnatural feeling, shutting himself down from others. He had to learn it – if he was to survive. Fortunately, the driver was not a great talker, but Blake couldn't risk being with someone long enough to raise their suspicions.

He looked at the map. If he didn't mind a long walk, he could get out fairly soon.

Thirty anxious minutes later, they came across a

petrol station that wasn't abandoned. Just as Blake was going to suggest stopping there, the driver announced he was pulling in.

They went into the shop together. All fuel had to be paid for in advance these days, the cashiers sitting behind grills. The driver paid with a hefty wad of notes.

While he was filling up, Blake chose some provisions, including sandwiches and tea bags, and tried to think of an excuse for leaving the truck.

Eventually, the driver came back into the shop and started looking at the cold pasties.

"Thanks a lot for the lift," Blake said, approaching him.

"You're welcome, pal. Is that you away now?"

"I'm meeting someone here then we're going on together." It was pathetic, Blake knew, but it didn't give anything away and would have to do.

The driver knew it was a lie, but in the code of the underworld, it was not to be questioned.

"Look after yourself."

Blake nodded and the bearded driver chose his snack, then paid and ambled out. Blake watched him drive off then paid for his own food and a map. Then he walked up the road on his own.

He soon came to a footpath sign, and climbed over the stile into an unplanted field. He walked for twenty minutes to get out of sight of the road before he sat on a log and looked at his map.

It was crisscrossed with lines and symbols, all indicators of man's taming of the landscape. He looked up at the fields, hedges and woods in front of him – they were all examples of man adapting nature to his requirements, as had been going on since the Stone Age. Previously, Britain had been covered in dense forest, quite unsuited to agriculture. How misguided the ecoists were when they thought living on a farm was going back to nature. Doing that properly, making no changes to the natural environment whatsoever – was that actually possible? Even animals and plants changed the environment they lived in by absorbing nutrients or building nests and burrows. So why shouldn't man?

Refocusing on his own survival, Blake studied the map and chose a part of the forest that looked especially dense and far from human habitation. He would be safe there. He set off on the twenty-mile walk to his hideout.

He was soon sweating with the July heat, despite tying all his clothes onto the straps of his backpack. Yet this was nothing compared with a desert, he told himself. He marvelled at how men had survived such journeys in the days before motorised transport, and how they had conquered the wildernesses of western North America.

He continued to pick his way along footpaths and across stiles, grateful for the map-reading he'd learned in the Scouts many decades ago. He'd never joined the army, as some of his friends had gone on to do, but he hoped his training would be enough to survive on. The army was dangerous enough when he was young, but now they were stripped of funding and continuously sent on tours to 'fix' other people's countries without a definition of victory, then prosecuted for doing their job – he was surprised anyone joined up.

After ten miles his feet were signalling the existence

of blisters. He didn't dare look, and wished he'd bought more than one pair of socks. He couldn't afford to get an infection – he'd forgotten to buy a first aid kit. What did people use before modern medicines? Suffer and possibly die, he presumed. Possibly some plant-based remedies would help. But what did he know about those? It was all about knowledge. In his previous life, he'd have looked them up on the Internet. But if the Internet Regulation Bill was passed, the web would be reduced to government sites and those companies rich enough to bribe their way through the red tape. He'd just have to use his wits. He'd be fine.

After a couple of hours, Blake's back and shoulders were really aching. At least his pack got lighter as he drank the water. But how on earth did pedlars and carriers used to manage? He longed to stop at a pub, eat a hearty meal and sleep in an upstairs bed, but he knew he couldn't. It was not the path he had chosen. Tonight he would literally have to make his own bed and lie in it, wherever that was.

Eventually, tired and hungry as it turned eight o'clock, he found himself looking at the remains of an amusement park. Beyond the torn-back, rusty fence with large 'Danger – Keep Out' signs, he saw the carcasses of rides and whatever had not been worth looting, covered in parasitic ivy. He knew what kind of engineering brains it took to build such things, and wondered what those people were doing now. Whatever it was, he bet it was relatively mundane. The fun had slowly gone out of the world over the last few years, as the burden of regulation and the repeated collapses of the economy had reduced people to merely staying alive.

He picked his way through the ruins and then plunged into the darkening forest on the other side. Looking at his map, he aimed for an area deep inside and the furthest from any paths. The air was cooler among the trees and sounds were subtly muffled. When he snapped a hidden stick by treading on it, the noise made him freeze. But there was no one to hear him. He carried on walking along paths and clearings strewn with prior years' beech and oak leaves, until he'd been in the forest for an hour. This should be enough, he thought.

He took the weighty burden off his back and almost danced with relief, he felt so light. He also felt starving. As he finished his second packet of sandwiches, he realised he would soon run out of food. But that problem could wait for tomorrow. Meanwhile, it was time for sleep. He cursed himself for forgetting to buy a ground mat, and instead made do with the survival bag and a raked bed of dried leaves with his sleeping bag on top. He climbed in wearing just his underwear and fell almost instantly asleep.

#

He dreamt of being pursued, of his brother's face, foaming at the mouth, and of climbing into his own house through a window…

~

He awoke with a start and looked at his watch. It was 6 a.m. He wondered if he'd been visited by any animals during the night. At first glance nothing seemed to have been disturbed, but he knew he should build some kind of shelter for himself, and particularly his food.

It had been more comfortable than the ditch, but as he stood up and tested his weary legs and back, he realised what he'd owed all these years to the inventor of the sprung mattress.

It was relatively cool under the deep canopy of leaves and he was desperate for a hot cup of tea. But how to conceal the smoke of a fire? He couldn't risk it while they might still be hot on his trail.

He made do with some cold water and some dried fruit. But he hankered after hot food. As he chewed the dried apricots, sitting on his rucksack, he pondered the day ahead and then the weeks beyond. It was strange. He had everything to do, and yet compared with his old life, almost nothing. His family were either dead, incarcerated or living with the enemy. His friends were being hunted down by the authorities and he couldn't help any of them.

He tried to find a bright side to look on. At least he didn't have to work harder and harder as taxes rose each year. He didn't have to comply with more and more regulations. He just had to live, using his own judgement, putting in whatever effort he decided. It was frightening, because he knew he couldn't afford a major mistake like injuring himself. And it was daunting, because there was so much to do, starting with almost nothing. But it was also exciting. He could see in his mind's eye the goal he wanted to achieve, then forming a plan and acting on it, without anyone else's permission or interference. He felt free.

He also felt hungry and thirsty still – the walk had been quite an effort. So he consumed some more food and drink from his purchases and thought about replenishing them soon.

Water – where could he get that? He studied the map and kicked himself for ignoring the point before. There were no streams within the forest but there were a few pools marked, possibly springs. He'd have to light fires to sterilise the water. Now, how could he avoid making telltale smoke? With a small fire and the right kind of dry wood, and with the thick canopy of leaves above, he'd probably be okay. But he'd keep thinking about a proper solution.

What happened when he ran out of matches? He had a knife. He'd keep an eye out for flints.

What about some food? He could build some traps and snares, if he could remember or work out how. There must be some nuts or seeds or fruits in the forest that he could eat, as well as wild plants he could forage. But which would be good for him? What about vegetables? He could probably grow some, but that would take time, and he'd need some seeds. He might be able to buy some from a farm. He'd have to find some greenery he could eat in the meantime.

What about shelter? It would soon be too cold to lie on the ground. But if he built a proper shelter it would be obvious he was living there, if people came this far into the forest. He resolved to keep an eye out for tracks and for suitable sites. Perhaps he should build several shelters and move between them, providing a backup and less of a permanent mark.

~

By the end of the day he'd scouted out three areas for building in, dug some pitfalls as traps, checked various pools for their water quality, and found some suitable stones for use as a hearth. He had built a fairly smoke-free fire on one of them and was cooking a dehydrated meal of beef bourguignon with rice.

As he watched the meal cook, he sipped tea without milk from his large tin mug and thought about his new life.

He was more free than he'd ever been. Even as a child he'd had various limits put on him by his parents, with good reason. Now he could do what he liked – or could he? There was no one else established in the forest so far as he could tell, so he had, as yet, no fear of being discovered, nor of his hard-won traps and shelters being taken from him. But there was one ever-present 'personality' that could not be ignored: nature. Only certain wood burned, only certain stones would not explode in a fire, only certain water was safe to drink, and only certain plants and animals could be safely eaten. 'Mother Nature' set the overall conditions of his existence. But within her domain, if he paid attention and learned her laws, then he could survive. He wasn't free to wish for anything, but he was free to use his mind to discover and create whatever helped him live. It reminded him of another passage he'd read in Dalton's manuscript.

He was about to fish the tablet out of his rucksack when he heard a sizzling, and turned to see his supper boiling over. Quickly he lifted it off the fire with a stick through the pot's handle and, sitting on a log, he tucked into it with a spoon.

After it was all gone, he swilled out the pan with water and fired-up the tablet. Its battery was low but he would try the solar charger tomorrow. Climbing into his sleeping bag, he read the draft of *The Proper Purpose of Government* for an hour before falling asleep.

~

Blake awoke and looked at his watch. It was 4:30 a.m. But it was light and his face was cold. Nature had woken him up. Today he would build a shelter, and hopefully enjoy a lie-in tomorrow.

He restarted the fire and was soon enjoying tea and porridge, albeit with water rather than milk.

As he felt the hot food inside him, he recalled a camping trip they'd taken as a family six years ago. It had been under canvas and on a proper camping site in South Wales, but James had loved running about the woods, building fires, following a set of tracking signs Blake had laid and building a rope bridge together between some trees.

Suddenly the tears came to his eyes and the porridge in his mouth would not go down. He felt the absence of his son like a missing lung. He choked as he struggled to breathe enough air. As he regained control, it struck him for the first time in his life that he could just stop. He'd lost his son. He would not see Marisa for years. His daughter didn't want to see him. His friends were all arrested. His company would soon be ruined. And he was living like a savage, while his brother unleashed the hell of ecoism on the country. What was there to live for?

He sat for a long while, waiting for the familiar energy to move. But all he could feel was his heart slowing down.

He'd been sitting motionless for what could have been hours, when he noticed a squirrel scampering past, quite close to him. It stopped and looked at him, then ran off. He saw the sunlight on the sides of the trees. He heard birdsong. He smelled the mustiness of damp leaves.

He swallowed back the lump in this throat and slowly stretched his leaden arms up, up to the light glinting through the canopy. This was his life now, and he was going to make the most of it. He started by uprooting a young birch tree and stripping its trunk for use as the ridge of his new shelter. As he worked, he wished he'd thought to buy an axe, but he made do with the knife and wire saw. Then he remembered what the earliest men had used for an axe, and went in search of flints.

After an hour he hadn't found any – it must be the wrong geology, he thought. He'd have to risk going back to the broken fairground and salvaging some piece of metal. Would he be able to find his way back to his campsite? He'd better lay a trail, but not an obvious one, just in case other people came along. He could destroy the signs on his way back.

Using sticks, stones and holly leaves, he left a trail on his way out to the edge of the forest.

When he finally reached the fairground, there was no one there. He ignored the 'Private Property' signs above a large hole in the fence and went in. He picked his way around the old rusting turnstiles on the lookout for something that might serve as an axe.

There were railings, gargantuan supports too big for anyone to move, heavy, curved pieces of track from an old roller coaster, large rusty gear wheels, a dog…

He locked eyes with it just before it barked. Which way would the owner come? He couldn't tell, it was such a maze, so he decided to brave it out.

The dog barked again and footsteps followed behind it. Blake turned to see a large, roughly shaven man in greasy overalls carrying a toolbox.

They stared at each other briefly, then moved off in different directions, both bearing the guilt of thieves. Men who could not create or bargain for what they wanted, but could only take it. Blake felt like a Dark Ages vagabond, plundering a Roman temple for a hearthstone. United in crime, he doubted the man would report him even if he recognised him. Still, he felt tainted by what he was doing, and started to look more earnestly so he could leave sooner.

Eventually a black metal chair caught his eye, and he managed to wrench off an arm rest. That would do, he thought. He could sharpen it later. Working his way through the wreckage then back through the forest, following his signs, he emerged at his campsite. It had taken all morning and now he was starving. Time to go and check his traps.

To his surprise and trepidation, there was a rabbit running around at the bottom of one of them, trying in vain to get out. Blake wasn't used to killing animals. But as he looked at the moving form, his hunger grew sharper. He didn't want to use up all his bought food, leaving none in reserve. Besides, he was tired of its blandness. Then he recalled that people usually hung game for some days before cooking it. Was that essential or just for better flavour? He didn't know. But in case it might otherwise make him ill, he decided on hanging it for a day. So the sooner he killed it the better.

He briefly pondered the philosophy of vegetarianism and its prohibition on using animals. If taken to its logical conclusion, men would never learn much biology, test their drugs before risking their own lives, build a house where a fox's den existed, or enjoy the many dishes involving meat. Reduced to such a state, ironically men would be more like animals themselves. If vegetarians worshipped animals, in a twisted way, it made sense.

Bolstered in the rightness of maintaining his own life, he brought down the armrest on the rabbit's head and killed it with a single blow. Then, remembering what else he could from his Scouting days, he gutted and hung it, making a bloody mess but determined to learn and to live.

~

He temporarily assuaged his hunger that day with reconstituted hotpot, rice and custard made with water.

As he stripped trees and made his shelter, he knew in the pit of his stomach exactly what had driven men to understand crops and irrigation, to perfect animal husbandry, to sail the seas for spices and to learn how to tin, freeze and dry food to preserve it. He would survive as best he could with his own knowledge, but living in a society of specialists in these areas would have been much better. If only men realised how fortunate they were, if only they felt the alternative as he did, then they might stop worshipping the planet and damning themselves.

That night, as he lay under his partially constructed shelter, he read some more of Dalton MacDermot's manuscript. The solar charger for the tablet had worked. What a gift it was, someone else's brainwaves captured and communicated to him on a device of such elegance and power. And with that nourishment of the soul, he fell asleep.

~

The rain on his face woke him the next morning, and

174

so Blake spent that day putting a roof of branches and ferns on his first shelter. In the evening he skinned, skewered and spit roasted the rabbit. It tasted good but he missed the accompaniment of potatoes.

Over the next few days he set more traps and snares and continued his 'home improvement'. As he added each detail – a raised floor, a window, a chimney – he was aware of constantly consulting his mind's eye for houses he'd seen in the past. How did lintels work? Nails? Lashings? Pegs? Joints? Hinges? How could he keep it all square and stop it twisting? How could he let the smoke out but not the rain in? Once upon a time, someone else had thought of all these things from scratch with no history to call upon. Blake felt humbled and indebted to those visionaries. Indebted because he couldn't pay them. Humbled because they had chosen to share their knowledge with others. They hadn't hidden away from men's gaze in a forest.

After a week he had started his 'second home', a good half-mile from his first. No 'non-primary dwelling tax' on this one, he chuckled wryly to himself. It was an improvement on the first, learning from it. This one received a roof of wooden tiles made of bark from a large, dead oak. He threaded them together with young, green branches, and lashed these rows to the underlying roof timbers. After two days he had finished and stood back to admire his work. It had taken longer than expected. Thank goodness he had the wire saw, knife and armrest. Without those, he'd have been stuck. Was he capable of making iron, let alone steel? He'd need the right rock, charcoal, a draught-enhanced fire... It would take him a long time. He said another silent prayer to the heroes of the past.

~

The next week, he realised he was now well into August. Perhaps some fields nearby were being harvested and he could buy some straw for bedding and thatching. He was also getting desperate for starch.

Blake set off in a different direction from before, aiming for the northern edge of the forest. As he walked, he realised he'd eventually run out of money. How would he pay for things then? He could supply dead rabbits, but how could he be sure they were acceptable? Trade required two parties to voluntarily agree. But it was impossible without revealing himself. He began to realise what it really meant to be an outlaw.

After a couple of hours he came to the forest edge and stopped in amazement, looking at the fields. There was a crop of wheat. But it was being harvested by hand. The lonely combine harvester stood abandoned at one end. Probably out of fuel, he guessed. A dozen men and women were cutting, gathering and bundling the crops with long-handled scythes and their bare hands.

Blake smiled bitterly at this idyllic image, knowing it had been eulogised by poets, painters and politicians for decades, but also seeing these people making painfully slow progress and occasionally stopping to stand and stretch their aching bodies.

He could come back later for straw. In the meantime, he skirted the forest's shadowed edge until he found an unpeopled field covered in green leaves. Were they the tops of potatoes? He'd dug them up as a child but had lived in cities too long to remember. He hadn't thought to bring any implements, so he tried kicking at the dried earth ridges and burrowing into them with his hands.

Within a couple of minutes he had extracted thirty palm-sized, red-skinned potatoes. That would keep him going for a while. But how to pay? A hundred yards away, in the middle of the field, stood a scarecrow in a suit – a mocking imitation of an executive. Trying to avoid the crops, he walked over to it and placed some coins in its pocket. He hoped the farmer was in a better state, despite the ruinously low prices the government had imposed on produce since farming had been declared a national resource. Touching the cloth, he noticed what fine material it had once been, and out of curiosity he opened it up. Inside was the remains of a purple silk lining, and sewn onto the inside breast was a name: Henry Booth. What on earth was it doing here?

He turned back towards the forest when suddenly there was a gunshot from somewhere behind him. Blake ran, stumbling in the soft, friable soil. He reached the trees safely. There were no more shots. He could see no one. Maybe it was only a bird scarer. He laughed at himself and his new fearful outlook on life. Would this forest experience change him forever?

#

As he sat one dry September evening on a chair he'd made from beech branches and hazel twigs fastened with willow bark, he pondered his situation, and caught himself talking to the air. He'd wanted to hear a voice, he realised. He hadn't had any friendly human contact since the lorry driver. He missed human company. He desperately wanted to talk to someone, even just to say hello. But how could he do that without risking being caught?

As he stroked his chin in contemplation, he realised the beard he'd grown for nearly three months would be quite a good disguise. Also his general appearance, and probably his smell, would not remind people of an IT executive. He strip-washed occasionally but had no deodorant. He would chance it. Just to see some normal people would cheer him up. He fetched his map and picked a smallish town about ten miles away.

That night he took ages to get to sleep, but when the sun woke him, he was raring to go. After tidying his camp, packing his remaining money, some water and a packet of cold rabbit and potatoes, then concealing the entrance, he set off.

It felt good to be on the move in the open air. He hoped his disguise would hold. It was worth the risk.

When he finally reached the town, after tramping many footpaths and narrow roads, he realised people were staring at him, then mostly avoiding him. He must look wild, he thought. Perhaps he should sit down and hold out a cup. That might make him seem more acceptable.

At the old town cross he saw another man doing just that. Occasionally people put a coin in his cup. Blake was going to give him one himself, but realised it would look very odd. Instead, he went and sat next to him.

"Where are you from?" Blake asked.

"London," replied the man, who smelled of body odour and meths.

"Me too," Blake said in a half-truth. "How come you're here?"

The grimy man smiled a wrinkled smile and showed a gold tooth. "I used to be a merchant banker at Hutchin & Co. But I lost my job, my wife and my children when the electricity quotas came in. I used to advise chemical and concrete manufacturers. They all went bust. I had large personal stakes in them. But it's no good complaining," he grinned, "I've got this." He patted his coat pocket. "Do you want some?" he asked, pulling out a glass bottle of purple liquid.

"I'm all right, thanks," Blake said, and he wondered what they both must look like, and whether the banker-bashers would be pleased with their work. Of course, some bankers were corrupt and took advantage of people. But tarnishing them all had always smelled to Blake like envy.

"Are you hungry?" he asked the man.

"When am I not!" he replied.

"Hold on, I'll get us something," and Blake went off.

Ten minutes later he returned with two steaming pasties. The man looked at him with a broad, grimy smile then attacked the Cornish staple. As they chewed the hot, peppered lamb and potato, they grinned at each other.

"What's your name?" Blake asked.

"Henry Booth," the man said proudly.

Blake chuckled. "I think I know where your suit jacket is."

"Really? It was the only good one I ever had. Made to measure. But I had to sell it."

Blake explained about the scarecrow as Henry laughed.

Blake was about to take his third large bite of pasty when out of the corner of his eye he saw a dayglo jacket and helmet.

In a second he had dropped his meal and was sprinting in the opposite direction. The streets got thicker with people as he ran, and soon he was obliged to slow down. He could hear the slap of the policeman's feet a short distance behind him. He didn't turn and look, but plunged into the crowd, hoping for safety in numbers.

It was market day and people crowded around makeshift stalls, hoping or haggling for a bargain. Despite the density of people, they made way for Blake, causing his progress to be obvious. He presumed it was his smell. He slipped between two stalls and hid in an alley between two buildings.

Pressed up against a wall with his heart pounding, he peered out. He could see the policeman's helmet above the crowd. He yanked his head back into the shadows.

After a minute, Blake ventured out. He could see the policeman fifty yards away, heading away from him. As he allowed his breathing to normalise, he wondered if he'd been recognised. Was he in danger, or was he free to continue wandering the town as just another vagrant? He decided to return to the countryside via some back streets.

As he passed a pile of uncollected rubbish bags beside a shuttered-up shop, he saw a newspaper sticking out and extracted it.

The headline was '*Business Chiefs Wreck Economy*'. He hadn't read any news for months. But a tramp using a newspaper for anything other than warmth might be conspicuous. It burned a hole in his coat pocket as he sneaked out of town. Once in a field, he sat behind a hedge and read it.

His brother had been busy. Since Blake's 'trial', the members of the BCF had all been sentenced and imprisoned for Carbon Crime. Their illegal use of carbon was said to endanger future generations. It also appeared that they had all deliberately flouted the law, rather than just negligently failed to follow it. Blake recognised this as a direct threat to Fabian's fragile ego. And for this they were branded serious threats to society and the economy.

He turned the page and saw the familiar flowing locks of Dalton MacDermot as he sat in the back of a police car. He was being taken from prison to a police cell, ready for a pre-appeal hearing which was happening the day after tomorrow. He felt a pang of anguish for Dalton. Given his own recent experience, he was unlikely to receive any justice. But he admired him for trying. He read on. The hearing was in a town only ten miles away.

Blake felt his pulse race. Could he do it? Why the hell not? This was not the time for holding back. He had everything to gain and almost nothing to lose. He pulled the tablet out of his rucksack and checked the map application. It covered the whole of the UK, pre-downloaded to a reasonable scale. He tried to determine the probable route of a police van. After a few minutes he had the beginnings of an audacious plan.

He folded the newspaper and shoved it into his rucksack along with the tablet. Then, checking carefully for hi-vis jackets, he made his way back to the market cross.

The banker tramp was still there, looking relatively

pleased with life.

"Henry, are you here every day?"

"Not many other places to be, have I."

"If I pay you, will you help me with something the day after tomorrow?"

"It depends what it is."

Blake explained.

#

Blake stood at the edge of the forest by a road. It had taken him all the previous day and most of the night, but tired as he was, he now felt he was ready. The adrenaline of action propelled through his arteries. He could hear the van coming. He pulled up his mask and moved into the middle of the highway.

Behind him was a seemingly massive pile of burning wood, forming a barricade. As they came round the bend, the prison officers had no choice but to screech to a halt.

Then Blake approached them menacingly, holding some metal tubing that looked like a sawn-off shotgun. They tried to reverse. But by then Henry had already positioned an old cart behind them using a horse, forming another barrier. The narrow lane afforded no way around.

The two officers behind the windscreen looked scared.

Blake gestured for them to get out with his homemade gun. When they stubbornly refused, he made a movement with the barrel and Henry let off one of the bird-scarers.

Blake could see them making frantic gestures with their radios and a mobile phone. He chuckled. Henry was breaking off the van's antenna and Blake had chosen the location because it had no mobile reception.

When they still refused to move, he stepped back to one of the logs in the barricade and released a taut rope attached to it.

Two seconds later a rock smashed through the windscreen.

The guards got out with their hands raised as Blake approached them, pointing his 'gun'.

"Open the back," he shouted, "and let out the prisoner MacDermot."

One of them nervously reached for his keys as Blake shepherded them to the back of the vehicle. There they found Henry, without a mask, but with a wild look and a stubbly beard, wielding a powerful looking bow and arrow. The guard unlocked the door. Two men in handcuffs climbed out, bewildered, but sensing freedom.

"Who's the other one?" Blake asked.

"His name's Oxley," Dalton MacDermot said. "He's a convicted murderer, being transferred to a more secure prison."

Blake tightened his grip on his 'gun'. "Unlock the cuffs on MacDermot," he ordered.

As the guard did so and Dalton rubbed his wrists, Oxley tried to run for it.

Blake had planned for this. As instructed beforehand, Henry aimed at Oxley's back and brought him down. Then he strung another arrow.

"Now pick him up and put him back in the van. And give me your keys."

The two officers did so, straining against Oxley's weight and residual resistance.

"Now in you go too." The officers reluctantly

climbed in after their charge.

Blake slammed the door and threw the keys to Henry. "You make a good rogue, you know."

"Ah, that'll be thanks to my ruthless dealings in the City." Henry's smile emerged from the grime.

"Take care, won't you," Blake said as he lead the horse with its cart back into the field it had come from.

"I'll be fine," Henry said, waving the banknotes Blake had given him and raising his hand. "Take care yourselves." And with a parting wave he climbed into the front of the van and reversed away down the lane.

Blake hoped he could see well enough through the shattered windscreen when he turned around.

#

It was early evening when Blake and Dalton reached Blake's camp, having tramped a circuitous route through fields, woods and streams, trying to put any pursuers off the scent.

They plumped down exhausted on a log and Blake's improvised chair.

"If I'd known I was going to be rescued, I'd have worn boots," Dalton said as he gingerly removed the brogues from his swollen feet.

"I presume you're glad you were?" Blake said, only half joking.

Dalton smiled. "Now, don't go doubting yourself Blake. You've saved my life, and at great risk to yourself. Thank you just isn't enough."

"You're welcome," Blake said, relaxing. "Of course I only did it because I needed some help with the camp."

"And look what a place you've built here. You must have been busy. When did you get here?"

"Nearly three months ago."

"It's grand. Now, let's have that cup of tea you mentioned and you can tell me more about the trial. Shall I get some wood?"

Once they had a steaming mug to share, Blake explained about the unorthodox setup of the court, and Dalton recognised the location: the Star Chamber. He then recounted its egregious history.

"I thought we'd moved on from that level of abuse of power in government," Blake said when he'd finished.

"So did I, until recently. But now we're all in danger. When a government is motivated by something other than securing the rights of its citizens, then anything can happen to them. That's why I've sent Grace abroad."

"You've what? Your wife's in another country now?"

"She's in Africa with her family."

"But when will you see her again?"

"I don't know." Dalton looked off into the forest and took a big swallow of the black tea. "I thought it was the safest thing. She's very vulnerable in a care home here. Not just from accidents during power cuts."

Blake nodded slowly and grimaced. "Ironically, they can't make it much worse for my wife. She's already in prison."

Dalton grunted.

Blake looked at him for a moment, then went into his shelter before emerging with a smile on his lips. "I've got something that might cheer you up." He presented Dalton with the tablet.

Dalton frowned, then took it and examined it. "and Jesus, it's my manuscript."

Blake grinned. "I've got a charger, too."

Dalton was frantically swiping the screen. "It's all here. Up to when I sent it to you. I've written some more since then but I can remember that easily enough. Oh, this is marvellous, Blake. I can carry on. I can finish it!" And the older man's eyes shone as he shook Blake's hand with both of his.

"I'd be happy to edit it," Blake said.

"Of course, of course. I'd like that."

"But once it's done, how will you publish it?"

"That depends on the Internet Regulation Bill. If it's passed and enforced, we might have to go the traditional route. You'll help me, I hope?"

Blake agreed with conviction, although he could hardly think past his next couple of meals.

Together they cooked supper, Dalton praising Blake's ingenuity and Blake explaining how he obtained the food, and how they could set more traps the next day.

After eating they sat and stared into the fire.

"That was one of the best meals I've ever had," Dalton said. "I apologise for being a bit morose earlier. This has put me in a much better mood, along with the tablet."

"You're welcome."

"You know, you've displayed a remarkable level of ingenuity, building this place. You weren't in the army, were you?"

"No, just the Scouts."

"Well, whatever training you had, it takes a lot of independent reasoning to achieve all this. And to work out how to rescue me."

"Thanks. I am pleased with myself in one way, but in

another I'm…" he broke off for a moment. "…I'm angry and disappointed. I may have used my brain well and kept out of prison, but look where I am. Look at how I'm actually living. I live off the land. I use no fossil fuels. My impact on the Earth is minimal. I'm the ultimate green. Despite everything I've done to oppose them, I've ended up becoming a first-class ecoist!"

"Now, I wouldn't say that—"

Blake stood up sharply. "But it's true. Look at me. Look at my family – dead, imprisoned or converted. Look at my business – begging for quotas to survive. I know I'm right to oppose Fabian and ecoism, but I feel like I'm being punished for it. For all the effort I make, my life just gets harder. I can't see a way out. Of here, or of the ecoist grip on the country."

Blake had never admitted to himself how he really felt about his situation. He'd been too focused on survival. But having Dalton there to listen made it all come out. He looked at him now, and saw his own desperation reflected in the sad sympathy on the other man's face.

"I know it's hard," Dalton said. "I've been fighting the same problem all my academic life. Here, have some more tea," and he poured some of the stewed liquid into Blake's outstretched cup. Blake sat down to drink it.

"The issue you're facing, the battle we're both fighting, has been going on for a long, long time. Centuries before we were born, in fact. But you'll be pleased to know," he said, smiling, "that the theme of my new book offers a solution. It's about how reason has been misused, misdefined and abused, such that we enslave ourselves. It's also about how to set us free."

"But what's reason got to do with politics? Surely that's just about popularity?"

"Indeed, in a democracy. Then the question is, what makes people popular?"

Blake waited for the answer, then realised Dalton was waiting for him. He'd been a science student from the age of sixteen and had never had much time for subjects like politics and philosophy. He realised now that he was being given the chance to catch up. At age fifty-four it was not in his comfort zone. He'd managed quite well for years without having to think hard about such matters. Or had he? What if his leaving these subjects to others, effectively eschewing responsibility, had been a mistake? He fought back the familiar fog that engulfed his brain when he tried to engage with such issues and decided to give it his best shot. Dalton wouldn't make him feel inferior in his ignorance, he was sure of it.

"Well," he screwed up his mind to help him focus, "what makes you popular is doing things for people. Providing them with benefits."

"But that's not what ecoism does, now is it?"

Blake hadn't thought of that before. It was true. Unlike socialism, it didn't offer to take from the rich and give to the poor. That was easy to understand. Ecoism, on the other hand, made everyone's life harder, whatever their income.

"No," Blake said. "But it must offer something, otherwise people wouldn't vote for it."

"Can you think what that might be?"

"Well, they say they're saving the planet for future generations."

"Why is it future generations, do you think, rather than the current generation?"

"Because…" Blake was starting to rack his brains now. This wasn't like calculating petabytes of storage or developing a sales strategy. "Because we're the ones who have messed up the planet, not them."

"I think it's very arguable that we've 'messed up the planet'. After all, we've only been trying to change it to suit our needs. If we didn't 'mess up' the planet, we wouldn't have had smartphones, cars, affordable heating, affordable clothes or abundant food. These things literally do not 'grow on trees'."

Blake had to admit he had a point. He'd never really questioned ecoism at that deep a level. He'd accepted that man was doing irreparable harm as a given. This was making his head hurt.

"Okay. I see that. But no one ever really puts it like that."

"Even though they might suspect it's true?"

"I suppose, on some level, yes."

"Then that leaves the rest of your sentence. Omit the part about messing up the planet and see what's left."

Blake worked it out. "Because… we're not them."

"Precisely."

Blake had to get this straight, it seemed to make no sense. "People buy into 'saving the planet for future generations' because it's not saving it for themselves?"

"Yes."

"Why?"

"Why do you think? Imagine someone saying the opposite: 'I'm using the planet for my own and my generation's benefit.' What would be wrong with that?"

Blake hesitated, although his mind prompted him with the answer. The answer that seemed to have been bred into him, that he'd heard repeated in endless stories, sayings, sermons and speeches. He answered slowly, "It's selfish."

"Yes. That's the whole trick to ecoism's popularity. It's anti-selfish. In a bigger way than any other political view for centuries."

Blake's head was like a pressure cooker. Selfishness was bad. It was why countries went to war. It was cruel and hurtful, indifferent to the sufferings of others. He wasn't that kind of person. And yet he was selfish in that he grew his own company and used the Earth's natural resources for his, his family's and his shareholders' benefit. How could he be selfish and not selfish? Was he partly selfish, and if so, was he a bad person?

It felt like writing a line of computer code that was too complex, that was trying to do too much. His mind was seizing up. When working on code, what did he do? He refactored. He broke up the problem into separate pieces and tried to come up with simpler, cleaner, more logical ways to group the pieces back together. But he couldn't do that with a concept like 'selfishness', could he?

Dalton was smiling at him gently while looking at him over the mug of shared tea.

Finally, Blake asked, "Are you saying selfishness is not wrong?"

"I am, when the concept is understood correctly."

"But that goes against every moral lesson we've ever learned. No party would get elected if it stood for selfishness."

"No. Not today. Yet look where today's parties have led us." He gestured to the darkening forest, but Blake knew he meant the state of the country beyond it. He wanted to disagree but he didn't know how. His mind felt as if it was underwater, where he could hear rough sounds but not distinguish them properly. When he strained to hear them, they still could not be grasped. He was getting annoyed now, and he knew it was frustration with himself, so he tried to keep the anger out of his voice as he thought of another question.

"You're not completely correct. The ecoists don't just talk about future generations. They say that if we don't act now, the oceans will rise, the ice-caps will melt, species will die and natural disasters will get worse. They appeal to our self-preservation in our own lifetime. They appeal to our selfishness."

"In a sense, yes. But consider this, Blake. How many of these predictions have come true? You've heard them all your life. Which of the earliest claims have actually happened?"

Blake paused. He knew that scientists had predicted global cooling back in the seventies. But that had to have simply been a mistake. He tried to integrate the claims he had mentioned with his own experience. He knew that people still went on expensive holidays to the Maldives with its low-lying atolls, so global ocean rise hadn't completely ruined them. He knew that food prices had generally gone down throughout his lifetime as a percentage of income, so plants hadn't been too badly affected by climate change. And he knew that fires, storms and droughts had occurred throughout history, long before recent industrialisation. Finally, despite his frustration, he had to answer.

"None of them, as far as I know."

"Do you think you're the only one who's capable of working that out?"

"No."

"Well then, why do people still buy into ecoism?"

Blake shrugged.

Dalton leant forward. "Consider the actual result of implementing all the ecoist policies. More taxes, more regulations, more restrictions. Less money in your pocket, less time to conduct your business your way, and fewer opportunities open to you. Why does no one complain about that and demand back their money, their time, their freedom to choose?"

Suddenly Blake's anger was extinguished, as if by a thick fire blanket. "Because it's selfish," he said slowly.

Dalton grinned. "You'd make a fine student of philosophy, given a bit of time."

"Thanks."

"But I for one am turning in. It's been a hell of a day. Thank you, again, for my life and my freedom."

He stood, stretched his legs, then smiled and gripped Blake's shoulder.

"You're welcome," Blake said, and as he watched Dalton clamber into the hut, Blake wondered if he needed setting free himself.

~

He awoke from a troubled sleep under the canopy of trees and started figuring out where to put a new shelter so they could have one each.

It wasn't long before Dalton appeared.

"Sleep okay?" Blake asked.

"Like a log," Dalton said, "while also sleeping on a log." He smiled. "Thanks for lending me your shelter.

Will you help me put up one of my own?"

"Just what I was thinking about," Blake said.

They made breakfast of tea and water-based porridge then set about gathering and stripping saplings for a new home.

As they worked, with the saw and knife from the garden centre and their own muscle power, Blake began thinking again about ecoism. Everything he was doing was 'destroying nature'. Stopping the saplings becoming trees. Ripping out the ferns that would have been spreading. He asked Dalton, "How do ecoists expect us to live if we can't alter nature?"

"Secretly, they don't."

"So how do they expect to survive themselves?"

"Secretly, they don't."

"Are you serious? They're like some kind of suicide cult? People would never willingly vote for that, surely?"

"That's why I said 'secretly'."

"So how come people don't uncover the secret?"

"Because it's cleverly disguised," Dalton said, picking up a pile of bracken. "If I put this on the roof now, when it's hardly got any rafters, it will hold, but it won't stand up to any serious test."

"But I can see it's not structurally sound."

"But what if I tell you that your eyesight's faulty? That you can't trust your own judgement?"

"I'd ignore you and check for myself."

"Did you do that, in depth, about climate change?"

"No," Blake admitted, grudgingly.

"Why not?"

Blake had to think. There was no point pretending or evading the question. Dalton wasn't trying to trick him. If he was honest about it, he might eventually figure out how to escape from the mess his life was in.

"I relied on experts," he eventually replied.

"Did you check their credentials? Examine their track record?"

"To be fair, no. I assumed someone else had. The politicians, I suppose."

"Do you think they did any checking?"

"Well, it sounds stupid to admit it, but of course not. They're always getting it wrong."

"So why trust them?"

"Because… because it's too hard to go against public opinion."

"Well, who makes public opinion, if the members of the public don't do it themselves?"

Blake chuckled.

Dalton went on. "There's no such thing as public opinion. Only the ideas of the people who make up the public. And they will differ to the extent that people think for themselves and come to different conclusions."

"But why don't people think for themselves more?"

"Why didn't you?"

Blake was silent and looked away.

Dalton looked at him for a while, then said, "Sorry Blake. I'm not trying to get at you, honestly. I'm trying to help you, through self-examination. It's just what I do."

"All right," Blake said, smiling slightly. "I'll be your pupil for now."

"And I'm yours as regards survival techniques. We can all learn from each other, if we accept that we can be wrong. And more importantly, if we learn how to be right. I have a question for you that might help. When you were at school, especially early on, did knowledge seem to come to you automatically? Was it natural to be good at sums and writing, for instance?"

"Yes, I was always near the top of my class."

"So learning seemed easy?"

"I suppose so."

"What about later?"

"It became harder, especially maths."

"And did you make mistakes?"

"Lots."

"Did you give up?"

Blake pondered this. "Not in the subjects I was interested in and needed for university. But I did give up history. I couldn't get my head around what I was supposed to say, what method I should use."

"I wouldn't be too hard on yourself. At least you've come out of the education system with some solid knowledge. Many people don't. They come out with their mental apparatus scarred for life." Dalton shook his head and silently copied Blake weaving branches into the new roof. Then he spoke again.

"If you think reason is automatic, and you sustain that belief into adulthood, then you will be embarrassed by your failures and shy away from ideas in case they reveal your mistakes. You will live in self-doubt outside your own particular field of knowledge, and have to cow-tow to the opinions of others. But if you understand what an error is, and how to correct it, you will be confident at using your own mind in any field."

Blake thought about it for a moment, then had a revelation. "It's funny you should say that. I recently had to get private tuition for my son, who…" He swallowed and tried again. "…who said how much clearer the tutor's explanations were. How he felt more empowered in his mind."

Dalton waited a moment. "I'm deeply sorry about James. He sounded like a fine lad."

"He was," Blake said, only partially stifling his tears.

They carried on building the shelter for a while, passing each other the bits they needed.

After a while, Blake asked, "So what's your opinion of the current school system?"

"You can see the results for yourself in society. There's an extraordinary fear of new ideas and almost total obedience to authority."

"I was refused permission to speak myself recently, at my daughter's school."

"It's inevitable given the attitude to knowledge I spoke about. The government sets targets with no means to reach them apart from rote learning. Teachers have no explanation besides, 'that's the way it is,' and, 'we don't have time for questions. Just pass your exams if you want a job.' So you see, early on, our lives become dependent on obedience. Once you have obedience, you can control people. And once people rate obedience above rationality, they will pounce on dissenters for you. Those who stray outside the norm will be condemned by society. Look at the attacks on you and the BCF."

"And on you, I bet."

"Well, that's par for the course as a political thinker, but the quality of attacks has plummeted recently. Have you been condemned as an 'extremist'?"

"Many times."

"Extremely what? Right? Mistaken? There's no argument there. You're just extremely different from the consensus. You're condemned for not falling in with their ideas."

"Why are people so vitriolic about it when they send me their death threats? Are you saying it's fear? Fear of new knowledge? Of being unable to think?"

Dalton's eyes sharpened. "I take it back. You are already a good philosophy student."

Blake smiled. It was so long since he'd been praised by another adult outside his family. Perhaps it was because people always expected him to know everything and be good at everything as the leader of his company. But it felt good. He picked up some bark and wondered if it could be turned into properly interlinked roof tiles. Maybe on the next iteration of their accommodation.

Continuing to thread bracken, he asked, "I understand the fear, but I don't fully understand why they attack me and other industry leaders so strongly. What good does it do them?"

"This won't come naturally to you, but try to put yourself in their position. They realise, on some level, that thinking is necessary, that for human beings, knowledge is key for survival. But like a bird unable to stretch its wings, they don't know how to get it. At school they get rote learning and at university, even in the sciences, they are told that nothing is certain, that no one can really be sure of their knowledge because they can't help being subjective."

"It sounds pretty stressful."

"It is. But it's not just an isolated event. It underlies every waking moment of every day."

"No wonder they think the world is going to collapse."

"Yes. But it's not the world, it's their own mental grip on the world. Their house of knowledge which they need to live in is built on shaky ground, and they know it."

"Unlike this fine piece of architecture," Blake said, grinning.

They worked on the new shelter for another hour until it was good enough for sleeping in.

"We'll be adding a porch and a veranda next week, then," Dalton joked.

"We do have plenty of time," Blake said.

"Actually, I was thinking about that. I realise we need to go hunting and keep this place up to scratch, but I was also wanting to get on with my book. Can we divide up the work to let me do that?"

Blake smiled. "Of course, as long as you read it to me later."

"It's a deal."

"I'll go out and check the traps this afternoon."

~

They carried out their plan and repeated roughly the same pattern over the next week: camp maintenance in the early morning; Dalton writing from mid-morning through to late afternoon, while Blake foraged and trapped their food; then reviewing Dalton's work and cooking and eating into the evening.

~

One day, after a particularly unfulfilling lunch, Blake took Dalton to the field with the potatoes and the scarecrow. There they managed to dig a few spuds out of the soil that had been missed by earlier pickers.

Blake again left some money in Henry's suit pocket. The earlier sum was still there, but what could he do without exposing his presence?

Looking forward to devouring the tubers with rumbling stomachs, they picked their way over fallen trees and through fern thickets back to the original camp.

The scene they returned to make their blood boil.

"Bastards!" Blake shouted. No one was there, but they had been. The fire gadgets were kicked over. The pots were missing. The shelters had been knocked over and torn apart. Their meagre possessions were strewn around the forest floor. Fortunately, Dalton had taken the tablet with him.

They started gathering up their property and searching the area for items that had been gleefully thrown there, as if specifically to make their lives harder.

"What kind of people do this?" Dalton asked. "Do you know what it reminds me of? The history of the Jews in Europe. How often they were forced to move and denied any property other than what they could carry."

"I remember Dickens making fun of 'portable property'."

"Yes, it was commonplace, sadly. And still is."

"But what good does it do them, making us suffer? They haven't even stolen anything, just smashed it up."

"I put it down to envy," Dalton said sadly. "Not of our possessions, but of our ability to create them. They cannot literally steal our ability so they try to erase it by destroying its products."

"But why?"

"Because our abilities make them feel so ashamed of their own lack."

"But they could learn from us rather than try to destroy us."

"They could, were it not for their moral code."

Blake looked at him, puzzled.

Dalton sighed. "It's a long story. We'd better get our accommodation sorted first. I'll tell you about it later."

They collected together what was intact of their portable property, and headed off to the second camp. Now that the first had been found, they'd have to abandon it in case the marauders returned.

They found camp two untouched, but spent some hours disguising it further with holly branches. They thought about digging a hidden moat as a protective measure around the site, but that would have taken an enormous effort and they didn't have a spade.

It was almost dark when they finally sat down and enjoyed a meal of potatoes and rabbit stew. They ate in silence as they fed their ravenous appetites. Blake was almost finished when he remembered Dalton's promise. "Now, what did you mean about *their* moral code?"

Dalton looked up from his plate, smiled, and wiped the juices from his chin. "I was hoping you'd bring that up. Most people wouldn't. But only because they don't see its importance. A moral code sounds terribly formal, and old-fashioned. The Ten Commandments. The teachings of Jesus, or other imposing religious figures. People think they're irrelevant but they're not. Mankind doesn't come with an instruction manual on how to live. You need some kind of general guidance.

So either you follow a system of morality, or you muddle along with a few sayings you've picked up and agree with, like 'do as you would be done by'."

"Or, 'think of others before yourself'."

"Exactly. In fact, it's that particular saying that causes all the trouble."

"Why? People don't really stick to it. They know it's an ideal, but on a day-to-day basis they have to think of themselves to stay alive."

"So how do you feel if someone gives you an impossible ideal? If someone asked you to create a computer system that had no bugs in it, that worked perfectly from day one and that would never need revising?"

"I'd walk away. It's impossible. On any serious scale, bugs creep in, improvements can always be found. I wouldn't sign a contract on such terms."

"So what happens if you try to live your life on those terms?"

Blake was silent, thinking of times early in his career when he'd taken jobs like that. Eventually, he came up with an answer. "You'd feel constantly inadequate, not in control, aggrieved about being in such a situation."

"Would you feel happy? Pleased with yourself?"

"No. I'd feel frustrated. Disappointed with myself."

"Guilty?"

"Of what?"

"Of failing to be a good person. Of failing to live up to the required standard."

"Yes. I suppose so." Blake felt a strange mixture of anger and indignation as he said it.

"So if you're a failure in your own eyes, are you surprised if no one comes asking for your help?"

Blake shook his head.

Dalton pressed on. "The ransackers of our camp won't ask how you built it, won't want to learn from you, because what you've done is for yourself. It's clearly not for other people. By their standard of morality, it's evil. That's why they destroyed it."

"But that's insane. Suicidal. You can't go on like that. On some level they know that you have to build and create things in order to survive."

"Yes. Deep down, buried in their psychology. And it leads them to be in eternal conflict, between what they ought to do, and what they need to do. You've never taken their standard that seriously, so you've protected yourself, to some extent. But for those who do, it's deadly. It tears them apart, and they can only keep going by two means: by contradicting themselves, leading to guilt; and by lashing out at those who 'cheat the system' by being, to some extent, selfish."

"Even if those 'cheats' are physically keeping them alive with houses, jobs, tools, fuel, food, medicine, computer services…?"

"The more they do that, the guiltier they are. Because their success comes from being selfish. No company makes cheaper or better products by working for their competitors. They succeed by working, thinking, planning, spending, saving, producing for themselves – their company, their shareholders, their customers and their families."

"But that's doing things for other people, surely?"

"Yes, but what's their motive?"

"To…" Blake felt like he was climbing his way up a cliff with his bare hands, but that he was near the top. "…to be successful," he continued.

"How selfish can you get!"

Blake laughed out loud. "But that's ridiculous. You can't win. If you succeed in helping other people, you're guilty of... of pride, of winning, of beating the competition, of following your own ideas. But if you fail in helping other people, if you don't go to work, you don't make food, or clothes, or computers to sell to people, or you make bad quality ones because you didn't focus your mind properly, you're guilty too. It's an impossible standard."

"It is."

"And you're saying it's what drives the destroyers?"

"Yes. And the majority of Western society, to the extent that people accept it. Technically, it's known as altruism."

Blake shook his head. "Surely altruism means being kind, considering others. What's wrong with that?"

"Definitions are important. In computing is a 'byte' defined as eight bits or seven? Every calculation would be different depending which it is."

"Of course. But there's no disagreement about that. It's eight."

"Quite. But what if it was defined as 'maybe eight but maybe seven or maybe some other number.' ?"

"It wouldn't work. Nothing the computer came up with would be reliable. You couldn't use it."

"Precisely. Now what if the definition of altruism was unusable? What if the key principle behind everyone's behaviour was impossible to act upon?"

"Everyone would be at a loss as to what to do. They would try and be altruistic but when it didn't work, do something else."

"It if wasn't altruistic, it would have to be selfish,

right?"

"Yes."

"And how would people feel about that, if they believed in altruism?"

"Like failures who hadn't come up to the mark."

"And who is easier to bully, someone who considers themselves a failure, or someone who holds their head up high?"

"You're saying altruism is a mechanism for bullies to control people?"

"And much worse. World Wars are started by altruism."

"That's a hell of a claim. You've not even convinced me about the definition. What I said, being kind and so on, doesn't lead to wars. How can it?"

"It can't. Consideration and kindness are crucial for living in a decent society. But that's not how the word altruism is used. Try this sentence: 'Blake altruistically held the door open for the person behind him.' "

"It seems too strong a word for such a simple act."

"It does. How about 'Blake altruistically held the door open for the next sixty minutes despite knowing that he would miss a dinner date with his wife.' "

"That's more like it. And it's not something I would ever do."

"Why not?" Dalton's face was tensely focused.

"Because having dinner with my wife is a huge value to me, much more than holding a door open for loads of strangers."

"So for you, holding the door open, would be a sacrifice?"

"Yes."

"So you're basically being selfish. Putting your own

interests first."

Blake frowned and Dalton pressed on. "Here's a dictionary definition of altruism, which I think is what you actually mean: 'showing a wish to help or bring advantages to others, even though it results in disadvantage for yourself'. It's the *disadvantage* that makes it different from kindness. Do you see? It's the sacrifice that's crucial."

"But surely I can be kind to people without sacrificing myself?"

"You can, but it isn't moral, not according to altruism."

"But what's the alternative?"

"Egoism."

"Did you say 'egoism'? Ego with a 'g'?"

"One letter can make so much difference."

"But that's…"

"'Outrageous.' 'Sinful.' 'Pure Evil.' I've heard it all, believe me."

"And you'd defend that position, the idea that egoism is good?"

"I'd stake my life on it. But not any more tonight. I need to rest. It's been quite a day. I'm sure you do, too."

Blake's mind was reeling. Who was this man he was sharing his life with? Everything he said made sense, and yet it felt so wrong. He realised he desperately needed sleep too. His anger at the ransackers, the rapid move and building up of camp two, and then this series of revelations – they had exhausted him.

"Goodnight, then," he said, and crawling into his sleeping bag, despite the turmoil of his mind, he fell swiftly into unconsciousness.

They spent much of the next day improving the camouflage of camp two, then Blake went off to a site he had in mind for camp three, while Dalton carried on with the PPOG.

When he found the site, Blake started clearing the ground and gathering branches, all the while thinking about egoism versus ecoism. What had Dalton revealed to him? Was it the answer to why he was in this situation? How would this new knowledge get him out? As his mind spun, he thought about improving his bows and arrows. Partly in case they came across any marauders, partly for killing other animals. He had seen deer on the edge of the forest and his mouth watered when he thought of venison.

When he got back to camp two, his mind was buzzing with questions.

"So, even though I'm here, in a forest, living a life as close to the ecoist ideal as you can imagine, I'm still a bad person? Because I'm supporting my own life, not other people's?"

"According to altruism, yes."

"And even if I did, say, create twenty camps and gave them to other people, I'd still be guilty, because…?"

"Because you didn't build fifty. Because you decided what you wanted to do rather than listening to others. Because you exploited the Earth's resources and denied them to others, including future generations. It's all about you, you, you. That's selfish. That's wrong."

"But how else am I supposed to live? I can't just switch off my mind."

"They think you should."

"Then how will anything get done?"

"You can still obey orders, can't you?"

"If I want to."

"Then you must want to."

"And if I don't?"

"Then they will make you. What do you think is the justification for all those regulations and laws you've been fighting? It's not to help you or anybody. It's to stop you thinking. Your thoughts are *your* thoughts. By their very nature they are selfish. Why are your thoughts better than anyone else's? By the standard of altruism, they can't be. Just like your life or your livelihood. So you'd better not indulge in them. For those that embrace altruism, regulation is perfect. It saves them the trouble of thinking and protects them from their competitors. For those that do not, it stops them in their tracks with fines and threats of prison. It's win-win, you see, for the altruists."

"And the ecoists are just a kind of altruist?"

"The most extreme."

Blake paced around, shaking his head. Eventually, he sat down and looked into the professor's perceptive blue eyes. "No wonder we're in trouble."

Dalton smiled.

Blake asked, "So what are we going to do?"

"I think, to start," Dalton said, getting up, "we should have a cup of tea." He went to their woodpile for some kindling and a few sticks, then got on his knees and blew the fire into life.

"Good. More heat for us and more CO_2 for the plants. You can't have one without the other. Which reminds me of another phrase: 'You can't make an omelette without breaking eggs.' Do you know who said that?"

Blake was watching the flames, beginning to understand why Dalton was always, ultimately, light-hearted. "No," he said.

"It was Lenin. He said it about the Kulaks – the farmers who he thought needed to be killed for communism to succeed."

"That was his justification for millions of deaths?"

"No, altruism was."

"Surely socialism and communism were economic systems, trying to make working people's lives better?"

"Did they succeed?"

Blake thought about it, mostly recalling his schoolboy history. It was funny how much of the curriculum had been given to studying dictatorships, and how little to capitalist countries. "They succeeded in one way: countries all over the world took up their system. After Russia came China, Vietnam, Eastern Europe, much of Africa…"

"But did they succeed, even on their own terms?"

"No. Everybody, particularly the poorest, became worse off."

"So why did people continue recommending it? Venezuela tried it and failed just recently."

"Because…" Blake could see where Dalton was going with this, but it just couldn't be that simple. "Because it was altruistic."

"Yes."

"But economically it's a disaster. It's obvious."

"So why does it spread?"

"I don't know," Blake admitted.

"Because morality trumps economics every time. How often have you argued with your daughter about the economic downside of some ecoist policy? Do you ever win her over?"

Blake shook his head.

"Consider these election slogans: 'Make society fairer by redistributing wealth,' or, 'Make yourself wealthier by enshrining property rights.' In this day and age, the latter sounds tainted even though the former requires the use of government force."

Reluctantly, Blake had to agree.

"Of course, now it's, 'Save the planet by reducing your impact on it,' versus, 'Save yourself by exploiting the planet.' No one says the latter – it's morally outrageous today. But throughout man's history, it's been treated as common sense. Morality has enormous power. It is what drives men to do things. They will always follow whatever is deemed good. But, what if their standard of the good is wrong? What if the good defined as 'anything that doesn't benefit yourself' is a mistake?"

Dalton paused. Blake knew from the expression in his eyes that this was what drove him. This pursuit for the truth. And that he was lucky to be witnessing it.

Seeing Dalton was still waiting, he replied, "It would be the most costly mistake in human history. It has probably caused death and misery to hundreds of millions of people. All while they thought they were being good, that they were doing the right thing." He paused, struggling to visualise what that meant. He asked, "How on earth did it happen? And more importantly, what's the alternative? What is the proper standard of the good?"

"How it happened is simply down to a few philosophers in history. More interesting, I think, is the mechanism by which it continues to 'convince' people. It's actually surprisingly simple to refute once you see the trick they're using."

"Go on." Blake sat forward, his tea forgotten, hoping that he was about to find a way out of his nightmare.

"In today's culture, 'selfishness' is morally wrong. The same word is used to describe the child preserving his toy by not sharing it, the exam student who keeps his answers to himself, the business owner who reaches an agreement with their employees that contradicts government rules, the drive-by killer, the robber and the fraudster. It's essential, if we want to live as civilised human beings, that we split the evaluation of selfish from its basic meaning – to act in our own self-interest. Then we can judge separately whether someone's action is good or bad. Making it bad just because the person who supposedly benefits is the same person taking the action is a monstrous intellectual fraud. What's automatically bad about trying to live *your* life? No one has ever answered that rationally."

Blake could feel the crack in his own mind opening between what he had always thought, and what he was coming to realise now. But this idea was so tightly enmeshed in his thinking, he couldn't simply change it, just like that. He looked at Dalton and answered, simply: "But it's selfish."

Dalton laughed. "You see?"

"It can't be that simple. Getting the meaning of a word wrong. It can't lead to holocausts, or corruption, or communism, or economic collapse."

"It led you here."

Blake couldn't deny it. Throughout his life, he had

been attacked for being selfish. By graffiti, by the media, by his brother and by his daughter. And he had felt indignant about their accusations, yet also undercut by them. Torn between doing what he felt he needed to do, but knowing that it was somehow wrong. This wasn't now just about getting out of the forest. Calmly he asked, "So, what is the standard of the good? What's the alternative?"

"That which furthers the life of a human being."

"It can't be that simple."

"Well, it's true that you have to unpack that idea and apply it, but essentially, yes, it is that simple."

"What do you mean, unpack it?"

"Human life is not automatic. You don't get out of bed, get washed, feed yourself, drive to work and make eight hours of productive effort all on instinct. Every step of the day, every action you take, requires thought. Either in the past, that you've now habituated, or in the present. You spend your day thinking and acting, and these only bring the results you desire if your thinking fits the facts. If your ideas do, in fact, identify reality. Rationality is the virtue of sticking to that principle, of correcting your ideas if they don't fit the facts, rather than wishing they did. So what I'm saying is the standard of life to aim for is that of the rational human."

"But that isn't much of a guide at all, for most people. They need specifics. They need rules. They're not as clever as you at being able to work them out."

Dalton looked at him very seriously for a moment, then he sighed and smiled wistfully. "Is that really what you think of your fellow man? That he is too stupid to use his own mind? Too stupid to determine what's in his own interest, whereas you are not? Blake, what you've just uttered is the whole problem in a nutshell. While you still believe what you said, you are part of the problem. Part of what put you here."

Blake stood up, affronted. He wanted to storm off. Get away from this man who made him feel so uncomfortable. But where could he go? Moreover, a small internal voice told him, how could he hide from his own ideas?

He walked off into the forest to think, and to cool down.

~

When he returned, Dalton was finishing the washing up. He looked up with sad, deep blue eyes. "Blake, I must apologise. I can hardly blame you for absorbing the ideas of the culture. And I owe you my so much. It was unkind."

Blake looked at him for a while, then sat down again. "Apology accepted."

"Thank you," Dalton said. Then he looked into the forest for a while before continuing. "Perhaps I can answer your question in a more constructive way. While it's true that rational morality requires a lot of individual thinking, there are guidelines which help. The most important one of which we have just suffered from being ignored: 'force is anti-mind'."

Blake looked puzzled.

"I'm talking about the scum who ransacked our camp. If we accept that each individual is an end in themselves, with the capacity to reason about the world and how to live in it, then we must accept that it is always wrong for others to try to force that individual to act against their own reason, either by harming their life or their property, or by threatening to do so."

"Even when we know they're making a mistake?"

"Yes. The ransackers probably thought you were making a mistake by building a fire because of the CO_2. But you'd decided you needed it for cooking. One must never come between a person's life and their means of sustaining it. Otherwise we might as well kill them outright."

"Well, I would never do that!" Blake said, sitting up in his seat.

"But unfortunately you do, albeit innocently. Look, with every regulation you accept, every tax you grudgingly pay, every trespass on your time, or your property, you are sanctioning the same to be done to others."

"But I try to oppose them. I started the BCF. I can't fight every tax, every regulation, every law that goes against my self-interest. I wouldn't be able to get any work done."

"Which is how the system functions. Keeping us all too busy earning a living to keep up with the burgeoning rules, which our earnings pay to police. I understand what you do. What we all do. I don't blame you. But look where obedience has led us."

Blake looked away and around at the camp. "So what can we do?"

"We must defend ourselves intellectually, but also physically. I'd feel safer if we had better camouflage and facilities at camp three. Shall we go there tomorrow? The book can wait for a day."

Blake agreed to this and they went to their separate shelters to sleep. Again, it was not a night of peaceful rest for Blake. His mind was full of flashing images of government inspectors, newspaper headlines and Candice's cross-looking face, but with Dalton's grey hair and blue eyes often in the background.

~

By the end of the next day they had finished camp three and disguised it, along with the paths that led to it. Whenever they entered or left their homes they were careful to cover their tracks, and they avoided using the same routes too frequently.

Blake also found a way to prevent smoke being discovered by placing an enclosure of wood and fern around the fire, and then adding a roof made of old sacking he had picked up from a barn. If he kept it wet, it didn't burn, but instead filtered most of the smoke out before letting the heat through. When he finally succeeded in killing a muntjac with his bow and arrow, he felt safe spit-roasting it for the longer time it required. All the time, though, Blake was mulling over what Dalton had said, and one evening as they sat down to venison and potatoes he was itching for a further debate.

"If it's up to individuals to guide their own lives, to work out what values to hold, what actions to take, what happens if they disagree with one another? What if, for instance, one person thinks that a car emitting CO_2 is a danger to the Earth and hence to life on Earth, while another thinks it's a benefit?"

"In a rational society, it would be up to the ecoist to prove it in a court of law. The question would be whose life and whose rights are being harmed by you driving your car?"

"They would claim the Earth has rights, as do future

generations."

"And in a rational court, such claims would be thrown out. The Earth is a big rock and future generations don't yet exist. The unborn and the inanimate can't have rights. What the ecoists want is for you to adopt their values. They value a more natural Earth than you do. But why should you give up your evaluations rather than them? You value rapid transport, but you're not forcing them to use it. In a rational society, each can have their own values and none can force them on another. The Earth has no value in itself. There are no values apart from valuers. To claim there are is part of their trick."

Blake digested this for a minute, while simultaneously chewing some meat.

"What about pollution? Don't some people suffer lung damage from diesel fumes?"

"Again, it would have to be proven that specific damage had occurred and that specific people had been harmed, then appropriate restoration could be made. But you don't ban all cars because some people are hurt by them inadvertently. The benefits of cars far outweigh the risks, otherwise people wouldn't drive them."

"I see. Cars exist because that's what most people actually want," Blake suggested.

"Exactly. But ecoists aren't interested in actual human beings. They only care about the Earth. To hide this they have become masters of re-definition. They use 'pollution' to mean 'any act of mankind affecting nature' regardless of its benefits. And they use 'climate-change' to mean 'all changes in the weather are the fault of human beings'."

"What about plastic in the oceans?"

"Again, plastic has great value to most people. The products made from it are endless. From syringes to fishing nets. From cellophane to felt-tipped pens. Dumping it for someone else to deal with is clearly wrong and should be punished. But so is banning it. Think of the lost value of such products to human life."

"So you're saying that each person should be free to decide their own values?"

"Yes, exactly."

"Provided they don't use force against someone else whilst pursuing their values?"

"Yes. They mustn't initiate force, to be precise. Retaliation is sometimes necessary. Courts exist to make such retaliation objective. It wouldn't be anarchy."

"Many claim it would, all those people and no rules."

"And those are the people who do not believe in reason as an individual faculty."

"What do you mean?"

Dalton sighed and smiled. "We've come to the root of it now. This is the link between the ecoists' morality of altruism and their method of thinking. They don't use reason, they use feelings. Using reason is hard work. And it only occurs in each person's head separately by their own effort."

"Tell me about it," Blake said, thinking of the headaches involved in keeping Caelum afloat.

"To reason, you have to ascertain the facts then assemble them in a logical way that fits with your existing knowledge. It's not always obvious. You often hit contradictions that need resolving. Sometimes you get stumped and you have to take a step back to see where you've gone wrong. Sometimes, you just don't know."

"So they're lazy thinkers, the ecoists?"

"No, worse than that. They fear thinking. Remember what I said the other day about automatic knowledge?"

Blake nodded.

"The ecoists literally don't believe knowledge requires reason. They think it just comes to you."

"So how do they know if an idea is true?"

"They consult their feelings and they consult other peoples'. 'Does it feel right', is all they ask."

"That's why so many government pronouncements don't make sense or contradict each other. They haven't actually thought them through."

"Exactly."

"And that's why they're always relying on opinion polls."

"Yes. And that's why they are against freedom. Freedom means individuals thinking for themselves and succeeding or failing in life based on that thinking. That way of life isn't open to ecoists. It's a threat. It shows them up as inadequate. They are afraid of making decisions and living their lives on their own judgements but they won't take the consequences. People who aren't afraid and succeed in life are an affront to them. That's why ecoists have to stifle innovation and hold back those who want to build prosperity."

Blake took a deep breath and stared into the distance, trying to take it in. Eventually he said, "Imagine that kind of attitude in the eighteenth century. It would have prevented the Industrial Revolution."

"It nearly did. But the anti-Enlightenment movement didn't have the traction it does today. People then were still in awe of reason. Reason is what led to science, and thence to the Industrial Revolution and the command of nature. It enabled humankind to live longer and spread further across the globe. It is the ultimate cause of our success, and ecoism's deadliest enemy."

"But ecoists are always claiming to be scientific, wheeling out climate scientists and graphs till kingdom come."

"Fine. Let them. But in a rational society, without government subsidies and government educators – both examples of the initiation of force – such 'scientists' would wither away. Their science without reason would not stand up to rational, human-loving scrutiny."

"I agree with you about subsidies, but what's your objection to government education? Surely we need state schools?"

"Did they teach your children about the space race? About man's incredible achievement of landing on the moon?"

"Not that I heard of."

"But I bet they did plenty of projects about man's exploitation of the Earth. Deforestation, melting ice-caps, lost species, global warming."

Blake nodded.

"If the ecoists had been active a little earlier, we would still not have left the Earth. Imagine that. You and I have witnessed those kinds of achievements.

What have today's children got to inspire them? A chart in every school showing how many carbon tonnes they've saved, not by reaching for some achievement but by doing nothing except hoping the sun shines long enough to provide some power, but not so long that it overheats the Earth. Where is the ambition in that? Where is the pride in being part of the human race? Where is the aspiration?"

"I loved the science of space travel when I was young," Blake exclaimed. "It probably inspired me to do what I've spent my life doing."

"And if we let the ecoists win, children will never experience such feelings again. Blake, you must realise what you're getting yourself into here. This is an epic battle for the future of humanity. Either ecoism is right and we need to abandon reason and reverse civilisation in order to save ourselves, or ecoism is wrong and we need to use reason and increase civilisation in order to save ourselves. But it's not a battle over science. It's a battle over man's right to exist as man. Is he an irrational creature, doomed to failure through destroying his environment; or is he a rational creature, able to understand and control nature, thus improving his environment? The answer to that determines your morality – selfishness is wrong and freedom must be curtailed, or selfishness is right and freedom must be worshipped. The future of your life, your family, your company and everything they provide is at stake."

Blake lay awake all night thinking, his mind as active as the night creatures he could hear. He had never questioned the reason for his company's existence. He had thought it was to produce a product, to provide jobs and to pay for public services. Secretly, he had said to himself that it was also about making a profit, not just for the shareholders but for himself. Secretly, he knew that increasing profits had been his main motivation. But he had never felt comfortable with that, nor had he shared his view with others, let alone printed it on the company's mission statement. He'd always felt a tug of war between his desire to make a profit and his need to placate society and the government. He'd accepted it as the norm, this feeling of tension – and guilt – for thirty years. What if he'd been wrong? What if such guilt had never been necessary? He saw what suffering he had brought upon himself and almost laughed and cried aloud. Instead, he sobbed inwardly and shook with the frustration of it.

~

When he awoke late the next morning, he felt as if he'd been running all night in his dreams.

He found Dalton a few yards away, sitting in the shade of some beeches, tapping vigorously on the tablet. As he looked up, Blake said, "What can I do to help?"

#

They developed a steady pattern of writing, editing and revision interspersed with campsite chores. The weather was largely fine, the charger worked as designed, and they made good progress.

One day Blake used the cardboard wrappers from his early dried meals and a biro he'd found in his jacket to write Candice a letter. It was no good writing to Marisa, as all her correspondence was screened. Now he knew so much about the ecoist cause and what he was going to do about it, he had to warn Candice. He had to do what he could to keep her safe. And he wanted to reach out to her, to let her know he was okay, to open the door for a proper discussion with her. But given that she lived at Fabian's, how could he do so without jeopardising the safety of either of them?

He concocted something that he hoped was sufficiently cryptic: '*If you can, meet me at the fairground where we once went on holiday and you poked that actor in the ghost ride. I'll be there every Monday at midday.*' He also told her for the first time about the threatening note he'd received after James had been killed, which the police had ignored. He hoped it would prompt her to consider properly whether all ecoists were benevolent.

As he was putting his note into a makeshift envelope, Dalton came over.

"Who are you writing to?"

"My daughter. I want to see her. I know it's a risk, but she's a sensible girl. If she wants to meet me, she'll be careful."

"I trust your judgement, Blake. Would you like a stamp?"

"How on earth do you still have one of those?"

"I was planning to write secretly to Grace when I was in prison, so I hid it in my shoe. But I was waiting until my appeal was over. You can have it."

Dalton took his left shoe off, and after rummaging around inside the footbed, produced a small plastic bag containing a stamp.

"I'm impressed," Blake said. "But are you sure?"

"If it weren't for you, I might have been dead by now, and I'd never be doing this." He held the tablet proprietorially.

"Thanks," Blake said, and affixed the stamp, hoping it was enough postage.

~

The next day he headed off early, and reached the petrol station he had started at several months before. There he paid a lorry driver with a Scottish flag on his cab to post the letter when he got home. Walking back by a circuitous route, he arrived at the camp shortly after dusk.

8

It was a chilly October morning when Fabian woke early, went to open the door of his flat within No. 10 Downing Street, and retrieved the personal post from the sideboard in the hall. The temperature there was much warmer than in the flat, so wasteful, but the curators of the historic building had insisted that damp was kept out – and as he had bigger battles to fight, he had acquiesced.

As he went back inside – holding his baggy extra jumper and dressing gown in place with one hand, and the letters in the other – one in particular caught his attention. It was in a cardboard envelope. On closer inspection he saw it was addressed by hand and that it had black, smudgy marks around the edges. For a moment he thought he recognised the handwriting. Then he looked at the addressee and put two and two together.

It had been odd living with a teenage girl, first in his house and now in the President's, but they had got used to each other, and while they ate rare meals together he had got to know her better and helped her understand the ecoist mission he was bent on fulfilling. Deciding instinctively that here was another occasion where, as her guardian, he needed to help his niece, he took the letters into his private study and locked the door.

~

An hour or so later, he insisted on cooking Candice some breakfast in their small kitchen. She was grateful, as it left her more time to prepare for school. As they sat at the small table eating toast, Fabian asked casually, "You know, Candice, we've been so busy this year, we haven't had time to go away on holiday. I imagine Blake would take you all away to some exotic locations. Or did you ever save the air-miles and stay in this country?"

It wasn't long before he found out what he needed to know. It was for her own good. When she had gone, he phoned his contacts in the police.

~

The following Monday, Blake made his way cautiously through the forest, using a different route from last time, and emerged into the apocalyptic looking ex-fairground. He knew there was little chance Candice would manage to get there without significant planning, if at all, but he had come for the second week, just in case.

This time, however, something was different. The temperature was a few degrees colder, perhaps that accounted for it. But it seemed much quieter. There were usually plenty of birds making their calls. Today, just a few crows in the distance.

And then he heard a different kind of noise. A man's voice, somehow garbled and crackly. He stopped dead, to work out where it was coming from. Then he stole over to an old 'shoot-em-up' gallery and peered round the side.

A policeman, with a dog, was talking softly into his radio.

Blake's heart jumped but he managed to creep quietly away from the man, and also away from the forest. He had to lead them away from Dalton. He had managed about thirty yards when he trod on some gravel and he heard the dog bark.

And then he ran. Weaving in and out of stalls and rides. Jumping over ruined crowd barriers. Until he saw another dog running towards him.

As he stopped to change direction, he felt a strong grip on his left arm. The first dog's teeth were sinking in. He tried moving away, but it was heavy and pulled in the opposite direction. He smacked it on the nose repeatedly, but it had been trained to resist such an attack.

The dog was trying to drag him down and he let himself be moved. There was an old metal tent peg nearby. If he could reach it he might be able to fight the animal off.

He lunged towards the dog, throwing it off balance for a moment, then picked up the peg. He brought it down on the dog's head, but still it clung on, gripping tighter. Then he managed to poke it in the eye. That made it let go.

As it whimpered and looked around, he ran. Past a merry-go-round, around a convoluted roller coaster, past the ghost ride.

And into a group of policemen. They tackled him to the ground and yanked his wrists behind him before clamping on some cuffs.

Panting for breath, Blake was dragged to his feet and stood glowering at his assailants. But as he took in their mean, determined faces, he felt a punch in his lower back and went down again, gasping in pain.

"That's for my dog, you bastard," said a voice above him.

When he'd recovered slightly, one of them asked, "So where's your friend?"

"I don't have any," Blake said.

"Don't give me that. We know all about you and your professor chum. Been playing Boy Scouts in the woods, have you?" The others laughed. "All right lads, use the dogs."

As Blake sat handcuffed to a bumper car, nursing his bruised kidney, he thought of what he had done. Presumably Candice had betrayed him. Was she that far gone? He didn't know, and it didn't matter now.

After nearly two hours he saw Dalton, scratched and bleeding, being marched out of the forest towards him, clutching the tablet.

#

Blake woke and stared at the low, grey stone ceiling. There were ancient iron rings set into it, but he couldn't fathom their purpose. This was a guardhouse now, but in the past who knows what it was used for.

He sat up from his thin mattress on the floor and checked on Dalton. He was still asleep, which good. Blake had been worried that Dalton's injuries would keep him awake. But he breathed soundly enough, which was remarkable considering what they'd gone through the previous day.

After being captured they had been bundled into a

police van with tiny windows, and driven for hours in what Blake estimated to be a roughly southerly direction, until they'd finally arrived at Westingham Castle.

Here they'd been unceremoniously yanked out, Dalton's wounds had been superficially seen to, and Blake had been told to spruce himself up before they were taken to meet the prison governor.

Oliver Furrow was a man of medium build and height but with very small eyes, a red puffy face, a receding chin and matching forehead. He had told them in his staccato high-pitched voice that the castle, turned into a prison due to lack of space in existing facilities, would be where they'd carry out their sentences. In Blake's case, it would be five years for intercepting government communications and ten years for Carbon Crime. For Dalton, nothing had changed. His sentence for Climate Change Denial was still death by hanging. He would be interned at Westingham pending his appeal, which, given his escape, was not likely to succeed.

Blake looked again at the peacefully slumbering professor. How could he remain calm enough to sleep, especially considering the final blow: their tablet had been taken for safekeeping by the governor. It had the only copy of Dalton's book on it. Given his situation with the authorities, it was likely they would put pressure on universities, publishers and bookshops to stop access to his other writing. The man's life's work was surely about to be erased. And yet he slept soundly.

A few minutes later a harsh voice shouted "Up", and banged on the door. Dalton slowly raised his grey head from the makeshift pillow, rubbed his eyes and yawned, then asked, "Is it breakfast time?"

He was proven right, and they were soon being marched across a large, grass-covered courtyard to a small wooden door in a towering wall.

Inside was the refectory. It was heaving with men and steaming with their smell and that of porridge. The guard went back the way he had come and they stood in line for their sustenance. Smiling slightly at the sloppy hot oats when they were doled out to him, Blake carried them over to the hard, wooden bench, where Dalton was waiting.

"Bon appétit," the professor said.

Blake snorted. "At least it's got milk in it for a change."

Making the most of it, and not having eaten for a day, they dug in. Life in the forest had been a lot more trying in many ways, Blake thought. They had had to learn how to live with nature and be resilient and patient. But there they had been free to solve their own problems and take the actions they saw fit. Here they would be at the beck and call of the guards, and those who drove them. It wasn't a situation he cared to put up with. For Dalton, there was a stronger imperative.

Looking around at the faces of his fellow diners, Blake failed to detect the menace and fear he associated with prisoners. Though rough-looking superficially, all the men seemed happy in their own skins, and if not actually smiling, they were eating unhurriedly and chatting to each other normally, as if at a lunch meeting.

"Do you know anything about this place?" he asked Dalton. "They all seem very collected. Not like the desperate villains I was expecting."

"Yes, I think I do. We'll find out soon enough, but I read about plans for such places when I was studying the Internet Regulation Bill. I believe this facility is for ideological prisoners. The bill must have become law while we were in the forest."

Dalton's suspicions were confirmed when they spoke to a fellow prisoner. He had been a blogger with a website that regularly criticised the government.

Suddenly, an ugly buzzing noise was emitted from a tannoy somewhere, and the prisoners gradually filed out.

"Not you two," said a guard by the small wooden door, and he marched them back to the gatehouse for a set of clothes, a shave and a haircut.

Emerging twenty minutes later in red jumpsuits and with the wind on their cheeks, they were taken to where a large group of prisoners were labouring over repairs to a wall.

The Norman structure had taken a beating over the centuries, especially during the Civil War. The prisoners were supervised by armed guards as they lifted heavy stones and mixed cement to mend the breaches. There was little time to talk, but Dalton could not resist passing comment upon the walls that businessmen built for themselves both in and out of prison.

It wasn't until that night, when they lay exhausted on their truckle beds in their allotted cell, high up in one of the towers, with its tiny, unglazed window and its bare stone floor, that Blake and Dalton could converse freely.

"These walls look pretty solid, but I'm buggered if

I'm going to stay in here for fifteen years," Blake said.

"You're thinking of escape?"

"Yes, of course."

"Good. So was I."

"You really don't have much choice."

"Unless my eloquence wins out at the appeal – which, despite full confidence in my logical powers of persuasion, I doubt – then no."

The single, eco-friendly bulb glared down at them. It looked too primitive to house any kind of listening device, but Blake took it out just in case, using a sock, and hid it in his pile of dirty clothes.

"Any ideas?" he asked, once he'd found his way back to bed.

"Oh, lots," Dalton said, and they talked into the night.

~

The next day Blake established that phone calls between prisons were not allowed, so he set about writing Marisa a letter. One of the guards who had shown them to their cell the day before helped him with this, explaining where the pens and paper were. He had even attempted a joke about their new accommodation, referring to it as 'Shangri-la'. Blake was familiar with introverts' attempts at humour through his long experience of recruiting them for his tech company. Perhaps this guard could be useful. Blake got talking to him and discovered his name was Ed Quinton, that he'd had a birthday the week before, and that he was ten years older than Blake. He even lent them money for a couple of stamps, which they offered to repay when their meagre 'wages' were distributed at the end of the month.

"They will be censored, you know," Quinton said as he handed over the postage.

"Thanks. I expected nothing less. I'm only going to write, 'wish you were here'."

Quinton grinned, and was equally cheerful when he told them a few days later that they'd received replies.

Dalton had sent his letter to Roger, who had been to see Grace and read it to her. He'd been visiting her regularly since Dalton's arrest, and had reconciled her to the need to move back to Africa. The sale of Dalton's house was apparently in its latter stages.

Marisa replied that she had been worried sick about Blake, not knowing if he was dead or alive while he was in the forest. So she was glad, in a way, that he was now in prison. Blake had explained how risky it would have been to write any earlier and that he had tried to contact Candice. That seemed to have mollified her. Her own situation was much the same, although her prison was filling up fast, mostly with dissenters of one kind or another. Blake felt a surge of mixed emotions reading her letter. It was joyous to be in contact with her again, but dispiriting that it had to be in such circumstances.

Just after reading these replies, as they ate their breakfast on the seventh day of their incarceration, a Sunday, the ugly buzzer sounded and was followed by a strange announcement: "Confession will begin in five minutes. Repeat, confession in five minutes. All prisoners to the chapel."

"What did he just say?" Blake asked the prisoner next to him.

"Ah, you've not had the pleasure of one of these before, have you. Well, us recalcitrants, we need our

231

minds corrected, don't we." He smiled when Blake looked aghast. "It's not that bad."

#

After leaving the refectory, Blake and Dalton joined a queue of other prisoners standing outside a part of the castle Blake had not noticed before. As they shuffled forward, he observed narrow windows of stained glass. This must have been where the previous occupants had gone for God's sanction before battle, or for His explanation when besieged.

Inside, the first thing Blake saw was a line of women, dressed like himself, filing in through a door in the opposite wall.

"I had no idea there were women prisoners here, too," he said to the prisoner in front, flabbergasted.

"No, you wouldn't," came the reply. "They have a separate courtyard and buildings all to themselves. Apparently it's not just men who can have the 'wrong' ideas."

They were directed to a male pew and squeezed up with the others. Looking around, Blake suddenly recognised several faces.

"This place isn't for any old dissenters, is it," he said to Dalton.

"No. I've recognised them too. I suggest it's particularly for those who were once at the pinnacle of society, and who have plummeted to the bottom as the result of recent laws." He paused. "I gather it's also the only new prison with an execution facility."

Blake stared.

Dalton continued, "Both of these factors mean we will probably be subjected to an unusual number of 'visitors'."

As Blake stared at his companion, wondering what he meant, there came a high-pitched voice over the chapel's speakers: "Prisoners, pay attention!" It was Furrow, standing at a lectern. As he opened his puffed, red face to speak again, Blake noticed two more things about him. He kept wiping his hands on his trousers, and there was a flash of silver on his lapel.

"Today we are gathered together for one of our special acts of rehabilitation: confession. All new inmates will perform this rite as part of reshaping themselves ready for one day, perhaps..." He paused briefly, looking at Dalton. "...re-entry to society. As usual, I will act as the confessor. I call upon Sam Tillman to come up to the front and confess."

Why hadn't he noticed him before? Blake asked himself, frustrated. Was he just too busy eating and working, or had he only just arrived? Now he watched as the short, wiry man with sandy hair launched himself towards the altar. He was on the step in no time, and turned his creased forehead towards the audience.

The governor began, "What offence has brought you to this facility?"

"Success," roared Tillman, who didn't need a microphone. The inmates laughed appreciatively.

"What particular law did you transgress?" the governor asked, testily.

"Carbon Crime," Tillman said.

The governor sucked his teeth and nodded wisely. "And how large was your transgression?"

"I manage a thousand large supermarkets."

"Did you leave the lights on at night?"

"Yes. It keeps down the burglaries."

"But what about the carbon emissions?"

"They are a consequence of providing a service that people wanted. A bit like the way breathing is a consequence of being alive."

The governor gave him a dark look, then continued.

"Did you use lots of wasteful packaging?"

"We use thousands of tonnes of useful packaging every year. It keeps the goods from being damaged."

Furrow looked flustered but ploughed on anyway, ignoring the convict's explanations.

"Did you sell foreign products that incurred unnecessary road miles?"

"The miles weren't unnecessary. Our customers deserve as wide a choice as possible."

"Did you encourage over-consumption with multi-buy offers?"

"We want to hand on a part of our bulk discounts to our customers."

"Did you heartlessly exploit people through excessive advertising?"

"We are proud of our work and want to gain as many customers as possible."

"Did you open more than five days a week?"

"We open for seven, because that's what our customers want."

"And," the governor was finding it hard to contain his contempt, "did you exploit foreign-born workers, bringing them to this already overcrowded island?"

"Yes. We give those that want it a new Western life."

The governor's voice quavered with indignation as he said, "I am shocked. Shocked. By such shameless transgressions. You seem to have no respect for the environment whatsoever. Is there anything you don't do?"

"Yes," Sam said, smiling. "We stopped selling the *National Voice* newspaper – to save 'waste'."

The audience laughed and burst into applause, while the governor looked livid.

Sam Tillman bowed and returned to his place.

The governor watched him go, his eyes like powerless lasers. Once their target had sat down, he remembered his next victim.

"I call Liz Blackwood to confess."

Blake nearly choked. So this was where the first meeting of the BCF would be held, he thought bitterly.

The tall, dark-haired woman with a stern face rose and walked calmly to the transept. As she reached the appointed spot, she turned her dark eyes on the audience. Blake thought some of her intensity had gone, but her upright posture revealed none of the hardships she'd doubtless been made to endure.

The governor cleared his throat. "For what crimes have you been sent to this facility, Ms Blackwood?"

"The elemental crimes."

"Could you elaborate for us," the governor said, sounding impatient.

"Carbon, and accepting guilt for being alive."

"What was the actual judgment?" the governor pressed.

"We failed to provide sufficient ethical lending. Under recent laws, my bank must lend at least as much money to low-carbon organisations on the government's approved list as to other, supposedly high-carbon ones. The idea is to offset the sin of Carbon Crime. Like being fined for smoking."

"But people aren't fined for smoking," the governor

blathered.

"What else would you call a non-voluntary payment at the point of sale?"

The governor had to think for a moment. "Oh, you mean duty?"

"Yes. It's apt that it has two meanings. Wouldn't you agree?"

"That's beside the point. Now, surely you realise the magnitude of your crime. We must be talking about millions going to companies that destroy the planet."

"Billions, actually. But they don't destroy it. They reshape it."

"Don't you see what your actions are doing to this country, to the world? What they will do to future generations?"

Liz Blackwood raised her chin higher and looked up at the stained-glass windows. "My actions, especially refusing to fund the Ecoist Party when pressed by Fabian Hardwicke to do so," the audience sucked in its breath, "will possibly give the country a chance to save itself, before it's too late."

The governor looked outraged and afraid. He said in a petulant voice, "Well, you can apologise to The President in person, as he's coming on a visit tomorrow."

Liz fixed him with her dark eyes, then walked back down the aisle, which was stunned into silence, as sedately as a queen. As she passed Blake and recognised him her stride faltered, but then he smiled at her broadly, and the corners of her mouth tilted slightly upwards.

Later that day, as they were locked in their cells for 'restoration', Blake wondered how many more BCF members were interned at Westingham. Was it a coincidence, or had the authorities somehow got hold of its list of members? He would have to find out.

He and Dalton spent the afternoon discussing the difficulties of escape, and reading the *National Voice*. It was the only paper allowed in the prison.

They were let out for the evening meal but Blake wasn't able to recognise any more of the prisoners. Their individuality was almost smothered by their uniform boiler suits.

When lockup came, Ed Quinton popped his head around the door as usual to check they were in, but then stood on the threshold awkwardly.

"Can I help you, Ed?" Dalton asked after a while.

Quinton looked at him and Blake, chewed his lip, then began to speak. "I was thinking I might be able to help you."

"We'd be very grateful if you could, Ed," Blake said, sitting up.

"I know you'll never get your business back – Caelum, I mean. And I know that even if you did, the Carbon Crime Laws would make it impossible to run. So I wanted to thank you for being part of the Internet Revolution, and for fighting against all those regulations the way you did."

"That's very good of you," Blake said, wondering where this was going. "I appreciate your support."

"I was a real believer in IT. I put all my pension savings into tech companies over the years, lately most of it into Congo. When they were forced out of the country over carbon quotas, my shares were forfeited to the government."

"That's scandalous," Dalton said. "Your retirement

plans must have been ruined."

"Why do you think I'm still working here?"

"Sorry," Blake said.

Ed shifted his weight, looked over his shoulder, then spoke again. "To come to the point, I think I can get your computer tablet back for you. Would that be worthwhile? I mean, it wouldn't be on the Internet or anything but…"

"That would be a godsend," Dalton interjected. "It's got my life's work on it. A book that has the potential to change the governing of this country forever. But how will you do it? We don't want you getting into trouble on our account."

Ed then told them what he knew about Oliver Furrow's office and his secretary, Rebecca.

9

Candice hated living at Number 10. Or rather, she hated aspects of it. The location, the prestige, the building itself was a privilege to be in – she knew all that. But the publicity that went with it was anathema. She often went out of the garden entrance, even though it meant a much longer walk to where she was going. Today would be one of those days. Her uncle would soon be leaving for a much publicised official visit to Westingham Castle, where her father was held. Fabian wanted people to focus on its eco-credentials and the business leaders, artists and scientists who had gone against ecoism and ended up imprisoned there. He explained how it was for their own good and how it would save the Earth, but she was beginning to think it was going too far.

Finding out her father was still alive had been a massive relief. More than that. She had gone to her room alone and cried. She wasn't sure why the news had affected her so much, but she suspected she had probably been involved in his capture.

As she and Fabian finished a hurried breakfast and

he was about to go out, she put down a letter from her friend Lucinda, and said, "Uncle Fabian, I read in the paper that my father was captured near Sherwood Forest. They made a joke about how he was the anti-Robin Hood."

"Yes, I believe so, Candice," Fabian said, looking for his woollen scarf.

"Do you know how they found him after all those months?"

He stopped looking and faced her.

"Not really. I think it was some walkers who noticed something suspicious and told the police."

"Oh. I see. Thanks."

Fabian smiled, looking relieved. "Now, you have a good day at school, won't you."

"Yes, Uncle. Enjoy your trip. Say… say hello to my father for me."

"Of course, Candice. Perhaps you'd like to see him yourself sometime. Now, I must get going. Bye." He waved a long, thin hand and was gone.

Candice thought he was lying. People didn't go on long walks for leisure these days. They were too exhausted from the manual labour their jobs required since fossil fuels and electricity had been rationed. Plus, it was too dangerous. The countryside was full of outlaws these days. Then there was the way her uncle had looked. It was just too coincidental. Asking about her holidays, her mentioning the rides at that amusement park, and her father being found a week after.

Then her skin went cold. What if Fabian worked out that she was onto him? He was the most powerful man in the country. He could make up some story about her secretly sympathising with her father and then get her, what? Locked up too? It seemed to be becoming the norm these days. The media was looking forward to gloating over the misfortunes of those who had ended up in Westingham.

She forced down her panic with some deep breaths and the remains of her tea. Then she continued reading the letter from Lucinda. It was good to hear from a friend. She might soon be needing as many as she could get.

#

Having consumed his lunch of potatoes and cabbage (meat being frowned upon as producing too much CO_2), Blake was lying on his bed enjoying a brief rest on his own — Dalton was still in the refectory — when he heard the unusual sound of three motors. He stood on a chair and peered through the turret window.

He could see a long, gleaming black car with flags on the bonnet and two motorcycle outriders drawing to a halt in the courtyard. Almost before it had stopped, a back door opened and his brother stepped out. The governor rushed across to meet him and they shook hands.

As they entered the prison's inner door, Blake noticed a horse and cart trundling slowly in the limousine's wake. From the sacks and open crates on the back, he deduced it was carrying food. It reminded him of a trip to Morocco many years before, where he'd seen donkeys still in daily, essential use, sharing the road with Range Rovers.

He returned to his bed and was about to lie down again when the tannoy buzzed for afternoon work to begin. It was his turn to do 'chores' rather than walls this afternoon, so he headed for the courtyard where he'd been told to report.

Meanwhile, the governor was entertaining Fabian in his office.

"It's such an honour, you coming to visit us, Lord Hardwicke. Here's your sherry. I hope you like it."

Fabian took it with a smile. "I'm sure I shall."

"And to be the first governor of a truly eco-friendly prison, is— well, also, as I'm sure you know, a great privilege for myself."

"Indeed," the President replied, and he looked at the red face of the governor glowing upwards at him. "You realise this will be a showcase for future prisons. There is a significant burden on your shoulders."

"Of course, Mr. President."

"I want this place to show that we live up to the high standards ecoism demands of us. It must show eco-justice in its best and truest light. It must make it abundantly clear to people that eco-crime is taken seriously, but also that eco-criminals are dealt with fairly."

"I assure you we are striving every day for those very ends, Mr. President."

"Good." Fabian looked out of the window down into the courtyard while he finished his sherry. It had a rather harsh taste. Unfortunately, food miles prevented imports of the decent stuff from Spain, but it was a price worth paying for the cause. He turned to the governor.

"Shall we take a tour, and you can show me how well the punishment fits the crime?"

"Of course, Mr. President. It's this way."

They proceeded back down the stone stairs and

through the Great Hall, where prisoners were hard at work scrubbing the floor. Fabian smiled as he recognised the grimy faces of former businessmen on their knees.

Passing through a door in the far corner, they emerged into a small inner courtyard which served as a garden for the governor.

Sam Tillman was sweeping the leaves from the flagstones with a twig broom.

Fabian smiled broadly. "How do you like your new job, Mr Tillman?"

Sam looked up and stopped his sweeping. "If it was a job, I'd be able to quit, Mr Hardwicke."

Fabian winced slightly. He had grown very attached to his title. Although it would be hard to punish Sam Tillman any further at the moment, he wished there was a law enforcing use of the correct forms of address towards state officials.

"That's enough of your lip, Tillman," the governor barked. "Get back to work, or you'll be put in solitary."

Sam turned away from them and recommenced his sweeping.

Fabian wondered why Tillman annoyed him so much, but he couldn't fully explain it. "Shall we move on?" he said eventually to his unctuous guide.

"Of course, yes. Let's visit the washhouse." They crossed another small courtyard and traversed a narrow corridor until they came to a locked door studded with iron nails. The governor took out a large bunch of keys and unlocked it. "This is the women's section," he explained.

The smell of hot, damp clothes made clear the purpose of the next building as they entered it. Inside were dozens of women in red jumpsuits, their sleeves rolled to their elbows. Some were rubbing clothes on boards in large buckets of steaming water. Some with red hands, not just from the dye, were rinsing clothes in buckets of cold water. Others were working mangles, or hanging clothes onto lines.

"No electricity used here," the governor said proudly.

Fabian nodded absent-mindedly. He was surveying all the high-flyers dressed as identical washerwomen, looking for someone in particular.

Eventually, his eyes rested on his quarry and he moved towards her.

"Good afternoon, Ms Blackwood," he said with mock formality.

The red hands of the red-dressed woman in front of him stopped at the sound of his voice. As she looked at him, Fabian felt a jolt of fear in his stomach. Without her make-up, her smooth facade was gone and the dark-eyed face she turned on him offered no blandishment of protection, no civilised veneer. He thought of Boadicea, and he knew that it would be a fight to the death to crush this woman, too. He tried to make light of it.

"Are you enjoying your stay? You know there are still ways it could be shortened?"

Liz stared at his scrawny figure and his supercilious smile as she took her time before replying.

"I could ask you the same about your term in office, although you can't seriously be trying to remain there. When you've completely ruined the country with your policies, what do you expect to rule over?"

A flash of discomfort skimmed his mind, so rather

than the witty repartee he had planned, he simply said, "We shall see," then moved on.

Liz watched him go, pleased to have got rid of him so quickly, but puzzled and concerned that perhaps he really didn't have an intelligible plan, and he knew it. When she put her hands back in the rinsing tub she shivered, but not from the cold water.

The governor swiftly directed Fabian back to the men's section and into their kitchen.

Here there was a food delivery being unloaded, pots being washed by hand and two fires under large chimneys being tended by kneeling figures, blowing them back into life. Fabian stepped over to one of them.

"Professor MacDermot, are you enjoying the repentance of your sins?"

The professor looked as surprised as if a toad had insulted him.

Before he had time to reply, Fabian smirked and wandered off.

As a final treat, and also in case there was an incident, the governor had agreed that the encounter between Fabian and his brother would be the last of their tour. They found him as expected – alone and sewing clothes by hand in a small room with one window.

Fabian asked to be left alone and the governor obligingly closed the door.

"How did the police find me?" Blake asked.

"I don't know the details, I believe it was some walkers coming across you."

"I see," Blake said. "Now you're in charge it'll be easy for you to cover your tracks. What else have you got planned, besides allowing people to die in hospitals and care homes?"

"As an elected leader, I will do what I have been asked to do by the voters. If you wish to discover what that is, you need only study my manifesto."

"Does it include gloating over the misfortunes of industrious people? The rich you've always envied?"

"Locking up eco-criminals is only one step. The main task of my leadership is yet to come. I plan to truly honour the principles of ecoism by going much further."

Blake looked at him. "What do you mean?"

Fabian regarded him coolly. "Blake, you'll never understand me. But I understand you. I knew you well enough to get you in here eventually. One word to the governor and I can have you starving and alone. Would you like that?"

Blake remained silent. He seemed curious, but not afraid.

Fabian continued, "Still, if you behave yourself, that may not be necessary. I am a just President, after all. Now, if you'll excuse me, I have a country to run."

And with a satisfied smile, he opened the door and left.

#

Back in his and Dalton's cell that night, Blake exploded with pent-up frustration as he recounted his meeting with Fabian, the threats and the reversal of justice they must all be feeling.

"I know he's wrong, and ultimately he will lose, but right now he's got us all in his power and it's utterly infuriating."

"I know it seems we're powerless," the professor

said, "and that Fabian holds all the cards, and yet you also know his actions make no sense and in the long run will lead to disaster. So how has he got to the position he's in? That's the question, isn't it?"

Blake nodded.

"Look Blake, there is a way out of this for you and the others, if not for me."

"What do you mean?"

"I've been given a death sentence. If my appeal fails, which I expect, and if we don't manage to escape, I am not long for this earth."

"You mustn't talk like that…"

"But it's the truth, and so we must face it. Anyway, there's something I think I can do first that should help you and your fellow inmates after I'm gone."

Blake swallowed. Dalton was right – he didn't really want to face up to what might happen. "What is it?" he said eventually.

"I'm going to give them a lecture. It's what I do best. The title will be 'Ecoism and Egoism: which has the real power?'"

"How are you going to deliver it? Furrow wouldn't let you, surely?"

"I expect I'll find a way. It's part of my theory: they have no real power because they literally don't understand what I'd be saying."

"Good luck with that. At least if you succeed in getting permission you'll have a captive audience."

Dalton laughed and Blake began to feel slightly more optimistic.

As the cheerful sounds died away, Blake could hear someone coming up the stairs. It was about the usual time.

"Lock up," said a voice outside, dangling some keys, then a face popped around the door. It was Ed Quinton.

"Good to hear you two laughing for a change," he said. "I've something here that might also cheer you up." He produced Blake's tablet from inside his tunic.

"You're a genius!" Dalton exclaimed, his eyes wide, taking it from him carefully. "Like Prometheus bearing light to mere mortals. How did you get it?"

"Well, for years, Rebecca, Furrow's secretary, was having an affair with the previous governor. He was moved to a prison in Scotland when the ecoists came to power and she was ordered to stay here. She's been looking for a chance for revenge ever since. So, after I mentioned your predicament to her, she took that one from his safe when he'd left it open one day, and replaced it with one she got from a garage sale."

"That's amazing, Ed," Blake said. "But what about the charger?"

Ed reached into a couple of pockets and pulled out a lead and a transformer. "This should do it. You can wire it up to the lamp socket when you need to, like people doing the ironing in the old days."

"How old did you say you were?" Blake said, grinning.

"Old enough to know a few tricks," Ed said. Blake could see how pleased he was with his work.

"I can't thank you enough," Dalton said, his eyes glittering.

"That's all right," said the rebellious guard. "Just do your best to bring this lot down. But when you do, you'd better have some good ideas about what to replace them with."

"We will," Dalton said, "you can be sure of that."

Smiling, Ed closed and locked the door, leaving the inmates to marvel over their good fortune.

#

The following Sunday, Blake's backache made him hunch as he walked gingerly to the chapel under the weak November sun. He'd had a hard few days of wall-building and was looking forward to sitting down and hearing more 'confessions'.

He recognised Paul Williams immediately as he was called up the aisle, although his face was surely closer in colour to that of his short greying hair than when he'd entered the prison. As Williams was CTO of Western Energy and a physics graduate from Cambridge, Blake had come across him on numerous social occasions, and he'd been quick to join the BCF. Now he expected to get to know him rather better.

The governor introduced him then withdrew to focus on playing with his mobile phone. Paul seemed to take particular notice of this, before beginning his speech.

"I confess," he glanced at the governor, who wasn't listening, "to refusing to support the Carbon Crime Bill. It's my own fault. There were plenty of warnings. A lot people were kind enough to camp outside my business every day and throw eggs, or sometimes bricks, at my car, to remind me what was best for me. And I know I was privileged to have had a personal visit from the Minister for Carbon to try to persuade me. But I was stupid and naive enough to believe I could ignore it, that it would all soon blow over and my life could carry on as if ecoism had never existed. When they shut down my power station and turfed me

249

out, I was still stupid enough to complain."

He paused, took a deep breath, then went on.

"I confess that I was instrumental in getting 'smart meters' off the ground. I confess that I stood by while the shale industry was regulated out of existence. And now," he spread his hands and gave a bitter smile, "I am paying for the error of my ways. My company, what's left of it, is now being run by one of my competitors, for 'essential purposes' only. A competitor who listened and obeyed. And I am here."

Shaking with what Blake presumed to be contained rage, Paul Williams descended the step and returned down the aisle. The prisoners watched him in sympathetic silence.

Eventually, the governor noticed no one was speaking and called a name that made Blake start.

"Clive Donaldson, it is your turn to confess."

Clive stood very slowly, with agonising effort and a bent back. Then, although he looked like he needed a stick, he made his way to the confessional step without one.

Finally, he turned to face his audience and raised his head level.

"I confess," he began in a low Scots drawl, "that I gave up freedom long ago, and now I too am paying the price. Some years ago the Minister for Competition came to me with a desire to lower voters' telecoms bills. I used this opportunity to crush my smaller rivals by having the government set price controls which I could afford, but which they could not. It was done by a simple equivocation of different services. I didn't explain these differences to the minister, and he wasn't expert enough to ask. Or perhaps," he paused to reflect, "he never was interested in fairness, despite his title. Anyway, when the Internet Regulation Bill came into being, which will soon destroy English Telecom, I had no leg to stand on."

He paused to look around the audience and his eyes landed upon Blake.

"Eventually, I confessed to myself what I had done, and decided to try to make amends. Firstly, I decided to resign. Secondly, I did some pro bono work for an old rival, which involved investigating the provision of power at care homes and hospitals around the country. Eventually, this took me to London."

There was the sound of footsteps on flagstones as the governor strode out of a door, his mobile pressed to his ear.

Clive continued. "London, for those of you who have not been there lately, is a much changed city. The Underground is even more unreliable than before. On one occasion, near Green Park, I had to climb off a train and walk with the other passengers through the tunnel back to the platform. Buses are regularly running out of fuel mid-route. Food prices, never cheap in the city, have rocketed, as trains and trucks have been cut to save carbon. A lot of people are leaving London by one means or another – horses, barges, bicycles. And those who can afford to remain have established privately patrolled vegetable gardens in Hyde Park. If you ever get out of here, you should consider carefully before returning to live in what was once a great capital."

He shifted his weight to rest on his other leg, grimacing as he did so.

"Anyway, to return to my investigation. I confirmed the facts that had led to Blake Hardwicke's arrest. Care homes and hospitals were being deliberately starved of fuel. I took a chance by quickly setting up a website and publishing everything I'd found, hoping there would be enough public support to help bring the government to account.

"However, I confess I must have made another mistake. Instead of becoming a national hero for blowing the whistle on a shocking scandal, I have been convicted of spying on the government and find myself here."

He bowed his head briefly as if receiving judgement from his peers, then walked slowly and haltingly back down the aisle.

As he passed Blake's seat, Blake noticed he was missing some fingernails.

Once the governor had returned and dismissed them with one of his ecoist homilies, Blake lingered behind to follow Clive out of the chapel.

"It's good to see you," Blake said.

"Aye, but I'd have preferred different circumstances," Clive said, smiling, but also wincing.

"When did you get here?"

"Yesterday."

"What did they do to you?" Blake pointed to his hands.

Clive paused. "On the police report it says I tripped down some stairs. But to be honest with you, they couldn't punish me more than I've already punished myself."

Blake stared sympathetically at his rival and friend. "Listen," he said quietly. "We'll get you out. Dalton and I have been making plans to escape."

"That's very kind of you, but I'm none too quick on

my feet at the moment."

"It's all right. It's not imminent. The truth is, we're finding it difficult to figure out. We're not experts in this kind of thing."

"Neither am I, but we've got to help ourselves. When can we meet?"

"I'll find you at breakfast."

Clive agreed, but then a guard approached to move them along and they returned to their sombre cells.

10

It was December, and Ahmed cursed how early night fell. In the old days, couples would saunter past, arm in arm, stopping now and again to point at potential necklaces or rings for Christmas. Now, after dark, in the absence of street lights, there would be no more customers.

Sighing after a meagre day's trade, he picked up his baseball bat, locked the shop from outside, and went to join his fellow shopkeepers at their regular vigil halfway down Hatton Garden.

He nodded and greeted his neighbours of all origins – Jews, Russians, Greeks, English – as he walked over to the chestnut cooker where several of them were warming their hands.

"No sign of any police today?" he enquired of a wizened old man named Nick.

"Not a sausage," Nick replied. "Mind you, if we did sell sausages, we'd be a lot more worth robbing. You can't eat gemstones."

"Too true," Ahmed said, smiling laconically. He wished someone would start cooking chestnuts soon.

He could almost smell them.

~

A hundred yards away, hidden down a side street, a short, thin man, his birthmark hidden by a black balaclava, hefted a brick in his hand and addressed his hand-picked troop of racist anarchists. "Right," Lee said, "have you all got enough bricks?"

They growled affirmatively and hoisted their holdalls for inspection.

"Good. When you've emptied the bags of bricks, you can fill 'em with jewels."

The group cackled with amusement.

"Now, show me the bombs," Lee ordered.

Half a dozen fume-laden bottles with rags inserted were made ready for inspection.

"Very nice," Lee said appreciatively. "Right, let's go."

As they started moving, a lookout came back with news. "The Paki owners are out there again with their bats." His hesitant tone didn't match his aggressive words.

"How many?" Lee asked.

"At least fifty."

He had probably exaggerated for effect, but Lee guessed there were still enough to scupper their plans. "Right. I'll put in a call," he said, lifting his balaclava and stretching his birthmark with a grin.

He pulled a two-way radio out of his pocket and spoke into it, too quietly for the gang to hear. Then he put it away and addressed them again.

"All right, let's go and see our friends. Don't light the bombs yet. I'll tell you when."

The gang members smirked at each other, then pulled up their hoodies and followed Lee out onto

Hatton Garden.

~

From further down the street, beside the glowing chestnut cooker, Ahmed called out, "Look!"

The other shopkeepers turned to face the direction he'd pointed in, tightening their grips on their baseball bats and iron bars. Then they saw the ominous crowd of hooded figures, bricks and bottles in hand.

"Oh no!" a Greek jewellery maker cried. "I'm going to call the police," and he returned to his shop.

The others formed a line across the road. If no one came to their aid, they would have to help themselves.

After a couple of minutes, Ahmed said, "Why aren't they moving?"

"I don't like it," an Irish ring maker said.

"Maybe it'll be all right. Maybe we've made them change their minds," Ahmed suggested, with more hope than conviction in his voice.

The standoff continued for another minute or two. Then they all heard the sound of a siren.

"I never thought I'd be so pleased to hear that sound," the Irishman said. "Maybe Alexsis got through to them."

The shopkeepers lowered their bats as a van screeched to a halt and a body of police in riot gear emerged from it.

"Follow me," Inspector Smith said to the officers, and he strode in front towards the two groups, his coat flapping.

"Jesus, Lee, it's the old Bill. Let's scarper," said a hoodie when he saw Smith and his armed attendants.

"Don't panic, mate," Lee replied calmly. "Just let the officers through. After all, we ain't done nothing wrong yet, have we?"

One or two hoodies ran off into the shadows, but the rest did as Lee ordered and made way for the police to come through.

The inspector noticed Lee as he strode past and gave him an imperceptible nod. Otherwise, he pretended the hoodies weren't there.

When he came to the group of shopkeepers, he signalled to his men to surround them.

Unarmed himself, but with the backing of twenty machine-gun carrying subordinates, Smith raised his voice to address the frightened looking merchants.

About time, Ahmed thought. *He's going to provide proper protection for us*, and he moved closer to Smith to hear more clearly.

"I am arresting you all for disturbing the peace, or intending to do so," Smith boomed. "And also for an unlicensed fire," he added, seeing the chestnut cooker.

Ahmed was astonished. Surely he must have meant the hoodies too. He was just going to address them separately. Then they could explain everything down at the station. That was it.

"What about the hoodies, sir?" asked a confused officer.

"These are the real villains," Smith replied in a lowered voice. "You've heard what the President has said about people harbouring luxuries such as jewels in a time like this. Bring them in."

The officers stepped forward and grabbed the nearest shopkeepers by the arm. Most were too surprised to react, except with astonishment. Ahmed thought about making a run for it, but he couldn't answer the question, *where to?* He lived here, with his family, above the shop. He couldn't leave it, or them.

A pair of rough hands grabbed his and cuffed them.

Ahmed felt numb. He had moved to England over twenty years ago to escape a police state. Now it was as if his past had caught up with him. He tried to put a smile on his face as he glanced towards his family looking out of their upstairs window. Then he was bundled into the police van.

In seconds it was full. The despondent shopkeepers looking at each other in bewilderment. Then Ahmed realised. There was only one van. In it were all his fellow tradesmen. None of them were hoodies.

Panicking, he struggled to climb over his friends and reach the back door.

"Amira, get out," he shouted to the upstairs window, just as the door was slammed in his face and locked. He banged it furiously as the van started to move.

Had they heard him?

He looked out desperately through the van's windows, but the only figures he could see were the silent hoodie-wearing thugs.

~

Lee watched the van drive away and then laughed. His gang looked at him as if he had performed a miracle.

"Right, let's have some fun," Lee shouted, and got a couple of bricks out of his bag.

The others followed his lead. Then they lurched towards each side of the street and cast their primitive weapons through the stainless windows at the beautifully hand-crafted jewellery. Alarms went off and frightened residents appeared on the street. But no more policemen came.

The gang smashed every window at ground level and occasionally grabbed some of their contents, as they marauded up the street.

When they reached the end, Lee turned and spoke softly through his sweaty balaclava.

"Now, let's light a couple of those bombs."

#

Manny scratched his balding head after he'd put down the phone summoning him to the President's palace. Over the last month, Fabian had been spending more time there than at Number 10. What could he want now? Surely he, Manny, was doing an outstanding job? He was keeping the people entertained through his programming of the GBMC, and he was keeping some of the harsher facts of recent life from them through editing the *National Voice*. He didn't like leaving his plush offices on Fleet Street and Portland Place more than was necessary. Not these days. But what could he do? Drawing a deep breath, he reminded himself that his GBMC chauffeur was a very competent ex-policeman. He should be fine.

As he was driven through the dark December evening, Manny surveyed the scene. The sporadic street lighting made it hard to be sure, but he thought he counted six empty shops on Regent Street, all with their windows broken.

In Trafalgar Square there were two burned-out cars, one still smouldering. In the run-up to Christmas these streets would usually have been heaving with shoppers, but tonight he saw only hooded gangs. No police were in sight.

With The Mall being closed except for ceremonial occasions, the driver turned into Whitehall, where the plentiful street lights revealed a different situation. Armed police stood outside all the government buildings and no windows appeared broken. People walked hurriedly by.

Emerging on Parliament Square, Manny looked up at the dark home of democracy. It had been closed to save CO_2. MPs and Lords now met in small rooms up and down Whitehall instead. Even Big Ben had been silenced, and its clock face unlit to show the government's commitment to Carbon Tonnes Saved.

The chauffeur navigated his way through the largely empty streets of Victoria until they eventually saw Buckingham Palace to their left. It was unscathed and protected by ranks of soldiers. As they drove through the security check, Manny looked up at the flag on the roof. Although he was a committed ecoist, he was secretly glad that it hadn't yet been changed to the green and red tree.

The car drew up at a set of steps, and after re-presenting his credentials, Manny was shown along picture-laden corridors attended by occasional armed guards until he was ushered into the ballroom. At the far end, surrounded by what looked like a large part of the Crown Jewels, including the orb and sceptre, Fabian sat in a black suit on a plush throne.

Manny was gobsmacked, but tried to hide it by turning and pretending to admire the decoration.

A thin man whom Manny recognised as Zac Rutter, the barrister, sat on a lower chair beside the President.

Fabian looked up from their close conversation and welcomed him. "My old friend, do come in." There was nowhere else to sit and Rutter showed no sign of moving, so Manny put on his best smile and went to stand at the foot of the throne.

"Zac has been helping me draft new measures for an important announcement."

"Really," Manny said, trying to hide his irritation at not being consulted first.

"And it's so important," Fabian continued, "that I wanted you to be involved before anyone else."

Manny relaxed somewhat, but Fabian was being unusually flattering. Why, when he was surrounded by so many trappings of power? Looking closely, he could see his old friend was, in fact, rather nervous. He kept wiping his hands on his trousers.

"You must know how out-of-hand things are getting around the country. You have a fine network of reporters, do you not?"

Manny nodded.

"So, to combat this anarchy, I am going to declare a National Emergency. This will give me the powers I need to restore order. Zac is determining how to do it legally." He paused and smiled at Manny. "And your very important job is to sell the idea to the public."

Manny felt both flattered and alarmed. His closeness to the President was well known, but he didn't want to become just a state mouthpiece. Who would believe his objectivity?

"I appreciate the honour of being given such a task," Manny began cautiously, "but wouldn't it be better coming from someone inside the government? Someone with an official position?"

Fabian looked at him steadily, then smiled. "As ever, you anticipate me, my old friend. Great minds do, indeed, think alike. As I was about to say, I'm offering you the post of Minister of Information, and a place in the Cabinet. I suggest you retain your positions at the GBMC and the *National Voice*, but delegate more of their day-to-day running to others."

Manny was speechless. He'd been interested in politics since his early teens. He'd spent innumerable hours at political rallies and protests in his student days. He'd canvassed hundreds of voters and distributed thousands of leaflets. He'd spent his career investigating and analysing government activities through the media. Now he had the opportunity to influence government directly, right at its heart.

"It comes with a ministerial car and a very generous stipend, of course," the President mentioned.

Now was his chance to really do something, for socialism, for ecoism, to really make a difference, and hopefully to stop things collapsing any further, thought Manny. An inner voice told him he was rationalising, and that if he accepted this job, he could kiss his independence goodbye. But he muffled that irritating sound as he visualised himself giving speeches outside 10 Downing Street, and making the world a better place.

"I'll take it," Manny said eagerly. "I accept," he said more slowly, trying to sound more sober, as dignified politicians should.

"Good," Fabian said, smiling broadly and letting out a long breath. "Very good."

Zac Rutter smiled, too.

Feeling ten feet tall and with a licence to change the world, Manny blurted out, "So, as Minister for Information, I need to know things myself, so I can explain them to the public. Why, for instance, has public order collapsed so quickly? Why are there so many food shortages, runs on banks, unplanned brownouts and blackouts? Why is what's left of the Internet getting slower and slower?" It was actually he who wanted desperately to know the answers, but Manny continued, "If I know, then I can give the right explanation to the people."

He looked at Fabian and saw his face turn a darkening shade of red.

"You already know why these things are happening. When mankind abuses the natural order, they are inevitable. When he selfishly exploits the world's resources, nature will turn against him. His behaviour is unsustainable. It's the key principle behind the whole environmental movement. Isn't that what's been driving all your green stories all these years?"

It was a rant not an explanation. Manny was becoming afraid as he heard the rising volume of his friend's voice, but it was not Fabian that scared him. "Yes, of course," he mumbled. "You're right."

"I'm glad we're in agreement," Fabian said, gradually cooling down. "The public like a strong, united government." He paused, then said, "Zac, will you go over the measures we've planned for the National Emergency Executive Order? I'm sure our new minister would like to hear them."

Zac cleared his throat and began reading from a notepad. "Carbon Crime to carry a capital punishment. Travel abroad to be forbidden, except on government business." He smiled thinly at Manny, then continued. "Properly enforcing the Internet Regulation Act by arresting those using it without a licence. A new Public Interest Committee to be appointed with the power to commute all sentences to capital ones." Zac looked up triumphantly.

Fabian was beaming as he said, "I'm sure the public will be glad to know we're taking decisive action. In fact, only this morning a private plane was shot down by the RAF as it tried to leave the country."

"But it wasn't a law this morning," Manny blurted out.

Fabian gave him a withering look and turned to Zac. "Do explain."

"Of course," Zac said. "The plane was being flown by one of the richest tycoons in the country, who 'made' his money from computers. I don't think the public will have too much sympathy for him. Do you?"

Manny shuddered involuntarily and shook his head, apparently in agreement.

"Well then, Minister," Fabian said, "is there anything else you need to know before you put it over to the public?"

Manny looked at the floor, his mind whirling with the implications of the new order. On the one hand, he'd always been against the death sentence, but on the other, since mankind really was destroying the planet, he deserved the strongest punishment. Again, he preferred the proper legal process to a committee's snap decision, but looking at the state of the country, something drastic had to be done. As for the Internet, he was in favour of free expression within reason, but he hated what it had done to newspaper circulation and it was full of fake news.

He looked up at Fabian's and Zac's expectant faces. He knew this was a critical moment for himself, and for the country. He drew a deep breath and focused on the here and now. "No, I think that's everything," he said.

~

As he almost ran down the corridors to escape into the outside air, he kept reminding himself how pleased his wife would be about his new position, now that he could really influence things.

#

Blake felt depressed as he trudged up the slight hill towards the chapel, pulling his blanket around him to repel the December wind. He normally looked forward to confession – he had given his own some weeks back and found it most cathartic – but he had just been reading about the declaration of National Emergency. Its implications for them all made him shiver, far more than the wind on its own.

Sitting in a pew with his thoughts bent again on escape, Blake was interrupted by the governor's announcement.

"We will now hear the confession of Timothy Campbell."

A tall, muscular man with a shaven, sun-tanned head stood up. Blake watched him as he marched briskly up the aisle. The prison guards instinctively touched their firearms.

In a loud, penetrating Glaswegian accent, the Brig began. "You probably all know from the papers why I'm here. For those that missed it, I was court-martialled, not for the first time, and found guilty of disobeying orders. I was told to abandon my post and withdraw my troops from defending Tilcot Power Station. I refused but was overruled. Now, you all know what happened next."

There was a general murmur among the convicts,

until Furrow shouted, "Order, I will have order! Campbell, get to the point."

The Brig smiled, and when he seemed ready, continued. "Despite the invasion and subsequent shutting down of Tilcot for good, I was found guilty not only of disobedience but also of aiding and abetting Carbon Crime, which is why I'm here. So I confess, I followed my own ideas and am being punished for it. However, I'm not hopeful that the punishment will be effective. My first court-martial was six years ago for rescuing the injured prince, ex-Prince Arthur, from a dangerous situation in the Middle East. He wanted to spare us and be left there, where the enemy would have had a field day parading his head on TV. But I confess, I disobeyed our rules of engagement by proactively fighting our way out.

"At that trial, my defence counsel argued for dismissing the charges and instead awarding me a medal. The prosecution, on the other hand, tried to make me reject my own judgement. When I explained that I'd rescued the Prince because it was the right thing to do for him, for my men, and for the country, he asked, 'How can you be so sure?' I replied as honestly as I could, and said that my judgement was the only one available to me. I couldn't make a decision using someone else's head."

The Brig shifted his weight and drew himself up before making his next point.

"The prosecutor then asked why I didn't just 'do as I was told' and obey my superiors, those who actually wrote the rules of engagement."

He gave a long sigh then continued.

"I've been a soldier for nearly thirty years and seen

action in Northern Ireland, Bosnia, the Gulf, Afghanistan and Syria, and I've commanded a lot of men. They don't join the army to give up their lives, but to fight for them. And they're not pliable little civil servants, bowing to every demand and hoping not to mess up their pensions. I explained this to the prosecutor. Both he and the two desk generals acting as judges went bright red."

He smiled at the memory.

"Of course, they found me guilty, but I was let off because the Prince's father intervened. Things have changed since then. There was no reprieve this time."

He shook his head in disbelief, then raised it again.

"I confess to having my own mind and my own standards, and if society's are now so different, perhaps this is the best place for me."

Blake and the rest of the congregation watched in silence as the Brig marched firmly back down the aisle. Although he himself had never been in the forces, Blake felt like shooting to his feet and saluting.

After the governor had dismissed them, Blake caught up with the ex-soldier on their way out and introduced himself.

"You escaped from your trial and lived in Sherwood Forest for months," the Brig said, smiling. "That was a fine piece of work. What gave you away?"

"I'm not sure. But I do have serious issues with some of my family."

The Brig nodded in understanding. "Not just your brother, then?"

"No. Anyway, we haven't much time now, but I'd like to talk to you about our escape plans."

"Well, you've come to the right man. How many of

you are there?"

"Three including yourself, possibly four."

"I see."

"It's not many, I know, but these prisoners are not physical types. They're businesspeople, artists, doctors."

The Brig nodded, then said, "A small number makes it easier. But what about after the escape? What's your plan then? You can't get recaptured a second time."

"I'm wondering if you might be able to help with that. Dalton and I, Professor MacDermot…"

"Didn't he live in the forest with you?"

"That's him. We've been wondering what the feeling is among the soldiers about the way things are going politically?"

"Well, I could tell you quite a bit about that…" He broke off as a guard approached. "…but not here."

They hurriedly arranged their next discussion before moving nonchalantly on.

11

As the rest of the prisoner congregation filed out of the chapel, Dalton waited for the governor to leave, then followed him back to his office.

There he approached Rebecca, his secretary, and asked for an interview. She betrayed no sign of what had passed regarding the tablet, except a broad smile as she gestured him to a seat.

Dalton waited patiently for the guard to let him in. When he was finally admitted after twenty minutes, he discovered the governor sitting at his desk, an illuminated piece of parchment in a frame on the wall behind his puffed, red face. Dalton remembered the governor had studied mediaeval theology. Perhaps it was from some renowned copy of the Bible. If it was an original, how had he managed to obtain it?

Interrupting Dalton's thoughts, the governor asked, "What do you want, MacDermot?"

"As there have been no new prisoners since the Brigadier arrived two weeks ago, I assume there are no outstanding confessions."

The governor struggled to see the point of this

conversation. "Yes. So what?"

"Therefore the chapel will be free." Dalton paused for confirmation.

"Get on with it," the governor said, drumming his fingers.

"I'd like to give a lecture to the other prisoners. It will be about ecoism."

The governor sat back in his chair as he tried to fathom this out. He knew MacDermot was famous for being anti-ecoist, so he knew he wasn't trying to earn brownie points. It was too late for that anyway. He was due to be executed sometime in the new year, depending on his appeal. He probably just wanted to feel in charge of his life for a short while, before it was ended for him. The governor thought himself a gracious man, and decided he'd be happy to grant a man's – almost – dying request. Besides what harm could it do, a lot of hot air among the incarcerated? The prison had little communication with the outside world. Visits were strictly limited and all ingoing and outgoing mail was censored. And despite MacDermot's ego, who knew if anyone would bother to turn up to listen? He wasn't dealing with students needing to pass an exam now.

"All right," the magnanimous governor said. "Go ahead. Make it the first Sunday of the new year."

"Thank you," Dalton said, and went to tell Blake the good news.

~

Christmas was a modest affair for the prisoners. There was no snow, so at least it was no colder than usual. Their rations were supplemented with turkey slices, gravy and a decent helping of Christmas pudding, but with runny custard. Blake enjoyed this the most. But he sorely missed his family. Christmas was always a joyous occasion, with their rituals of present opening, eating and games. James still enjoyed it even though he was… *would have been* nearly nineteen.

As he lay down to sleep on New Year's Eve, utterly sober, Blake thought of the tumultuous year that had passed: the loss of his son, the estrangement of his daughter, the certain end of his career and his business, and then becoming imprisoned with no chance of seeing his wife. Everything supporting his life had gone. Almost. He could still cling on to the functioning of his mind and the chance of escape, as well as the friendship of Dalton MacDermot.

But what would the future bring – for Dalton and everyone? With the country under a National Emergency, almost anything could happen.

~

The first Sunday of the new year came, and as he stood at the lectern in the chapel, Dalton looked out at his 'flock'. Nearly every prisoner was there, which pleased him. They didn't have to come, unlike confession.

He knew he didn't have much time. It was a race to finish the PPOG before he was executed. A successful escape might extend that period, but he couldn't count on it. Today was a boost for him and an insurance policy.

The guard today comprised solely of Ed Quinton. That boded well. There was no sign of the governor – Dalton hadn't expected him – so when no one else seemed to be coming in, and knowing it might be the last lecture he ever gave, he began.

"Thank you all for coming, ladies and gentlemen. I know you have busy schedules and I appreciate your taking time out from them."

The prisoners laughed gently.

"In case some of you wish to leave, I'll remind you what we're here for today. I'm not giving another confession, but instead a lecture on egoism versus ecoism, and the massive difference one letter and one fundamental idea can make."

He paused. "No leavers? Then I'll begin."

He took a deep breath and said, "What are we really here for?" Before continuing, he looked around to gauge the audience's attention, and saw Ed Quinton staring at him with a question in his eyes.

"Superficially, of course, we are here for the crimes we have been convicted of. Crimes that occurred as we pursued our values." Dalton looked around the room until he saw the Brigadier's bald, tanned head, then said, "Freedom!" "Energy!" as he found Paul Williams, "Telecoms!" when he saw the thinning red hair of Clive Donaldson, and "Food!" when his eyes alighted on Sam Tillman. "And above all, what everyone here seeks in one way or another: profit." His eyes came to rest on Liz Blackwood. Her prison attire failed to dim the intensity of the look she returned him.

"However, fundamentally, we are here for another reason. Something recently has changed in the world. Not long ago, all of your so-called offences would have been praised as virtues. People like yourself did not go to jail. But now, an ancient philosophical battle has come to a head, and you have been made the first victims. On one side is egoism, or self-interest. Each of you has sought, while committing your 'offence', to improve your life by gaining or increasing what matters to you. That is the essence of selfishness, not trampling on other people. On the other side is ecoism – the epitome of self-sacrifice – today's newly dominant philosophy. It condemns what you have done, because improving life is not its goal. It seeks to reduce energy production, cut down computer usage, make less profit, and provide less choice of food.

"In other words, it seeks to decrease what matters to you. How does it justify such a radical position? After all, if mankind had followed its advice, we would never have left the cave. Ecoism claims that there are not enough resources in the world to share around, that if we keep consuming oil, minerals, water, oxygen and land, we as a species will run out.

"Their focus on 'climate change' amounts to the same thing. If the Earth heats up and the oceans flood the land, there will be less land to live on and to grow crops on, so it will run out sooner. The same goes for 'pollution' – they claim it reduces the quality of resources available.

"On the face of it, this all seems plausible. But not if you dig a little deeper.

"Look at the decline of the country since you have been locked up here."

Dalton held up a recent newspaper, whose headline was, '*Oxford Street Riot Kills 20.*'

"Without you running your businesses – thereby creating value from resources – food, transport and jobs are in shorter supply, which provides some people with an excuse to riot and thieve.

"Your imprisonment has scared other high-flyers

into hiding. Now, with the National Emergency laws in place, they potentially face death for continuing in their jobs. These laws also put a brake on international trade – if you can't leave the country without special permission, you can't transport foreign goods or extend your own business abroad.

"And with Climate Change Denial a crime and the Internet Regulation Act passed, you can't debate those problems in public.

"Could our beloved President have predicted these consequences? As an Oxford graduate, you would hope so. Can he be evading the fact that the country is falling apart? That seems impossible. So why are you all still here, instead of being pardoned and begged to return to work?

"We are closing in on an answer. But first consider the simple flaw in the basic logic of ecoism. Supposedly, its basic moral premise is that the good consists of conserving resources. But for whom? For future generations, we are told. But who should *they* be conserving *their* resources for? Their future offspring. And so on, ad infinitum. Under ecoism, no one ever gets to enjoy the fruits of their labour for themselves. And therein lies the real explanation of the ecoists' behaviour. It is not the future that requires the pursuit of values and the subsequent joy they bring. It is life today. Without values we are doomed. And ecoists hate this fact. They hate it because it makes them feel afraid. They fear it, because they themselves do not want to pursue values, to live.

"Why? It's a question of their psychology and their refusal to engage their reason. They prefer spouting platitudes like 'saving the planet' to the hard thinking required to see if they make sense. They can evade that effort, but as living beings who cannot survive without values, they cannot help but feel guilty. And guilt being a terrible burden, they need someone else to help carry it, so they punish you instead. If you stop achieving values, it blocks out the fact of their own impotence, and of their implicit, suicidal death wish. Sadly for them, ecoism is worse than normal religion, for under the Church, there is…" He looked up at the ceiling. "… apparently forgiveness. Under the inner jury of your own ego, there is not.

"And so, to conclude this brief explanation, the fundamental reason why you are all here is that you want to live, while the ecoists want you to die."

Without a planned intention, Blake suddenly stood up and looked around the chapel for Liz Blackwood. She too was standing and looking at him, but whereas he had feelings of pain-free joy, clarity and vindication, she had a scowl on her face above her tightly folded arms.

#

The priceless Ormolu clock chimed eleven and Fabian stopped pacing the empty ballroom. He had been there for over an hour. The agreeable warmth and the dazzling light from the electric chandeliers should have been a comfort, given that so many others were missing them on this freezing January night. But for Fabian they were not enough. In fact, they were an annoyance, a reprimand. Who was he to be enjoying such luxuries when they cost the earth? Perhaps he should get right of them then. But someone had to lead, someone had to make sacrifices. It might as well be him. It was too late to stop now. Nevertheless, he hammered the immaculately painted wall with his fist so that it hurt. Then he was pacing again.

Why was he so 'unhappy', he wanted to say, but the closest he could come was 'irritated'. With all his plans going so well and all the resources of the state at his disposal, he could do almost anything. So why was he feeling so frustrated? There must be something he needed to do. Something his body was telling him. He tried to remember when he had last felt really happy. Searching back through the days since Christmas and then before that, he realised it was when he was at Westingham. This gave him an idea. He rang the gilt-embroidered bell pull and almost instantly a guard arrived.

"Bring me the Lord Chief Justice," Fabian barked, and the guard left to comply.

Fabian knew he wouldn't have to wait long. The Lord Chief Justice, such a pompous title when he himself held all the power, had been appointed recently by him, and was extremely willing to please.

As he waited he visualised the Carbon Crime prisoners, and hoped the winter wind was biting them smartly through the gaps in the castle walls. He especially hoped his brother was feeling it. After decades of being the better runner, the better student, the most befriended and the richer of the two of them, Blake was now where he belonged, paying for the consequences of his success, while he, Fabian, was on top – in fact, as high as you could go.

He walked to the gilded sovereign's chair and sat down, enjoying the feeling of the plush velvet. He thought of how many people he could command to stand before him, and of how many people would grovel to attend a banquet in this room and then hang on his every word.

A sharp twinge of guilt touched him and he reminded himself not to get too big-headed, that he was only there to serve a higher cause, that the trappings of power were necessary, but as with all things, only temporary. He must play his part, that was all. Besides, his work was far from over. Recently, he had heard reports of sympathy growing for these eco-criminals. Rumours of a grassroots movement to have their cases reviewed. Such activists could and should be stopped. Well, he could see to that.

Before long, the Lord Chief Justice was announced and came scampering across the floor towards him.

For a moment Fabian recoiled as the sweaty, shaven head bowed deeply before him, but he steeled himself with the thought that you had to deal with all sorts of people in order to get things done. He noted the man's bitten nails. Really, at his age.

"Lord Chief Justice," Fabian began, knowing how much this man liked his new title.

"Mr. President," the Justice replied, obsequiously.

"I summoned you here for urgent instruction on a matter of national importance."

"Thank you, sir," the Justice replied, wearing only a slight frown of apprehension.

"I would like you to instruct the Public Interest Committee to review the cases of all the prisoners at Westingham Castle, and to find that they all deserve the death penalty."

There was a pause before the Justice bowed his head and asked, "What grounds shall I give them, sir?"

Fabian knew the Justice's character too well to

suspect him of insolence, so instead he enjoyed yet another opportunity to fill the void of an empty mind.

"You will explain that it is in the national, which is to say public, interest. The prisoners have all defied planet-saving laws, and in these times of limited resources they must be made an example of, otherwise people will go on behaving as they always did – buying and selling their grubby goods and making dirty great profits at the expense of the exploited poor. Besides, there are too many people. We have to start somewhere."

"Indeed, sir," the Justice said as he finished jotting this down on his notepad. "Perhaps, sir, I could also add that these people deny the future its heritage?"

Fabian smiled at the pliancy of his new head of the legal system.

The Justice smiled back and nodded. Fabian knew there would be some pathetic legal attempt by others to stop him, quoting ancient principles, or suggesting that future generations might think differently. But this was an emergency and he had the responsibility of saving the Earth. That trumped all other considerations. However, to rub the message in, he would enact another idea he'd been brooding over.

"I would also like you to contact the governor of Westingham and instruct him to set up public viewing times, so people can learn by seeing these reprobates in the flesh."

Confused by these two conflicting requests, the justice asked timidly, "Err, if they are to be executed, how will they also be viewable, as it were, sir?"

Fabian sighed. It was a burden doing everyone else's thinking for them, but he magnanimously rose to the challenge. "My dear Adrian, let me explain. As you know, it would be quite wrong to execute them all immediately. They should be allowed plenty of time for appeal. That would only be fair." And it would keep the public in fear, he added to himself.

The Justice smiled and wrote this down. Then he dared to express a thought of his own. "Of course, the prisoner Dalton MacDermot is at Westingham for Climate Change Denial, and already sentenced to death. We could deal with him much sooner."

Fabian grinned at the ruthlessness of the legal mind. "Yes, we should."

He dismissed the Justice then rang for a drink, before settling himself down on the gilded chair, feeling highly satisfied.

#

It was snowing as Blake headed to the canteen, so like all the others, he was looking forward to breakfast and being back inside more than usual.

He queued up for his gruel and thought about the dismal day ahead of breaking up stone into pieces for building. At least the frost might have made it easier, he thought hopefully.

As he sat down to eat, he noticed an orderly coming round with the mail. He had an unusually large stack of white envelopes. Blake presumed it was some kind of bureaucratic notice and carried on spooning the grey mixture into his mouth.

Then he heard a tray crash to the floor. He swung round to see who it was. Paul Williams was on his feet, his mouth hanging open, his eyes wide in disbelief, clutching a letter. Blake looked along the table from where Paul was sitting. It was like a tsunami had hit them. The slow, white wave bearing dreadful news washed away the composure of each in turn.

A man one bench away shouted in desperation, "But I was only in for tax avoidance!" Before Blake could ask what he meant, the wave reached him.

He opened the white envelope with his name on it. The letter was pompously headed "From the Committee for Environmental Offences (sub-committee of the Public Interest Committee)." Its contents were simple and to the point: "Blake Lorenzo Hardwicke, you are serving a custodial sentence for Carbon Crime and have had your sentence changed to death by hanging. The committee has decided this as a result of the level of damage your crime has caused to the environment."

Blake was too surprised and confused to react emotionally. Could they do this? Surely not. But then the National Emergency seemed to bypass legal procedures that had been in place for centuries. Before he could figure it out, the governor walked in and the guards shouted for silence.

Sir Oliver Furrow had enjoyed watching the mass hysteria through a window in an adjoining room. He was glad these so-called high flyers were going to get their comeuppance. He was looking forward to going down in history as the first prison governor of the twenty-first century to oversee the actual use of the death penalty. Although it had been reintroduced for terrorist offences some years earlier, it had never been employed. First, however, these prisoners needed to be kept alive a little longer.

"Inmates," he began in as strong a voice as his high pitch allowed him, "you will be pleased to know that the government is not so callous as to arrange your executions immediately, even though we do have the necessary authority. Instead, you will each have three months to appeal."

He watched their sighs of relief. It was fun, toying with them.

"During this time," he continued, "there will be special visitor viewings where the public can come and see you all, and pay their final respects, or perhaps offer some support. We will also be increasing the level of security, in case any of you are now planning to escape. That is all." He left the room, a broad grin on his puffed, red face.

The prisoners stared aghast at one another. Dalton came over to Blake's table. Blake noticed his hands were empty. Now he knew what he must have been feeling for months. He felt fear, dread and paralysis. Force and mind really were opposites.

"You must write to your wife, Blake, find out if she's been affected."

"Yes, you're right." Blake had been too stunned to think of it.

"And we must step up our plans for escape."

#

It was still January but the snow had turned to ice-cold rain when Blake and his fellow prisoners filed through the narrow passages from where they'd been working and into the main bailey. They'd been instructed to do this by 12 p.m., but had been given no reason why.

As Blake arrived in the large, enclosed space and saw all the other inmates gathering together to keep off some of the rain, he began to understand.

They were all assembling there, including the female

prisoners. There were also extra armed guards he hadn't seen before, looking on menacingly.

Among the crowd he spotted a tall, dark-haired woman moving in his direction. He hadn't been able to talk to Liz Blackwood since his cellmate's lecture. He knew she had some serious issues with it, but he would need her support if his plans succeeded. She reached his group and was about to speak when they all turned towards the noise of the main gate being unbarred and heaved open. As Blake looked, he noticed something new – a long rope barrier stretching the length of the opposite side of the bailey. Into the space behind, a steady collection of umbrella-holding people were moving. They seemed to be of all ages, but under no duress – the guards were all on this side of the rope. Were they new prisoners?

Then this crowd of people started pointing, laughing and taking pictures, their impotent auto-flashes going off against the dark sky, and Blake knew who they were.

Suddenly he felt a gun barrel in his back and heard the words "Move along" in his ear. A guard was spreading out the prisoners so the visitors could get a better view. As Blake turned to him, the guard said, "How are the mighty fallen," and smirked broadly.

Blake moved as instructed, but arranged himself so he could still speak to Liz.

Whispering in her ear so as not to attract the guards' attention, he asked, "Have you been given the death sentence too?"

She turned to him, her dark eyes challenging and yet also desperate. "Aren't we all condemned to death, the minute we are born?"

He knew her religious background and smiled gently at her. "Not really," he said. "I'd say we are given a life and it's up to us to create our own happiness with it."

He felt her hand against his and then she grabbed it, squeezing it as hard as she could. He didn't withdraw. Instead, when she finally relaxed her grip, he said, "I've heard from my wife. This retrospective death sentence is not being applied to other prisons. It's just for us."

"That is a relief," Liz said, but she sounded tense.

Escape was now more urgent than ever. He hadn't planned to meet the Brig but this might be a good opportunity. He excused himself from Liz and gradually squeezed his way towards the soldier. As he drew closer, he saw him. He was moving away from the relative shelter of the others and towards one of the spectators who seemed to be holding up a sign. Blake looked more closely and read the word, '*Sorry*'. For what? Blake wondered. As he peered, he recognised the person holding it. Beneath a shaggy beard and a large-brimmed hat, he made out the features of the ex-prince.

The Brigadier had stopped advancing. Presumably he'd also seen through the disguise. He couldn't move any closer to the Prince without attracting attention. So he was just standing in the rain and grinning at him. Blake couldn't read the expression on the Prince's face, but under his left arm he could see a crutch. Under his left knee, there was no leg.

Blake decided not to interrupt them. Instead, he too stood in the icy rain, feeling the bitter loss of normal, human contact, perhaps forever.

After about fifteen more soaking minutes, the show was brought to an end by a whistle and the guards prodded the prisoners back the way they'd come. Men one way, women the other. Blake looked to see where Liz was, but when he located her it was to see the back of her head dipping through a doorway.

~

Candice Hardwicke stood angry and perplexed in the rain, having just been escorted from the castle prison along with the other spectators. She had stood well hidden by the crowd of umbrellas and watched her father being soaked and pointed at in his red jumpsuit. She still hated him for having been such an unapologetic exploiter of the environment. But she admired him for surviving on the run for so long, and she felt guilty about her part in his capture. He wasn't just being punished now. He was being killed, and she would have to try to stop it. As she waited damply for the government coach taking them back to the station, she strained her brain, thinking of what she could do.

She knew her uncle was not to be trusted. She had found a letter to her from her father hidden in Fabian's study, inside a book he thought she'd never open – Snyder's *Capitalism the Creator*. In it she'd learned that her father had received a note threatening her life, shortly after James had died. He'd never mentioned it before, trying to protect her. Given her uncle's deceit, she guessed he'd had something to do with it, possibly even with James's death. How could he be so evil? She shuddered at the thought of returning to live with him. At least he was spending less and less time at Number 10 and more at the palace. It occurred to her this might present an opportunity. Since she had discovered his betrayal and spying on her correspondence, she had been spying on him. With the help of a camera phone hidden on his bookshelves, she now knew his computer password. Next time he was out for the day, she would return early from school with a fake stomach ache and go through his email. Perhaps she could learn more about his plans for her father and disrupt them. Perhaps she could use his account to impersonate him and have her father released, or something. She knew it would be dangerous and unlikely to succeed, but if she didn't do something soon, he would die.

These thoughts galvanised her spirits and made her eager to get home. The more she thought about it, the more ideas she had. Is this what it was like to be an adult, planning all the time, taking risks all the time? School hadn't prepared her for this. Who could she turn to for advice? Someone who'd help her, stop her from doing something stupid, whom she could confide in? The only person who sprang to mind was Lucinda. She would try to meet her. Other communication was not safe. She knew Lucinda was worried about her own father – not in prison yet, but out on bail, awaiting trial for Carbon Crime. They could work together. And she could ask Lucinda if she'd heard anything about the youth rallies at their old Green Shoots meetings. She'd heard about them at her own local group as an exciting chance to meet others later in the year. When she'd asked her uncle about it, he'd been evasive.

12

It was a dull February afternoon, but Dalton still enjoyed the fresh air and the change of scene as he was led from the prison van, across a car park, and finally into the town hall which had been hastily converted into an appeal courtroom.

He looked around and saw two hundred raised seats packed with people. Were they well-wishers or ill-wishers? He couldn't tell. At the other end of the stage was a long bench. At a table to one side was his lawyer and ex-pupil Roger Newton, who stood up as he was led to a chair in the centre of the floor, and who looked worried. Dalton smiled at him for reassurance.

As he waited, Dalton slid the irritating handcuffs up and down his wrists. This appeal took away vital time from finishing the PPOG. He was just beginning to edit the final draft, but it was taking much longer than he'd expected thanks to all the prison work. Fortunately, it wasn't long before three judges appeared and processed towards the bench. One was fat, one thin and one short, but in their wigs they looked much the same. Once they were seated everyone else sat down too.

The fat judge invited Roger to explain his grounds for appeal.

"My Lords," Roger began, "we appeal on the grounds of protecting the public interest. Professor MacDermot's writings on climate change are not in fact a danger to the public, but a help. They contrast with prevailing wisdom, thus allowing that wisdom to be seen clearly and sharply in its proper light. Without such opposing opinions, the public might think that climate change was merely dogma and therefore take it less seriously. By allowing opposing views, the case for climate change can be strengthened."

This approach surprised and pleased the judges. They put their heads together and conferred quietly. Then the fat one pointed out that if they accepted this line of reasoning, the courts would be swamped with appeals and the government's credibility would not hold. In such uncertain times, that could not be allowed to happen. Besides, they wanted to keep their jobs.

"I'm afraid," the thin judge said, "that in the present climate, the unity of the nation overrules the need for education, therefore we reject your appeal on such grounds."

The audience started talking and Roger rose to his feet.

"But is it possible," the judge continued, trying to help Roger without sounding condescending, "that Professor MacDermot was not of sound mind when he wrote his book? After all, everyone knows climate change to be beyond dispute."

Roger put his head in his hands. He knew this was

the worst possible suggestion the judge could have made.

"May I address the court, so as to prove my sanity?" came a voice from the dock.

"Er, if you think that would help," the thin judge said hesitantly.

"My Lords, one is insane when one cannot perceive the world normally. In considering the evidence for climate change, by which is meant catastrophic, regular weather events caused by human industrial activity, I have perceived a great many things I would challenge any sane person not to perceive. To name a few: the clothes worn in pictures painted in the Middle Ages; the flourishing of plant life under high levels of CO_2; the massive variation in temperature according to latitude; the cold and wet winters of the early 2000s and the ability of mankind to innovate.

"Newspapers would not sell as many copies if their headlines said, '*Everything normal yesterday*'. For the same reason, those organisations and people who want climate change to be true cast as 'unnatural' any weather event or pattern that might cause fear and panic in the population.

"Therefore, it is not I who am insane, but the climate change alarmists who distort their own perception of reality and try to do the same to others."

The judges looked from one to another with serious expressions as if considering Dalton's argument. In fact, none of them had ever read up on the subject of climate change, and despite the facts in Dalton's speech being common knowledge, they had never integrated them. They knew this and the looks they gave each other were their way of brazenly evading it.

Eventually, the short judge spoke.

"Professor MacDermot, it is not for you to pass judgment on such matters. After all, your subject is philosophy, not science. It is up to experts to educate society and for society to decide whether climate change is true. The opinions of millions of people, I hope you would agree, cannot be wrong."

Dalton, who was still on his feet, smiled to himself at their childish mocking of his subject and at their puerile form of reasoning. He said, "My Lords, if someone makes a mistake or invents a lie and others repeat it uncritically, like a congregation singing a hymn from a dusty book without considering the words, then the original untruth is simply amplified, not corrected."

The judges looked at each other again. They knew he had a point, and they knew it was their responsibility to consider it and find out the full truth regarding climate change. But both these courses of action were onerous, and both would bring them into conflict with society and the government. It was much easier to let this arrogant man die than open that can of worms. How dare he make them look like fools! They nodded to each other as they usually did, and then the fat one spoke.

"Dalton MacDermot, your appeal has failed to convince this panel that your original conviction was unsound. Therefore, you are to return to prison and await your original sentence. Case dismissed."

The audience erupted – mostly with cries of "Yes!" but with the occasional indignant "No!"

Roger bowed and shook his head, then went over to his client.

"Sorry."

"It's to be expected. We tried. How is Grace? Have you heard anything?"

"She's arrived safely in Cameroon. She's with her family now."

"Thank you," Dalton said, and breathed a sigh of relief.

#

March was not the most comfortable month for traversing the countryside on foot and living rough, but it was literally now or never, particularly for Dalton. Blake had heard his report of the appeal with bitter resignation. Justice was a thing of the past in Britain now. Blake's own appeal was looking similarly grim. His lawyer, Xavier Atkinson, had been replaced by an ineffective old man from the same firm who was preoccupied with retiring and trout fishing. Xavier had apparently disappeared. The old man blamed Blake, suggesting he'd followed his cue. Good luck to him, Blake thought.

And good luck was what they needed in abundance now. The planning was done, the preparations were made, but many factors were beyond their control. They all knew it: himself, Dalton and the Brig. Despite being urged to join them, Clive had bowed out saying that his state of health would only slow them down.

The basic plan was to reach some old military colleagues of the Brig and hide with them, then to gather an army of dissatisfied soldiers – there were plenty who'd been hung out to dry by politicians over the years – and rebel against the ecoist regime. It was audacious. It was a military coup. It would need public support to succeed, but it was the best plan they had.

As he stepped out of the chapel after hearing another confession – this time from a doctor who continued to use plastic to protect himself and his patients despite the ban – Blake could see his breath. Cold and clear was better than warm and wet, so said the Brig.

They had not sat together in chapel, and as planned, they remained separated at lunch. It was only on their way out of the refectory that they seemed to meet up accidentally.

"All set?" the Brig asked.

Blake and Dalton nodded.

"Right then, let's get this show on the road."

They peeled off in separate directions: Dalton to the kitchens, Blake to the laundry, and the Brig to the building supplies storeroom. These work areas were not patrolled much on the day of rest.

Exactly ten minutes later they reconvened in a corridor that led to the governor's office. As Rebecca had pointed out, it possessed the virtue of a wooden roof. They piled up the scaffold poles, dry clothes and vegetable oil they had collected. Then, with a flint and steel from the kitchen, Blake set the pile alight. Once it was blazing nicely, they ran outside and shouted, "Fire! Fire!"

Quickly the Brig went to hide near the gates to the outer bailey. It wasn't long before they were opened and some guards rushed through carrying buckets. He slipped past them.

Meanwhile, Blake and Dalton had gone to an obscure corner of the castle where the old, dry well stood. There was a solid iron grate protecting it. With several huge heaves they managed to pull it slightly across. Then they took the ropes the Brig had fetched and tied loops in them, before securing them to the grid and dropping them down the well shaft.

As fast as they could they donned the oversized prison guards' jackets and trousers Blake had acquired, pulling them on over their own clothes. Dalton was careful to stow the tablet inside his prison jumpsuit. Then they tied themselves to the two ropes, as the Brig had demonstrated, and lowered themselves slowly down inside the well.

There was a narrow ledge inside to rest their feet on, but they would need to shifting position once in a while to avoid cramp. And they had to hope that the gap at the top of the well didn't show. All they could do now was wait.

The Brig, in the meantime, had climbed the inner wall using another rope then broken through the outer wall in a place he had weakened with faulty mortar during work hours. He was soon sprinting down the hill and into the valley.

It felt good to be out in the open again. He was only carrying some spare clothes tied to his back with a rope, so he made rapid progress. He didn't worry about being seen or leaving a trail. That was part of the plan.

Oh, the joy of stretching his legs properly – the prison didn't provide enough exercise for a man like him – of breathing in the cold, fresh air, tinged with the smells of agriculture. He didn't know what the punishment would be for escape (if he was caught) but since he was already under a death sentence it didn't matter.

After five minutes, he turned to confirm the fire was properly ablaze. Thick clouds of brown smoke were indeed billowing up from the castle. He hoped the governor was feeling toasty. Then, after another twenty minutes or so, he heard a cannon fire. They knew of his escape, he reckoned, and would now set the dogs on him. Well, he had about half an hour head start. That would be enough.

He ran along the south side of the river, along the edges of partly ploughed fields. Twice, he startled some deer.

After about an hour, he came to the bridge Ed had described where a road crossed the river. He hid under it and changed into his alternative, dark grey guard's uniform. Bundling his bright red prison garb into a ball with the rope attached, he waited for a suitable vehicle to come his way. Just as he was getting anxious, a slow-moving farmer's horse and cart approached. There was no one in the back – just some cabbages. As it went over the bridge, he ran up the bank and along behind it, eventually managing to tie the rope attached to his clothes around a chain that was keeping the back of the cart shut. He quickly hid at the side of the road and watched with pride as the 'drag' took his scent steadily away. As far as he could tell, the farmer hadn't seen him. When he'd turned a corner, the Brig went back to the river and began the fun task of wading upstream, back the way he had come.

It was freezing cold, and although it slowed him down, the rough wool of the uniform did help. It was harsh, but he'd done much worse things to his body during his career. Every now and again he reached up and grabbed an overhanging branch, hauling himself out of the water for some respite. Then, after a minute, he went back in. At times he had to swim a little, but for the most part it was shallow enough to walk, just as Ed had suggested.

It didn't seem long before the inevitable came. Luckily, the wind was blowing towards him so he had plenty of warning. The dogs and their masters were barking their way along the south bank in his direction. He had to judge the right point to hide. Too shallow and they might come into the water, in case he'd used it as a crossing. Too deep and he wouldn't be able to last long enough until they'd passed. Then the sound of his pursuers was too close, and he had to choose his spot. Under the south bank, in the shelter of a bush that was slipping down, he crouched with the water up to his chest. It was the best place he could find.

The barking and whining drew closer. He could hear it approaching above his head. Then he could hear the dogs panting and their handlers directing them. Suddenly there was a splash, as one of the dogs went in – but it was downstream, and after letting it have a sniff, its handler pulled it back up the bank.

His fingers and feet were already numb. But as long as he could move his arms and legs, he would be fine.

It took five interminable minutes for the whole party of dogs and men to pass, but then he allowed himself to breathe normally and began wading slowly further upstream, to where he could climb out of the river. There was no sound of danger, just the dogs moving away in the distance. He smiled to himself as he eased himself onto the bank and stood, dripping. He could still do it, even at his age. He congratulated himself again on not becoming a mere desk officer.

~

By nightfall Blake's and Dalton's arms and legs were almost stiff beyond endurance, stifled of blood flow by the ropes holding them up.

Then, as the temperature was descending along with the darkness, they heard a tap on the metal grating. They tensed, trying not to breathe. Then came the rest of the taps they were expecting: SOS in morse. It had to be Ed. They raised their faces towards the moonlight streaming into the top of the well and saw his silhouette.

"All right, then?" Ed whispered.

"Just cramped," Blake said, keeping his voice low to stop it echoing.

"I'll help you up, but you'll have to climb too," Ed said.

The first rope he found was Dalton's. Fortunately, Ed was still a strong man and Dalton's time in the forest and prison had only made him lighter. With huge but largely silent efforts on the part of both men, Dalton was hauled over the lip of the well, where he rested for a moment, panting. Then, once he was over, the two of them pulled Blake up.

"Quick, get this down you," Ed said, producing a hipflask from inside his uniform. They swigged it gratefully then shook out their limbs, trying to warm up and regain some control. Then, stiffly but as normally as possible, they marched away from the well and into the adjoining courtyard. It was lit with burning torches rather than floodlights, and for once Blake was glad of an ecoist measure.

As they came to an inner gate, Ed put his face to the barred window cut into the door and was let through. He then spoke urgently to the guard about the day's events without giving him a chance to close the door. Dalton and Blake slipped through unnoticed.

"They think you've already escaped," Ed said as they walked steadily across the bailey.

Forty yards from the outer gate, Dalton and Blake split off and continued slowly in the shadow of the wall. Ed approached the guardhouse at a run.

A guard stepped out. "Where have you been? Jim had to go back on fire duty. I've been on my own since then."

"I'm so sorry, it took ages," Ed said breathing hard.

"What's wrong with you, mate?" the guard said. "Is it that bloody porridge bunging you up?"

"Might be," Ed said. "If only we could still buy prunes."

"Anyway, it's your turn for a break now. How about bringing back a couple of mugs of tea?"

"You know we're not supposed to leave just one duty, especially after today's escape."

"It's a bit late for that, isn't it?" Ed said. "Besides, when you get back we can add some brandy if you like." He showed him his hipflask.

"Good plan," the guard said, and after checking his commanding officer wasn't anywhere to be seen, he sauntered off.

After a few moments, Blake and Dalton emerged from the shadows. Ed ushered them quickly into the guardhouse and gave them a map and compass he had hidden there. Then he unlocked the door to the other side.

"Good luck," he said.

"Thanks," Blake said.

"You've not put yourself in any danger, I trust?"

Dalton asked.

"Don't worry about me. I'll be fine. Now, get out of here and do your worst."

They shook hands firmly and then the two guard-convicts strode off into the night. In their uniforms they had nothing to fear from onlookers, and they marched smartly down the hill and through the village at its foot. As they reached its end and started to rely on the moon and starlight, they slipped off the road and clambered through some bushes to arrive under the bridge over the river.

The Brig was already there.

"What kept you?" he asked, half-jokingly.

"A bit of cramp," Blake said.

"Nothing a good walk won't cure," Dalton said wryly.

"You look a bit wet, though."

"I wouldn't say no to a change of clothes, I'll admit to that."

"Well, that's easily solved," Blake said, taking off his guard's clothes and giving them to the Brig.

The old soldier peeled off his wet clothes and hid them, then donned the warm, grey outfit.

"If anyone sees me," Blake said, in his red jumpsuit now, "you can always pretend to be my escort."

"Good thinking," Dalton said. "Shall we go?"

They left the protection of the bridge, clambered back onto the road, and began walking the empty country miles.

They saw no cars, but after five miles they encountered what passed for a main road and turned west on it, as Rebecca had suggested.

When the occasional vehicle approached, they

simply marched boldly on, taking the chance that anyone out at that hour was probably also in trouble with the law and would speed past them. There was the slim possibility of a police car seeing them, but they knew it was unlikely given the ecoist insistence on reducing resource usage of all kinds. Besides, few people signed up for the police these days. There was genuine confusion about their role. Were the police meant to protect the people, or just follow politicians' orders?

Marching on in the crisp, starlit air was invigorating to them all, the lack of visibility adding an edge of excitement. They chatted briefly, but generally kept quiet, just in case nearby cottagers poked their heads out.

After another seven miles they reached the petrol station. It was closed, but at 3 a.m. it was what they'd expected. According to Rebecca, who had been there recently to fill up the governor's car, there was a delivery due at about six. This was the most dangerous time for their plan, but all they could do was wait.

As they sat on a decaying picnic bench tucked behind the station, probably used by its staff, they talked in low voices.

"Why is it," the Brig mused, "that people like the governor have large, petrol-guzzling cars, yet at the same time condemn anyone else who has one as 'selfish and greedy'?"

Dalton sighed. "To identify a contradiction requires an act of integration, a practice that is not widely taught or admired these days."

"What?"

"Seeing if your ideas are consistent with each other

and with your behaviour."

"Surely that's what you lot at universities do, isn't it?"

"Sadly not for some time. While I try to encourage it, my colleagues generally consider such operations of the mind unhelpful. If you accuse someone of supporting a contradiction, your criticism is condemned as selfish, and if your skin is white, racist."

"That's nonsense," the Brig snorted. "It depends on the person. I've seen racism and prejudice in people of all colours. Your colleagues should visit the Middle East."

"Again, I'm sorry to disillusion you, but basing one's ideas on actual evidence gathered from looking at the world is not considered necessary or practical."

"So how do they decide who's right if they have a disagreement, your so-called professors?"

"Whoever has the most followers."

"Jesus!"

"Precisely," Dalton said, smiling sadly.

They talked and waited until the sky had lightened slightly and 6 a.m. approached. Then, as expected, an employee turned up on his bicycle and began to unlock. Fifteen minutes later, they heard the rumbling of a truck and the grinding of gears as an ancient tanker entered from the road and rolled slowly to the back of the forecourt.

Again they waited, as the grey-haired and grizzled driver unloaded the fuel and liaised with the employee. It took a good half an hour's more patience until the process was complete.

Just as the man had finished stowing the hoses and was closing off the various valves, they climbed into his cab to await him.

He got the shock of his life when he was halfway up to his seat and saw them opposite.

"Who the—"

The Brig pulled him all the way in and Blake leaned round to close the door.

"If you wouldn't mind, we'd like you to drive off as normal and we'll explain later," Dalton said.

The driver was confused by the mixture of brute force and politeness. They couldn't be after the fuel. He'd just emptied it. Afraid but also curious he fired up the engine and drove off.

"What's all this about?" he asked. "You know interfering with carbon-based product distribution is a serious offence?"

"As are so many things these days," Dalton said, "but you see, we've caused so much offence already it would be hard to care about any more." He showed the driver his prison outfit.

"Ah, I see," said the driver. "You're carbon criminals then, are you?"

"Something like that," Dalton said. "We were wondering if you'd be kind enough to drop us off a few miles from your depot. About here," and he pointed to a spot on the map.

"That shouldn't be a problem. But what's in it for me?"

"I admire your attitude, sir," Dalton said, looking at him appraisingly. "Were you, perhaps involved in the drivers' fuel strike of 2000?"

"Indeed I was," the man said proudly. "That put the wind up 'em."

"It certainly did," Dalton said. "I take it you're not a

fan of government interference then?"

"I think it just makes things worse. Take this Carbon Crime Law, …"

As with many drivers, he relished some good conversation, and they paid their way in that form for the next three hours.

After the driver had let them out and driven off with a wave, they consulted the map and compass, and being mid-morning, trudged off across some fields to avoid the roads.

The ground was frost-hard and awkward to walk over, but they each found a suitable branch to act as a staff. Going through woods when they could and skirting hedges when they couldn't, after another six miles that seemed like twelve they emerged, tired and hungry but confident, on a road. It was bordered by a high, chain-link fence with barbed wire on the top.

"That'll be the barracks," the Brig said.

"Here goes," Blake said, and they walked, more speedily than before, until they reached the main gate. A young soldier was in the sentry booth. He stepped out holding a submachine gun, frowning.

"What do you want?" he asked the older men, his courage no doubt bolstered by his weapon.

The Brig stepped forward. "We'd like to see Major General Macleod, if you please."

"I'm afraid he's been removed from his post, sir."

As the Brig looked stunned, the soldier said, "He's no longer here, sir." After an awkward pause he spoke again. "What are your names and what's your business?"

Blake was already beginning to feel uneasy when he noticed a silver oak tree shining from the young man's lapel.

The Brig said, "Well, it was him we wanted to see. If he's not here, we'll just be on our way."

"Hold on a minute," said the soldier, pointing at Blake. "Why are you dressed in a prison outfit?"

"We're escorting him to a special meeting with the Major General, and as he's not here, there's no point us staying."

They turned and started walking back away from the gate.

Then they heard the clicking metal of a gun being cocked.

"Stop. I need to check this out. I can't see how you could make an appointment with a man who's been missing for a month."

They started running, but managed only a few strides before they heard bullets over their heads. The soldier's field of view was too clear. They had no weapons. Next time, he would no doubt shoot lower.

They stopped and turned around, their hands raised in the air.

~

After a brief interrogation, as they were being driven back to Westingham by some policemen, Blake realised their attempt to escape had been naive. Ecoism was too embedded in the culture. It had too many supporters. They stood perhaps a 50/50 chance of meeting with sympathy rather than betrayal when they came across someone.

But what if the odds became less than 50/50? What if ecoism continued to grow, and those who disobeyed or questioned it continued to be imprisoned or to hide themselves? Had that been the Major General's fate?

What would be left of the country?

He could only see one way forward. Leaning over to whisper in Dalton's ear, he said, "You must stop the tablet from being taken. You must finish your book."

Dalton nodded, clasped his chest tighter, and looked worried. The Brig too, alert to the actions of his friends, understood the situation.

After being bounced around in a metal box for several hours, they were glad when the van came to a final halt and they emerged into the twilight and the familiar profile of Westingham Castle.

The police driver and his sidekick escorted them in handcuffs to the prison gate and knocked loudly on the door. After some eyes peered through, two bodies emerged to take charge of the prisoners. One of them was Ed.

"I heard you were coming and managed to change my shift," he said in a low voice as he manhandled them back through the door. Dalton gave him the broadest of smiles, such that the other guard could not see.

#

The prison didn't have enough space for solitary confinement so they were put on half-rations as punishment for escape, but still made to work. As a reward for their courage, several other prisoners happily donated part of their own meagre portions so that the escapees didn't suffer too much.

Somehow the story of the escape made it into the papers. It cheered the prisoners up to know that the public were aware of their situation.

In the evenings and on Sundays, the Professor worked feverishly at the tablet, stopping only to hand it to Blake for further editing whilst he carried on writing notes on paper that Ed had smuggled in. Blake made sure he remembered to eat.

~

Towards the end of April, Dalton started getting up early and working on PPOG before breakfast as well. Blake knew why. The end of the book was near, but so was the date of Dalton's execution.

Late one evening Blake watched from his bed as Dalton sat on his, bent double over the tablet, his eyes blinking with the strain of focusing, his jaw clenched in a manner that brooked no interruption. Blake had never seen anyone work so hard. The physical labour of wall-building seemed easy by comparison. Eventually, the older man's hands began to shake and he leant back against the wall, putting the tablet carefully aside.

"A good session?" asked Blake.

Dalton nodded, then in a weary voice said, "We're almost there."

~

On May 1st, after an interminably rainy Sunday afternoon, Dalton handed the tablet to Blake, stood up, stretched and smiled broadly. "I've finished," he said.

Blake had never seen him, or anyone look so happy. Dalton's face wore the look of joy carried by a child getting just what they wanted for Christmas and the look of triumph borne by an Olympic athlete on the gold medal platform.

"Let's celebrate," said Dalton and he produced from behind a loose stone in the wall, a miniature hip-flask.

"Ed?" asked Blake. Dalton nodded.

"Here's to the future," said Dalton brightly, "your

future," and he drank from the flask before handing it to his cellmate.

Blake took it, but didn't know what to say, nor if he did, how to get the words passed the lump in his throat, so he simply drank. It was whisky, the aromas of heather and leather and associations with bygone times hit his senses as hard as the burning in his mouth and throat. Eventually he handed it back to Dalton.

"We tried," was all he could say.

"To escape, you mean?" Blake nodded. "We succeeded," said Dalton. "We just happened to get recaptured. Nothing we did was wrong, or inadequate or a failure. We planned, we acted, we achieved what we expected. That's all life is. That's all you can ask of yourself. If others interfere with your plans, that's their action not yours. What you achieve by your actions is yours. What they achieve by theirs is theirs. If you create a great value, whether it's a successful company," he broke off for a moment, "or a life, the creation is yours and it is a success and reward for your virtue. If someone takes a value from you by force, you are not to blame, and they are in your debt. Without your creation they would have nothing to take. They would be impotent.

"Evil has no real power besides what it takes by force, and that cannot last if people refuse to keep creating values to be stolen. Ultimately, although it appears that evil has all the strength and will always win, it is nothing and it has nothing without its victims. They are the creators. They make life possible. They are the ones you must reach with my book." He smiled, took a swig from the flask and offered it back to Blake.

Blake said, "You finish it."

Dalton did so, licking his lips. "And you must finish our work."

"How?" asked Blake desperately. "We're all being executed in August."

"Evil has no real power. There is no reason to surrender to it. Instead, use your mind. It's the most powerful thing on the planet."

13

Dalton lay on his thin prison mattress and watched the walls of his isolated room come into existence as the dawn crept in. He had not slept. He had been going over the episodes of his life.

He was now sixty-six. Too young to die by modern medicine's standards, but then that was not today's standard. However, he could not complain. He'd had a good life. A great life, actually, smiling to himself as he recalled it.

It was funny what memories had flown in unbidden to light up his mind during the hours of darkness.

Roger, his greatest pupil and protégé – until Blake – who had become one of the youngest people ever to be called to the Bar now headed up a highly sought-after firm in Middle Temple. Dalton liked to think it was his own arguments against determinism that had persuaded the young man to ignore the cultural focus on his skin colour and fight for actual justice for all.

The Proper Purpose of Government had been a painstaking process of early days and late nights for many years, as he fitted his magnum opus around his teaching and other commitments. The ideas had come to him at all hours and occasions, and he had struggled to record them, organise them and – hardest of all – integrate them into a work that was new, clear, compelling and accessible to laymen. He knew he had done his very best. And he knew that it was good. He was certain that somehow it would survive and have its deserved impact upon the world. But by God, it had been hard work. He remembered one day sitting in their garden, struggling for a clear example to show the connection between values and trade, when he saw a red admiral on the verbena against the yellow fence. He had pointed it out to Grace, who had planted it.

She had been an athlete, a professional sprinter, before they'd met, and had topped many a podium in her youth, including an Olympic one. Then she had become a coach and teacher at a centre for sports science. They had met as speakers at a literature festival and made each other laugh from the first. After their first date, they never looked back. They had married after just over a year and spent as much time together as they could, interlacing their relationship with their careers. Whenever they had saved enough money, they treated themselves to lavish trips abroad. His favourites had been to Florence and Antigua. Wandering the art-filled city together by day and indulging in Italian food by night had enriched their lives forever. Dancing in the moonlight on a beach of seashells had brought them even close together. And then, on a trip to Africa, she had contracted cerebral malaria and suffered ever since. But that was in the past. They had done what they had done and been to each other what they had been. And he had been superbly happy, he knew.

He was roused from his reveries by the sound of steps growing gradually louder.

A heavy key undid the cell-door lock and two guards came in. Without words they waited for him to stand and then escorted him as planned along the narrow, stone passages to the door of another room, which one of them unlocked and swung open.

"I wanted to see my recent home one more time," Dalton explained simply and smiled at Blake, who looked haggard and dishevelled. From beneath his bloodshot eyes, Blake tried to smile back.

"Come on then, both of you," one of the guards said nervously. Dalton wondered if he was worried about being on time, or about the execution.

Blake stood up and they were marched between the guards down the stairs and into the courtyard. Here the whole prison population, inmates and guards, had been gathered in the steady, late spring drizzle to witness the proceedings.

In the centre of the courtyard was the recently erected scaffold. It was a hastily made wooden affair, as if the builder had been keen to finish his task.

Away to one side, but still with a good view, was an awning-covered platform sheltering a few dignitaries, including Fabian Hardwicke, and a microphone on a stand.

Several tall and narrow wooden towers had been built and were dotted around the courtyard, giving the GBMC cameras on top an excellent view. They were the only television company still licensed to operate. Dalton was sure the new Minister for Information was enjoying that, yet today Manny Schweizer seemed to be absent. Why, when he could witness his greatest eradication of free speech so far? Dalton cared no more about him than about something unpleasant stuck to his shoe, so he gave the man no more thought.

Soon the brief hiatus was over, and he was led away from Blake and onto the scaffold. He could see the governor was watching carefully from his sheltered position. Protected from the rain, but not from the consequences of his actions, thought Dalton. Suddenly, he felt someone grab his arms. The executioner tied them behind his back. They seemed secure. The governor nodded to Fabian, who coughed into the microphone, satisfying himself that it worked. Then he began to speak.

"Today marks a return to one of the greatest traditions of this country – justice. For those that obey the law, the opportunities for success are unlimited. For those that disobey it, the ultimate penalty is once again available.

"May I remind you that Dalton MacDermot has been found guilty of Climate Change Denial, and therefore is complicit in the wanton destruction of our planet. Today he is only receiving that which he deserves.

"He, and all of you, must recognise the logic and fairness of our new ecoist regime. Its principles infiltrate every area of your lives for the good of mankind, forever. Even today's method of execution has been carefully chosen to avoid using nasty chemicals or wasting precious electricity."

Yes, its primitiveness did mirror the barbaric nature of the ecoists' minds, Dalton thought ruefully.

"I hope that today's ceremony will remind you, and the country, of the power and fairness of my leadership. And I remind the other prisoners here today that most of them also face a sentence of death."

He smiled slightly and looked at them. Then he turned to the platform and said through gritted teeth, "Dalton MacDermot, do you have any last words?"

Dalton's grey hair was being blown gently by the wind despite the dampness of the rain. He thought for a moment, then opened his mouth to speak.

"I am innocent," he said loudly, keeping his voice as deep and steady as he could and feeling proud of the result. "As you know, it is egoism that I advocate, and to those of you left behind I say, remember who and what you live for. Not anonymous future inhabitants, or rocks, trees and plants. These will not save you now. You may well value such things, but it is you yourself that must be valued and preserved above all other things, for without you, there is no one to give them value.

"Any action against your life is the bad. Any action that promotes it, in the long term, is the good. This is a fact of nature and I urge you to embrace it."

He paused and noticed Fabian's rigid grimace and his clenching and unclenching hands. He realised yet again how powerless the evil was – without its victims, it was nothing. He stared at the President, making him wait, smiling slightly. He would not give permission for his own execution. Thirty seconds' silence elapsed. Eventually, growing puce with frustration, Fabian nodded to the executioner, who slipped the heavy rope over Dalton's head and pulled it tight, then stepped away.

Fabian raised his arm like a Roman emperor at the games, holding his thumb level.

How strange it was that he, Dalton, who had so much to offer the world, instead of being received gratefully, was being snuffed out. Then he reminded himself that the world of Fabian Hardwicke did not itself want to live, hence it wanted him to die.

He thought of his book. He thought of Grace. He smiled. He thought no more.

#

As Dalton's legs disappeared through a trapdoor, Blake looked away and noticed many others doing the same. Among them were two guards who were throwing up. He turned back to look at Fabian. He was smiling broadly, relief spreading across his face. Then their eyes met, and Blake hardly recognised the face that was partly his. He was like some kind of abominable monster, unthinking, unfeeling, ready to perform any deed so long as it achieved his goal of saving the planet. Rage began to fill him and he pushed his way towards the podium, but was stopped by a guard with a gun.

"I want to see my brother," he said firmly. The guard ignored him.

"Fabian, you bastard," he shouted over the man's shoulder. His brother must have heard him, because moments later a uniformed man with a birthmark came down from the platform and gestured with his gun, grunting, "This way."

He was directed from behind, sometimes with the barrel of the gun, down some steps, along a damp stone passage, and into a room he had never seen before. The man followed him in. There was a wooden baton in a corner.

They waited while Blake's pulse raced up and down,

rehearsing in his mind what he was going to say.

Finally, the door opened and Fabian walked in, saw the man with the gun stand to attention, and closed the door behind him.

"I'm glad we've got time for this little interview, Blake," Fabian said. "There are some things I've been wanting to let you know."

"Where's Candice?"

Fabian looked surprised. "She's at Number 10, as far as I know. Probably watching the telly like the rest of the country."

"You bastard," Blake said, clenching his fists. "You've just killed…" He struggled for the right words. "…one of my best friends, and one of the greatest minds in this country."

"It wasn't me," Fabian said. "He was killed by his own beliefs. I'm just helping nature defend herself. Much as I was trying to do when your son's car veered off the road."

"You what?" Blake shouted, the sound bouncing off the thick, deadening walls.

"It was you we were trying to stop that night, on the way to the BCF meeting."

Blake looked at the birthmarked man, who simply smirked.

Fabian continued, "We couldn't let that meeting go ahead. It would have put doubt in people's minds. It might have led to our green targets not being met. We don't have time for recalcitrants or debate." He was getting worked up himself now. "The science is settled. If we don't act now, the planet will be ruined. There will be nothing left."

Blake launched himself at his brother, trying to get

his hands around Fabian's neck. But the other man was ready. He brought the baton down on Blake's head repeatedly, until the pain and his blurred vision made him stop. From a sitting position on the floor, once he could focus again, Blake stared at his brother. "You would kill your own nephew, who had done nothing wrong, just for your absurd beliefs?"

"And he won't be the last," Fabian spat back at him. "We have a mission, and we intend to carry it out."

He opened the door and left the room. The other man gave Blake a kick and then followed.

#

That night, as he lay with a still-throbbing head and bruised ribs on the remaining bed in his room, Blake heard the key turn in the lock. Nothing worse could happen today, he said to himself, and didn't even bother to brace.

It was Ed Quinton.

"I never thought I'd see that in this country," he said. "Not for anything other than psychopaths or terrorists. We can't let this go any further."

"But what can we do to stop it? How many other people in this country feel like you?"

"I don't know. But I do know that a good number of the guards agree with me. Maybe a dozen or more."

"That's a help, but it's just not enough."

"Well, actually, it might be. There's been a change of policy recently. They clearly don't trust very many people, including us. From next week, they're cutting the ammunition allowance. Most of our guns will have blanks, not real bullets. We can't hide any real ones. The ammo is counted in and out each day."

PART THREE: INNOCENCE

14

The heat from the low evening sun lingered in the stone of the city, though the people standing around the burned-out cars in Trafalgar Square did not seem to be enjoying it. From Manny's backseat viewpoint they seemed quiet and subdued, much as he did. But he could not spend a quiet Sunday evening at home – he had been summoned.

He dragged himself out of the comfortable car and up the stone steps of Buckingham Palace, then with a somnambulist's certainty walked past the guards and along the corridors to the Throne Room.

Just outside he was awakened – by singing. Putting his ear to the door, he could hear a light accompaniment on a harpsichord and some snatches of words:

"…a future strong and true
We'll sacrifice… the few
…so emerge a better one
When… our work is done."

The harpsichord stopped but the singing continued. Was that Fabian singing? He looked up at the stone-faced guard who silently opened the door for him.

Manny slipped in to witness the President waltzing with himself as he sang and moved around the room, holding a sheet of paper. The guards inside looked on with po-faces.

Eventually, Fabian noticed Manny, and finished the verse he was on while looking directly at his old friend:

"The noble shall extol our creed
And from this sultry earth be freed."

"Well, Manny," Fabian said, slightly out of breath. "It's good to see you. I thought you'd like to come over and celebrate." Fabian moved to pour a couple of drinks from the decanter on top of the harpsichord.

"Anything in particular?" Manny asked.

Fabian chuckled nervously. "Ah, you can still make me laugh. That's one of the many reasons I still like you so much. I'm talking about the demise of our favourite enemy, of course. Here," and he handed his friend a glass of whisky.

Manny took it and recalled that morning, after he'd watched the execution on live television. He had organised the coverage personally at Fabian's behest. Then he'd spent an hour in the bathroom retching, but had been unable to actually be sick. Now the thought of whisky inflaming his tired oesophagus kept his hand at a distance.

"Cheers," Fabian said, raising his glass.

Manny did the same, chinking their cut-crystal glasses. But he only pretended to drink. The aroma of the thirty-five-year-old malt was normally something he would savour. But tonight it repelled him.

"Guards," Fabian called, "you may leave."

After they'd gone, he turned to Manny with a broad

smile.

"Your coverage of the event, both the GBMC and the *National Voice*, was... exquisite."

"Thanks," Manny said quietly.

His friend didn't seem to notice his mood.

Fabian moved off to stand looking at the golden, sunlit garden through the large French doors.

"Beautiful, isn't it?"

Manny took the hint and moved to stand next to him. "Yes. Very."

"It's a shame, but there's only so much of it, isn't there?"

"Yes, of course." Manny was clueless as to what he was driving at.

"So many people will never get the chance to see it, will they?"

"No, I suppose not. But you could open the grounds more often to the public."

Fabian looked at him. "That's not what I mean." He took a deep breath and continued. "You know how we've both been environmentalists since the early nineties, when we were laughed at more often than not? Then, after constant campaigning, people came round to our way of thinking, until eventually it became the status quo? From children through to pensioners, they all agree on how important the environment is. That's why my party was voted in."

Manny grunted his affirmation, giving his friend a chance to breathe.

"Well, now we're in a position to really put our ideas into action."

"You can do almost anything," Manny said without thinking.

"Exactly," Fabian continued. "You remember what drove us in those early days, what we vowed to do?"

"To save the world?" Manny asked hesitantly.

"Yes, and now we can do it. I have a plan for drastically reducing the population permanently, for putting an end to man's rape of the planet." Fabian turned to Manny with a smile that showed both excitement and fear.

Manny knew that he should say something like, "That's great news." But even with his expert composition of headlines, all he could say was, "Do tell."

Fabian was on a roll, oblivious to Manny's lack of enthusiasm. "I plan to hold a dozen large-scale Green Shoots rallies across the whole country, simultaneously. There will be stalls giving away eco-friendly products, not charging for them. There will be music and speeches, all focused on our movement. But the climax will be a speech by me, broadcast simultaneously at all venues, followed by the premiere of the new National Anthem, which you just heard. And then…"

Fabian turned to look at Manny, who could see a twitch under his friend's right eye.

He continued. "Near the end of the song, at the third chorus, when they really know it and can sing it with real vigour, we release the smallpox virus into the air-conditioning systems at each venue."

Manny was flabbergasted. "Did you say smallpox?"

"Yes, I know it's been eradicated, but there are still labs and military establishments that have some. As head of the armed services, I can access them very easily."

"How dangerous is it?" Manny's hands had gone

cold and clammy.

"I'm told there is one strain which is 95 per cent effective. Of course, it's only 50 per cent if it's treated, but that's still a good number, wouldn't you say?"

Manny nodded automatically.

"And of course, it leaves terrible scars on those that do survive, which will hopefully cut down their mating opportunities."

"Don't people get vaccinated for it anymore?"

"Fortunately not. That would rather ruin things. The virus must be allowed to do its work. To allow all those young people to take the path of virtue, to help save the planet and society, to be noble, to make the ultimate sacrifice for their country and for the world."

Fabian smiled, and Manny wondered what kind of man could find mass murder enjoyable. But then he wondered what kind of men enjoy such company. He saw a reflection of his head in the window – an old, hairless ghost with sunken eyes – and he knew the answer.

Fabian stared at him silently and Manny knew he was waiting for an opinion, but his throat seemed blocked. He wanted to scream but his body wouldn't let him. Perhaps out of fear – how would Fabian react to disloyalty? But perhaps out of integrity – because he agreed with all the underlying ideas and had done for decades.

Eventually, he croaked out, "It's brilliant."

"Thank you. Of course, only a small number of people must know about this. You and the Inner Circle. They will be in charge of releasing the virus at the right time. All with masks on, obviously. What I need you to do is promote the rallies in editorials and on television and radio. People need to feel that the idea is not coming directly from the government. They've been lied to so often over the years that they won't trust what it says. Not without corroboration. You can do that for us. And also, you must continue to emphasise the damage men are doing to the planet. I'm sure you have plenty of material for that."

Acting on autopilot, Manny cleared his throat. "Yes, I'd be delighted to help."

"Good," the President said. "I'll call you tomorrow and we can start going over the details." He paused, then put out his hand. "Thanks for coming over. It's good to have someone I can really trust." He looked Manny in the eye, and Manny could see a small reflection of himself in them. He shook the proffered hand.

"Of course. Any time."

Minutes later, having run from the palace, he was breathing the fresher air of Pall Mall.

Hours later, long past midnight, he was still sitting hidden by the dark in his garden, the cool breeze on his moist face, unable to move, thinking about his daughter Laura – a Green Shoot – and what he had done.

#

Blake awoke from a troubled night's sleep.

It had been a week since Dalton's death and he still automatically looked over to his bed, expecting him to be there. When he remembered why it was empty, his veins filled with blood and his jaw clenched. Then he thought of Fabian's killing of James and his whole body tensed. He could not explode into action now, he told himself, but soon.

He had not been idle. The tablet with its completed manuscript was hidden more safely in his cell, in a plastic bag in a gap between two walls, which he had found by removing a loose stone. Importantly, he had managed to copy the electronic book onto a memory stick provided by Ed, who had taken it home for safekeeping. The question now was how to get the PPOG published and read by enough people to make a difference. Ed wouldn't be able to do it on his own, certainly not without risking his life. Blake couldn't do it alone either, and clearly not from within a prison. But he knew some highly talented people who ought to be easy to motivate. That was the next question: how to set them free.

He heard the unlocking of his door and realised he must have been thinking for some time.

Ed poked his head in and greeted him.

"Is the governor going to be at confession today?" Blake asked.

"Not likely. He's visiting Bedford Prison to help them set up the hangings." He swallowed hard and Blake could see his jaw clench.

"Good," Blake said. "Who's on guard in the chapel today?"

"Me and some new bloke. I don't know much about him, except he's quite young."

Blake considered his options. "I want to change the format a little. Are you okay with that?"

"As long as the governor wouldn't approve."

Blake grinned. "I can guarantee that."

They left the cell – Ed to unlock more, Blake to eat some breakfast. He took a pen and paper with him.

In the canteen, he ate toast with one hand and made

notes with the other. Slurping his tea, he looked up at the pale faces of his fellow prisoners. This might colour their cheeks, he thought, and carried on writing. Before he knew it, the tannoy sounded and they all rose and left.

The sun was shining through the chapel windows as he went in. It cast a kaleidoscope across the stone effigy of a reposing knight.

The governor normally acted as MC at confession, but in his absence they would sit quietly, contemplating their 'eco-sins', unless someone volunteered. Today Blake waited a few moments, then trod the flagstones and tomb lids up to the front. On the step he faced the prisoners and, holding his notes, began his speech.

"It is a week now since our friend and mentor, Dalton MacDermot, was sacrificed in front of us, and I believe it is high time he was given a eulogy."

A general murmur of approval echoed off the stone walls.

"Dalton was a professor of philosophy who spent his life in pursuit of the truth, by using logic. His unremitting approach led to many enemies and a few friends. I count myself lucky to have been one of the latter, and to have this opportunity to celebrate his life and reveal the truth about his death.

"He was born in Belfast, to a schoolteacher and a chemist. At school he excelled at history and could name all the Kings and Queens of England and Scotland, all the Roman Emperors and all the US Presidents, with their dates, by the age of ten. However, unlike most people, he could also summarise what they did.

"At Oxford University, where he read philosophy and history, his talent really flourished.

"Despite being surrounded by communist professors and living in a culture dominated by militant unions and leftist ideas, he stood up for the rational, this-worldly approach of Aristotle and rejected the conventional view of man as a hopeless neurotic, unable to survive outside the group, and doomed to sacrifice himself for their sake.

"He persevered in his academic career, winning prizes for his teaching, students for his cause, and several fellowships. He also published a number of books, some for academics and some for the general public. Reading one of those is how I began to know and admire him.

"It was also how he met his wife, Grace. They were both promoting their books at a literature festival. Hers on her career as an athlete, his on the philosophical value of achievement through sport. They attended each other's talks and subsequent book-signings, then stayed up until dawn. In a year, they were married.

"However, while his ideas led to the greatest joy in his life, they also led to him collecting many adversaries. He identified the evil nature of ecoism long before it took over from socialism as the Left's weapon of mass destruction, and received many attacks both in writing and in person.

"Yet despite these, and attempts to expel him from academia and destroy his career, he refused to be silenced and continued writing and teaching his views of the truth. It was this intransigent commitment to his right to free speech that eventually gave his enemies the chance to arrest him, and ultimately to execute him.

His only crime was speaking his mind.

"Like him, you are not in prison for committing a real crime like murder, but a bogus one – Carbon Crime, the crime of wanting a better life. And you specifically have been chosen as the first victims because, like Dalton, you have stood against ecoist ideas, and refused to cooperate with them one way or another. You are also prominent enough to be made a fearful example of. If you are executed, millions of others will fear to speak out against this regime and give Fabian and his cohorts what they crave – control. Believe me, they will stop at nothing to gain it. Fabian recently confessed to me that he'd arranged for the murder of my son in a car accident."

The audience started talking. Blake let them. Then he said, "To stop them will be no easy task, but I believe it can be done if we treat it as a battle of ideas. Dalton's greatest legacy is that he has given me the ability to understand how the ecoists' minds work, and therefore how to defeat them.

"Now, I'm not going soft, but I believe the key to an ecoist's personality and actions is that they are desperately unhappy. And they are this way because, for some reason, very early in life, they determined they were incapable of achieving values and therefore unworthy of being happy. Other people's happiness reinforced their self-condemnation. Thus their main purpose as a young children became to destroy other children's toys and games. This was the pattern with my brother Fabian. At school he became an arch-socialist, writing pro-Soviet newsletters and joining industrial strikes. At university, when the wall came down, he became a convert to ecoism. This gave him his perfect purpose, more consistently than socialism – namely, to stop others using the Earth's resources to enrich their lives. If they were allowed to carry on as they were, and become happier as a result, it would condemn and confirm him as incompetent to live. Reflecting on his own unhappiness, admitting he'd been wrong and deciding to do something about it, was not an option his twisted pride would allow. And so ecoism became his vehicle to destroy others.

"Moving from its psychology to its stated philosophy, ecoism claims that man's use of nature to provide material goods is evil, and so tries to curtail or stop it. It claims man should reject the means to live, which implies that he should die, sacrificing himself on the altar of nature. For Fabian and ecoists everywhere, the destruction of mankind is preferable to the destruction of their own twisted egos. Creating a proper ego, founded on reason and geared towards achieving one's own happiness, is exactly the challenge ecoists have refused to meet. And centuries of philosophical attacks on reason and selfishness have provided fertile cultural soil in which to propagate their alternative morality of death. This much I learned from Dalton."

Blake paused to look in earnest at the faces of the congregation. They were bathed in coloured light from the stained-glass windows. Never had he felt the power of ideas before, and never had he known so strongly that they were right.

"All of you here today are arch-egoists, who have achieved great happiness through your careers and who stand as arch-examples of the success that comes from thinking and acting for oneself. That is why, in the regime's eyes, you must be destroyed. I urge you not to let that happen, but instead to follow your selfish hearts and fight back, to avenge Dalton MacDermot's death and to honour your own lives."

#

Brigadier Timothy Campbell stood up sharply. The word 'fight' had triggered a reaction in him. He had sat engrossed by Blake's speech. Professor MacDermot's courage had hugely impressed him, and while soldiers cared relatively little for environmentalism, he recognised the common theme that linked their worlds: sacrifice.

Soldiers were always being told to do it by politicians. But that was never the reason people joined up, nor why they would risk a hail of bullets to drag a mate off the battlefield. What they wanted was life, not death. Soldiering was a way to protect it.

A plan had been forming in his mind. He and Blake had been discussing it since their recapture. Now it was clicking into place. Would the others accept it? It didn't matter. He had to express it. He smiled as he thought of Dalton. It was the only logical thing to do.

He glanced around and found they were all looking at him already. He didn't remember standing up, but that would help. He eyed the doors, then he spoke, moving slowly towards one of them as he did so.

"When I was in Bosnia and Iraq and Afghanistan, I was often told that it was good to sacrifice myself and my men for the greater good. We didn't really believe it, and carried on fighting for our own reasons. But Blake's words have made me realise we were not being egoistic enough. We didn't allow ourselves the moral praise we deserved for staying alive."

He had reached the main door now.

"There is the chance you will win your appeals, but I believe the same moral choice is before us now. To accept Fabian's plans for us and go meekly to our own slaughter, or to demand justice for ourselves and fight back. I say we take over the prison."

A low roar of approval emanated from the congregation, then grew as it echoed off the stones of centuries past.

The Brig watched the guards. Ed Quinton was grinning. The other, a younger one, was looking worried. His hand was on his holster, but he was not removing the weapon. Suddenly, he ran towards the door the Brig was guarding. He tried to use his speed to cannon through him, but the Brig was ready. He grabbed him in a low rugby tackle as he went by and the young guard clattered to the floor. Blake and Paul Williams jumped on him. Sam Tillman ripped the cord from an ancient flagpole and ran over to tie him up. He struggled in vain under the weight of three men, and soon he was gagged and bound.

The attackers looked at one another, grinning broadly.

"What shall we do with this one?" Sam asked.

Ed stepped forward. "I know a remote cell that's not being used. I can keep him there."

"You're happy to join us, then?" the Brig asked, already knowing the answer but wanting the others to be reassured.

"I never was much of an ecoist, but I thought it was pretty harmless. Now it's gone way too far. I'm sick of it," Ed replied.

The Brig eyed him appraisingly, then nodded.

Turning to the guard on the floor, he said, "Let's not forget his weapon," and removed the pistol. Studying it he said with surprise, "It's not loaded."

"Almost none of them are," Ed said cheerfully, and fired his own pistol at the stained-glass depiction of St Antony. It only emitted a click.

Blake explained to the prisoners, "It makes perfect sense. The regime doesn't trust people with guns in case they turn around and fire on them. Which means the only thing keeping us here is our own fear. It's like ecoism. They couldn't enforce it with real police – it would take too many. But they can if we police ourselves. If we pre-judge ourselves as guilty for having our own ideas and wanting to live."

"Don't forget the ones that do carry loaded weapons. There are a few that are trusted," Ed reminded him, glad now that he wasn't one of them.

"Right," Blake said. "There will be some risk there, but if we plan sufficiently, we should be able to take over with very few casualties." He paused to look at the congregation, all on their feet and crowded around him now. "Who's for following the Brig's plan, and who's for waiting for the results of their appeal? Those against taking over should go and stand behind Ed, who will arrange for your alternative accommodation."

The congregation all looked around, trying to read each other's faces, then seeing their own hesitation reflected there, looked inwards at themselves.

Sam Tillman recalled sitting in his office, swearing with frustration, the day the outlawing of free shopping bags was announced. He had known it would only make his customers' lives more difficult. And he had allowed the government to blackmail him into accepting the new law over his use of foreign workers. Why?

Clive Donaldson looked down at the missing fingernails on his right hand. They still hurt. He had tried to get justice for those in hospitals and care homes. Would he do the same again? Yes. So why was he hesitating to join Blake? He thought of his son Keith, seventeen and academically brilliant, but completely lost to ecoism. The rows they'd had around the dining table. His threats to leave home and go and live on a commune. Should he have argued with him like that, or compromised and maybe kept him? Was there still a chance to do so? Having been punished so much already, might his appeal succeed?

Paul Williams remembered the day he'd sat on the government's panel of energy experts and said nothing when they asked for objections to 'intelligent supply'. Now every house in the country had the technology fitted to its electricity meter, allowing the government to create blackouts as desired. Why had he not spoken up then?

Liz Blackwood stood and worried about her two teenage daughters, Helen and Sophie. If she rebelled would they be persecuted, even used as blackmail? But if she simply sat in a cell, hoping for a reprieve, and watched Blake's takeover fail, he would surely be hanged and she would lose the only man she had felt exhilarated by for a long time. Then she thought of the creeping environmentalism over the years – the hints, then the threats, and then the regulations that had sucked the profits and the pride out of banking and other industries – and she knew she had not opposed them strongly enough. She felt a surge of regret and then of indignation, and knew that was what she must hold on to. The feeling that she and her bank and her customers deserved justice, and that the cause they needed to fight for was their own freedom – to make their own decisions according to their own best judgement, and to act on them. To accept the intrusion of the law into virtually every decision they made was an act of gross self-sacrifice, for which there was no rational justification. She saw that only egoism could defeat this envious enemy, but as a Christian it seemed impossibly wrong.

Blake had been studying Liz's face for a while. When he saw her look up, her face frowning with thought, he smiled in encouragement. Then he looked at the others in turn.

Paul met his glance and smiled back involuntarily. Then he knew that he – particularly as a gay man, and especially in a church – had the right to be proud of what he'd achieved in life, and that he couldn't let his character down now.

Clive willed Blake to turn his way, to help him decide, and when he did Clive simply nodded and bowed his head in acceptance. The only way to get his son back, and to save his own life, was to stop compromising with the evil of Fabian and those who preached ecoism from their phoney moral high ground, and to condemn it instead by forcibly demanding his own right to live by his own values.

Sam had been thinking over all the other government mandates he had caved in to during the decades he'd spent in retailing. From the 'low-fat' campaigns, which had increased diabetes, to the anti-packaging legislation which had increased waste food, to the localism campaign which had put limits on overnight refrigeration, increasing food poisoning. He had betrayed his customers, his shareholders, and most importantly himself. It had seemed the only option. To defy the government and society had felt impossible. But that was then. Now he had been confronted with the eventual outcome of those decisions. He would kowtow no more. He would throw off ecoism's envious grip and redeem himself. He looked up at Blake and nodded with a hard-won smile.

Blake smiled in acknowledgement, then looked around at the determined faces of all the other prisoners in the church. None of them moved to leave.

15

It was a hot July afternoon – two days, one incarcerated guard and several secret meetings later – when the sea of red-suited prisoners was again met by the piercing taunts and gesticulations of the gawping public safely behind their screen. Blake was used to it by now, since it happened once a month, and he consoled himself with the thought that this might be the last such indignity if their plans came to fruition, and perhaps if they didn't.

As he waited at their rendezvous point, watching the uncivil civilians, he saw a face that made his heart jerk. It was Candice. And she wasn't jeering, she was just staring at him, her expression unfathomable within a hoodie that shadowed her face. Blake could still tell that Candice wanted to talk to him. But about what? The last time they'd exchanged physical words was at James's funeral, and that hadn't gone well. Plus, he still didn't know whether Candice had betrayed his whereabouts in the forest to Fabian.

As he waited for the gawping to finish and for permission to go, Blake looked around for Ed Quinton.

On locating him he drew slowly closer, until the bell rang and he was able to speak.

"Ed, how's our new prisoner?"

"He's fine. He's adjusting to his new situation quite quickly. Helped by the persuasion I gave him with this." He tapped his sidearm, then whispered, "I found some bullets."

"Excellent," Blake said. Then he continued in a low voice. "Listen, I've just seen my daughter in the crowd – tallish, blond hair with a fringe. She's sixteen. We haven't spoken in a long time. She must have something important to say, and there are things I want to tell her about her uncle that I don't want overheard. Can you be the one to supervise us in the Visitors' Room?"

"I don't see why not," Ed said quietly. "Move along now," he said more loudly, and then gave Blake a convincing shove.

Blake made his way to the Visitors' Room. It was packed with the prisoners' loved ones, looking more anxious then ever since the hanging. But they weren't all there. Space was limited and you needed an appointment. He scanned the room for Candice and saw her sitting at a table, her hoodie down now. She looked thinner than when Blake last saw her. But maybe that was just the effect of time. She did look a lot calmer, though. Blake felt a surge of love for his daughter, now his only child. He wanted to get through to her, to wipe the slate clean, to speak openly with her. But it was people with ideas like Candice's who had helped raise Fabian to power, and it was possible she had put Blake where he was. He wanted to tell her everything, but he couldn't. Not until he knew why Candice was there.

He saw Ed move into position near Candice's table, then went over himself and sat opposite her, the stifling of his speech causing him a pain in his throat.

"Candice, I almost didn't recognise you with your hoodie up," he began, as lightly as he could.

"I tend to wear it when I'm out. It stops me being hassled all the time."

"Are people hurting you?"

"No, they either point and stare a lot, or they come and ask how my dad is."

"They what?"

"And I can't really tell them, as you never write now."

Blake was silent for a few moments. "When I gave you a clue that I was in Sherwood Forest, a clue only you could have guessed, did you tell your uncle where I was?"

Candice looked down at her phone. Blake braced himself. Then she looked up, her eyes brimming with tears. "I didn't mean to. He kept the letter from me. I found it much later, hidden in his study. He asked me about our holidays over breakfast one day. I had no idea!"

Blake exhaled, then reached over and held her hand. It was against the rules, but the guards generally turned a blind eye to it since the prisoners were all sentenced to death.

She squeezed his in return. "I'm so sorry."

"It's all right. It isn't your fault. I'm afraid I have something worse to tell you about your uncle."

She frowned but didn't try to defend him.

"He had James killed. They were trying to kill me on

the way to the BCF launch, but James went out early in the car and they assumed I was with him."

Candice looked like she was going to be sick. Blake squeezed her hand. "Listen. I know this because he told me, just after Dalton's execution. I think he was bragging."

Candice looked away, and took a few deep breaths. Then she turned back, her face pale. "I think I might have been part of that, too. Mrs Oakley, my old Green Shoots leader, was asking me about the BCF two weeks or so before it happened. And I told her about the car." She looked at Blake in anguish. "Then I saw her on the platform at the Ecoist Party rally. She smiled at me."

She looked so distraught, her face crumpled and tear-lined, her mascara running. He took both her hands and stared straight into her eyes. "It's not your fault, Candice. You didn't plan to get manipulated. These are nasty people you're dealing with."

She wiped her eyes and sniffed loudly. Then in a croaky whisper said, "I've left the Green Shoots—" Blake smiled. "—at least in my mind. I've got to stay because I need to find out what they're planning."

Blake was concerned. "How do you mean?"

She glanced at the guard.

"It's all right. Ed is okay," Blake reassured her.

She breathed. "I've been in it now for five years, and have been given quite a high rank: Junior Major."

Blake recalled his dismay when Candice had joined the youth arm of the ecoist movement rather than the Guides or the Scouts. But that wasn't important. What he needed to do now, perhaps for the first time in years, he admitted, was to listen.

"So I know things," Candice said, "that are coming

up, that we've been ordered to help with." She leant closer to her father. "In just over a month's time, they're organising multiple nationwide rallies. We've been promoting them by putting up posters everywhere and by texting everyone under eighteen that we know."

Blake nodded. "I remember seeing something in the paper about it. Go on."

"They're all supposed to happen simultaneously, because Uncle Fabian is going to reveal a new National Anthem and he wants the whole country to hear it at once."

"Why can't everyone just tune in to the radio?"

"I don't know. But here's what I'm worried about." She leaned in. "The venues: Wembley, Cardiff Arena, Bridgewater Hall, Glasgow Hydro and so on, all match the labels I've seen attached to these masks that are piled up in his room in Number 10."

She showed him a picture on her phone. It resembled a gas mask but more sophisticated than those he'd seen in museums about the war. Next to it was the box it had been in, with a label on it: '*Reading Hexagon*'.

"Are you going to one of these rallies?"

"I'm supposed to be going to Wembley."

"Do you have to?"

"Uncle Fabian keeps mentioning it."

Blake bit his lip.

"Do you mind if I show this to someone? You'll get it back before you go."

"Okay. Oh, and here's a list I've made of the venues, in case you haven't read about them."

Blake took the phone and the list, scanning it for a

pattern. He beckoned Ed over.

"Can you show this picture to the Brig somehow, and then get the phone back to Candice on her way out?"

Ed said nothing but surreptitiously slid the phone up his sleeve and slowly patrolled the separate tables, moving indirectly towards the Brig's. As Blake looked harder he recognised the Brig's visitor. He had a thick beard and a metal lower leg poking out from beneath his trousers. He was taking a risk, thought Blake. Then he turned back to his daughter.

"You've done brilliantly well, finding all this out. I'll get to the bottom of it. I've a feeling you were right to be concerned. But never mind that. How is Uncle Fabian treating you?"

She smiled slightly. "Oh, fine. I hardly see him nowadays. He's at the palace most of the time now, not Number 10. I cook and shop for myself mostly. If there's anything else I need, the staff are very helpful."

Blake was relieved. She seemed safe, as least in the short term. "Have you heard from Mum?"

Candice brightened. "I'm going to see her next week. It's a bit of a trek, but Uncle Fabian's been giving me some pocket money which I've saved up. She's worried about you. It's one of the reasons I came today. So I could tell her how you are."

Blake smiled. "And how do you find me?"

She paused, contemplating him. "Surprisingly positive, considering." Then she leaned across the table. "Oh Dad, what's going to happen to you? Does your appeal have a chance, especially after your escape? What if it fails?" Her face furrowed in concern.

"Earlier you said something about people in general

asking about me. Is that true?"

She wiped her eyes quickly. "Yes. When I'm recognised, they want to know what's happening with you. They don't trust the papers. You're quite a celebrity, you know. But I don't know what to say." Her voice croaked again.

"Listen Candice. It's going to be all right. I have plans in place, in case things go wrong at the appeal. And I have lots of people here who want to help me. I can't tell you the details. But you mustn't worry."

Candice reached for his hand again and nodded while a tear rolled down her cheek.

Blake said, "Write your number down for me and we can keep in touch. I know someone who will relay text messages. But don't put anything secret."

"Okay, Dad." She gave him her number.

"Now, about this rally at Wembley. I think you should go, but be careful. And steal one of those masks for yourself. They must be important."

"What about my friend Lucinda? She's going too."

Blake thought hard for a moment. He didn't know what the ecoists were planning but he had his suspicions. On the other hand, he didn't want Candice put in any danger. Finally he said, "I suggest you take an extra mask for her, but don't tell her about it. If you need them, you can help her."

"Why can't I tell her?"

"This is important, Candice. I'm telling you this to protect you, and possibly me. I want you to read about Coventry during World War Two. It got heavily bombed and suffered a lot of casualties. Even though the Allies knew the attacks were coming, they didn't warn anyone."

"Why not?"

"I need you to look up Bletchley Park so you'll understand. It has to do with computers. You should like that. Will you do it?"

"Yes, if you really think it matters."

"It does. Now, you'll have to go soon. Are you okay for getting back to London?"

She nodded. He reached over and held both her hands. "Thanks for coming to see me."

"I-I wanted to say, I'm sorry we argued so much. I've found out a lot recently which has made me think you might have been right, about a lot of things. I didn't want us to… part as enemies."

Blake smiled. "We were never that, Candice. I always admired your feisty determination to prove me wrong. And we're not parting for good. Only for now."

He squeezed her hands.

Ed came over and coughed. They got up.

"Bye, Dad."

Blake said his goodbyes, and despite the rules he hugged his daughter. Then, as she left, Ed stealthily gave her back her phone.

Waves of emotion came over him – anger, regret, fear, compassion, indignation – but Blake knew what he had to do next. He took a deep breath and left the room.

The Brig saw him go. He signalled to Ed, who was now free to 'guard' his own conversation.

Ed approached the guard nearest the Brig's table. "I'll take over if you like. My one's gone."

"Oh, thanks," the guard said, fumbling with a cigarette packet before he reached the door.

The Brig gave Ed a fake look of disgust and carried

on talking, but now more openly.

"That mask in the photo. What do you think?"

"It's like the ones we wear with the noddy suits."

"What's the threat? Chemical, biological? Surely not nuclear?"

The Prince shook his head. "Biological most likely. It spreads the best. But why has his daughter got one?"

"I'll find out. It looks bad, though."

The Prince nodded and pulled at his beard.

The Brig continued, "So, back to what I was saying. Can you rally the TA in our support?"

The Prince grinned. "You know as soon as the government finds out I'm helping you, I'm going to be hunted down?"

"All the more reason to get some decent defence."

"True. It shouldn't be too hard to get a few battalions together. I met a lot of them when I used to give inspections. And you wouldn't believe how pissed off they've got, being sent on dangerous foreign missions all the time because the government won't pay for a decent size regular army."

The Brig smiled ruefully. "I can believe it," he said. "At the last count, there were two TA soldiers for every regular one." He paused, thinking of all the poor bastards who'd joined up for weekends in Wales and ended up having their legs blown off in the Middle East. Then he had an idea. "You know who else you could try?"

"Who?"

"Major General Macleod. He wasn't at the barracks when we got there, I think he's gone into hiding. See if you can find him. He may be able to rally the whole division."

"That's a tall order. You know I'm okay while they still think of me as a crippled mascot, encouraging others, but not really doing anything for myself. As soon as I start organising something, something the government won't like, something that looks like a rebellion, I'm in deep trouble."

"Do you want to see us all die? And I don't just mean us in here. You know where this government is heading. Parliament is virtually closed. The opposition parties, such as they are, can't force an election."

"I know you're right." The Prince looked out of the narrow stone window for a moment. "Perhaps we're long overdue a shake-up in this country. God knows we've been taking it lying down for long enough. Look at my family – ousted for daring to speak up for charities."

"Exactly. If you can't even defend people who volunteer their time and money, what will you be allowed to say?"

The Prince cogitated this for a few moments. Then he took a deep breath but kept his tone low. "I can get you the weapons fairly quickly. The TA and the brigade – that will take more time. How are you going to hold out until then?"

"We're holding a special meeting next Sunday to work out the details."

"Have you thought about air cover?"

The Brig grinned. "I know. It's a big risk. One or two well placed bombs and we're toast."

"Well, don't wave your hanky just yet. I still speak to a lot of my old mates in the RAF, and they aren't happy about being asked to shoot down private planes trying to leave the country. I don't think they'll turn on their own countrymen, even if they are rebellious prisoners."

"Good. I should think not."

"But they could be forced to. They're not really ready to mutiny. They've got no one to lead them, and they've got no kind of plan."

"Well, I think we can satisfy both those demands now."

"Really?"

"You lead them, and I'll give you a plan."

The Prince's eyes gleamed. "Go on."

"Get all the attack aircraft out of the way, where the pilots and their planes can't be got at. It'll be a one-way trip, for some time. But it's the only way to keep them and us safe."

The Prince mulled it over. "We'd better make it somewhere nice, then. I'm not sure about Ascension, maybe Bermuda. That's nice. Or Canada. Much nearer, and they can speak to my family for moral support."

"You decide. Any aircraft that can't make it a safe distance away must be scuppered. Sand in the petrol tank. That kind of thing."

"I'm sure we can working something out. You realise it would be leaving the country virtually undefended?" the Prince said thoughtfully.

"Yes. But I can't think of any country wanting to take us over, given the state we're in. Besides, most of them are bankrupt too. They can't afford an invasion. Now, regarding all these forces you're going to lead – do you think you can command enough loyalty?"

"I'll try to get it, if you can tell me where this is all heading."

The Brig took a deep breath, then lowered his voice

even further. "We're going to take back the country. Oust the current regime. Replace it with something much better."

"What?" The Prince's raised voice caused several nearby conversations to stop and look his way.

"Keep it down, you idiot," the Brig chastised. As the watching eyes eventually turned away, he continued. "We're talking about a new constitution. One that guarantees freedom. But we need to convince enough people to make it stick."

"How will you do that?"

"You'll have to wait and see." The Brig paused. He could see the enthusiasm on the Prince's shining, eager face, despite the beard. "Will you do it?"

A buzzer sounded, signalling the end of visiting hours.

"Of course. For you, Brig, nothing is too much." He grinned. "Even changing the course of history. After all, if it wasn't for you I'd have been beheaded by the Islamists by now, or worse, shamed, tortured and humiliated on the Internet." He stood up, as did the Brig, but managed to avoid saluting.

The Brig said, "You know some regiments use 'Rule Britannia' as their march? We're going to give those words about slavery some real meaning again."

"I'm up for that," the Prince said, and swivelling on his stick, he left.

The Brig let out a deep sigh. Ambitious wasn't the word for it. Insane? Ridiculously idealistic? He couldn't find the right term, but he knew it was the only option they had to survive, and he knew it made sense.

A voice from the past reminded him not to be too

arrogant. Regime change was far from easy. Nevertheless, when the visitors had gone and the prisoners were allowed to move again, he walked serenely out of the room and found Blake waiting for him in the yard. He nodded.

"He'll do it, then?" Blake asked.

"Yes. I think he really will. And your daughter? What's she doing with a military-grade hazmat mask?"

The light was dawning across Blake's face even as the furrows deepened on his brow. "Candice told me Fabian is planning a series of mass rallies that he's trying to get the country's youth to attend. Then he's going to unveil a new National Anthem."

"What?"

"I know. Each venue has a number of those masks being sent to it." Blake gave him the list.

The Brig studied it for a minute. "I see what's common to all these places. They're all indoors. Good for spreading a biological weapon. I'll get a text message to Arthur, get him to investigate."

Blake stopped breathing. Had he just sent his daughter into a death trap? What if her mask didn't work or she couldn't get it on properly?

"Are you all right?" the Brig asked.

Blake took an inrush of air. Then he blurted out, "Yes, I'm fine. But we have to stop him. He can't be allowed to destroy any more children."

"We will," the Brig said calmly and gravely. "But first we have to save ourselves."

#

"These two gentlemen, Ed and Greg," Blake said, gesturing to the tall, grey-haired guard, then to the short, stocky ginger one, "have agreed to help."

346

The governor was absent from the chapel again as the 'confessing' prisoners looked on appraisingly.

"Since our decision last week," Blake continued, "we have come up with some plans for the takeover, and have also heard some very disturbing news. As you probably know, the ecoists are planning mass rallies for young people across the country in a month's time. We have reason to believe that they will release a deadly virus at each of the venues. We don't yet know exactly what."

The audience erupted in alarm.

When they'd settled, Blake continued. "The suspected key moment will come when a new National Anthem is simultaneously broadcast at all the rallies. And we know all this from one of their unwitting acolytes in the Green Shoots – my daughter, Candice. So we now have two problems: taking over the prison to prevent our own deaths, and preventing the rallies from causing the deaths of millions of children."

Someone piped up, "Couldn't we just warn them? Tell them not to go?"

"Unfortunately we can't. Letting the enemy know that we know their plans will lead them straight to our informant – my daughter. Then they will simply eliminate her and try something else, later. Besides, I will not allow her to be sacrificed, even for millions of other children."

The audience murmured.

Blake continued. "But if we stop it happening at the last minute, and expose the plot to everyone, then it should be enough to shock people out of their complacent obedience to ecoism and turn them against it."

The prisoners talked among themselves.

Then another one asked, "Can we be sure this mass infection plot is true? It's so evil. He's your brother – how can the leader of the country be that bad?"

"I don't recognise your face," Blake said. "Are you new?"

"Yes, for my sins, which included 'fixing' smart readers so their owners could override them."

"Well, you probably don't know my brother's track record. I was originally arrested for discovering that he was starving hospitals and care homes of fuel. I suspect many deaths in both places said to be flu, are actually cover-ups for hypothermia, cancelled operations, and accidents caused by a lack of light or power."

"Surely that would have come out by now, if it were true? The Office for National Statistics has a duty to verify these things."

"How independent do you think a government appointed office really is? And you should know by now not to trust government numbers. They've been banging on about climate change for decades, and nothing's really changed. Have you moved house or suffered severe damage due to the weather? There's been no catastrophe beyond those normally caused by nature. All 'global warming' has achieved is a state of fear and guilt in those who believe in it, as well as a collapsing economy."

There were more discussions among the congregation.

"So," Blake said, "if there aren't any more questions, we need some plans to deal with both emergencies. Brigadier Campbell and I have made some initial progress already. Brigadier?"

The Brig went to stand next to Blake at the front, and addressed the crowd.

"We need short-term and medium-term plans to deal with this. In the short term, I've started obtaining some guns and Tasers, with help from Ed."

Greg looked at his colleague in surprise and admiration. Ed smiled and nodded.

"In the medium term," the Brig continued, "I've been in contact with my services colleagues to try to prevent any airborne response from the government, and to persuade them not to attack us. However, once the takeover is complete, we do anticipate some form of attack and/or a siege."

"But the police, let alone the army, are a massive force compared with us. How are we supposed to win against them?" one of the prisoners blurted out.

"We don't need to defeat them," the Brig continued. "We just need to put up enough resistance to show we're serious. Any attackers need to know, individually, that they risk their lives. Once we've broken their will to attack, we need to persuade them to join us. We need enough time to get through to the rational ones among them. To appeal to their own sense of self-preservation and of justice. Blake and the late Professor MacDermot have convinced me, so I know it can be done. The key issue is self-sacrifice versus self-interest, ecoism versus egoism. I know it won't be easy to convince them of this. We've all been indoctrinated with the idea that sacrifice is good. It's embedded in our psyches. But there will be some who choose to listen and think, and with them we have a chance."

From the back came a high-pitched voice. "Why

don't we just escape once we've taken over, rather than risk death in a siege? Isn't that self-sacrifice, getting killed?"

Blake was glad the issue had been brought up. He needed everyone thoroughly convinced of their cause. He glanced at the Brig, then replied, "No. In the long term, which is all that really matters, staying in the castle is not self-sacrifice. Outside, we would soon be captured and reimprisoned. Inside, we have a chance of surviving long enough to convince some of our attackers to switch allegiance, maybe also some of the public. It also gives us a chance to stop the rallies, provided we can keep the takeover secret for a couple of weeks."

There was a general murmur of approval, but the voice came again. "I think I'll take my chances anyway."

Blake kept his voice even as he replied. "That would mean alerting the authorities before we're ready to defend ourselves. You would be sacrificing the rest of us to your cowardice. I can't allow that to happen."

There was silence as the whole congregation turned to the owner of the voice. He was thick-set and average height. He moved slowly towards the door. The other prisoners began to surround him. Before he was trapped, he put his head down and charged. Two or three other prisoners were knocked to the floor, but Ed, Sam Tillman and Paul Williams were ready and waiting at the exit. They bundled him to the ground, then tied and gagged him. It was easier the second time. Their first victim, the guard from the previous week, was still in his remote cell. His family were told he was self-isolating due to an infection.

Breathing hard with their efforts, they looked back at the congregation with their faces set.

Blake nodded his thanks, then asked, "Is there anyone else who'd prefer to step out?"

The prisoners laughed grimly. They knew they were all in it now.

"Right, as I said, assuming we're not bombed out straight away, we're going to have to survive a siege. It will be weeks, possibly longer, and we have a short time to organise ourselves and obtain supplies. Who would like to help?"

Immediately, Sam replied, "I'll be responsible for organising food and water. I've already started counting the stock in the kitchen, but I'll need some help fixing the old well in the courtyard. I bet the first thing they do is cut off our water."

The Brig raised an appreciative eyebrow.

"I'll help," and, "Count me in," replied several voices, and several more hands were raised.

Sam went over to take their names.

"I think our next problem will be power," Paul Williams said.

Blake nodded. They didn't need much, but good lighting would act as a deterrent and show they were capable of surviving in a civilised manner. It might even draw people to their cause, seeing as they would be breaking the lighting curfew.

"We should be able to use the prison's generators," Paul continued, "but our major problem will be fuel. Again, they'll cut off the mains electricity as soon as they find out. We need to get stocks of wood, coal, even diesel if possible. It might be warm now, in July, but we don't know how long this will last."

Again, the hands of engineers, businessmen and women, playwrights and teachers shot up. They knew their lives were now in their own hands.

Clive Donaldson was next to speak. He raised his injured hand. "If we want to get through to those besieging us, probably the army, it would be ideal if we could jam and control their communications. I can do that, but I'll need some help from the Brigadier."

Campbell nodded his assent.

Liz was next. "We're going to need to buy some supplies, particularly in that window before the takeover is discovered. We'll need to manage our limited funds very carefully, as well as the logistics of people and assets. I'm keen to do that."

Knowing her reputation in business, there were nods all round.

Blake knew there was one major role left to fill. "I'll find a way to stop this virus being released. But I'll need to do it from outside the castle, and I'll need a working party to help me."

Several volunteered their services. More than he'd expected. He smiled in gratitude. Sometimes people were much braver than he gave them credit for. Dalton would not have been so cynical. He felt a massive hole open up in his chest when he recalled his friend's absence. But he knew he must channel that feeling into action to honour Dalton's memory. That way, he wouldn't be quite so missing. The hole filled with ice-cold resolve that galvanised him into making his most ambitious announcement.

"After we take over the prison, stop the virus, and withstand a siege with the army's help, the government will be in a state of chaos. With their evil intentions revealed, they will no longer be able to govern. We do not want anarchy. But neither is it any good relying on what's left of the old political parties to organise an election. Without the sovereign as head of state, we have no constitutional means of bridging that gap. But mainly, the problem is that the old parties are too weak and too invested in ecoism to govern the country properly. They're to blame for the state we're in as much as Fabian."

Blake let that sink in while he took a deep breath.

"As I see it," he continued, "there is only one option. We need to take over the government. I know we're businesspeople and artists, not politicians, and I know we're not elected, but somebody has to do it. If things go as planned, we'll have the support of at least some of the army, and once people know we've saved their children from death, they'll be on our side too. It will take time, but eventually it will be safe to reinstate democracy – this time with better safeguards."

The congregation rumbled with excited conversation. Blake heard the occasional phrase: "He's right", "It's audacious", "Who else?" He waited a moment then spoke.

"I realise this is a huge undertaking and that there's a lot to think about, and to plan, for it to work. But the first thing we need to do is save ourselves by taking over the prison. I propose sooner rather than later. How about a week tomorrow?"

This focused their minds. There was silence as they faced the idea of risking their lives to save their lives, and accepted there was no credible alternative.

"Any objections?" Blake asked. None came. "Right, that's settled. Now, we need to start collecting weapons. Ed, can we have yours, and some ammunition?"

Ed handed over his pistol, saying, "I'll tell them I've dropped it down the well while checking for hidden prisoners." Blake chuckled. Ed added, "I'll get some ammo for it."

"Greg?" Blake asked.

The other guard hesitated. This wasn't part of his training. His gun actually had some ammunition in it.

"If you don't help us," Blake said, "you know what the ecoists will do to your children. I presume they're going to the rally?"

Greg knew they were. Since signing up to attend, they had been inundated with text messages. It would look odd if a trusted government servant such as himself did not send his children without good reason. Josh and Ethan were eight and ten, and football crazy. They actually wanted to go to the rally in Wembley, because he'd promised them they could also visit the hallowed ground. A lump came to this throat as he thought of them playing together. He checked the safety catch and handed over his gun.

"Thanks," Blake said, seeing the conflict in the man's face. "Now, I need both of you to get as many guards on our side as possible. We need to figure out who we can trust."

16

Blake looked at his watch again. It said 5:59 a.m. He'd been checking it all night. The last two hours had been light enough to read it without its internal light.

He'd been running it all through in his head. Clive's idea to use colour codes on the guards' radios. His other idea to cut the landlines. The disarming and weapons training given by the Brig. Liz stepping in as comms coordinator. So much could go wrong. But so much could go right. It was up to them now.

He heard the guard coming up the stone steps. The heavy iron key in the lock. The bang on the door.

When the footsteps had faded, he sprang off his bed and out through the cell door. He knew the guards wouldn't all be exactly where they expected them. He hoped his fellow prisoners would be able to improvise if necessary. What was he worrying about? They were CEOs and professionals. They'd been dealing with a rapidly changing world all their lives. All the same, he was relieved to see his target as predicted: in the laundry courtyard. But he was talking with several other guards who were vaping. They couldn't all be tackled at once.

Then he saw the Brig hiding behind a doorframe. They surreptitiously nodded to each other. But where were the other prisoner teams? Perhaps they were hidden too. It didn't matter. He and the Brig had to focus on their own guard. Especially as, to speed things up, they'd decided to form a team of two not three.

It was 06:08. Then he noticed a prisoner coming towards him. It was Sam Tillman, unmistakable from a distance because of his sandy hair. He was walking casually but Blake could tell he was on tenterhooks. He was looking around more than usual and kicking at the dust, which he never did. The guards didn't notice. They were too busy talking among themselves. Sam had acknowledged Blake's presence, so Blake had to move into the courtyard proper.

"Morning, Sam," Blake said.

"How are you?" Sam said.

"Much the same," Blake said.

It was 06:11. Almost zero hour. What would they do if all the guards were together?

"It's, err, quite busy this morning, isn't it?" Sam said. Obviously he was thinking the same thing.

Just then the Brig strode forward, straight towards the guards. He spoke to their target. The guard headed off, out of the courtyard.

Blake and the Brig sauntered towards each other.

"I told him the governor wanted to see him," the Brig said.

"Clever," Sam said.

"But now we've got to catch him," the Brig continued.

"Good luck," Blake said to Sam, and he and the Brig left as casually as they could, following the guard, leaving Sam with the other two.

Once out of sight they ran, stopping at every corner until they saw him. He was walking smartly across a shadowed yard in the direction of the governor's office. They had to stop him soon.

Then Blake had an idea. He said to the Brig, "Go round through the kitchen yard and come from the other way, while I distract him."

"Okay," the Brig said, and sprinted off.

Blake stood hidden in a corridor, then called out loudly, "Oi, Steven!"

He'd had time to do a little research since last Sunday.

The guard turned around. Blake could see his wolf-like eyes piercing the gloom. "I hear Kayley's been seeing one of the other guards behind your back."

"Show yourself. Now," Steven shouted.

Blake walked into the yard slowly, continuing to talk. "I thought you might like to know."

"Who's been saying that?"

"Well, I can't remember all the details. Perhaps if you were to do something for me in return…"

Steven gasped as the Brig grabbed him from behind. Blake went in low and they both wrestled him to the ground. The Brig pinned Steven's arms behind him and Blake took his gun. He checked the magazine – it was loaded.

Pointing the gun at the guard, he said, "One peep out of you and I'll fire. We don't want any noise."

Too late, Blake realised the contradiction. Steven wasn't that stupid.

The guard bared his teeth. "So you want it nice and quiet, eh?" He took a deep breath, ready to shout.

The Brig punched a knockout blow to his head. Only a moan and a rush of air left the guard's lips.

"Should have got the gag organised sooner," the Brig said. "Let's hope the others think of that." He tied one in place before hoisting him over his shoulder. "Get his radio."

Blake extracted it from the man's uniform and changed the frequency.

"This is team six. Black. Repeat, black. Over."

"Black five, green one," came Liz's terse reply.

"That's good," Blake said to the Brig.

"But we need to find that green. Let's dump this one first."

The agreed collection point for the guards was an old dungeon now used as a cold store near the centre of the castle. The prisoners on kitchen duty had ready access to it, and the location gave everyone roughly the same length journey.

Blake and the Brig jogged cautiously down corridors and across yards. They came to the laundry yard. It was empty. The plan seemed to be working.

Blake took the guard's legs as they manoeuvred him down some steps and into the cold store.

They dumped him, still unconscious, on the floor next to another guard, who was gagged but awake. Blake looked around. Seven other guards were now on the floor, trussed securely. Two more to go, Blake thought optimistically.

Clive was sitting on a chair holding a wet cloth to one eye.

Blake asked, "Are you all right?"

"I've had worse," grinned the fifty-year-old Scot. "The lines are down."

Blake smiled in appreciation. Then he looked around the room.

The capture teams were standing around congratulating each other. Several were still pointing guns at the guards.

The Brig approached one of them, whose hand was shaking. "I could use that, if you don't mind," he said, and the ex-prisoner handed it over. The guards weren't going anywhere soon.

"We can leave them to this," the Brig said, handing Blake the gun. "Let's go." He ran out of the door, with Blake following.

"Where?" he gasped from behind.

"The governor's office," the Brig said. "That's where any rogue guards will go if they want to report what's happened. It's also where some spare guns are kept."

They raced along the most direct route to the office, free to move around without guards.

Panting hard, they found six ex-prisoners outside and a guard unconscious on the floor.

"He slipped through my hands," said Gobind, the ex-doctor, "so we chased him here."

"Ours has got inside and locked the door," Paul said, nursing his jaw and looking disappointed.

"Stand clear," the Brig ordered. He shot twice at the lock. The old wooden door splintered, sending sharp slivers into the backs of his hands. He fired again. This time the door fell open. He rushed inside, followed by Blake.

The governor had a mobile phone to his ear and a gun in his hand. The guard inside stood back with his hands up as Blake and the Brig pointed their guns.

"You're too late," the governor smirked. "It's already ringing."

Blake couldn't resist. "How ironic. You despise the makers of mobile phones and networks for 'destroying' the environment, and yet you rely on them."

The governor shrugged. "Logic was never part of our plan. I thought you knew that." Then he glared at the phone. "Voicemail!"

Before the greeting could end, both Blake and the Brig shot him. As he slumped to the floor his gun went off, lodging a bullet harmlessly in the old plaster ceiling.

#

They had three weeks maximum, Blake told them. It turned out that the governor's last call had been to the Home Secretary, an ecoist of long standing. However, Blake calculated that, as he hadn't noticed the missed call and rung back already, he had probably ignored it. No doubt he had more important things to do, such as toadying-up to the President, or worse, helping him with the death rallies. If he did phone back, he would be directed to voicemail. The landlines had been reconnected and the governor's secretary, Rebecca, had agreed to join the prisoners. She took any incoming calls as if nothing had happened. She wrote to the families of the captured guards, explaining they would not be returning home for three weeks due to a special training regime. People and deliveries came and went as usual, but if any got too inquisitive, she invented an excuse involving national security. After years of obeying orders, she was thrilled to be creating them herself.

~

Meanwhile, the prisoners who had volunteered to prepare for the siege had put their plans into high gear with the help of their teams. Clive was pleased with his preparations to take over a besieging army's battlefield communications. He had set his colleagues the task of stripping the prison's PA system of wire and components, and within two days they had come up trumps. Three tables in the guards' old social room, high in one of the towers, were now littered with copper wire and circuit boards. From these he was constructing an aerial and transmitter. He had also put an order into a local electronics firm for some more components, hoping that individually they were innocuous enough not to attract attention. Then again, with the governor's official seal being used on the requisition, it was unlikely to be questioned.

He was helped in this by Ed and Greg. They manned the front gate and met the supply trucks that came and went, making everything seem as normal as possible.

Only two other guards had been persuaded to help the prisoners. The rest were due to be released at the end of three weeks' captivity. They were a drain on resources.

~

Sam's preparations were also in full swing. The guards had been moved from the cold store to an ancient thick-walled room away from the main part of the castle. They were fed and exercised once a day, with several guns pointing at them. None tried to escape. They knew what had befallen the governor. The cold store was now rapidly being filled with perishable foodstuffs, particularly fruit and vegetables.

Nearby, another room was for stockpiling tins and dried goods. Sam had placed orders with several different suppliers besides the prison's usual ones. He hoped this would avoid the suspicion of a large increase in demand. The goods were sent on account, but he had no idea when they would be paid. He couldn't send the invoices off to the Treasury without arousing their suspicion. And once the takeover was discovered... well, he hoped the suppliers wouldn't begrudge them. Food was no good without water, and this was where he'd enlisted Blake's help with the old well.

~

As usual with castles, the prison was on top of a hill, making gravity useless for transporting water. The castle had seen sieges before, hence the well. However, it hadn't been used for centuries. There was no mechanism for hauling the water up, and once he'd abseiled down, Blake found it blocked with building debris and general rubbish. But it did seem damp. He put his ear to the side wall and was sure he could hear a trickle of water.

Knowing how crucial water was to their survival, there were plenty of volunteers offering to help. First, they rigged up a pulley system using rope from the scaffold and wheels from a couple of sack trucks. Then they attached this to the axle of the governor's car and use it to winch the rubble and rubbish out of the well in sacks.

After two days, with the help of others both in and above the well, the rubbish was cleared and a thin but steady stream of water was visible by torchlight at the bottom. It boded well that it still flowed in high summer, Blake reasoned. Now all they had to do was extract it. It was a daunting task, and one he could not afford to fail at, for all their sakes. That night, as he fell into a fitful sleep, Blake's subconscious worked on the problem.

When he woke up he clearly recalled a Jacquard loom and waterwheel he and his family had seen working at an industrial heritage site while on holiday.

That day he started putting his idea into action. The basis of the wheel he found in an old, weathered cable drum, left by the National Grid many moons ago. The rotating buckets took a bit more work. Luckily, plastic was still allowed in certain applications, and cleaning was one of them. The hardest bit was getting the water back to the surface. With Paul's help he did some energy calculations and figured that the stream itself was powerful enough to lift some of the water flowing by, if it had enough gearing. It was more complex than using a mechanical pump but he needed to preserve electricity and diesel, so it was worth it. After four days' work with his team, using lightweight rope, plastic buckets and some toothed wheels that had once been used to raise the drawbridge, Blake managed to create a self-powered well. At the brief opening ceremony, Blake accepted the ex-prisoners' praise, and gave thanks to the engineers of the Industrial Revolution.

~

Paul Williams' task of providing heat and electricity was almost as crucial. As he'd anticipated, the prison's generators were fully functioning – like everywhere else, the prison had to cope with frequent electricity outages. But the problem was fuel. It would look suspicious if he ordered substantially more diesel than usual, even on the governor's authorisation, so he needed an alternative fuel source.

He chuckled as the word 'alternative' came to mind. In recent parlance it was synonymous with eco-friendly, so-called 'renewable' fuel sources. But the wind and the sun did not exist continuously as humans did – when they died down, the ex-prisoners did not want to go with them. Then Paul remembered reading about the local area, and the massive steelworks that had once provided metal to the country and employment to thousands of people. It had been located there for two reasons – a plentiful supply of ironstone, discovered during the cuttings made for the railways, and a history of near-surface coal mining.

In the governor's office he found a detailed map. It didn't specify the geology but it did show a number of promising street names: Grey Lane, Quarry Road and Blackpit Lane. He sent members of his team out to have a look while he thought about how to extract any coal they found. It wouldn't be easy, because they didn't want to draw attention to themselves, yet they would be bound to need either large machinery or explosives to get the stuff out – where would he get those?

The team leaders had a brief progress meeting every morning, and it was at one of those that the Brig solved Paul's second problem.

"I've been bargaining with the foreman of a stone quarry a couple of miles away for my own purposes. I can get you some gunpowder."

"What does it cost?" Paul asked.

"Don't worry. You'd be surprised how much some of

the governor's possessions will fetch. His gold watch was particularly lucrative."

With that problem solved, Paul turned to the issue of removing it discreetly. They had a van used for transporting prisoners. They had picks and shovels used for the wall-building work. What if… he laughed grimly to himself.

It took some persuading, but eventually he had a dozen volunteers prepared to put their red jumpsuits back on and go digging.

After driving around for a couple of hours, the third site they looked at seemed the most promising from an access point of view. It was near a farm, so there wouldn't be too many onlookers.

Ed knocked at the farm door and told them the prison needed some more stone for building. Then he and Greg shepherded the prisoners over to the chosen site at gunpoint. Paul knew very little about setting explosive charges, but thanks to his sabotage training, the Brig did.

After four explosions, there was a substantial amount of coal on the surface. Over two sweaty days, they drove it away.

Then Paul started adapting the generator and heating system to use coal.

~

The Brig stood on the battlements of the castle. He was glad the ancient cannons hadn't all been made into pavement bollards like those he'd seen in London. Gunpowder was no problem. Ironically, the recent clampdown on trade and chemicals by the ecoists had made this basic explosive relatively plentiful. It was still stockpiled by various manufacturers but was not being bought. There was even a good supply of cannonballs – several pyramids had been arranged around the castle to impress the tourists when it was still open to the public as a historic monument.

The only problem was that most of the cannons had been spiked – put out of action by having too-large cannonballs melted into their ends. He couldn't risk blasting them out – the breeches might simply explode. That was a risk with all the cannons, given their age. Could he melt them? That would require more energy than they had. What about just loosening them somehow? What if the balls were just welded in? If he could melt the joint where they met the barrel, they would fall out. But how could he do that?

He remembered Paul telling him about the history of the area. The steelworks had been shut down long ago by high carbon taxes, but there was a chance some materials were left over that he could use. After all, steelmaking required intense temperatures.

One day in the middle of August, when the cannons had all been moved into position and their balls arranged in readiness, he donned some civilian clothes belonging to the captured guards and went searching.

The steelworks was not hard to find. Its various buildings stood towering above the countryside, their paint slowly peeling from the wind and the sun. The structures seemed to have been relatively new when they were forcibly shut down by law. How gentle nature is compared with man, he thought.

The place was obviously worth preserving, at least in the eyes of its owners. They still paid for a strong fence and a man to guard it. The Brig went to speak to him.

"It's an impressive sight," the Brig began.

"It used to be the most modern steelworks in the country, many moons ago," the lonely guard replied.

"Why do they keep it like this, rather than break it up and sell it?"

"Well, I'm just the guard, but I do have my theories."

"Go on."

"First of all, it would be very expensive to transport it, what with the taxes on fuel. And second of all, who would buy it? Heavy industry has been shut down all over Europe, thanks to the greens."

"So why not let it rot? Why guard it?"

The stocky man in his early fifties smiled with a sombre twinkle in his eyes. "They won't give up hoping that it will open again. One day. That must be what keeps them going."

Campbell nodded in appreciation. He knew the power of hope from many bad situations on the battlefield. More than once he'd had to hold off an ever growing number of insurgents with just a handful of men, hoping that air cover and reinforcements would come before they were overwhelmed. They always had. It was hope, followed by planning and action, that had kept them going long enough.

"Of course, they don't pay me much," the security guard said, noticing that Campbell had gone silent.

"These are hard times," the Brig said sympathetically. "Do you need to do a patrol sometime soon?"

"Funnily enough, I do," the man said, and he was out of his office and locking the door in a trice.

They walked around the main buildings, the security guard largely letting Campbell lead the way. After touring most of the site, Campbell pointed to a squat concrete room, isolated from the other buildings. "What's in there?"

"Ah, that's where they used to keep the more dangerous chemicals. Probably still some in there, what with there being so many regulations around getting rid of them."

"Mind if I look?"

The man hesitated. Campbell produced some cash he had gained earlier in exchange for one of the governor's gold rings.

"Go ahead," the man said, licking his lips as he counted the notes.

Campbell took the relevant key and opened it up.

The air inside was pungent, so he stood aside to let it clear for a minute, then went in, turning his torch on outside the building to avoid sparks.

Inside were rows of barrels with chemical labels sitting on shelves, just as the security guard had predicted. Eventually, he found one he recognised from a trip down a mine in his youth. Under the skull and crossbones it read, '*Calcium Carbide*'. He heaved it onto a sack truck nearby and wheeled it out.

"How much for this?"

After haggling they settled on £600 for two barrels.

Two trips to the van by the gate, and the Brig was driving off with a big grin on his face.

Two hours later, an iron ball fell from the mouth of a cannon as he torched it with acetylene.

~

As each team came and went from the castle, Liz Blackwood tracked what they were doing. When they needed money or items to barter with from the central pot, she handed it out and logged it in her ledger.

She chuckled as she realised that what she was doing was like the central planning of socialism. The difference was no one had to stay, except the guards, and this really was a life-and-death situation, not a fantasy about the failure of capitalism. The ex-prisoners knew it, and they were happy to leave her to her financial tasks while they tackled theirs.

She looked at the figures: money, food, fuel, gunpowder, people. She calculated they could withstand a siege until the New Year, as long as they kicked the imprisoned guards out now. At the following Sunday meeting, the ex-prisoners all agreed it was worth the risk, since the government would find out sooner or later about the takeover and they now felt better prepared to cope with the consequences. Liz watched them tramp away down the hill the following day. Good riddance, she thought. None of them had been prepared to stop the executions.

But then she wondered, could she blame them? They were only following orders after all, and someone had to give them. Most people she knew were passive. Decades of ecoism had made them even more so. They needed to be told what to do. That was the purpose of the government running healthcare, education and pensions. Without them, people would suffer, unable to obtain those things themselves. Especially the poor. She had clashed with Blake on this subject, even more since he got to know MacDermot. But she was sure she was right. She couldn't see any other way. But that could all wait. First they needed to survive in the castle, then convince people of the evil of ecoism, and only then set about resurrecting the government. It seemed an impossible task.

She wondered, as a banker, what she would do if she had to restart the financial system from scratch. That seemed impossible too – until she remembered the history of banking and the physical commodity which had underlain it. A substance which could not be created by a committee's tap on a keyboard: gold. Her family still had access to it, she hoped.

~

After three weeks of arduous but freely chosen work, the ex-prisoners felt in need of a celebration – to praise what they had done and to bolster their spirits for the future. Thanks to Rebecca, and by maintaining many of their former routines, they had avoided detection by the authorities for long enough to secure their situation. Now the prison officers had been released there was no point in hiding the takeover, so they arranged a ceremony to hoist a new flag – of the Brig's design – over the prison. It depicted a yellow light bulb with crenellations in place of the filament. His idea was to illustrate *'an Englishman's home is his castle'*, but protected by an invention of the mind. He said it was inspired by Dalton. As it ran up the flagpole the ex-prisoners cheered.

Liz organised a modest banquet in the main hall, and when it transpired that Greg the guard had musical talent, she asked him to play. From up in the minstrels' gallery, his acoustic guitar resounded from the castle walls as the industrialists and businesspeople ate rationed portions of potatoes and corned beef, while drinking dry the remains of the governor's cellar.

Laughing at the expressions of joy on his compatriots' faces – which had not seen such exuberance for months, if not years – Blake turned to Liz and remarked, "Isn't it amazing how much we've all done in such little time. It's like we're different people."

"We are the same, but the circumstances are different," Liz said.

"Yes," Blake said, laughing. "We don't have to spend all our effort complying with regulations. Here in our prison, we are truly free."

Liz smiled back, but she couldn't fully agree.

17

Inspector Smith had arranged an appointment as soon as he'd found out. Then he'd sworn the police in Westingham to silence. It would be his triumph alone. He struggled up the palace steps. His shoes were too tight and he kept putting on weight despite his best efforts to lose it. It must be the food companies, he thought, making him eat more with their addictive flavours and lack of concern about his needs. He was tall too, which meant he had to eat lots. Why couldn't they devise some range of diet products for him? They should be made to. Recalling the force of the law refocused him on the reason for his visit.

If he conducted himself well, he could move right up in the Ecoist Party ranks, as well as those of the police. He'd always wanted to be chief inspector. But if he failed, if the President blamed him for what he was about to hear, then he and his family would likely be back in the two-up two-down where they'd started – or worse.

As he showed his credentials to the armed guards and walked slowly down the red-carpeted corridor, he stroked his unkempt beard and ran his finger round the inside of his shirt collar – too tight. He could still go back. No, he'd calculated correctly, he was sure. The President would want to hear what he had to say, and wouldn't blame him.

Finally, at a pair of tall, ornately moulded doors, a footman showed him in.

The President was sitting on a throne, his head bowed in concentration over some documents. In front of him on a desk were several deep piles of paper.

Smith tiptoed up to the dais, his hat in hand. At what seemed a safe distance, he stopped and waited.

After what felt like thirty minutes from the aching in his feet, the President addressed him.

"Ah, Smith. How nice to see you. I believe you did some excellent work during the riots last year."

"Thank you, Lord Hardwicke."

"What brings you here today? It must be important."

"It is," Smith replied nervously. Important people never like bad news, he thought, running his finger round his collar. But it was too late now. "It's about the prison at Westingham Castle. I thought you should be the first to know, what with your brother being there, and the important example it sets to the public."

The President leaned forward. "Go on."

"The prisoners have—" he cleared his throat, "—taken over the prison."

"What!" the President shouted.

"It's like this, Mr. President," Smith spluttered. "One of your men, Lee Procter, was trying to contact the governor at the prison, Sir Oliver Furrow."

"Yes, I know who the governor is. Go on."

"Well, he didn't respond to phone messages for

several days, so Procter asked me to investigate. So I went there yesterday, and as I was about to drive up the hill to the castle, I saw a large group of dishevelled looking men in prison officers' uniforms coming down. I stopped and asked them what had happened." Smith opened his notebook. "They said 'the prisoners have taken over the castle, and the governor has been shot dead.' I thought you should be the first to know."

Smith waited, sweating, at the foot of the throne, not daring to look at the President's face.

Finally, he reacted. "Ha," Lord Hardwicke exclaimed, smiling broadly. Smith exhaled.

"You've made my day," the President said. "I'm so glad you told me."

Promotion it was, then, Smith thought, relieved.

"It's a shame about Furrow, of course. He was a good man, though a little overambitious."

"Right," Smith said, suppressing his expectations.

"But the prisoners like it so much, they prefer to stay in prison than escape! That's priceless. They must be afraid to come out." Fabian looked at the gilded dentils on the far side of the room. "Well, as long as they stay there, I'm content. Don't let any of them leave. I want them to stew in their own juices." He smiled at the thought, then continued. "I will, of course, continue executing them, slowly over time. The public must see that justice is being done. But we'll get them to come out one at a time when we need them, possibly to avoid their children being executed in their place, something like that."

Smith's mouth went strangely dry.

The President continued. "I'm putting you personally in charge of monitoring the situation there.

Don't make a fuss. Keep them guessing what we'll do next. But let me know immediately of any changes or movements."

"Yes sir," the Inspector replied.

"I'm trusting you with this, Smith."

"Thank you, sir."

"I need your attention on the matter while I focus on more important things." He looked around at his piles of papers. "Do you have any children, Smith?"

Smith was pleased the President had asked such a personal question. "Yes sir. One son. Jake. He's fourteen. He's been in the Green Shoots for five years now, and loves it."

Fabian smiled. "And will he be attending the National Youth Rally next week?"

#

It promised to be a hot July day, Blake observed as he stood beside the van with all the ex-prisoners.

"Would you mind holding the fort till I get back?" he asked the Brig.

"Very witty," the Brig said, handing him a taser gun.

The others nearby also smiled.

Liz looked more anxious. "Good luck. Come back safely," she said. Blake thought she was going to add something, but she didn't.

As he climbed into the prison van with Clive and Sam, he apologised to Paul. "Sorry about having to use some of your precious diesel."

"That's okay. Just make sure you save the future of this country. No pressure."

Blake smiled back, but they both knew it was no laughing matter. Many of the ex-prisoners had teenage children, and none of them had warned their offspring.

It had been extremely hard to keep silent. But they knew the alternative would surely mean the death of Candice Hardwicke, to whom they were indebted for the information. Also, unless the evil of ecoism was exposed for all to see, it would soon destroy them anyway. Instead, they were relying on Blake and his team.

Dressed in a prison guard's uniform, Sam drove the van out of the main gate, over the moat and towards the road. At the junction he turned right, towards London.

Inspector Smith was in his unmarked car behind some bushes on the opposite side of the road. He had trusted no one with the important mission the President had given him. He was alone. Having just eaten a heavy meal, he was also asleep.

The van made slow progress on the ill-maintained roads, made even slower when they got to the outskirts of London by the throngs of Green Shoots marching happily to their rallying points. Most, Blake guessed, were heading for Wembley Arena.

Clive was constantly but cautiously peering out of the window, hoping to see his son Keith, but knowing that he must not see him for fear of giving the game away. Besides, if he got out, he would be terribly conspicuous. There was not a single person over twenty-one to be seen. There must be a rule about no parents or guardians, thought Clive. Easier to control them without more mature views around.

Hopefully Candice was somewhere among them, their hidden accomplice. She was going to text them to help time their interception, and to report back if it had worked.

Sam drove on, heading obliquely, then away from the direction of the crowds, towards Blake's old firm.

After nearly two hours they drew up outside Caelum. The enormous car park was almost deserted. Blake thought the buildings looked neglected. Peeling white paint was flaking off here and there. It made sense – since the Internet Regulation Act there was no possible growth here, only decay. But it was unlikely that in only a year its crucial role of managing the telecoms traffic on the main communications highway in the UK had changed. The presence of several guards suggested not. They were wearing military style uniforms. Not employees that were likely to recognise him.

Sam drove up to the main gate and Blake, also wearing a prison guard's uniform, leant out.

"We're here to pick up some new prisoners."

"I haven't heard anything about that," said the bemused guard. The way he held his rifle, with the barrel pointing idly at his own foot and with the safety off, suggested he didn't know much else of importance either.

"Let us in, and we'll get your boss to call you and explain. You can always stop us leaving until you get the authorisation you're looking for."

The guard cogitated. That seemed to make sense. If they were here to nick stuff, which is what most people tried to do, he could easily stop them getting away. He had a gun.

"All right. But make sure you get authorisation from him to leave."

"Will do." Blake smiled and they drove into his old stomping ground. Figuring there would be fewer guards round the back, they headed there. On the way they passed the standby diesel generators. Blake's jaw tightened as he recalled the events of the previous spring.

There was one guard attempting to keep people out of the rear of the building. They gave him the same spiel as the other guard, but he refused to move. Blake and his team had no time to lose. As Sam got out of the van to talk to the guard in more detail, Blake came up behind and tasered him. Once he was trussed and gagged they entered the building through a fire exit that had been propped open, presumably for ventilation. Air conditioning was essential for large numbers of computers but it needed a quota which had probably been reduced.

Blake knew his way round well. Though an executive, he had overseen the plans for the building fifteen years earlier, wanting to ensure the place was efficient but also safe, especially given the thousands of servers chuntering away, using megawatts of power. They were silenced now by the Internet Regulation and Carbon Crime Acts, except for a few. As Blake stepped along the corridors and through server rooms, it felt eerie. An electronic *Marie Celeste*. A lot of equipment was not just silent, it had been moved. Dangling wires showed where it had been ripped out. However, unless things had radically changed, there would still be some systems connected to what was left of the Internet, and thence to the rest of the world.

Finally they reached a gallery that looked down upon the main Network Operations Centre, with its wall of screens – now mostly blank – and rows of benches covered in keyboards, mice and monitors. At one of these a balding, lone technician in his late thirties was sitting with his feet up, chewing a carrot, reading a dog-eared magazine. They went down to address him.

"Hi," Blake said. "We need to use your terminal."

"What?" the technician said, throwing the magazine aside and jumping to his feet.

"I said—"

"Wait, I recognise you. You're Blake Hardwicke. You're supposed to be in jail."

"I escaped. I need access to your screen."

"Hang on mate. I shouldn't even be allowing anyone in here, really."

"I built this place. I still own a lot of it," Blake said in frustration.

"No you don't. This is a government facility now. It was requisitioned after your trial."

"Look, I don't have time to argue with you. We're on a mission here to save millions of lives. Are you going to stand in our way?"

"Well, I'll have to ring my boss to check it's okay," the technician said, but he didn't move. Blake could see the fear in his eyes as they flicked back and forth beneath his glistening forehead.

Clive walked up behind the frozen man and tasered him. "'When all that counts as knowledge must come through others, then no one is free to have a thought of their own,' or something like that," Clive said recalling a passage from one of Dalton's books.

Blake sighed in recognition as they trussed and gagged the impotent man and carried him out of their way. Then he sat down at a console. It was still logged in. It was his job to hack into the power networks used by the rally venues. He quickly sent another text to Candice, then passed Greg's son's mobile phone to Clive.

"See what you can find out. There's another console logged in over there." He pointed to a keyboard under a lit screen across the room. Clive was in charge of sending an appropriate message to all the Green Shoots at the critical moment.

Sam, meanwhile, did his best to barricade the room they were in, in case of interruption. His son Liam was ten, and while not a member of the Green Shoots, he could easily have been caught up in the excitement of the day and gone to a rally with friends. Sam hadn't warned him.

"It looks like a lot of communication has been by text," Clive said. "Not surprising, given the crackdown on the Internet. Listen to these: 'Two weeks to go. Strike a blow for the Earth!'; 'Ten days and counting. Join the campaign we're mounting!'; 'The rallies are today. Meet your mates along the way'; 'At 4 p.m., the President's Speech and National Song. For you pure happiness won't be long.' That confirms what Candice said, so at least we know when it is. I'd better get on with the new message. How many servers have you got?" Clive asked.

"There used to be about five thousand," Blake replied wistfully. "I doubt there's more than two hundred now, judging by the lack of noise."

"That should still be enough. We can parallelise the program quite easily. It'll depend on how fat the pipe still is to the GSM network. If it's not looking good, I can always hack into my own servers at English Telecom and send some messages from there. What network addresses should I be looking for?"

Blake told him, based on his memory of how things had been set up, then got to work himself.

Paul Williams had given him an idea on where to start. In their bid to reduce CO_2, successive governments had extended the smart meter programme from homes to businesses. When they deemed too much CO_2 was being produced by electricity usage, the systems controlled by the Department of Energy and Climate Change, also known as the DECC, could cut the power instantly at any house, office or factory. Except for some businesses that had successfully pleaded for exemptions. Paul's Western Energy had obtained one based on the release of extra CO_2 if their power plants were shut down and restarted too frequently. The DECC had grudgingly agreed, but only to a temporary exemption. Like zero per cent VAT on food, the government reserved the 'right' to take control in the future. So the mechanisms for blacking out were all in place. But Paul had been given a password that disabled them. It was this that he gave to Blake.

Caelum's own servers were subject to blackouts, but because of his generators Blake had never tried to bypass them. Now he regretted his easy compliance. He had about two hours to undo years of evasions and government controls.

After twenty minutes of network tracing and struggling to reverse engineer how the blackout system worked, Blake looked away from his screen for a breather. "How are you getting on?" he asked as he shuttled across to Clive on his wheeled chair.

"All right, thanks," Clive said. He was rather

enjoying doing some low-level programming for the first time in years. He was putting the finishing touches to some code which would create text messages for all the phone numbers between 07000000000 and 07999999999. A billion messages was a lot, but it didn't matter if all the numbers were in service or not. It was better to hit all of them. He had already persuaded a hundred servers at Caelum to host his code and queue it up for execution. Next he would try to find a similar number at English Telecom. With the ability to fork the program into multiple copies of itself, he only needed each copy on each server to send out a relatively small number of messages, say 50,000. That way, they should all get out in time.

Blake, meanwhile, had found the key control server at the DECC. Hacking into it would take too much time. He needed Paul's password to work. Facing the 'login' prompt, he entered the details Paul had given him. He pressed 'return'.

He was in!

Excitedly, he looked around the system. What kind of software was it running? What kinds of databases? Were there any obvious ways he could access the central management system?

After a short time, but with only thirty minutes to go, he had discovered a lot. He had located the rally venues in the database. He knew their 'IDs' for priming the blackout software. But he also knew how limited the permissions of Paul's login were. He needed more authority.

He sat back, his hands trembling slightly, his eyes raw with staring, and breathed deeply. What would someone at the DECC use for a root password?

Something they wouldn't forget. Something tricky enough they wouldn't have to change it too often. He had a password-cracking program running against the system, but he needed a seed, something to narrow the search process…

~

She was standing with Lucinda in the top back row of Wembley Arena. Just like last time, Candice had been offered VIP seats at the front. Unlike last time, she had swapped them with someone else. From her position she could avoid any kind of panic, if there was one. She also had a good view of the attendees.

There were thousands of them. All within a few years of her own age. Mostly wearing the Green Shoots uniform: a green top with a red scarf. Many also wearing the emaciated look of either serious ecoists – denying themselves all but the minimum of the Earth's resources – or those who could no longer afford to eat well. International trade in food had been curtailed to save 'food miles' and prices had rocketed. They reminded her of monks and saints she'd seen in woodcuts from the Middle Ages. The difference was that ecoism offered them no afterlife.

A few seconds later, six giant screens around the arena flickered on. They showed a picture of the ecoist flag: a green oak tree like a mushroom cloud, on a red map of Great Britain, superimposed with smiling young faces of marchers on the way to their nearest rally. In the background some popular chart music was playing. She wondered if the artists knew what they were endorsing.

She checked her watch. It was 3:45 p.m. The big moment was at 4 p.m. She had a large rucksack at her feet, containing her stuff for the sleepover she had arranged with Lucinda. It also contained the masks. Would she need to use them? She had texted her father, who had somehow almost immediately replied: '*Send text during second chorus. Allow 30s delay*'. It was her responsibility to get the timing right.

Just then there was a blast of trumpets over the tannoy, and the long, wasted face of her uncle appeared on the screens, sitting on a throne, presumably in Buckingham Palace.

"My brave and noble children," he began. "Today you've travelled many miles to congregate with your friends throughout the country. Today marks the beginning of a new relationship between man and Earth, a new relationship, in which you will be the first, and bravest, to take part…"

Candice looked at the crowd. Many were standing to stiff attention, tears in their eyes. They wanted to be taken seriously, to be given a mission, to make the world a better place. Others were moving among the crowds, holding baskets, handing out mementoes of the day: flags, badges, rosettes. Eight months ago she would have been with them. A chill ran down her back as she thought how many of those smiling faces could soon be lifeless. It was up to her to save them. But when would be the right moment? Too soon, and the ecoists might have time to recover the situation and carry on. Too late, and…

Candice had her text ready. Her thumb hovered over the 'Send' button. How could she factor in the delay her father had highlighted? Was that thirty seconds before he got it, or thirty seconds for him to receive it and thirty more for him to do his bit? She didn't know.

Perhaps somewhere between the two. Wait… wait… the President's voice droned on. How long did it take to sing a chorus or a verse?

Then finally it stopped. The camera panned back to show the President standing and smiling in front of the ecoist flag. And then came a melody she hadn't heard before. The crowd was transfixed, as the screens showed waving flags and smiling boys and girls, the infectious tune playing in the background as a soundtrack. It was soon accompanied by words:

"We'll build a future strong and true,
We'll sacrifice, our sinful few,
And so emerge a better race,
For giving up our selfish space…"

Candice's mind woke up when it heard the word 'selfish'. What was she thinking? Why hadn't she acted? She pressed 'Send' and hoped it wasn't too late.

There was an agonising wait. How could thirty seconds feel so long? Then the double-bleep of a text on her phone: '*OK*'.

The hideous new National Anthem went on, the crowd picking up the chorus, reading the words from the enormous screens, their heads held high, waving their new flags.

Candice reached for her rucksack. The top was tied with a knot. Her fingers fumbled as she tried to undo it.

Then, suddenly, everything went black and silent.

~

Three Inner Circle guards were crammed into the roof space next to a whining air-conditioning system. When the lights went, the whining stopped. One of them ripped off his mask. He was claustrophobic. As he did so, he dropped the vial and swore. But he didn't hear it break. He felt around on the floor but couldn't find it in the dark. When he stood up, he heard the crunch of glass. A minute later, he sneezed.

~

As Candice rooted around in her rucksack, thousands of bleeps erupted round the stadium, in quick succession. The children nearby were comparing their screens. Lucinda showed Candice hers. It read, *'Sorry for the interruption of power. This will take some time to fix. Please proceed to the nearest exit.'*

Used to blackouts, they all produced torches or used their phones as lights and moved slowly out of the building.

Exactly forty minutes later, when they were all outside, they received another message: *'We, the egoists, have saved you from a smallpox attack via the air conditioning. Look for the men in masks.'*

Thousands of faces started looking about them. Soon, they began pointing in one direction. Candice could see a group of men wearing the uniforms of the President's Inner Circle heading towards a security van. They were all wearing full, rubber face masks. She opened the rucksack and started explaining things to Lucinda.

18

The blood-red sky of the early August dawn penetrated the windows of the throne room, drenching the tall, thin figure inside it who oscillated from one wall to another.

Fabian had been up all night, pacing manically, shouting at anyone who came near, his face puce and his eyes bulging as he tried to accept the massive failure of his plan.

How had it gone wrong? Manny was on his way. He'd better have an explanation. He had been in charge of making the rallies run smoothly. Instead, the power had gone off at all the venues simultaneously and none of the backup systems had worked. Some of the guards had still broken their vials, but the smallpox had not spread, except perhaps among them. And those texts! Going to the whole nation! Who the hell were they, the 'egoists'?

~

Manny sweated as he hurried along the red-carpeted corridors, which felt warm, despite the early hour. Were there always this many armed guards? He couldn't remember. Perhaps he was just being paranoid. He reached the throne room, braced himself, and was shown in.

"Manny." Fabian sounded genuinely pleased to see him. He hoped the mood would hold.

"Fabian, I've been up all night, working out what happened, and I have an answer."

"Go on." Fabian's voice was pleading.

"It wasn't some kids mucking around, it was done very professionally. The power control commands came from your brother's old Caelum headquarters."

"He couldn't have, he's…" The dawn light made Fabian's face even redder as he crossed the room, opened a door, and shouted at a guard outside, "Get me Inspector Smith on the phone." The guard hurried away.

Fabian turned to Manny. "And the texts?"

Manny cleared his throat. "Ultimately, the same."

"Aargh!" Fabian uttered, clenching his fists. "How could this be allowed to happen?"

"He's a resourceful man, your brother. He was probably helped by Clive Donaldson, another prisoner, because some of the new texts came from English Telecom's servers."

"Don't these people have any security?" the President raged.

"I believe their guards were attacked with tasers, but also your brother was driving a prison van which managed to deflect the bullets fired at it on its way out."

Fabian appeared stuck for words. Manny prompted him.

"Have you thought what you'd like us to report on

the matter? We've broadcast a holding pattern as you suggested, along the lines of—"

"I know, I know," Fabian said, pacing in frustration.

"Couldn't you just appear on television to reassure people we are investigating, and tell them the facts so far?" Manny suggested.

"The facts!" Fabian blurted out. "That mass death is good for the nation, for the race, for the planet?"

Those weren't the exact facts Manny had meant. But then, he wasn't sure which facts they could get away with.

Fabian carried on. "The people wouldn't understand. They don't know what's good for them. Particularly parents. They're typically so obsessed with their children they'd put them before almost anything else."

Manny heard a tone in his friend's voice, one he'd never heard – or perhaps never noticed – before. It was almost one of petulance. He wondered what it meant for a moment, but then his spin doctor brain kicked in and played out a strategy. As he spoke, he felt he was on automatic pilot. In one way, he was impressed; in another, slightly frightened.

"We can say the people in masks were simply soldiers carrying out a security exercise, assuring the safety of the children."

"And the power cut?"

"Part of the same drill."

"And the texts?"

"Also part of the drill. To see whether the government could contact everyone in times of emergency."

"And the word 'egoists'?"

"A mistake caused by predictive text."

Fabian stopped pacing and looked up, straight at Manny. Manny felt a surge of dread. Had he gone too far this time? Would he believe the public were that gullible?

"It's brilliant," Fabian said. "Put out that story right away. On all media. The people will trust me even more. Tell them we're slaving away to keep everyone safe."

He paused to breathe, then continued. "When the time is right, we will try again to reduce man's impact on the Earth. But next time, we won't allow any mistakes to happen."

Manny took the hint and the opportunity to leave.

As he strode back down the plush carpets to the entrance, he felt the exhilaration of power, but also the pit of dread in his stomach. What was he doing, covering for a man like that? Part of him knew it was logical, wanting to protect the Earth from man. But a deeper part was screaming something was dreadfully wrong. His daughter had been kept safely away from the rallies. But what about everyone else's? The thought rose like reflux in his mind. It was growing harder to suppress his doubts about what he was doing.

The chill air of the early morning hit him as he reached the top of the entrance steps. He swallowed hard and got into the car that awaited him, though he felt like running in the opposite direction.

~

Fabian, meanwhile, had Inspector Smith on the phone.

"Did you see them? Are they all still there? What the

hell's going on? I trusted you to do this properly."

Smith was sweatily calculating on the other end of the line.

"Speak up, man!" Fabian yelled.

"Yes sir!" Smith burbled. "The, er, prisoners are still in the castle. I saw some of them drive in late last night."

"How do you know they're all there? Did you count them out as well as back?"

Smith hesitated. He could lie. He was quite good at that. Years of interrogation had taught him how. But if he did, he'd have to explain why he didn't alert anyone when he saw the van leave. He decided to take his chances with the truth. Hopefully, the President would respect that.

"No sir," Smith said. "I must have missed them."

"You mean you were asleep, or you weren't there?"

"I must have dozed off briefly, sir."

"I see."

Quick, he thought, I need to redeem myself somehow.

"Mr. President, I believe I know something you might find important. I recognised the driver of the van. It was your brother, Blake Hardwicke."

The line went deathly still for several moments.

"That will be all, Smith. Stay at your post and call back if there are any more movements."

Fabian hung up.

He went to the door and spoke to one of the Inner Circle guards. "Inspector Smith is outside Westingham Castle. Find him and shoot him. He's a traitor." The guard nodded and left.

Then Fabian dialled his secretary. "Get me General

Kettle."

~

Five minutes later, General William Kettle, the Chief of the Army, answered his telephone. He did not like being called this early in the morning. It had better be urgent.

"Kettle, this is Fabian Hardwicke."

"Good morning, Mr. President," Kettle said through clenched teeth.

"I need you to take some soldiers to Westingham Castle and lay siege to it. Due to incredible incompetence the prisoners have taken control of the prison, and they need to be made an example of. When they surrender, starving and hopeless, we will deal with them in the full light of television. But if any try to escape beforehand, shoot them."

There was no reply.

"Is that clear, General?"

"Perfectly, sir."

"Then see to it," Fabian said and hung up.

Kettle slammed the phone down, seething. Hardwicke's way of ordering him around like a lackey was outrageous. And he didn't even have the courtesy to talk to him face to face. Coward, he thought.

But then what am I? he wondered. He despised the new President and regarded ecoism as a belief system run amok, ruining the country, but he had done nothing about it. On the other hand, Hardwicke had been voted in. Who was he, Kettle, to do anything other than obey? If he didn't, would he end up in the same boat as Brigadier Campbell, whom he had court-martialled for disobedience? Or worse? The irony and the justice made him shiver. He needed a hot cup of tea. He decided he would comply with the order, after breakfast. But he would not authorise any use of weapons without his own direct say so, except in clear self-defence. Attacking peaceful, British citizens was not what he had dedicated his life to.

#

As Blake stepped from the sunlit courtyard into the cold, dark chapel, a great cheer echoed off the ancient walls and rattled the stained-glass windows.

Clive and Sam were already sitting at giants' height, raised on the shoulders of others: those who had received text messages from their loved ones, confirming events at the rallies.

Paul Williams was waiting near the door as Blake came in.

"I don't know how to thank you," he said, clasping Blake's hand in both of his.

"What for?"

"My nephew, Gavin, a naive ecoist. He was at the rally in Cardiff."

"What happened?"

"He saw the masked guards. When the children approached them, they ran. He doesn't think it was a drill." There were tears in Paul's eyes.

Blake gave him a big hug. He himself had been worried about Candice, but according to a recent text she seemed safe enough at her friend's house.

After several more personal thank-yous, Blake stood on the altar step and called for silence.

"Thank you. We've had reports from all the rallies now, and as far as we can tell, there were no deliberate releases of smallpox. All the air-conditioning systems were stopped in time. But it's possible some accidents have happened and incompetent guards have infected themselves. This could spread if untreated, and we know the government's attitude to healthcare."

The audience murmured.

"This we will have to address if we get out of here. But for now," Blake continued, "we must focus on what we have achieved. We have averted a true disaster and embarrassed the regime. But there will be consequences. From the news on the radio just now, it looks like Fabian is trying to claim the whole thing was just a safety drill, and that our text should have said 'ecoists' not 'egoists'."

There was a cry of consternation from the crowd.

"He is a master of manipulating the narrative, so it's highly likely he will get away with it and remain in power."

"What if his plan had worked? What was he expecting to do after that?" one of the ex-prisoners asked.

"Who knows, or cares. Hopefully he'd have been lynched. But right now he's alive, and once he's figured out that we stopped him, he will come after us. It probably won't be a direct attack. He needs to build credibility as a compassionate President, not a mass murderer. So I expect we will have to cope with a siege. How ready are we? Sam?"

Sam stood and walked to the front.

"There are seventy-one of us altogether. If you don't mind roughing it a bit, we can last a year. We'll run out of fresh food fairly quickly, but if this siege is going to last, we may as well try growing some ourselves. Are there any keen gardeners among us?"

Half a dozen hands went up.

"Let's get together after this meeting," Sam said, and stood down.

"Paul," Blake asked, "how's the fuel?"

"The governor's credit is wearing a bit thin, but we've assembled enough diesel, wood and local coal for between six months and a year. It depends on how cold it gets, and how many jumpers you're prepared to wear. We bought a pile of those, too."

"Excellent," Blake said. "Clive, any progress with the army communications?"

"It's been tricky getting hold of components. Radio hams are even less common than train spotters these days. But within a range of one kilometre, we should be able to jam their radio signals and replace them with our own." Clive was grinning. Blake suspected he'd enjoyed the late nights, soldering.

"Thanks Clive. I suspect we'll need to. Liz?"

"We've spent all the cash we had, and most of the valuable watches and jewellery. But I think it's all been wisely invested. Anyway, if a siege starts soon, we won't be needing any money for trips to the shops."

"Quite." Blake smiled as they all laughed a little. It helped to be cheered up before facing the worst-case scenario. "If they get fed up with waiting and actually attack us, Brigadier, how ready are we to repel them?"

"We've got thirty-six rifles and eight working cannons covering the different approaches to the castle. They will do some serious damage if used correctly, and they should also act as a deterrent. I would like to perform some test firings, but these are ancient pieces of iron, so it's rather risky."

"Let's leave that until we have to use them. There's no point injuring ourselves or anyone who accidentally gets in the way. Or giving the authorities any excuse to attack us."

Campbell nodded.

"Gobind? How's the hospital shaping up?"

The pharmacist executive and ex-doctor spoke up. "We have ten beds ready and one operating room. As you can imagine, it is a bit primitive, but we've gradually been building up supplies thanks to the guards and their families, many of whom have now gone into hiding for their own safety." He indicated those that were left with a raised hand. "They've been presenting their doctors with a wide variety of symptoms, only to recover quickly then present with something else. It will be quite a conundrum if the authorities ever analyse the data."

Blake grinned. "I'm sure we'll have other things to worry about by then." He looked around at the 'army' of ability before him.

"Thank you all for your reports and your efforts. That leaves me. You'll be pleased to hear that the water system is fully functioning – but don't expect a hot bath every day. And if they block our drains as a way to degrade our environment, we'll go back to the old days and simply tip everything over the wall, hopefully onto any spies."

They all laughed, somewhat grimly.

Blake turned to the guards, who no longer wore uniforms but still had a habit of sticking together.

"Thank you for helping us get this far. Now is the last time you can leave. I know you have families nearby."

The guards looked at one another. Then Ed Quinton spoke. "You've saved our children. And you've saved us from being part of this." He indicated the entire castle. "We know we're risking our lives here, but in the long run, if the ecoists stay in power, our lives won't be worth living. We'd like to stay."

Blake smiled broadly and the rest of the ex-prisoners applauded. After some more back-slapping and hurried conversations, he went up to the highest tower with Ed's mobile and called Marisa. He hoped the authorities had not got round to blocking Ed's number.

It rang. It was the usual hour allowed for incoming calls and visitors, at least it had been over a year ago. It kept ringing. He looked out over the peaceful valley, which held no obvious trace of its previous conflicts. What had ended those? How much bloodshed had there been? A rough voice came on the line. Blake asked for his wife and claimed to be a solicitor. Then he waited. What would he say? There was so much after so long. Yet his call was sure to be recorded. If the siege happened, all mobile signals would be cut. If they surrendered…

"Hello?" It was Marisa's voice. Hesitant but clear.

"It's me."

"Oh my God. Blake. How are you? Where are you? Have you seen Candice? What do you know about those children's rallies? We've heard rumours…"

"Listen, darling. We probably don't have much time, or privacy. Can I tell you what I need you to know?"

They spoke for five minutes before she was forced to end it.

#

As Fabian Hardwicke addressed the 'War Cabinet' in the yellow room at Buckingham Palace, General William Kettle looked out of the window at the autumn leaves and noticed that Hardwicke's face was also turning a dull crimson. Quite a contrast to its dull pallor when he'd last seen him – laying the wreath at the Cenotaph in a poor imitation of royalty.

Kettle had obeyed the order to attend but was mainly there to stop things getting out of hand. There were only seventy-odd prisoners – hardly an army – and they hadn't committed any acts of violence – not since killing the governor, who to be fair was going to kill all of them. Indeed, they had let all the guards go who wanted to, rather than taking them hostage. The prisoners were still in prison and were no threat to anyone.

"Kettle?"

The General's reverie was interrupted.

"Yes?"

Fabian took a deep breath before repeating himself.

"What's the situation at the castle?"

Kettle had received a full report that morning.

"No one has gone in or out of the castle since we began the siege. And no weapons have been used by either side. The prisoners have been safely contained."

"Well, what on earth are they doing in there then? I cannot believe they're just playing Scrabble and waiting for the food to run out."

"As far as we can tell, they're not doing very much, except producing significant volumes of smoke—"

"Which is illegal," Fabian interrupted, getting up and pacing while toying with his ring.

Kettle stared at him before continuing, "—and lighting up the walls at night—"

"Also illegal," Fabian said, again not noticing Kettle's expression.

"—presumably to deter scaling." He paused, then thought there would be no harm mentioning another act of the prisoners. One he rather admired. "They've also raised their own flag from the highest turret. It seems to be their own invention. It shows a castle tower inside a light bulb."

Fabian snorted but couldn't think of a law preventing flag flying, so silently fumed.

Manny, as Minister for Information, felt obliged to chip in. "My reporters and other sources are at the scene, and have some interesting additional information."

Kettle scowled. He'd wanted to control the situation, to avoid provoking the President, who might easily escalate it.

"Yes, what is it?" Fabian snapped.

"It seems," Manny continued, "that despite their landline being cut and all the nearby mobile phone masts being switched off, the prisoners still get messages in and out via Chinese balloons."

"What? Those paper lantern things?"

"Yes, Mr. President."

"Well, what are they sending? Who's reading them?"

Thinking carefully, unsure who in the Cabinet knew of Fabian's real intentions, Manny continued. "They've been trying to take credit for preventing some supposed attack at the Youth Rallies. The messages aren't directed at anyone in particular. But crowds of people are waiting nearby, trying to catch one. Any spare accommodation has been taken."

"Why?" Fabian asked.

"Well, it seems they've been drawn by the sight of the so-called 'rebellion', Mr. President. They're calling the prison 'Castle Ego'."

Fabian stopped pacing the room and fell silent while he stared at Manny.

To look at the President's face, Kettle thought, was like watching a red balloon steadily inflate but going deeper, not lighter, in colour.

"Attack the castle!" the President shouted at him, relieving some of the pressure. "Kill all the prisoners!"

Manny gasped involuntarily.

Kettle looked at him with scorn. What did he expect?

After a suitable pause, hoping Hardwicke would come to his senses, the General responded.

"I'm afraid I cannot order such an action," he said calmly. "These are British citizens who are not using violence. My men will not attack them."

"You will do your duty, General Kettle, or you will be court-martialled," Fabian said icily.

"Doing my duty does not equate to obeying you," Kettle replied. "I resign." He stood. "And I will see you in court." Then he strode across the room towards the door.

"Stop him," shouted a desperate and apoplectic Fabian to the one guard by the door.

But Kettle had already drawn his pistol and was pointing it at the guard who had been too slow.

He relieved him of his gun.

As he turned before closing the door behind him, Kettle looked at the red-faced Fabian, the open-mouthed Manny Schweizer, and the other men and women of the Cabinet crouching behind their chairs. He had sworn to uphold the government, but not this. Not these sycophantic accomplices to murder.

He locked the door behind him and marched swiftly

down the corridors. Hardwicke would call in time for someone to try to stop him. But he had two weapons now. These would get him out of the palace, but where then? There was his family's ancient lodge on the Isle of Coll. He was pretty sure the enmity between the Scottish and English governments would make him safe there for a while. As he stepped into the back of his staff car, he gave the order to his driver to take them north. Then he phoned Lieutenant Colonel Peters, who was in command at the castle.

~

Back in the yellow room, Fabian was indeed making a call, but not to his guards. "Get me Lieutenant General Limpett," he barked, then resumed pacing the room. The rest of the Cabinet sat silently, afraid of saying the wrong thing.

"Limpett?" Fabian eventually said into the phone.

"Yes, Mr. President, what can I do for you?" Darren Limpett was surprised and flattered by such direct communication from the highest authority.

"You are now a full general. I am promoting you with immediate effect."

Limpett was gobsmacked. He hadn't done anything to warrant such a promotion. He'd spent the last several years keeping his head down at a desk job in Whitehall, writing occasional reports and looking forward to his pension. Did Lord Hardwicke even have the authority for this promotion? With all the constitutional upheaval since the Royal Family's departure, he probably did. Limpett didn't care to question it.

"Thank you, sir. How can I be of service?"

"I need you to go down to Westingham Castle and

storm it, making sure all the prisoners die in the process."

Limpett coughed and swallowed hard before answering. "Yes sir." Then he thought of something. It's a very sudden appointment Mr. President. Would you mind giving it to me in writing? And the orders? It would expedite matters with the officers on the ground."

"Yes, all right. But this is extremely urgent."

"I'll be over immediately." This would definitely improve his pension.

#

Brigadier Campbell could feel the cold stone of the parapet's floor seeping into his feet, but he stamped them up and down and kept his eyes to his binoculars. Now the sun was coming up he could see more clearly what the army was up to.

Next to him, with a blanket around his shoulders, stood Blake.

"They're packing up and moving back," the Brig said, squinting against the sunlight.

"If they're retreating, doesn't that mean we've won?" Blake asked incredulously.

"I'm afraid not. I suspect they're retreating to a safe distance. Then they can fire artillery without being in range themselves. I suggest you give everyone a last chance to leave."

Blake digested the Brig's unpalatable words, then spoke. "I'll organise an emergency meeting in the chapel." He began speaking into his radio.

As he did so, the Brig lit half a dozen Chinese lanterns made with blue paper which he'd retrieved from a nearby turret.

"What on earth are those for?" Blake asked.

"Hopefully someone will see them. It's a signal." He smiled grimly.

Ten minutes later, apart from the Brig, the ex-prisoners and ex-guards were all assembled in the chapel.

"It looks like we will be shelled quite soon," Blake announced sombrely. "If they put any effort into it, the castle will not survive longer than a day."

Murmurs went around the ancient sanctuary, until Clive spoke up. "Lord Hardwicke will not let us survive outside the castle, either. If we give in, and if he doesn't hang us first, which I'm sure he'd love to do, and if one day we're allowed to return to our businesses, we would not be permitted to run them, except as he and his strangling regulations allow. Avoiding the noose and begging for favours is all we could hope for."

The chapel stared in silence. None could disagree.

Eventually, Blake said, "Is there anyone who wants to leave?"

For a while, no one moved or said a word. Then Sam said, "You know, I've enjoyed myself in here, in prison since the takeover, more than when I was part of normal society. I've felt…" He paused. "…free."

They all looked at him as he said these words, knowing exactly what he meant.

After a minute, nobody had moved to leave.

Blake smiled. "Thank you all for your friendship and your self-belief. Together we have achieved more in a few weeks than our businesses have achieved in years. Together we can do far more. Let us not give up just yet. It's time to go to your posts, for the defence of your lives and for everything you care about."

A massive cheer went up from the determined crowd as it left the chapel, causing the rooks on the roof to fly in panic, and a soldier in the regular army, who saw the birds, to wonder why. A split second later he heard a sound like a rumbling rugby crowd.

~

It was two in the afternoon when the first missile struck the castle walls. It did not strike exactly where its aimer had intended, but it did not miss. Instead of hitting the outer gate, it hit a guard tower. On its roof were two businessmen – one a chemist, one a philanthropist – armed with rifles obtained by the Brigadier. They both fell to their deaths as the tower collapsed beneath them.

The artillery gunner adjusted his aim as his commander looked for signs of damage and defeat. But the castle tower in its light bulb still fluttered bravely from the highest turret.

The Brig gave the order for all his cannons to fire. None struck far enough to reach the hiding army, but at least he now knew their range. Simultaneously, he released ten red-coloured Chinese lanterns with the words, *'God's speed'*.

The commander of the smoking army gun saw that it was an unequal match and ordered his men to take their time reloading. When asked to report to his superior officer, he said the gun was jammed.

Not all the other commanders were so scrupulous. Their batteries were set a safe distance back on the same side as the main gate or on the western flank. The other sides were far too steep and offered only a glancing shot. While some shots deliberately missed their targets and over- or under-shot the castle walls, a strike per minute began to shatter the ancient structure.

Tomasz Kolodziejczuk was a mathematician who had been imprisoned for contradicting the figures produced by the government's climate scientists. He was in the visitors-cum-arms room, loading and checking his rifle for the expected final assault, when the roof exploded. Its pillars toppled, pinning him to the stone-flagged floor, rubble blocking out the light.

His right arm was broken – he could feel it. His legs, he could not. That didn't bode well, he thought, but he cried out for help, not giving up yet.

It seemed like hours before voices came amid the thundering bombs, and after the sound of heaving stones, they gently lifted him away. But still he could not see.

"You're safe now," said a voice. He recognised it as Gobind, who was still a registered doctor.

"Thank you," Tomasz tried to say. He marvelled yet again at what men would do for each other without any kind of order, given the chance. As he lay on his back, detaching himself from the pain, he thought of the people he'd loved – especially his wife and child – and the joy he'd felt in his life through solving mathematical problems, and how he'd relished working each day to apply them to real-world issues. He also recalled his favourite music, Chopin, and knew he had been happy because all the values he had chosen had been his. Then he closed his eyelids and let the forces he could not control take their course.

~

The Brigadier still manned the cannons facing front, ready to repel any personal attack. His cheek was bleeding from the cut of a shrapnel shard, but he'd sprayed it with a hydrogel dressing and stayed at his post. Blake ran hunched over from the central keep, where he'd been seeing to the injured, and joined him on the wall.

"We've already got three dead and seven injured. Do you think they'll keep it up, that rate of firing?"

Campbell reflected a moment. It had only been thirty minutes. "That remains to be seen," he said through gritted teeth.

Just then, a mortar bomb exploded in the courtyard behind them. It shattered the stonework surrounding the well that Blake had made work again.

"Destruction is easy, isn't it," he said to the Brig as he dusted himself off and noticed some shrapnel cuts to his hands.

The Brig snorted in reply.

Blake thought for a moment, torn.

"If we surrender," Blake said, recalling something Dalton had told him, "we're showing them that destruction succeeds, even if it's only for the short term. But if we never surrender, there can be no doubt about what they've achieved."

The Brig looked at him, marvelling at words he wished had passed his own lips on the battlefield. "Yes, I do believe you're right. But maybe it won't come to that."

He had heard a distant drone, like a thundering bee, and was training his binoculars on the skies to the north. Hard to see at this angle, head on, a well-recognised shape slowly grew as it moved towards him and a grin formed on his blood-soaked face. When he handed the binoculars to Blake, there were tears in his eyes.

"This is something you should see."

Blake had heard the sound but couldn't explain it. Now, with the glasses, he understood. The unforgettable deep throb of the engine grew louder and louder, and suddenly the Spitfire was streaking past them at a hundred miles an hour. He followed it with his own eyes now and saw a flag of red, gold and blue streaming behind the pilot's canopy. It couldn't be! Could it?

The graceful defender of the Isles banked and came around again. This time it unleashed a thunderous pummelling of exploding lead upon the bewildered soldiers standing by their guns and looking up. They fell like ninepins, caught out, with no expectations of attack from the air and no weapons to repel it.

The invincible killer rounded on them again, and this time dropped a cluster of bombs in its wake that smashed the landscape and several guns to smithereens.

The Prince tilted the plane and looked down from his cockpit window. The army crews on the ground were running now – the army he had once served with. But they knew the rules, and they could see from his flag who he was. They could surrender, or they could face the consequences. He would chase them until they understood.

He banked the plane again. It wasn't easy with one false leg, but he smiled as he thought of Bader and knew he had no right to complain. The Spitfire had been the best option he could find after the RAF had spread itself to the four winds, as he'd implored them to. The mechanics were simple and easier to get help with than modern planes. As for the ammunition, luckily he knew a collector who had some stashed away in Norfolk, and he'd flown there to collect it.

He strafed his ex-colleagues again and estimated his remaining number of rounds. Hopefully a couple more passes would do it. They'd tried firing rifles at him, but he didn't care and most were too scared to get too close, even to rescue their dying mates.

He came around again, readying his bombs. But then, out of the corner of his eye, he caught sight of a stream of floating green lanterns coming from the castle. Looking back at the enemy, he saw a white square on the fields to the south, marked out on the ground with sheets. He laughed through his teeth and barrel-rolled across the Northamptonshire sky, before waggling his wings as he flew across the castle and back to his base, glad it was over for now, but preparing to reload.

19

Darren Limpett was sitting safely at his desk in an obscure office of the MoD in Whitehall – but he didn't feel safe. He liked his new promotion, but he didn't like what came with it. He slicked back what remained of his hair for the umpteenth time, then made the call.

"Lord Hardwicke?"

"Yes?"

"It's General Limpett."

"Yes, I was wondering when you'd get round to calling."

"Ah. So you've heard the news then."

"Of the ceasefire, yes. Was there something else you wanted to tell me?"

"Lieutenant Colonel Peters arranged the ceasefire. It was his idea. I've been extremely busy, trying to convince the troops to fight, but they simply won't."

"And you did all this difficult persuasion from your desk, did you?"

Limpett hesitated. "Yes sir."

"I see."

There was a long pause. Limpett could hear the

President breathing.

"Stay at your desk and don't make any more calls. I'll let you know when I need you to do something."

"Yes sir." The relieved general put down the phone. Had he just got away with it? Or had he just suffered the shortest promotion since the Charge of the Light Brigade?

Meanwhile, Fabian got back on the phone. "Manny, I need your services. We're going to Westingham."

~

Manny had conflicting feelings about the trip as they sat in Fabian's official car, making their way to the castle. On the one hand, it was key that he was at the centre of government. He had the best possible access to information and a special channel through which to try to control events. On the other – what was he thinking? It was one thing to move the world surreptitiously towards socialism, but it was quite another to be party to attempted genocide.

Or was it? He remembered the books written just after the Wall came down, exposing the millions of Soviet deaths caused by socialist policies towards farmers. Then similar books came out about Mao's Red China. He hadn't been able to finish reading any of them. As for Fabian's government – he was in too deep to get out now, but shouldn't he try to do something? He had unleashed a monster on the world. A monster now sitting opposite him, looking calculatingly out of the window. Or had he? Wasn't history inevitable? That's what Marxism had always said.

He admitted he was just trying to find excuses. And he knew he would have to explain himself before long. The editorial page of his own newspaper stared up at him. Besides the leading articles, there was a letter to the editor titled '*Fallen Heroes*'. It reflected on the recent Remembrance Day parade and urged readers to consider what those soldiers died for, suggesting one reason was to avoid another Holocaust.

Manny felt the opposite of a hero. He knew that he had aided and abetted an attempt at mass murder. That he had abused his official positions. That he was about to assist in the destruction of seventy political prisoners. But what could he do? The bulletproof black Range Rovers of the Inner Circle were hemming him in at front and rear, but not as tightly as his own fear.

As they eventually neared Westingham, having been held up by horses, potholes and a puncture, Fabian came out of his own reverie. "I will speak first, but when I give the signal, I would like you to address the troops also. Give them your best patriotic guff. Whatever gets them back on side and ready to attack that castle."

"Yes, of course," Manny replied.

~

When they arrived at the camp, Fabian's car drove across the frosty field to where the men were assembled in uniformed ranks. As soon as it came to a halt, Fabian sprang out. "Peters!" he shouted. "Lieutenant Colonel Peters!"

A tall man of about forty in combat dress walked calmly towards him. When he stopped, he saluted.

"Peters, I am relieving you of your command, with immediate effect."

The officer hesitated momentarily, then saluted again and marched off. As he did so, Manny noticed him glancing back at the castle.

With the help of a set of steps retrieved from the one of the Range Rovers, Fabian climbed onto its roof and addressed the troops through a megaphone.

"As you know, Remembrance Day has just passed. While I was at the Cenotaph, you were holding your own service here. That day is a reminder to us, of the noble and immense sacrifices your forefathers made in past wars for the sake of this beloved country.

"You are the proud inheritors of a tradition of military prowess that is not only highly honourable, but which underpins the peace and civilisation of a country which demands obedience to the law. Normally, civil disputes are the police's responsibility, but in extreme circumstances such as these—" he pointed at the castle, "—it is you, that must defend the country from anarchy. This is your vital role in Britain's ancient constitution. If you do not fulfil it, if you do not accept and act upon your duty, you must ask, 'Who are we?', 'What are we here for?'"

There was a very long pause. Then, with his CO dismissed, Sergeant Ian King decided the speech was over and it was time for action. If no one else was going to take up the call to arms, he would. Stirred by the President's words – and, in the back of his mind, thinking of a promotion – he yelled, "Right, lads, on the double," and led a squad of a dozen men with rifles and a mortar gun towards the castle.

Fabian smiled broadly. "When this battle is won, they will be the ones who are honoured," he declared from the top of the car as the other troops stood and watched.

King couldn't hear any approaching aircraft nor see any signs of serious opposition as he led his team towards the castle. There were some ancient looking cannons on the battlements, but he doubted anyone could work them properly any more. At a distance he judged suitable for attack he ordered his men to set up the mortar and kneel in firing position. His plan was to enter through the main gate by blowing it up, then to pick off with rifle fire anyone guarding it .

"Fire!" he ordered, and the mortar was loaded then shot away with a dull thud. It sailed just over the wall above the main gate. An explosion, followed by cries of pain, came from within.

Adjusting the aim down slightly, the mortar operator reloaded and waited for the command to fire.

It was the last action he took. The Brig's aim was not so bad. The cannonball hit the ground just in front of the mortar gun then bounced into the squad of men, taking off the crouching operator's head and the right arm of his mate.

Then came a series of whizzing sounds, and it was the squad's turn to cry out in pain. One of the ex-prisoners had won medals for amateur marksmanship at Bisley, and had not lost his touch.

Ian King took a bullet to his left thigh, but still managed to limp and hop back the way he'd come. Lacking instructions, the rest of his men retreated, leaving the body and the arm behind.

The remaining soldiers, still on parade beside Fabian's car, looked on in horror. The President himself had a look of fear frozen on his wasted face.

The firing stopped, but then a more dangerous weapon attacked them all. The voice of an unafraid man.

"This is Blake Hardwicke. I am speaking to you from

the castle you have just attacked."

The soldiers looked round in confusion for the source of the disembodied words. It was coming from all their radios, simultaneously.

"I see that only a small number of you recommenced hostilities. I realise you must be torn between obeying orders – as you've been trained to do, as an army must do if it is to achieve victory – and staying alive. You know now that you will be shot from the land and the air if you attack, and while you as a collective might eventually win, your individual chances of survival are poor.

"I can help you decide. If you attack us, we who are due to be hanged for running our businesses with fossil-based fuels, consider what you risk throwing your lives away for. Since you can remember, you have been lectured by politicians about sacrifice. About giving up your tax money, your freedom, your ambition, even your life, while the country recovers, or to help the poor, or the health service, or foreigners, or the planet. But always at a loss to yourself. Always harming your own self-interest.

"Ecoism, the philosophy now ruling this country, is yet another example. It has taken away your cars, your heating, your lighting, your food, your foreign travel and your ability to prosper. It has reversed the Industrial Revolution. The leader of this movement, and of this country, my brother, has followed this philosophy several logical steps further.

"Firstly he attempted to kill me and my son as we drove to an anti-ecoist meeting. As it happened, only my son was in the car and he died as the result of a staged accident. Fabian admitted this to me himself.

"Secondly, he held my trial for espionage in secret because I had uncovered his plot to kill the sick and elderly. This was, and is, being done by failing to provide backup heating and power to hospitals and care homes, leaving them to fate when a blackout hits.

"My brother is also the architect of the attempt to sacrifice a whole generation to ecoism. Your children narrowly avoided being infected with a deadly virus at the Youth Rallies. Fabian claims it was just a drill for their safety. That the text message had a misspelling. But in fact, it was me and my fellow prisoners who cut the power and sent the messages. And it was we who discovered that the secure store of smallpox in Porton Down had recently been withdrawn on Fabian's orders. For that, the President has ordered you to attack the whole castle. Believe me, if you succeed in killing us and turning it back into a prison, you will have sealed your own fate. Fabian will see to it that our cells are quickly filled by other dissenters who will be hanged, and then by others, until there's no opposition left and the entire country acts in obedience to him.

"All of the President's actions, and all of the rhetoric he uses on you, is driven by the principle that self-sacrifice is noble. Do not fall for it.

"Your life, and your children's lives, are your own. There is no reason why sacrificing them is good for you, and every reason why it is not. Self-sacrifice, altruism, and now ecoism – its most deadly form – have been rammed down your throats as the only moral way to live. My brother and his genocidal actions are the logical result, for if sacrifice is the good, living your life according to your values is the bad. You now have to make a momentous choice. To continue to be pawns in the sick ambitions of my deluded brother and his followers, where the best kind of world is one without humans. Or to break with the inhuman, anti-human morality of self-sacrifice, and try to live and prosper instead."

#

LC Neil Peters had forgotten about the anger and fear in his heart from being so easily dismissed. The words from the radio had made it irrelevant, like an anaesthetic. In the silence that followed, the anger and Peters' guilt and confusion came rushing back.

Who was he supposed to take orders from? Kettle had ordered him not to attack. Limpett had said he had to. But when he did, the Prince, his fellow officer, had attacked them. Now the President had assumed command, but he was sure his troops wouldn't obey such a man. Was he supposed to relay the President's orders without official command? Or should he break from political authority and lead the army himself? There was no one to make up his mind for him. This time he would have to ask his own conscience.

He'd almost forgotten about his friend and mentor, Brigadier Campbell, whom he had attacked earlier. He knew he should have come forward to defend the Brig at his trial, but he hadn't. He'd convinced himself he would be putting his own family at risk – perhaps he would have been convicted, too. Now he accepted that had been excuse. The danger to his family, and everyone's families, was far greater thanks to his inaction, which had led to the imprisonment of heroes like the Brig. Now the danger to himself, from the Prince's strafing, was very real too. He smiled grimly. At least there was justice in that.

So how had the President gained so much power when – as seemed obvious now – his goal was to destroy the country?

He recalled the mantras of his upbringing: 'Do more with less', 'Save the planet', 'Don't rape the Earth', 'Production is Pollution'. They had always been there, and he had always, sometimes grudgingly, accepted them. Then taught his children to respect them.

He remembered the last barbecue they'd had as a family before the ban. It had been a gorgeous, warm August afternoon, and they had sat around the fire-pit until late at night, cooking meat, laughing and singing, watching the embers slowly fade, yet never questioning whether the ban was really needed.

As a soldier, he often had to burn wood when there was nothing else available. What real harm can it do, he wondered, burning charcoal at home, or coal in power stations, especially with scrubbers attached to them as Paul Williams had explained up at Tilcot? The ban had certainly harmed his family's enjoyment of summer life, and the carbon-adjusted price of winter heating had certainly made them poorer. Could the planet, as such, ever really be 'harmed'? It was a good question. At Sandhurst he had read Sun Tzu. But the army had also sponsored his degree in philosophy. He realised he had allowed his critical faculty to atrophy since his college days. Now he tried hard to kick it into gear.

The planet couldn't feel, or think, or suffer the cold. It wasn't alive. It was just the place where living things lived – or tried to. What sense was there in human beings denying themselves life-enhancing things for the sake of an unfeeling world that couldn't care?

Another question leapt to the front of his mind, as if it had been lying in its depths, waiting for an opportunity to pounce. If people alive today used some of the Earth's resources, as they had to, to stay alive, did they really harm the chances of future generations? For a start, the future generations wouldn't exist unless the current ones looked after themselves. Also, the Earth was not like an empty supermarket shelf after a panic buy. It was more like an unexplored, almost infinite larder. Throughout the ages, men had used their ingenuity to discover and unpack these resources, just as he and his men did in the wild – until other men stopped them, as had happened with shale. If you believed that man's moral aim should be self-destruction, then stopping his attempts to live was logical. The next slogan could easily be 'People are Pollution', followed by laws to clear them up. He felt a shudder and the replacement of his earlier anger with indignation. This was the kind of feeling that had led him to join the army in the first place. A desire to fight for justice against those who used violence on the innocent. The reconnection with his values made him smile.

He knew what he had to do now. He would obey himself.

~

While LC Peters was beginning to feel happy, Manny Schweizer was beginning to feel his blood run cold. He knew about most of the bad things Fabian had done; he had helped cover them up. But he hadn't known about the hospitals and care homes, and he didn't need to check the evidence. It sounded too like Fabian to be untrue. The letter to the editor about Remembrance

Day was still etched on his conscience. For once, he couldn't stop his mind putting two and two together. His ancestry wouldn't let him: Fabian and ecoism were worse than the Nazis, because they wanted to destroy the whole of mankind, not just a part of it. A wave of dread and nausea rushed through him, bringing with it a tide of self-incrimination.

He had never bothered to check the truth of all the eco-scare stories he had published over the decades. He had enjoyed the boost in sales and the level of interest in his paper's articles. He had enjoyed being an authority and being interviewed on serious news programmes. He had enjoyed being made head of the GBMC, then the Minister of Information. He had enjoyed putting down Dalton MacDermot in public debate. When MacDermot was executed, he had felt a little sick, but no remorse for his part in it.

Why?

He had never dared answer that question before. But now he knew the price he was to pay for unleashing the monster that was ecoism and its chief feeder, Fabian Hardwicke. It was to unleash his conscience upon himself. He, Manny Schweizer, was a power-luster. He lived to make people do what he wanted, to react to his wishes, and to live out the same moods and fears as him. He was a second-hander of the worst sort – his existence depending on others' duplicity. It was a double fraud since he didn't really believe what he wrote himself. Being an activist for socialism and ecoism had given his life meaning. Now he knew just what that meaning was.

Fabian had passed him the megaphone some time ago. He held it clutched in his hand.

"Speak!" Fabian screamed at him. "Tell them what to think!"

Manny felt the weight of a thousand tombstones where the megaphone was. He couldn't have lifted it to his mouth if he'd tried. But he did have one choice left to him. It was all he could do to redeem a sliver of his soul before it was condemned, by himself and by history.

He looked Fabian squarely in the face, not caring, for once, to modulate how he looked himself. He saw for the first time, in the bloodshot, pinched face of his friend, the fear and malice of the thing he had helped create.

Slowly and clearly, he said, "No."

As he did so, he let go of the megaphone. It struck a rock as it hit the ground, its plastic case cracking open and its components spilling out.

For a moment, Fabian looked as if part of him had broken with it. Then he visibly took a deep breath.

"This is a war situation," he shouted, unamplified from the top of the car. "I am in supreme command of the army. All deserters and disobeyers must be shot. Starting with him." He thrust an arm at Manny.

The nearby soldiers grasped their weapons more tightly and looked around at each other. After a few seconds, nothing had happened.

Lee Procter, now a senior member of the Inner Circle guard, raised his pistol and pointed it at Manny, who raised his hands in surrender. Lee knew the danger of disobedience. It involved questioning oneself. It was something he was afraid to do. He aimed at Manny's heart and pulled the trigger.

#

The famous newspaper editor, Director General of the GBMC and Minister for Information crumpled to the ground – like a puppet who'd had his strings cut, Lee thought, smiling.

The rest of the Inner Circle, torn between fear of death and loyalty to their President, surrounded Fabian and pointed their pistols at the army. But they did not fire.

From fifty yards away, LC Peters felt anger and disgust at the sight of the summary execution. Like his colleagues, he hadn't raised his gun at the Inner Circle. It was too absurd. How had such brutal automatons got the idea they could take on the British Army? Instead, he walked slowly back to the Range Rover and then raised his voice.

"Lord Hardwicke," he said, addressing the perspiring face of the President, "you are a weak, pathetic fraudster. Your only power is destruction. Your only skill is to make people hate themselves and fear the future. That's what a belief in ecoism does. You must know this, you're smart enough. So you're either some kind of sadist," he looked at the man who had shot the editor, "or you're so afraid of the future yourself, you need others to feel the same so you can pretend it's normal." He scrutinised the darting eyes of the President and tried to work out which vice it was.

"Either way," he continued, there being no authority to interrupt him, "I will not take orders, opinions or threats from such a man," and he slowly raised his rifle to point at Fabian's chest.

A second later, the nearest hundred soldiers did the same, training their sights on Fabian or the Inner Circle. A dozen of Fabian's most loyal guards dropped their pistols immediately and raised their hands. Peters signalled them to move away and accept capture. The rest, around thirty, continued to point their guns at the soldiers.

"Shoot them!" Fabian screamed.

Both sides opened fire. In an instant a ring of bodies lay on the ground. The soldiers among them, who were all wearing body armour, were only injured or wounded. The Inner Circle, in their striking but impractical uniforms, were all dead. Fabian had been hit multiple times, and he fell from the Range Rover to lie in the mud below.

Peters covered him with his rifle. He could see the President was bleeding heavily from his abdomen. "You could live, if we treat you quickly."

Fabian could feel the sticky wetness against his side. He touched it with his hand then examined it. It was dark red.

A feeling of exultation came over him. He realised this was what he'd always wanted. He felt vindicated. It gave him the strength to address the crowd around him.

"You think you've won, don't you. You think you're good, puffed up in your uniforms, looking forward to more medals. But your pomposity is just a show. You're just as pathetic as the rest of us. You live in an industrial civilisation that you didn't make. You are usurpers. Not just of the modern world and all its technology – technology you rely on but do not understand, like your guns and your radios – but also of the positions you hold. You did not earn your places in the world. You simply copied what others before you had done, then slipped into their shoes. You need the prestige of a good job, of a career, just as you need the supermarket food you wouldn't know how to grow, and the heat from the electricity you wouldn't know how to generate."

He paused for breath. Somehow, his very weakness made his convictions stronger.

"You depend on all these things, but you cannot earn them. You exist in this world, but you have no right to any of it, no more than the next man, or the poorest hut dweller in the developing world."

He grinned through a pain-tightened jaw.

"I have done my best to bring this country to its knees, through years of regulations, prison sentences and rationing – to help you realise the true position you're in."

He paused again, feeling a huge relief at saying these things out loud for the first time.

"Now you know your total worthlessness, you cannot go on as the charlatans and freaks of nature that you are. Charlatans because you have no right to what you haven't earned. Freaks because you somehow still manage to be happy. How can you be happy when your whole life is built on lies? The animals are not happy. They're honest. They take nature as it is and don't continually try to change it. They accept their position and capabilities and let nature take its course. But mankind, smiling, striving, greedy, dominant mankind, you have the gall to think you are better than the animals. That you know better, how to change the world, better than your parents, better than previous generations. And so you strive against nature in pursuit of your selfish gain, calling yourselves heroes, while you leave destruction in your wake."

He paused again, panting. His blood was getting warmer and wetter round his stomach, but now he had started down the road where his speech had led him, he had to finish.

"You fight against nature. You fake scientific knowledge, which is all just guesswork. You know no one can be certain of anything. And you clamber over each other in careers, in sport, in personal relationships, struggling to get ahead. And yet, you claim you are happy. That it was all worth it. I cannot understand you. I cannot believe you. You cannot be happy. It isn't possible. How can you be happy?"

He stopped himself from saying what was really on his mind: how can I be happy? He knew he felt it sometimes, but when? Breaking his brother's toys, winning the election, watching MacDermot hang, watching prisoners on their knees, planning the Youth Rallies. These had all given him a feeling of excitement, of pleasure. But each was tinged with a streak of guilt, and none of them had lasted. He had to keep creating such opportunities, so he could feel happy again. He had to keep…

He could not finish those words, even in his mind. He had admitted, for the first time, who and what he was. He felt paralysed.

~

LC Peters had been listening behind his rifle with increasing horror to the contorted creature in front of him. And he knew now it was not just physical pain. He lowered his gun because he saw that it wasn't necessary. Instead, he used a more deadly weapon. He finished Fabian's thoughts for him.

"You don't want to live."

"No," Fabian rasped.

"But you do want us to die."

"Yes!"

"You envy our desire to live."

There was no reply.

Their eyes met, and what Peters saw was hardly human.

Slowly, and with difficulty, Fabian reached inside his jacket with his blood-covered left hand. The blue pill had been nestling in his inner pocket for a long time. He had intended to take it if the rallies had been successful. But they hadn't. Yet again, his perfect, boastful, vain, smiling brother had beaten him. His happy, accomplished, rich, popular brother Blake was about to win again by defying the army and keeping the castle. Well, there was one thing Blake could not do. One thing he, Fabian, the younger one, the smaller one, who'd never had a chance, could do. And his brother would not be able to stop him.

He put the pill in his mouth, and with the help of some blood pooled in his hand, he chewed and swallowed it.

LC Peters watched in disgust as the ex-President of his country writhed in obvious agony on the ground before him. It seemed fitting that all the energy of Fabian's last act was used for the same purpose he had lived his life. Finally, he stopped moving.

20

Blake handed the binoculars back to the Brig. They had heard the volley of gunshots and Blake had seen his brother fall from the Range Rover. But now the car obscured their vision. Was Fabian dead or just injured?

Blake felt his heart racing. There were no more shots. Who was in charge now? Would they order another, more concerted attack? It would be hard to repel if they did. The Prince could only carry so much ammunition. He and the Brig exchanged glances then watched and waited mutely.

A crackle of static came from Blake's radio.

"This is Lieutenant Colonel Neil Peters."

The Brig looked up, frowning. He hadn't forgotten Peters' betrayal at the power station.

After a short silence, the radio continued. "The President is dead. We offer a truce."

The Brig shouted, "Yes!" punching the air.

Blake gasped as he felt a flood of jostling emotions. They surged through him, leaving him powerless to examine them, only able to respond automatically. Incredulity – his brother was dead, but had he really wanted that? Relief – he wouldn't have to fight for his own life any more. Vindication – the plans, the interception, the takeover, the forest, the investigation – they had all been worth it. Avenged – James's and Dalton's killer was dead himself. Anger – all the mental and physical pain that he and his ex-prisoners had had to endure, the casualties of the siege, the privations they'd all accepted for years – all of which had been caused by Fabian. Sadness – that his marriage, his son, his daughter, and his business had all been taken away from him by ecoism. Fear – he knew he had brought down the nation's government, and that he now had a responsibility for raising up a better one. Strength – he had succeeded in what he had tried – he had survived in a forest, he had saved himself from the noose, and he had helped save everyone in the castle. Confidence – he would succeed again in his next endeavour, because he had reason on his side, and because egoism was good and efficacious.

The Brig had been looking at Blake for a while as he leant on the battlements, drawing deep breaths. When he seemed to have regained control, he asked, "Shall we accept?"

Blake looked up, astonished to find someone else so close by. "I'm sorry, what?"

"The truce. Shall we accept the truce?"

Blake stood up and breathed in the cold winter air, feeling the stones under his feet. He looked at the Brig, who raised his eyebrows.

"Yes," Blake said.

"Lieutenant Colonel Peters, we accept," the Brig said into the radio. "We will meet you at your camp shortly, to discuss terms."

A roaring cheer went up around the castle. They had all been listening in on the same frequency.

The Brig changed channels on the radio. "Clive. Can you and a couple of the others with cannon training get up here and take our positions?"

An affirmative reply came back.

"Just a precaution," the Brig said when Blake looked at him. "I know Peters well. He was under my command for several tours. I trust him, even though he didn't defend me at my court-martial. We just don't yet know the level of command he's got, or the state of the army."

As they proceeded down the tower steps at the end of the battlements, they met Clive, who was running up to meet them.

"Reporting for duty, sir," he said, mock-saluting, the stone dust falling from his sleeve.

"At ease," the Brig replied, grinning.

"You're in charge of the castle now," Blake said.

"All right. Call me when you're coming back and I'll put the kettle on."

Blake chuckled. Then he and the Brig descended to the ground and walked out of the main gate and up the drive.

As they went, Blake said, "I see you've brought your pistols."

"I want them to know we're not pacifists," the Brig said lightly. Then he added more seriously, "As Dalton once said, we do have a right to defend our own lives. If everyone stuck to self-defence, we'd never need to use them."

As they arrived at the camp, Blake hoped that would indeed be the case.

A tall soldier greeted them with a salute. "This is Lieutenant Colonel Peters," the Brig said, and introduced Blake.

"I'm sorry about Tilcot Brig," Peters said. "You were right."

The Brig nodded in acceptance then Peters led them to the scene of devastation around the Range Rover. Some soldiers stood in disorganised groups surrounding the scene, their guns shouldered, while others applied field dressings to their injured colleagues. The bodies of Manny Schweizer and Fabian Hardwicke lay on their backs, touching the soil of the earth which they had both held more dear than their lives. Around them lay the guards of the Inner Circle who had not surrendered, blood congealing on their pale faces and black uniforms. There was nothing to be done for them.

They looked at the carnage, which was what remained of the leadership of the nation.

The Brig said, "How on earth did it come to this?"

Blake looked at the bodies, then in his mind's eye at the elderly in care homes, and the patients in hospitals, and the cold, shivering families throughout the land, waiting for the government to remotely switch on their electric fires. And he pictured James's too-young body, lifeless on the operating table. Then he spoke with full understanding, in a voice as deep as the grave.

"It took just one extremely poisonous idea – self-sacrifice as a moral ideal – and its believers' envy of those who would not comply."

As he recalled Dalton's words, the series of ideas stretched out in his mind and he raised his voice to address all those who could hear.

"This ignoble idea, self-sacrifice, has been afflicting our country for centuries and now it has reached its inevitable climax. There is almost nothing and no one left to sacrifice. The nation has been bled dry, and all that's left for the collectors of sacrifice to do is sacrifice themselves.

"Britain cannot continue with these leaders and these ideas. It must start again. It cannot simply resume 'business as usual', because the goal of this and many previous Parliaments has been to destroy business. Now that goal has been achieved. We prisoners in the castle were taken away from our work, and the country has quickly collapsed as other businesspeople have resigned rather than risk imprisonment and hanging.

"The government is packed with ecoists because voters shared their ideas. The events here, once they get out, will not be enough to make people change their minds. We must convince them with winning arguments, or we will face this same tragedy again sometime soon.

"The castle behind me was once part of a bloody civil war that ran for many years. Let it not become so again."

He turned to the Brig. "Brigadier Campbell. These men, it seems, have lost their leader. I suggest you return to your old post. Once we've cleared away the debris, I invite them all to a celebration at the castle."

The Brig grinned and climbed up to address the troops from on top of the Range Rover. "I am resuming command. This siege is now over. You are to cease treating the occupants of the castle as the enemy, and allow them free passage. Hostilities are over. I repeat, over. Are there any questions?"

No one said a word. Then Peters led a cheer that resounded like the winning goal in a stadium football match.

When it had died down, Peters addressed Blake. "I want to help you spread the right ideas. I have a degree in philosophy, which might help."

"Indeed, Colonel," Blake said, "then we should enjoy a lengthy discussion."

As Blake and Peters turned back towards the castle, the Brig asked, "What shall we do with the bodies?"

Blake looked at what was left of his brother and his acolytes, lying twisted on the ground. He felt anger mixed with pity. Were they victims themselves? After all they had not originated the ideas that caused such self-destruction. But they had chosen to accept them, or just blindly to obey.

"Find out who they are, then bury them in a corner of the church on the side of the hill. Simple grave markers will do."

"Even your brother?"

Blake felt a moment's pity, then the thoughts of what Fabian had done to him washed it away. "Yes. Make it basic but very clear. We don't want anyone thinking their President is in hiding somewhere."

~

Back at the castle, Blake checked how the injured were doing, then went up to his room and returned carrying the tablet.

"Colonel…"

"Neil, please."

"Neil, I recommend that you read this." He handed him the final draft of Dalton's *Proper Purpose of*

Government. "It explains where the need for a government comes from, where the British system went wrong, and how to fix it. I helped with the editing."

"It sounds like quite an undertaking."

"It was," Blake said, smiling. "I think you'll find it clear and easy to understand. But getting enough people to read it – and accept it as a blueprint for a new society – will require an enormous effort."

Peters was silent, reading for a moment. Then he raised his head. "If the book is as good as you say it is, one of our first tasks will be to print a large number of copies and distribute them to the men. If there's going to be any fighting, they'll need to know what it's for."

~

Peters put all his energies into studying the book. Besides reading it and making copious notes, he spent many more hours discussing its details with Blake. How, for instance, did Dalton expect a government to be funded, if force was banished? What was his proof for saying that 'history is driven by concepts'? Why did he think that reason was humans' essential means of survival? Blake recalled as much of Dalton's personal remarks as he could and slowly, Peters' objections were answered. At the end of an intense two weeks, whilst he didn't fully agree with all of Dalton's ideas, Peters had come to agree with Blake's estimate. The book was clear and accessible to the man in the street. The ideas were radical but made sense. And they offered the best way forward for their broken country.

They agreed the next task was to gain more allies. Through the Prince's contacts they quickly contacted Major General Macleod, the Brig's old friend, who

432

soon came out of hiding to see them at the castle. After four days of talks, he left with an electronic copy of PPOG and a plan to take over his old regiment. Within a week they heard of his success and contacted other army regiments, who were happy to accept orders once they knew Macleod and Prince Arthur were involved. Their previous chains of command had lost all moral authority.

As soon as the phones were fixed, Blake called Marisa. Even in prison, news of the victory had got through. They laughed and talked openly for over an hour, the prison guards being unsure what to do. "I'll come for you soon darling," Blake said as they ended the call. "I'll wait," she said, laughing.

Sam spent his time organising supplies of food and drink for the banquet. When the many supporters staying in the area heard about their victory, there was no problem finding what he needed.

The Brig and his troops set up mess tables for them all inside the castle's courtyard.

When the Prince heard about the truce via yellow balloons, he hid the Spitfire in a disused barn and drove to the castle in an old RAF fire engine. It had a manual gearbox, but he managed anyway.

Liz Blackwood busied herself working out how to distribute the castle's supplies. Some of the ex-prisoners were going back to their homes to spread the news in their communities. They needed the wherewithal to sustain them. Most of them, though, were joining the 'March to London'. This was Blake's idea, to travel the British Isles with the army as support, giving speeches and holding meetings to educate people about what needed to be done to rebuild a lasting nation after the scourge of ecoism.

Liz was not going to join him on that. He was still showing no more than polite interest in her, and he must be looking forward to seeing his wife during the tour, if not freeing her. Instead, Liz sighed to herself, she would do what she did best: work. She had the beginnings of a plan to use her family's wealth to restart the economy but she hadn't had time to discuss it yet with anyone except Paul Williams. Besides, her immediate concern was to arrange safe journeys for her daughters, Helen and Sophie. At eighteen and fifteen they were old enough to look after themselves, and they had been alone at her Berkshire home since Liz's arrest. But now that the phones were working again, thanks to Clive, she had managed to speak to them, and they were coming to stay for Christmas. Previously they had exchanged censored letters, but now she'd heard their voices, she was beginning to realise how they'd reacted to the threat of her execution.

Clive's first act once he'd fixed the telephone systems had been to call his wife, Fiona. Having begun bracing herself for his death, she had been overwhelmed with relief at his news. Now she and Keith, their son, were also coming to Westingham for Christmas. The prospect of grey stone walls and cold damp cells was not enough to stop them. Keith, who had been at one of the rallies and had seen a guard taken away in a secure army ambulance, had been unusually emotional down the phone to him. He had quit the Green Shoots and persuaded most of his friends to do the same. Clive reassured him as best he could over the phone, and sent him a copy of Dalton's book on a memory stick.

Sam's wife, Yvonne, and his son, Liam, were also set to arrive by Christmas. She had told him over the phone about the state of his supermarkets. Basically, they were half empty. With such severe fuel rationing and restrictions on running their computers and their fridges, products were either not making it to the stores at all, or going bad in situ. Sam smiled bitterly to himself when he remembered the history of the 'food miles' campaign. Well, they'd got what they wanted now. He promised his wife the best bottle of wine he could find and went in search of it – as well as plenty of beer for the troops – within a ten-mile radius of the castle.

Paul Williams was desperately looking forward to the arrival of his partner, Oliver. They had been together for twenty years, since before he'd come out to his parents. They had rejected him then, and despite his contacting them every year, they hadn't been in touch since. His parents' marriage had been built on rows and regular separation, so he'd always wondered who they were to lecture him about relationships. But then, perhaps that was the point. They had been envious of his happiness and wanted to destroy it to justify their own misery. What he'd learned from Blake about Fabian had opened his eyes to a lot of similar situations. Envy was rife. But it was so destructive, how could it run the world? The answer was now unfolding – it couldn't. And it had only survived so long because it had been tolerated and supported by the envied. He felt the familiar pang of guilt about supporting smart meters in people's homes. Well, that was a mistake which wouldn't matter now. His contribution to getting the nation back on its feet would be to recreate the old Central Electricity Generating Board, run by the new government, but without ecoist policies. His recent talks with Liz about funding made him think he could do it.

In among the excitement of visitors and planning the future came the sombre task of burying the five prisoners who had died in the battle. They eventually managed to contact their relatives, who made arrangements for the bodies. All except one, Tomasz, whose family was all in Poland. The ex-prisoners held a service in the church on the hill. When he was asked to say a few words, Blake concluded with this: "He did not make the ultimate sacrifice. None of his life's actions consisted of giving up a greater value for a lesser one. He believed in himself, and through his work and his courage, he showed what kind of happiness is possible to men. He died defending his life from those who would take it away from him. Let him live on in our memories."

Another serious job was assigned to Gobind Grewal. As a pharmaceutical executive, he was in the best position to arrange mass production of a smallpox vaccine, in case the vials given to the Inner Circle were deliberately or accidentally released. There was no news about the guards' surviving members at present, but Blake and Macleod agreed it was best to be prepared. With Macleod's help, Gobind began calculating the stores of vaccine the army already had, then went on a trip to his company's main factory to organise production of more and visit his family at the same time.

One more person Blake was quick to inform about

the siege's end was Roger Newton, Dalton's QC. As they sat in the governor's office, Roger explained why it had taken him three days to get to the castle from London. News of the President's death had spread quickly, even though what remained of the official channels denied it. Everyone from bus drivers to policemen, to bankers, to shopkeepers, was so used to being regulated and told what to do by rules that changed almost daily, that for a week or so, the whole city had just stood still, waiting. When they realised they could do what they wanted, they were so out of practice at deciding what to do, they still did nothing. The Bank of England was unsure whether to continue printing money or not. The banks were unsure whether to approve loans or not. The police were unsure whether to prosecute Carbon Crime perpetrators or not. The train companies, whose license to operate had just expired, were unsure which services to run, if any. No one knew what was 'sustainable' or 'eco-friendly' any more, because there was no one to tell them. The whole place had ground to a halt and Roger had to walk most of the way to Westingham.

"I'd like to say I'm sorry your brother is dead."

"Don't be," Blake said. "He more than deserved it after what he did to Professor MacDermot."

Roger nodded. "And he left us in a huge mess. London and the other cities will soon turn to anarchy and chaos. Lord Hardwicke wouldn't appoint a deputy, so there is no official line of succession. Parliament has been closed for the last year, apart from ceremonial occasions. There is no one in control."

Blake smiled wryly, and Roger saw him looking into the far distance. Then he spoke. "We will all have to do as Adam Smith described many years ago, only unlike him we must not be ashamed of it. We must use our reason to be self-interested, as Dalton explained."

Roger knew his professor's work inside out, but some part of him had never fully accepted the necessity of self-interest. He asked, "But won't that simply act as a licence for people to do what they want, to commit fraud, murder, rape, burglary, so as to fulfil their self-interest?"

"No," Blake said. "That's why I've asked you here. You know Dalton MacDermot's work better than any QC or solicitor. What I need you to do is help me frame a new constitution that lays out, in principle, what actually is in people's rational self-interest, and then to spell out the laws a new government would uphold to realise it in practice. Self-interest is not synonymous with short-term self-gratification. Ask a long-term drug addict, or a robber who has run out of victims."

"Or a man who spends ten years writing a book," Roger said, thinking of Dalton. He sat back in the wooden chair he was perched on. His mind boggled as he thought of daring to emulate the great legal minds of the past such as Black, Montesquieu and Coke.

"I know it's a tall order," Blake said, seeing Roger's face, "but with Dalton's help, we can do it. A lot of the existing laws are perfectly rational. That can be proven because they follow Dalton's basic rule of social interaction: 'Those who initiate the use of physical force are in the wrong and bear the blame for what follows.' Your task, the task of the law, is to spell out and limit what follows objectively. To re-establish property rights, proper rules of evidence, and proper sentencing, based on what is in the self-interest of a rational human being. Otherwise people will take the law into their own hands and there really will be chaos."

Roger knew Blake's reasoning was right. He had always followed logic and it had never lied. Even if it didn't 'feel' right, he would have to do it anyway. When it came to convincing others to accept the constitution, what other methods did he have apart from reason and logic? Faith wouldn't do it: 'That way insoluble conflict lies,' he thought, quoting Dalton's summary of all the religious wars in history.

But he knew men could cooperate and achieve great things. He had seen the way the ex-prisoners had transformed the castle, and he had read British history. He would do his best as well.

"What shall we do with all the laws on the statute books that violate the new constitution?" he asked Blake. "We can't just leave them all there like Brexit. They'll never get removed."

Happy to see Roger had picked up the gauntlet, Blake told him what he'd thought of so far. "We can either declare a whole list of Acts to be invalid – and God knows that's most of them from the last sixty years – or we can leave them in place and wait for people to challenge them in a constitutional court, then rule on them one at a time."

Roger thought for a moment. "Or both," he said. "That's a lot of work – reviewing every statute and deciding if it comes up to scratch. Many probably need reworking, rather than scrapping altogether, so we can extract just the valid elements. It would be impossible to do it in a reasonable time, and people need to know, otherwise the courts will be gridlocked and businesses won't risk acting while legislation that affects them is in doubt. Another lesson from Brexit. Instead, why don't we identify the worst Acts – as many as we can in, say, six months – and declare these invalid from day one. Then deal with the rest piecemeal as cases come up."

Blake liked the approach. "You're right. There's only so much we here can do. We need to persuade a lot more people to get on our side and help. Unless the vast majority of people agree with what we say, ecoism and other self-sacrificing dogmas will simply make a comeback. Remember the far-left coalition?"

"I don't want that to happen again," Roger said, shuddering. During that episode the nation had been partly renationalised, and thus swiftly plunged into recession. That had led to the three-way coalition and then to the ecoist victory. He'd lost his mentor and hero to the ecoists. "Let's do everything we can think of to stop that," he said resolutely.

"I'll drink to that," Blake said, and he charged their glasses with the little that was left in the governor's whisky decanter.

~

The week before Christmas, Candice arrived at the castle by car. She looked older, Blake thought as she stepped out. Then she ran and hugged him, and he felt her body and her tears as he hugged her back. How long had it been since they'd done that? He couldn't remember at first, then it came to him: when she had won a hundred-metre race in the last year of her primary school.

He had taken the afternoon off work to be at her sports day. The sun had shone and the difficulties of his job were forgotten as he witnessed the children running, jumping, throwing and hurdling as if their lives depended on it. Candice had been overjoyed to win. It had taken all her effort and she had only done so by a matter of inches. Marisa had been at her job in the city, and he had been the parent that counted that day. Candice had proudly worn her medal for days afterwards. Two months later she had gone to secondary school. Shortly after that she had joined the Green Shoots, and they had argued ever since.

"You did well," he told her as they broke their embrace.

"What do you mean?" she asked, wiping her eyes with a tissue.

"Giving us the timing for the blackout."

"But you actually did it."

"It was a team effort," Blake said, smiling.

She smiled back. "I've told Lucinda all about it. Oh sorry…" She looked embarrassed. "This is John, Lucinda's dad. He drove me all the way here."

A shortish man with greying hair and casual but impeccable clothes stepped forward and shook hands with Blake.

"Thank you for everything you did."

"That's all right."

"I realise why you had to wait until the last moment to stop things. Many people now know what might have happened, and have stopped accepting the government's propaganda, or what's left of it."

"Good."

"But here's the thing. Now the President's gone, what will happen next?"

"It's up to us," Blake said. "Countries don't make

themselves. Come into the castle for a drink. There are some people I'd like you to meet."

Several hours later, John left, clutching a memory stick in his hand (the army had raided its own electronic supplies) and the nugget of a revolutionary idea in his head. As the dawn started coming up, Blake stopped talking to Candice and insisted she go to bed.

~

The banquet was held on Christmas Day. Blake jokingly referred to it as the Third Coming. But all the ex-prisoners knew they had only just succeeded in cheating death. A year before they had all been facing the noose, thanks to the National Emergency. It was with this perspective that they celebrated like they had never celebrated before. The Great Hall, the courtyards and every room of any size in the castle was crammed with ex-prisoners, their families and the soldiers, all making merry.

Without much electricity, there was lots of live singing and instrument playing. Without television – the GBMC having collapsed without Schweizer and without tax-money – there were numerous skits, tricks, feats and stories being told and performed by all and sundry, including some children. Blake laughed out loud at a farce set in a French language school. It was almost a hundred years old, and yet it still united people in joy.

Blake missed his son, but the wound was beginning to scar over, helped by the presence of Candice and the prospect of travelling to see Marisa. He also missed his friend, but Dalton would have been proud of what they'd achieved. His chest swelled uncontrollably when he thought of it.

The following week was spent partly clearing up and partly having more celebrations. People staying or living nearby saw the firelight and heard the sounds, and being curious for news they approached the castle. The soldiers let them in, explained what was going on, and issued them with early copies of *The Proper Purpose of Government*. A few stayed and lent their expertise to planning the march that was to follow. The rest withdrew to their homes and read about what the future might bring.

While Blake, Roger, Peters, Prince Arthur and the others debated and planned what to do in the coming weeks, months and years, the army, under Major General Macleod, spent its time gathering supplies and organising the mass printing of Dalton's book. Electricity, the Internet and the mobile phone network were no longer reliable, but fortunately some old-fashioned printing companies had survived, and the army provided them with paper and fuel from government supplies. Blake observed them unloading a truckful of copies one day and thought, with irony, how it compared to Mao's Little Red Book. But then he also thought of the Putney Debates Dalton had spoken of, and how those had turned out. It was up to him, and all those who agreed with him, to persuade others why they were right.

He made sure one of the first boxes went to Marisa. He wanted her released, but he knew he shouldn't abuse his position and relationship with the army. He wanted her to be freed legally, by argument and persuasion, but he didn't know how. He did know that the clearer the ideas they put forward were, the more chance they had of spreading successfully. With that in mind, he had begun writing a speech to give at public meetings as they marched around the nation.

In the middle of January, Gobind returned to the castle with enough smallpox vaccine to protect all those going on tour, and proceeded to administer it. By the end of January, the army and the retinue of ex-prisoners and other supporters were ready to move out, armed with more batches of vaccine and thousands of copies of PPOG.

Their first stop of significant size was Leicester. Here they followed their agreed plan, first establishing whether there was a smallpox outbreak – and performing voluntary mass vaccinations if so – then setting up a large-scale public meeting for debate and book distribution. Blake had tried to persuade Prince Arthur to open proceedings but he had firmly refused: "I don't want to become a figurehead. I don't want people to think this is a return to some fictitious golden age of monarchy. This is something new. And I don't want them seeing me as some kind of authority to which they have to defer. We've had enough of that in this country. Centuries of it."

Blake could tell that the Prince had taken on board what Dalton had written. So it was left to him to do most of the speaking.

He reiterated what he thought were the most important of Dalton's ideas, and of other writers from history who had put pieces of the puzzle together of how to live side by side in harmony and be rational. He also examined the many flaws of ecoism and exposed the deadly hospital, care home and youth rally plots. But although there was some applause for his

444

speech, it was not the thunderous reception he expected. And he could tell from the questions that it hadn't really sunk in. He had talked about freedom, reason and property, and how the government could only guarantee the first and encourage the second by securing the third. But then people had asked: "What about state pensions? What about the poor? What about childcare vouchers? What about free healthcare?" making him realise there was a lot of explaining to do. But how to get through to them? He hoped reading and thinking about the books they distributed at every meeting would eventually be sufficient. But would the country survive long enough for that to happen?

They marched to several other towns and cities, army medics administering vaccinations where needed and then holding similar meetings. They visited Nottingham, Leeds, York, Newcastle and Edinburgh, but Blake's speech always resulted in a similarly lacklustre response. Why could these people not see what he did? The nation had deteriorated rapidly under the Ecoist Party's rule and now, with government funds cut off, it was going downhill even quicker. And yet people were not doing anything to help themselves. Why?

While Blake was having difficulty getting his ideas across, Major General Macleod was having difficulty trying to prevent anarchy. One of their agreed tasks in each town was to secure the prisons. Since the collapse of central government, staff had not been paid and many had left their posts. Macleod agreed to leave an army unit or two at each prison, but as they visited more towns, their ranks were wearing thing. What

Macleod needed was more troops, but each time they arrived at a barracks, they found it empty.

It was at Glasgow that they discovered why. On the northern edge of the city centre and in the nearby parks, General Kettle, two ranks higher than Macleod, had assembled tens of thousands of troops, their regimental banners showing that they came from all around the country. They appeared to be keeping the peace and preventing most of the looting, but what were their long-term intentions? Leaving the Brig in charge and Blake to his speechwriting, Macleod and Peters went to Kettle's HQ in Maryhill to find out.

Their uniforms and weapons gave them quick access to the commander, whom they found standing in the officers' mess. He was wearing a holstered pistol while surrounded by large-scale pictures of battles and heroes from ages past. Peters wondered how many of them had been fighting for freedom, and how many for self-sacrifice. More importantly, how did Kettle see it? He could sense the tension behind Kettle's moustache. There was no functioning government now, and so no political structure to enforce the command hierarchy in the army. He realised that between them they had the chance to start or avoid a civil war.

He looked at Macleod, who nodded slowly. Then they both stood to attention and saluted.

Kettle immediately saluted back, then said, "At ease, gentlemen."

As Peters relaxed his stance he could feel the atmosphere soften.

"Take a seat," Kettle said, and they took up positions on the edge of worn leather armchairs, their guns pushed to one side.

Then Kettle began. "Now, I never thought I'd have to say these words about this country, but here's how I see it. The government has turned against its people, has lost its leader, and is in the process of collapsing. The normal mechanisms of Parliament have failed and it's up to us to do something about it, before anarchy takes hold. Having been intimately involved with recent events, I'm looking to you for information and ideas. What can you tell me?"

As agreed, Peters slowly reached into his tunic and produced a copy of PPOG, then held it out to Kettle.

"What's this?" he bristled.

"It's a work of political philosophy," Peters said, "written by one of the prisoners at Westingham. He saw the whole thing coming, at least in principle, having started it years ago. Sadly, he did not live to see it published."

"Now, I want you both to know that I never condoned attacking that castle. In fact, as Peters will attest, I forbade it."

"So I heard," Macleod said in his broad Scots accent. "Then like me, when you disobeyed orders and were dismissed, you went into hiding?"

"That's right."

"Rest assured, sir," Peters said, "we are not here to blame you for the author's death. He was Dalton MacDermot."

"Ah. The one who was executed. Nasty business. I thought I'd witnessed the last of that with ISIL. Let's see it, then," and he reached towards Peters and took the book.

"I'm having it mass produced," Macleod said. "We have several thousand copies with us now in a couple of trucks, if you're interested."

"I see. You must think highly of it. To be frank, I haven't read much in the genre since Sandhurst. Give me a quick summary."

"It outlines a new constitution," Peters said, "one that protects individuals' rights much as the common law does, but with a much deeper foundation. It's like the American Declaration of Independence in that it lists grievances against the current government and states the principles for a fair and just one. The difference is, it doesn't claim they are self-evident. Nor does it appeal to God. It justifies them in terms of mankind's very nature. And, crucially, it rejects the morality of self-sacrifice. It's the most rational book on the subject I've ever read."

"And you think that troops and people in general will understand it?"

"Yes. If they choose to exercise their minds."

"Surely it's not that simple – people read it, are convinced by it, and we live in peace and harmony forever after?"

"Of course it's not that simple," Peters said exasperatedly. He took a breath and remembered the situation. "But consider the long-term consequences of these publications: *The Communist Manifesto*, *Mein Kampf*, *The Rights of Man*."

"You have a point," Kettle said.

"But you're right, it will take time for enough people to change their minds."

"Which is why we're here," Macleod interjected. "Think of it like the end of World War Two. The Allies set the groundwork for new constitutions in Germany and Japan, which they went on to refine and successfully live by. Like them, we can't go back to the way things were."

"Agreed," Kettle said. "Fabian Hardwicke was one of the most evil and dangerous people I've ever met."

He went on to describe his escape from Buckingham Palace, and how he had immediately begun plans for extracting the army from Fabian's command. Macleod and Peters in their turn related events at the castle and the rallies. They returned to their camp some four hours later, leaving PPOG with Kettle.

"You look exhausted, but you're smiling," Blake said when he saw them.

"I think we've got him on side," Peters said, sighing with relief.

"And avoided a war," Macleod said.

They all looked at each other, and feeling the gravity of the situation, were glad of the others' support.

Over the next two weeks, Kettle read and discussed PPOG with them at length and attended Blake's public meetings. He then agreed to them joining forces.

After a brief discussion among the officers, the first thing they did was ramp up the printing and distribution of the book. The second was to send a battalion, under the Brig, down to the power station at Tilcot. With Paul Williams's help they were to take it back from the 'protestors' – if any were left – and restart it. Kettle was keen to make amends for 'sacking' Brigadier Campbell there two years previously.

When they arrived at Tilcot, the huge buildings that had empowered generations of Britons to achieve their dreams were empty and desolate, their windows broken, their chimneys smokeless.

A dozen protestors bundled up in dirty, greying

clothes met them at the gate.

"You can't come in here," said a wiry-haired woman who seemed to be in charge. "We're stopping this ever being used again to pollute the planet."

"And do you own this power plant, madam?" the Brig asked.

"We do. On behalf of the people."

"Which people? These ones?" He pointed to the ranks of soldiers behind him.

"On behalf of the government."

"There is no government."

"But it's ours. We've occupied it."

"Squatting isn't an entitlement to property. It's just a form of theft. If it belongs to anyone, it belongs to this man who used to run it." He indicated Paul.

The woman recognised him and sneered. "You have no right to force us out of here."

"But you had no right to force yourselves in there. With or without government help, it's still force. We're simply rectifying the situation."

"What about climate justice?"

"I look forward to debating with the sun, moon and clouds in court."

The woman shrieked and spat.

"We'll give you half an hour to pack up and leave, then we will evict you." Then he raised his voice so the soldiers behind him could hear. "We want to live in an industrialised world of technology, energy and innovation. If you do not, go and live in a jungle somewhere, but don't try to impose your views on us. They are immoral, irrational and impractical."

The men cheered.

The woman was stunned. None of the other

protestors said a word. The Brig suspected they'd never been accused of being immoral. He enjoyed the feeling of efficacy such words gave him, knowing they were right.

Within half an hour the squatters had left, with only mild persuasion from the soldiers being required.

~

From Glasgow, Blake travelled with Macleod's army to Belfast to give speeches, distribute books and find out the situation there. It was dire. With industrial collapse on the mainland, Northern Ireland's economy had been devastated. People had fled to the south, but the Republic's worship of ecoism had been only marginally less severe. Many had then paid for passage to America, much as their ancestors had. Those that remained were living on their meagre reserves of food, or begging, or looting. Whereas in the past they would have resented an influx of soldiers, these people now saw them as a source of rations. After they'd heard Blake's speeches, they also saw them as a source of hope.

Candice had been watching her father's efforts, and had a go at public speaking herself. She addressed a hall full of schoolchildren, recounting her experience of the rally and explaining why she had switched from ecoist to egoist. "The future is in your hands," she told them. Later, when they spoke to their parents about what they had heard and noted the shame in their faces, they knew Candice was right.

The egoists returned to England via Liverpool, and it was here that they had a welcome surprise: Xavier Atkinson had been hiding in the area since Blake's trial. He had grown a beard and his hair was now shoulder length, but he still had the ruthless gleam in his eye that had encouraged Blake to hire him. He had been given (and later rejected) a strict Catholic upbringing, so it didn't take him long to see the connection between ecoism and self-sacrifice. Soon he was working ten-hour days with Roger on the new constitution. Roger had joined the tour to discuss his ongoing work with Blake, and was very glad of another legal mind to help him.

After several speeches, again with a muted response, they moved on to Manchester. The people came in their thousands to hear what Blake had to say. He reminded them of their city's revolutionary role in the past, but again they were not easily won over. The ethics of socialism still had them in their grip, making Blake realise it would take something more to loosen it. One person, though, was quickly convinced: Henry Booth, whom Blake had last seen driving off in a prison van, having helped rescue Dalton. Despite being a fugitive for over a year, he had smartened himself up and was almost unrecognisable from the tramp Blake had first met. Apparently, he had been making himself useful since the government's collapse as an organiser of basic necessities for the growing number of desperate people on and around Manchester's streets. His banking experience made him extremely good with numbers, and highly helpful to the charities who were struggling to preserve human dignity. Blake left him with extra pallets of books to distribute, and Henry vowed to help set the city back on its path to industrial glory once the new government was established.

It was as the tour turned south into Cheshire that they came to Ironview prison where Marisa was held.

As soon as they arrived Blake made arrangements to meet her, and they were soon sitting opposite each other, separated only by a plastic screen and overlooked by the soldiers guarding the prison.

He hadn't seen her in two years. He couldn't believe it was so long. He couldn't believe how much his heart ached when she smiled at him. Her face was thinner but had lost none of its beauty. For a few moments they couldn't speak, and then the words came tumbling out from him, then from her, then both overlapping like waves upon a shore. There was so much to say, and yet hanging over them was the question of when they would see each other again.

The next day it was Candice's turn. She cried when she saw her mother and realised how much she needed her, and how much she needed her forgiveness. After the soldiers called time, she tore herself away from the plastic screen and went to her father.

"Can't you free her or something? She's not done anything wrong really. It was self-defence. And she's paid already by being in prison so long. You've got the whole army on your side. They could just order the soldiers to let her out, couldn't they?"

Blake felt his daughter's desperation as she squeezed his hands and pleaded with her eyes. He told her he would think about it, and that night he did nothing else. Lying on his camp bed, feeling the chill of the spring night, he longed to have his wife beside him again. His hands tore at the blanket and his face contorted with the pain of having her so close but kept from him. He had not allowed himself to feel like this for years now, but his longing had clearly always been there, waiting for a chance to pounce on his peaceful state of mind. For lack of a solid wall, he thumped the ground with his fists as he tried to think what to do.

The next morning, having been on a dawn walk of several miles, he spoke to Macleod.

"I'd like you to organise a second trial of my wife, and then of all the political prisoners as we go around the country."

"That sounds reasonable, but I'll have to confer with General Kettle."

"Of course." He had to accept the country was effectively under military law for the time being. But that didn't mean no law, and it didn't mean favouritism for those close to the top brass. As much as he wanted to find a quick way to release Marisa, he knew that if he was to convince the country that egoism wasn't the same as doing whatever you felt like, he would have to lead by example.

~

It was a month and four towns later that Blake returned to Marisa's prison for the trial. It was held in a large, communal hall. He sat with Candice at the back, so as not to be seen to be interfering. Their future, as much as hers, rested on the legitimacy of the result.

After several hours going over the evidence with the new jury there was an adjournment, and then it was Marisa's turn to speak. Being in prison already, she didn't have to wear handcuffs. Listening to her give evidence, Blake realised she could never truly be captive. Her spirit would always be free.

"When I pushed the ecoist attacker down the escalator, I was protecting my life and my livelihood – for what is one without the other?"

Blake smiled as he recognised the phrase from

PPOG.

"Not only was he using force against me right there, by hitting and grabbing me, he was using force against me in the future by smashing up our offices, preventing me from earning a living. Life does not sustain itself. It has to be constantly nurtured and fed, and that can only be done by the mind, a mind free to create the values its owner requires, and free to keep those values from thieves and destroyers. I knew that if I did not fight back, if I accepted his force destroying my office, then I would also be accepting government force destroying my company. At my previous trial, the jury found against me but our business survived. In the intervening years, ecoist regulations shut it down. Today you have the chance to set a new precedent and put that right."

Blake had never seen her more alive, and he had never loved her more. Her felt Candice squeeze his hand and, turning, saw the tears in her eyes.

While the jury conferred they waited, first in the courtroom-cum-hall, then outside, where they ate some army food in the fresh air. Finally, after nearly five hours, the jury was back. He noticed one or two were carrying copies of PPOG, and that none wore a silver oak tree badge.

"The prisoner will rise," the clerk ordered.

Marisa stood, her face calmly expectant.

"What is your verdict?" the judge asked.

"Not guilty on all charges," the foreman replied.

Marisa beamed with joy.

"You are free to go," the judge ordered. "This trial is over."

As the courtroom erupted with conversation, Blake

and Candice ran to the front, meeting Marisa as she came down off the stand.

Blake lifted her off her feet as he crushed her in his arms. Then they kissed with an intensity Blake hadn't known since the weeks when they had first met. When they eventually broke apart, he heard a voice.

"What about me?" It was Candice, and he released his wife so they too could embrace.

As he watched them showing the strongest affection for each other that he'd witnessed in years, he thought of his missing son, and felt a wound where his existence had been dragged out. He also girded his loins to avenge him fully.

~

The tour of Britain continued, with Blake trying to convince people of the merits of egoism and audiences continuing to ask questions revealing that they just didn't get it. People were not being inspired to help themselves out of economic depression. They seemed to still expect the government to save them.

He lay awake most nights, talking to Marisa about it and trying to find an answer in his own mind. This happened day after day as they marched through the slowly thawing countryside from Cheshire, to Staffordshire and Shropshire, then through Wales, Gloucestershire, Somerset, Devon, Cornwall, Dorset, Hampshire and Berkshire. He spoke at many different venues, from town halls to theatres, to shopping centres, until at the end of one occasion, a member of the audience said something to him in private. Not wanting to be overheard, he explained what he saw as the main problem to Blake in a low voice: "The reason why we need the NHS, state schools and state pensions is that most people can't think for themselves. They don't know what's best for them, especially in the long term. They're not as intelligent as you and me." He said it matter-of-factly and slightly sadly, as if it were a well understood and inevitable truth. Blake heard it, and in his mind it was as if a thousand cogs had slipped into place. He could now see what made their minds turn.

At their next stop – Cliveden, high above the Thames in Buckinghamshire, where he knew *'Rule Britannia'* had first been performed – Blake warned the soldiers on guard, then, standing on the terrace looking out over the formal gardens to the river and sky beyond, he began his speech with something quite different.

"You are all stupid," he shouted with his amplified voice. "You are all thick, unintelligent, immoral people, who don't know what's good for you. When we form the next government, we are going to control every aspect of your lives and do all your thinking for you. Anyone who disagrees," he barked, "and goes against our ideas will be heavily fined or thrown in prison."

The crowd erupted, shouting their protests to the open sky where they dissolved in the cold, blue air. Blake just stood there, smiling. The crowd were shouting at the soldiers, asking how they could countenance such rot, but the soldiers just stood there placidly, holding but not using their rifles and bayonets. After several minutes the shouting stopped, as people realised Blake and the soldiers had done nothing and that Blake had a broad grin on his face. When it was quiet he resumed.

"That is not – I repeat, not – our policy. That is what *you* have voted for in the last twenty general elections.

Ecoism is only the logical outcome. The results are all around for you to see."

He paused, waiting for this undeniable observation to sink in. Then he continued with his normal speech, but added phrases that emphasised the efficacy of everyone's mind, if they chose to use it, and explained how the government as such creates nothing. When he had finished – there had been no heckling, for a change – he thought of one more remark which might hit home.

"If you create a nanny state, you will end up with a nation of children."

There was a long silence and then the questions began, but this time no one asked, "what about the poor?" They knew with their own, intelligent minds what the answer was.

This pattern continued at each town they visited, and each time it worked. With more people being convinced by Blake's arguments, more were coming forward to discuss them and to tell tales of woe regarding their experiences under ecoism. Many business owners and executives had shut down their operations or quit their jobs as a direct result of the Carbon Crime Act. It was literally too dangerous, both financially and personally, to keep going. Blake reassured them that the next government would repeal the Act on day one, along with many others. He also emphasised that their next priority would be re-establishing law and order. Organising, re-educating and funding the police, courts and the army along egoist lines was essential. It was a lot of work. Would they like to help? A few in each town said yes and joined Blake and the others on their tour, using the time to learn about, argue about, and then propagate their view of a new system of government.

Blake realised he needed to revisit some of their earlier venues with his improved speech, and so they circled the nation again. It did no harm that people who had remained silent on his first visit had now had time to think it over, and were able to ask their questions.

#

By the time they reached London, having covered the nation again from Dover to Penzance, to Cardiff, to Carlisle, to Northern Ireland, to Scotland, to Yarmouth, there were thousands of people marching, ready to commit their time to fixing their country. However, what greeted them in London was worse than they had expected.

Some on the march had feared a confrontation with angry protestors, possibly violence. But, in fact, the opposite was the case – and it was worse.

London had collapsed. From a still thriving, buzzing, restless city only two years before, it had become a wasteland. It was worse in a way than the Blitz, because then at least people were pulling together to help each other and planning one day to rebuild. This time London was a ghost town that had lost its soul. Without carbon-fuelled transport, there was almost no food coming into the city. Without gardens, there was nowhere to grow it. Without businesses, there were no jobs to go to; and without jobs, there was no way to pay the rents and mortgages, nor to acquire any basic necessities of life.

Some people stole and scavenged, but most simply packed up and left. The intelligentsia of Islington had fled to socialist Paris. The pretend capitalists of Kensington had fled to China. With the collapse in house prices, the Russians and other large property owners had gone back to their native countries. And the others who could not afford to travel to America had dissipated to their roots in the countryside. Those that remained were either too feeble to travel, or had stockpiled food and were living off that. Unfortunately, that made them easy targets for the gangs of looters that remained in the city, picking scraps off the nearly dead civilisation they had always relied on but never supported. When the army arrived, they scattered like rats in a cellar after the light is switched on. Besides them, there was very little opposition. All the marches and protests demanding redistribution of wealth from some people to others had vanished – there was no wealth left to be envious of any more. All the clamour for further ecoist controls had stopped too – they had achieved their goal, the collapse of industrial civilisation.

Once they reached the City of London, Marisa made a beeline for Leadenhall Street. She took Paul Williams with her, as he had given up on restarting Tilcot. She wanted to see what was left of her old office and what could be salvaged.

The heavy metal and glass doors to what had once been an inner sanctum of international trade stood half open. There were no guards and no one on was in reception. The atrium floor was covered in golden glass that seemed to have come from lights in the broken ceiling. As they trod carefully over it and made their way slowly up the stationary escalator, Marisa smiled at her return to familiar ground, but grimaced at the wreckage all around her.

Computer screens had been smashed, chairs ripped apart and filing cabinets over-turned. It was as if the looters had been frustrated and turned to pure destruction for relief. But she knew it was inevitable. Without reliable electricity, the computers were useless. Without the freedom to participate in international energy markets, there were no profits to be made. Without profits, no one could or would work for her old firm.

She turned to Paul, whose mouth was gaping open, and let out a large sigh.

He smiled weakly in return. "What will it take, do you think, to get this up and running again?"

"A civilised society," she said grimly. "One that doesn't licence hooligans as eco-warriors."

He nodded slowly. "I've been talking to Liz Blackwood, the banker, about it."

"How did you manage that? She's at Westingham, isn't she?" Marisa had heard a lot about Liz Blackwood from Blake and was aware of her fierce determination.

"We did it by text mostly, although it takes several days now to get one through."

"So what has she been saying?"

Paul looked at his shoes then faced her. "It's just not going to be possible to do what Blake wants, to restart industry on a new basis, to scrap the old, government-controlled eco-focused economy and start again with a free one. I've tried it at Tilcot. There's just too much to put right. Too much confusion about what's legal and what's not. Businesses are afraid to invest because they are afraid of taking the wrong action and being penalised for it later. They also worry about missing out on a subsidy their competitors get, or a new regulation that suddenly ruins their business model. They want to start again exactly as we were, then maybe change things later."

He looked at her, his eyebrows pointing up and in.

She studied him, and wondered if he'd actually read PPOG. "You mean, set things up to their advantage using the regulations they had either helped create or had capitulated to so as to discourage any real competition?"

"Well, not exactly, that would perhaps just be a consequence of resurrecting the old system…"

"And would you call that being rationally selfish?"

"Well, yes and no. It's a question of time. If we don't act quickly to restore things, there will soon be nothing left." He gestured to the remains of her office.

"But it will just entrench the practice of government control over everything again, whether the justification is saving the planet or helping society get back on its feet. Look what happened after World War Two. Food rationing continued for nine more years – far longer than the war itself."

Paul had no answer to that and lapsed into silence.

After discovering the graffitied boardroom, they decided it was time to leave.

~

Later that night, Marisa discussed her visit with Blake. "I'm looking at the mess and the lack of activity but I'm thinking about how to get things going again. It wouldn't be that hard. The people that created energy markets and wrote software and made computers all still exist. We can use their knowledge to rebuild. But all Paul could see was fear and inertia.

People waiting to be told what to do. Afraid of making their own decisions."

Blake sighed. "He's a good manager and he understand the irrationality of ecoism, but he lacks the courage to lead with his ideas. Even if he knows they're right. He prefers to give in to the majority, to conform. Perhaps he's just had enough of arguing with people. It can be pretty exhausting. Did he mention Liz Blackwood?"

Marisa's ears pricked up. "He said he'd been talking to her about the difficulty of restarting the economy."

"So have I."

Marisa stared at him.

Blake smiled. "I've been using the army relays. She's a very competent, well connected and rich woman. But we've had major disagreements. When we joined forces with General Kettle, I thought we'd solved our biggest problem. Now I think we've got a bigger one. If you want to come with the rest of us to the Bank of England tomorrow, I think you'll see some kind of showdown."

She nodded in agreement, then wrapped her arms around him.

~

The next morning a large group of them, including Candice and a platoon of soldiers, made their way on foot to Threadneedle Street. While she relished being out in the open and back in the City, Marisa also felt indignant at the ransacking and destruction that had been meted out to this cradle of creativity and abundance. Windows were shattered, burned out cars were rammed into buildings. Graffiti was on the walls and the streets. It was much worse than the anticapitalist rampage of '99 which she had witnessed. She had spoken to a policeman the day after and asked why he and his men hadn't stopped it. He'd said they'd wanted to and knew how to, but orders from the PM of the day had stopped them. The PM had said these were valid protestors. She thought of all the PMs since then, and all the subsequent attacks on the City, both physical and legislative. They had tried to kill it, despite or perhaps because of its life-giving power, and had nearly succeeded. No more, she resolved to herself.

The doors to the Bank of England hung open. They trooped inside and found Liz Blackwood, Paul Williams and some others waiting in the lobby.

Marisa was prepared for the sights that met them as they toured the building, unlike most of the others. Candice looked appalled as she trod carefully around the broken glass and stared at the smashed-in doors. Liz scowled at the loose sheets of paper everywhere and the paintings of previous governors ripped from the walls and slashed.

Down in the vaults someone had spray-painted in red a massive message: '*Where is it bastards?*'

Where indeed, Marisa thought. There had been no gold in the Bank of England for decades. Just as there had been no mettle to most politicians for at least as long. They and the looters had simply waited to take from some and give to others, including themselves. After decades of such practice, it should be no surprise there was nothing left.

Marisa herself was depressed but calm, knowing that the inevitable logic of ecoism, socialism and all the other forms of envy had finally played out. She also realised that guilt for being selfish was what had empowered the envious. There needed to be a wholesale political and cultural shift in favour of egoism to stop such destruction recurring. The old ways did not work.

Liz Blackwood, however, wouldn't see it that way, Marisa predicted, and she was soon proved right. As they ascended to the ground floor and walked dejectedly across a courtyard filled with toppled statues, Liz climbed onto one of the empty plinths and gave a speech.

"Despite what you have seen today, we can rebuild. This great institution, the power behind the British government and once the envy of the world, can be resurrected and restarted. My family have the funds to back a new government, and as in previous crises, we are willing to lend them to the nation."

There was a muted round of applause. Then Blake spoke up.

"I agree that a government must have funds, but I don't agree that a central bank is the way to get them. Is that what you were suggesting?"

"It is. Why do you object?" Liz asked testily.

"It will not work. Have you forgotten the Ethical Lending Laws that landed you in prison? If you recreate a central bank with a legal monopoly on what counts as money, you render it, and everyone who uses money, subject to government regulation. If the government creates an organisation and empowers it, it can control and manipulate it for political purposes. Look at the GBMC, the NHS and the state schools."

"You would stop those coming back to life?"

"Yes, I would. They have no justification in a country

that respects individual choice. They simply force the government of the day's views upon us. Look where that has led." He gestured to the wrecked courtyard.

Paul stood on another empty plinth. "I realise it's not ideal, but we don't have time to remodel society. People are starving. It will take years for ideas to change, and before that happens industry and the institutions we rely on will have collapsed. There will be no country left for individuals to enjoy."

"I disagree," Blake said calmly, still on the floor of the courtyard. "Starting again with flawed principles can only lead to flawed results. We need to reset government. Limit it to its proper purpose. With that foundation, of freedom, the right to their property and to pursue their own happiness, people will quickly learn to flourish. They are much more intelligent and able than the so-called intelligentsia think. To make those principles stick, however, nothing less than a moral and political revolution will do."

"Who says?" Liz shouted. "We've believed in the same fundamental morality for centuries. Kindness, caring for the poor, generosity. Who are you to change all that?"

"I'm not," Blake said. "I'm simply saying people's choices should be respected rather being constantly overridden by the force of the state."

"But that would overturn a society-oriented morality that has lasted for millennia."

"I realise that."

"But it isn't right. What you want is too much change. You are... you are an extremist."

The emotionally charged word exploded, leaving only silence among the debris.

Eventually, Blake said firmly, "I think we will have to agree to differ."

"But your disagreement is impractical. People can't be allowed to 'do their own thing'. It will be anarchy."

"And that is where we differ," Blake said quietly, and moved towards an exit.

As he left, Candice piped up.

"You remember my friend Lucinda? You met her dad – John. You gave him the book."

"Oh yes."

"I think you should ask him about financing the government. He's also a banker."

"That's a good idea. I'd forgotten about him. Thank you, Candice."

"You're welcome," she said, beaming.

Marisa saw them and took Blake's arm. Despite everything, they were beginning to feel like a family again.

~

Over the next few days, Marisa met with several of her old colleagues and started to gather support for creating new energy markets that would be able to power-up the country again. All they required was a reliable currency – not a government one prone to manipulation – and the upholding of contracts. Blake also held talks, but was less successful. One night, as they sat on their camp beds on Richmond Common, eating cold corned beef, he explained the situation.

"Liz is right, we are running out of time."

"You're not going to give in to her ideas, are you?"

"No. But the situation needs resolving. People can't work or plan or invest. They need to know what the new government will do for them, or to them."

"So what are you going to do?" Marisa couldn't stifle the anxiety in her voice. She feared some kind of botched coalition which would negate everything they'd worked for.

"I've spoken to Macleod and we're going to organise a ballot of the army, both here and in Glasgow. The question will be, 'Do you want a new constitution based on individual rights, or do you want to return to the laws and institutions we had before?'"

"Will they be able to understand it?"

Blake looked at her ruefully.

"Sorry," she said, embarrassed. "Force of habit. It's really hard to shake off."

Blake laughed. "Yes. Which is why we need to do it."

"When's the vote?"

"A week on Sunday."

"Have Liz and her faction agreed to accept the result?"

"They have."

"But what if you lose? Will you be sent back to prison? She called you an extremist."

"I'll just have to rely on you getting me out, won't I."

"No way. I'll be in there with you."

"You know they keep men and women separate in prison?"

She smiled, her lips widening. "We'd better make the most of what we've got now then, hadn't we," and she pushed aside his rationed meal before giving him the most bountiful kiss she knew how.

~

With Clive's telecoms knowledge and the logistical efficiency of the army, it didn't take long to print the ballot papers, arrange for ballot boxes around

Richmond Common and in Glasgow's Dawsholm and Ruchill parks, and to rig up a sound relay between the armies' locations. Counting was to be done by a mixture of volunteers from each side. The rest of the week was spent in passionate debate. Blake circulated the draft constitution that Roger and Xavier had created, while Liz's team circulated their ideas on continuity. The soldiers, who were trained to obey orders, for the first time most of them could remember were deciding their own destiny. As they debated with and challenged each other without preference for rank, some found they had an ability to persuade and to reason that they didn't know they had. When the day for the ballot came, they were primed and ready.

~

It was a chilly April morning when the official debates began. Blake was supported by Clive and Sam, and Liz by Paul and Gobind. Although Prince Arthur was asked to speak, he refused, not wanting to nurture any bias among his old comrades. For the same reason, Macleod, Peters and Kettle likewise stepped aside.

The soldiers did not stand in regimented rank and file. Instead, they sat in whatever groups they preferred, clutching their ballot papers and listening via their radios to the speeches.

Marisa and Candice listened from camping chairs in front of their tent.

First to broadcast was Gobind Grewal. He explained his support for going back to the way things were by describing his work with the NHS. His company had supplied vital drugs to the NHS and he detailed the life-saving results their partnership had achieved. He simply could not imagine the country without the

NHS. Its reach was so wide and it systems so complex it would take decades to change it. Wouldn't that effort be better spent on treating people?

Listening intently, Marisa couldn't deny his facts. But she thought he lacked the ability to see the big picture. It was always easier to see the number of people who were treated than the number who weren't due to waste, mismanagement and political interference. How could he forget to mention the care home scandal? Couldn't healthcare be reimagined somehow? After all, most hospitals had their origins in large donations or public subscriptions.

"Surely feeding people is more important than treating them," Candice said, "but we seemed to manage without a National Food Service." Marisa smiled.

Next up was Sam Tillman. He made the case for deregulating the food industry and all the others it depended on, particularly farming and transport. Ecoist laws had slowly but surely suffocated then almost destroyed the growing, processing, importing and distribution of food. He described the years of plenty, when prices fell and food was grown wherever it grew best before being shipped quickly around the world. Then he catalogued the failures of supply and escalation of prices they had all seen in recent years, but which had now reached a climax. Millions of people around the country were close to starvation. The army had distributed its own supplies where the need was greatest but that could not go on. What was needed was more production, more importation, and free markets unfettered by bogus fears of climate change.

Marisa suddenly realised how much she had taken for granted. The orange juice on the breakfast table. The cheap bananas at any time of year. She loved English strawberries but she knew they couldn't be grown all year round. Seasonal food was all very well, but human life continued as normal regardless of the seasons. At least, it did in the industrialised countries, until recently. But that, of course, was the result of the food miles campaign and the ultimate goal of ecoism – to stop life continuing as normal. She hoped the soldiers listening realised it, too. With no media to massage their thoughts they had only their own minds to rely on. Could they be trusted? That was the ultimate question.

Paul Williams spoke next on his plan for a nationalised electricity generating system. He argued it was the only way to get power back into people's houses quickly. The National Grid existed, as did the smart-meter rationing system, and would be the fastest and safest way to get industry back on its feet and people warm in their houses. All it needed was central organisation and tax funds to set it going.

"Who first made electricity to sell?" Candice asked.

"Edison," Marisa replied. She had seen the building he'd used in Holburn. Why did people think a government would be expert at generating and distributing energy? She knew from her job that the more open the market was, the more innovations would occur. What about gas? What about shale? What about wind or solar power, but not subsidised – used where it actually was efficient? These were all questions that 'the market' could resolve. Unfortunately, Paul, like many people, didn't make the connection between 'the market' and the people who comprised it – the wholesale buyers and sellers of energy, and ultimately the consumers in firms and houses. The market wasn't some evil, anonymous, money-grubbing monster. It was just people and the choices they made. Government control and the morality of ecoism could only suppress them. She hoped one of the other speakers would mention that.

Next up was Clive Donaldson. His Scottish lowlands accent was a soothing change. Older by some margin than the previous speakers, he talked about his experience in different telecoms companies over the years, the massive benefit of breaking up the state telecoms monopoly in the 1980s, and the subsequent halting slide back into a government-controlled sector. He admitted his errors: the legislation to stifle competition he had supported and his cowardice in not defying the law curtailing free speech. He knew his actions had allowed state control to be seen as the 'new normal' and empowered the transmission of ecoist ideas at the price of its opponents'. But he also proudly mentioned what he had done since to restore his character, including his involvement in preventing the smallpox attacks. This drew the first round of general applause which echoed around the common.

"What was it like when the government ran the Post Office, Mum?" Candice asked as they waited for the next speaker.

"It took weeks, sometimes months to get a new phone. And they were all grey, or muddy green."

Candice, who was old enough to remember when mobile phone shops offered new products every week and let you walk out with a working phone within minutes, gaped in disbelief.

The next speaker was Liz Blackwood.

"London is in ruins," she began. "Britain is in ruins. People are starving. Will you stand by and let this happen, you whose job it is to defend the nation? I hope not. I hope I can trust your humanity to rescue you from the idealistic, unworkable plans of my opponent, Blake Hardwicke. He thinks selfishness is the answer to everything. That left to their own devices, people will solve these tremendous national problems on their own. I believe he is wrong. It will be chaos. Wasteful, expensive chaos, as people fight with each other for the few resources we have. Don't get me wrong. I don't think we should return to the 1970s and near-complete state control, but we do need regulation. Carefully considered rules that create a level playing field and allow competition but not anarchy. We cannot afford inefficiency in this emergency situation. And we cannot afford to jettison two thousand years of Christian teaching. Selfishness might be fine for the rich and the able. They can afford to indulge themselves. But for most people it is wrong. We need to care for each other, to share our resources, to harness the profits of enterprise and use them for the common good. The good of everyone. The good of the country."

Liz paused, Marisa guessed to gauge the audience reaction. There was none. They had heard it all before, Marisa thought, and wanted something new. It was clear to her, and therefore plenty of the army, that Liz had just made the perfect case for ecoism, just replaying the panic over global warming with one over starvation.

Liz continued to talk about how dedicated a leader

she would be and how tirelessly she would work to make Britain great again, but Marisa wasn't really listening. She was wondering whether Liz had actually read PPOG. If she had, she certainly hadn't integrated it with the rest of her knowledge. Surely Liz knew about the huge amount of charity that people were willing to give each year despite enormous taxes? Or about the legions of volunteers who made things happen in all areas of life, from soup kitchens to choirs? Everyone knew this was a more efficient and less coercive way of helping people than organising a government programme, didn't they? And then it dawned on Marisa that Liz had probably never done such work. She could only conceive of help being given to people for money, and that people would never relinquish their money without being forced to by the state.

What a sad view of human nature, Marisa thought. Money was important. Crucial. It enabled saving and investment and encouraged ingenuity and creation. And it was a prerequisite to being charitable. But it wasn't the ultimate reason people did things for each other. They did things because they wanted the world to better express their values. They didn't need to be bullied or bribed into it.

The more Marisa listened to Liz, the more she realised the irony of a supposedly capitalist banker reiterating the sad worldview of Karl Marx. It was also clear that Liz treated this as a leadership election, as if she needed people to obey her in order to justify her existence. A bit like God, Marisa thought.

When Liz had finished her speech, Candice turned and said, "She just wants to be in charge of us doesn't she, Mum."

"Yes, Candice." She smiled at her daughter's perspicuity. She would make a fine thinker in whichever career she eventually chose, assuming she wasn't locked up for being an extremist. That was a possibility under Liz's plans for a regime. With the security and recovery of the state set as the country's goals, it was inevitable that individuals who disagreed would have to be sacrificed. Her husband had a chance to stop that, and she listened eagerly for the beginning of his speech.

The radio soon crackled into life and Blake's voice, deeper and more measured than she had ever heard it before, emerged from the radio.

"My fellow countrymen, thank you for lending me your ears. You do not have to vote and you do not have to listen, so I appreciate you doing so. Thank you also for marching around the country with me, trying to spread ideas. The late Professor MacDermot's book is, I believe, a sorely needed antidote to the poison of ecoism that has ravaged this country, the effects of which you have seen for yourselves. But it is easy to criticise a folly. It is much harder to correct one, and so I want to highlight today the new outlook on human life that MacDermot proposed and what it would mean for you.

"Consider this question: how do you feel when you choose to help someone, versus when you're forced to do so? When you hand over some of your rations to children in a war zone, versus when you hand over your taxes to subsidise wind farms? I imagine the first leaves you with a sense of satisfaction while the second leaves you numb. Even if you happen to believe in wind farms, the emotional reward of 'helping' them would be dulled by one thing: you had no choice. Literally. Pay your taxes or go to prison.

"Imagine if every action you took was dictated to you. From what you ate to what you did for a job, to how you performed that job, to what kind of transport you may use, to where you can go on holiday. But wait, you don't need to imagine it. You know what it's like because that's exactly how the army operates. Now, you joined it voluntarily for your own reasons. But imagine this: what if you could never leave? What if, when you retired, life would be exactly the same minus the actual fighting? What if the whole of society was like that: one almighty organisation in which any individual choice was crushed. That is what communism means for North Koreans. That is what ecoism was like in this country. And that is what will happen again if obedience to state rules, regulations and institutions is valued more highly than individual choice. Life would contain no happiness, because nothing you did would be of personal value to you. Because nothing would be done by your personal choice.

"Ecoism was all about denying yourself for the sake of the planet. Statism, which I believe is what my opponent wants, is all about denying yourself for the sake of the state. I want to alert you to the fact that this will not only deny you happiness, it will make you poor. Statist politicians always say that if we pull together as a nation, if we 'do our bit', if we sacrifice our freedom to them, then we'll all be better off. This is simply not true. History does not bear it out – look at the countries that sacrificed the most for the supposed common good: Soviet Russia, Communist China, Iron Curtain Eastern Europe, Vietnam, North Korea, Cuba, Venezuela. Nor does the logic of human nature bear it out.

"Life is only worth living – it only gives you the emotional rewards of joy and happiness – if you serve your own values. In the army, you know well what service means. But would you stay in the army if that service meant going against your own values? I would hope not, and would expect not given the refusal of many of you to fight at Westingham Castle. The decision you made then to turn against the President is why we are here today. And it is your decision next, on your ballot papers, that will determine what happens to this country tomorrow. As you cast your votes, I urge you to consider this:

"The means you will use to make that decision lies in all of us: it is called reason. It is what enables us to choose, to make plans and to gain new knowledge. Without it humankind is not human. We owe it to ourselves to use our minds to the best of our ability, to make the best we can of our lives. Therefore, we owe the same to everyone else in this country. The freedom to choose what ideas to print, what broadcasters to support, what transport to use, what websites to read, what fuel to heat and cook with, what banks to trust and what curriculum to teach our children by.

"A society based on rational self-interest, on egoism, allows everyone the freedom to reach their own decisions in these matters and then act on them. A society based on statism, such as ecoism, forbids the individual to decide. It is your vote that will determine which kind of society we live in. As you cast it, consider this as well. There is a difference between the state and society. The state is the means of governing society. It is not the same as society. One kind of state will force society to act one way only, to sacrifice individual choice to that purpose, and ensure conformity by fining, imprisoning or executing those who are disloyal to it. But it does not have to be like that. A state can also allow society to be free, only using force in retaliation against those who initiate it. If the state's purpose is to secure freedom, then disloyalty to the state consists of being against freedom. It is up to you which kind of state we will live in.

"Nearly four hundred years ago, not far from here in Putney, the New Model Army tried and failed to decide upon a new and better constitution for this country. Its failure eventually led to nationalism and the state we are in today. I urge you to fix history, and set this country free."

As the echo of Blake's voice dissipated around Richmond Common, silence reigned. Marisa, who had known Blake for twenty years, had never heard him speak like that. She was stunned. Her mind was in suspense, still existing in the world he had described. And then, suddenly, there was an eruption of noise all around her, and she realised the soldiers were talking, arguing, discussing and getting to their feet, then proceeding to form long queues at their ballot boxes.

Candice touched her arm. "Are you all right, Mum?"

"I'm fine," Marisa said, wiping her eyes while smiling.

She pulled Candice close to her and watched as the soldiers moved past, waiting for her own soldier to return.

It was almost an hour before Blake reached them. Marisa held him in her arms for a long time.

"You did it," she said hoarsely.

"I did my best," he replied, and separated them so he could look at her.

She smiled up at him, then beckoned for Candice to join them.

"Were you 'channelling' Professor MacDermot?" Candice asked as Blake put his arm round her.

"I was trying to," Blake smiled.

"I wish I'd met him."

~

By early evening the votes had all been cast in both London and Glasgow, and the counting was well under way. Blake came back from supervising the proceedings and lit a fire outside their tent to keep warm. One or two soldiers walking past looked at it in horror, then saw Blake and realised that, for now, such things were not banned by the government.

As they finished their supervisory role, others came to join them, including Clive and Sam. They sat around the blaze, drinking tea, eating baked potatoes, singing songs and telling stories.

Marisa watched the joy on their faces and listened to their laughter. Was this their last night of freedom – Liz's faction would not tolerate criticism or competition, she was sure of that – or was this the beginning of a new way of life, for them and the country? She looked at the sparks ascending into the void of the sky and wondered…

~

She awoke from a troubled sleep with a start. It was light outside the tent. She vaguely remembered

479

crawling into her sleeping bag sometime after midnight, still waiting for the result.

She opened the tent flap and put her head out. It was frosty but the sun was up and beginning to burn away the mist on the common.

The chairs round the fire were empty now but it was still smouldering gently.

Suddenly she saw a firework – an orange rocket bursting in the sky half a mile away. What did it mean? Then she heard cheering. The deep sound of male British voices, off in the distance. Who for?

She clambered out of the tent properly, pulling her sleeping bag round her, straining her eyesight for some clue.

Suddenly, through the mist, she saw him. Blake was sprinting towards her. She couldn't read his expression.

She saw his arms widen to embrace her before she saw his grinning face.

"We won," he shouted, gasping for breath but with a joy she hadn't heard from him since James was born.

Then, with an overwhelming force, he embraced her and lifted her off her feet, and swung her around until he was exhausted. After that they kissed for some time before he finally told her the story.

"We won by a lot: 63 per cent to 37. Liz and her party have officially accepted it. They want to work with us."

"Of course they do," Marisa said. "They want power any way they can get it."

"'Keep your enemies close,' isn't that what they say?"

"I suppose," Marisa said, finally starting to relax.

"She spoke to me alone for a minute afterwards. I

think the result shocked her. And I think my speech surprised her. She wants to learn what Dalton taught me."

"She wants to be close to power."

"I don't have any power, except perhaps to persuade some people. As soon as the army can organise it and the basic constitution is in place, we'll have to have full elections."

"Are you going to stand?"

"Do you want me to?"

She smiled broadly. "Not just yet. I want you to myself. We have a lot of catching up to do."

They kissed again, and it was as they had done when they'd first met. They stopped when Candice appeared to give her the good news.

#

Late that afternoon, after much celebration, the Hardwickes visited Westminster. The army had camps in Parliament Square, St James's Park and Green Park. Besides them only a few people were about. One or two approached and asked about the vote. Others saw the soldiers and ran away. In the shadow of Parliament, its windows broken and its lights extinguished, Blake found an old man wearing a shabby overcoat and shiny shoes, who was carrying bundles of paper under his arm. Having heard various accounts of what had happened in London, he wondered whether this man's perspective could add something.

"Once it was known the President was dead, along with his mouthpiece at the GBMC, the MPs and Lords tried for a short while to agree on a coalition, but they couldn't. Nothing united them, except ecoism, and everyone could see the destructive results of that all around them. Then the rumours started to spread about Lord Hardwicke having planned to kill all those children at the Youth Rallies with smallpox. The MPs didn't want to be associated with that – their constituents would turn nasty. When they heard the army was on the side of the Westingham prisoners, it was the last straw. They all quietly slunk away. Back to being the non-entities they mostly were."

"What about all the civil servants?" Blake asked.

"You're looking at one of them now, Mr Hardwicke," the old man said with sadness in his eyes. "Clearly the government of this nation had gone off the rails, but there was still law and order to keep. However, as you would know, the state has been technically bankrupt for a long time, and once the ministers had gone there was no one to authorise continuing the farce of money printing, so no way to pay the wages of the police, or us more clerical civil servants. When a government collapses, I'm afraid the good bits go down with the bad."

Blake and Marisa looked at each other. The situation was perfectly logical, but it still shocked them. They were promising to put the nation back together again, but it was in such a mess!

Candice asked the old man, "What have you bothered to come back for?" indicating the papers under his arm.

The man clutched them to his side defiantly. "These are some of the original vellum statutes, my dear, kept in the Victoria Tower, of laws that I believe should be preserved in any civilised country. Among others I have here the Bill of Rights and the Magna Carta." He held them proudly. In answer to their faces he said, "I wouldn't want them destroyed if the looters start a fire in the Tower."

"You might be interested in this," Blake said, handing him a copy of PPOG.

"I've read it," said the man. "I think these documents support it," and he patted the scrolls.

"What position did you hold in the civil service, might I ask?" Blake said.

The old man smiled, with the lines and the far-off look of decades of wisdom. "Many years ago, I was the Chief Secretary to the Chancellor."

"Are you retired?" Blake asked.

"Aren't we all?" the man smiled.

"Would you like to work again?"

"If you mean, would I like to help get my country back on its feet, then the answer is yes."

Blake smiled. "Here's someone you should talk to," and he gave him Roger Newton's contact details, before wishing him well as he departed.

Marisa said, "Bearing in mind what he said about fires and looting, shouldn't we secure these buildings somehow?"

"You're right," Blake said, and they went in search of army commanders. To their pleasant surprise, they not only found Major General Macleod but also Prince Arthur, shorn of his beard and back in army uniform. When Blake suggested securing the buildings, Macleod agreed, but when Blake suggested lighting up the inside, especially Big Ben, he laughed.

"There's no diesel to be had for love nor money, except for transport. We've barely enough for our own emergency lighting."

Candice, who had been staring at the Prince, suddenly grabbed her father's arm. "Dad, listen, I might be able to help. If you can get the generators, I know where there might be lots of diesel."

The Prince raised an eyebrow at her.

"But Candice," Blake said mockingly, "that would mean polluting the environment with CO_2 and using up valuable resources."

"Ha, ha," Candice said. "You know I've given up the Green Shoots. Completely. You talk about values – well, that diesel is far more valuable providing light here than it is stuck in a tank at Waterloo."

She went on to describe an aborted plan of her ex-group: to set off a bomb that would empty the hidden tanks of diesel held in emergency reserve for the trains. But at the last minute they hadn't gone through with it for fear of pollution, so they had just left it.

"One for you, I think," Macleod said to the Prince.

"Right. Lead the way, then," Arthur said to Candice.

She took him and a bomb disposal team to the sidings where the old Eurostar trains had once stood.

"Down there." She pointed to some stairs that led beneath the tracks.

"Leave this to me," the Prince said, and led his men down the steps, limping slightly.

As she waited for what seemed an age, Candice winced at her naïveté in joining the Green Shoots. Why had she ignored all her father's arguments? Had she just wanted to rebel against him?

Suddenly, she heard a muffled boom. Her heart froze. A minute later nothing else had happened. She was starting to descend the steps when the Prince emerged, sooty and grimy but uninjured. She gasped then smiled with relief at him. He grinned and gave her the thumbs up.

A couple of hours later, they returned to Parliament with a tanker full of diesel. Soon the clock within the tower was running and its face was once again shining out over London.

As Big Ben chimed seven o'clock, Blake checked his watch and noted it was April 5th. People from around Westminster and Lambeth came to stand and look. It was a friendly, familiar sight, associated with Great Britain in times gone by. As they watched, the lights of Parliament came on in sections, streaming out into the gathering gloom and illuminating a benighted city.

"I say, that's a sight for sore eyes," came a Scottish voice, and Blake turned to find its owner. He shook hands with and then bear-hugged a big man in army fatigues.

"Marisa, this is Brigadier Timothy Campbell, a fellow ex-inmate and escapee."

She shook his hand and was surprised by its strength. "He's told me a lot about you," she said.

"Aye, all good if I'm not mistaken."

"So what brings you here?" Blake asked.

"I've come down from the castle to find out what's going on," the Brig said, "and to bring you this." He handed over the tattered but distinct flag that had flown over Westingham during the siege. "I thought you could use it."

Blake felt the faded yellow cloth in his hands but then handed it back. "Why don't you raise it yourself, on the Victoria Tower? We could use a new symbol for this country."

The Brig nodded, and headed off to speak with the

soldiers guarding the gates beneath the venerable building.

Twenty minutes later, the red, white and blue overlay of national flags had been replaced by a picture of a grey castle inside a yellow light bulb, itself lit by a spotlight.

The Brig soon came down to admire his work. He, Macleod and the Prince stood together with Blake, Marisa and Candice, watching and smiling but with tears of joy, exhaustion and relief on their cheeks.

They were soon joined by Clive and Sam, and then a bit later by Liz and Paul, all of them drawn to the sight.

Blake said to them, "Today used to be known as the beginning of the new tax year. We need a different name. How about 'National Rational Self-Interest Day'?"

Candice groaned. "Oh Dad, it's a great idea but it doesn't exactly roll off the tongue!"

The lines on their weary faces creased as they all laughed, cheered and hugged each other. The ecoist era was over.

***

THE END

Further Information

Author's Note

Surprising though it may seem, this book was conceived and practically finished before the outbreak of COVID-19. Such is the power of ideas, particularly philosophical ones.

To learn more about the author's work and to receive a free short story, go to this web address and add your contact details:

richardgbrooke.com/contact

Printed in Great Britain
by Amazon